the gift of darkness

V.M. Giambanco was born in Italy. She started working in films as an editor's apprentice in a 35mm cutting room and since then has worked on many award-winning UK and US pictures, from small independent projects to large studio productions. She lives in London.

V.M. GIAMBANCO

the gift of darkness

For Claudio Giambanco and Giulio Cardi,
my father and my grandfather

First published in Great Britain in 2013 by Quercus Editions Ltd
This paperback edition published in 2014 by

Quercus Editions Ltd
55 Baker Street
7th Floor, South Block
London W1U 8EW

A CIP catalogue record for this book is available
from the British Library

PB ISBN 978 1 78087 873 7
EBOOK ISBN 978 1 78087 872 0

10 9 8 7 6 5 4 3 2

Printed and bound in Great Britain by Clays Ltd, St Ives plc

Typeset by Ellipsis Books Limited, Glasgow

A sky so blue it hurts to look at it. Ancient trees rise a hundred feet, red and yellow cedars next to black cottonwood and vine maples, their roots twisting out of deep green slippery moss and rotting wood. The boy runs barefoot. He stops in a small clearing, breathing hard and fast, and listens. Eleven maybe twelve years old, dark eyes wide. His jeans are torn where dead branches have been caught and snapped, the muddy gray T-shirt is stained with sweat on his back and the sleeves cling to his thin arms. Skin shows through where the fabric has been cut and blood covers his arms and hands as if they have been dipped in it.

The boy sweeps a strand of hair from his eyes and throws up what little is left in his stomach. He steadies himself against a tree and then, down-hill. His body pulled by gravity, losing his balance, wading through the fallen leaves. Under his feet the world crackles and shifts.

Last night

Darkness. The waves roared and crashed against the pebble beach. It was the loudest sound James Sinclair had ever heard and it filled his whole body as if poured into him.

He couldn't remember waking up and walking across the lawn and down to the pier. A cold wind brushed his face and something hot and dry started to spread through his lungs. He panicked and tried to wake up; instead he tasted blood and heard himself cry out: the bed he lay on, the blindfold, the wire around his neck and hands. He thought of his children, he thought of his wife.

Chapter 1

On a good night you can smell the sea from way up on University Hill. Alice Madison rolled down her window a couple of inches and sniffed the air. The night was cold and December mist hung low and damp between the houses and the naked trees. Christmas was two weeks away and the students who could afford to live on that side of the hill had already left for the holidays, gone back to homes all over Washington State.

The clock on the dashboard said 4.15 a.m. Detective Sergeant Brown, a dark shape sitting next to her, had put the seal on the evening hours before.

'After all the coffee has been drunk and all the talk has been talked, stake-outs are just long stretches of time with little to do, for people who would like to be doing something else, somewhere else, in somebody else's company.'

It was a pretty fair description of their partnership, she thought.

Her breath was vapor on the pane. It was a choice between being cold and being reminded of other men's hours of boredom and sweat. She'd rather be cold.

Brown turned around to look at the other end of the street and she caught a whiff of aftershave, cool and not unpleasant. Madison knew that they had been sent out there with next to zero chances; Brown was not a happy man.

Gary Stevens – white male, 23, no priors – was hot favorite for the murder of a 19-year-old student from the campus. Handcuffed to a radiator, Janice Hiller was sitting up with her back to the wall when the police found her, dead from a single blow to the head. A half-drunk cup of coffee was neatly placed next to her right hand.

The day she had joined Seattle Homicide, four weeks earlier, Alice Madison visited her grandparents' grave in a cemetery near Burien. She put a bunch of white roses by the stone and stood there alone. In their heart they would know, wherever they were, that she was who she was because of them, and their love was a blessing she carried like gold, on her skin and out of sight. That night Madison went home, fixed herself dinner – nothing frozen, nothing canned – and slept for ten hours straight.

Brown had since been neither cold nor unhelpful, just detached. He was as good a cop as they come, better than most. They would never be friends, that much she knew, yet she would trust him with her own life any day. Maybe that was enough.

Brown and Madison had not discussed the nature of evil when they saw the ring of seared flesh around Janice Hiller's wrist, the radiator heating up the metal of the handcuff at regular intervals; they just got busy trying to save the next victim, working steady and fast to get the innocent out of the path of the hurricane.

At the other end of the street two men in a dark Ford Sedan were trying to keep each other awake, long out of coffee and dirty jokes. Madison would much rather have spent the evening in their company: detectives Spencer and Dunne had been partners for three years, knew each other from the Academy and worked well together. They were an odd couple. Spencer was second-generation Japanese, married with three kids and a degree in Criminology from night school. Dunne, on the other hand, was Irish red, put himself through college with a football scholarship and dated women whose short skirts were part of the mythology of the precinct. They knew each other's thoughts and could anticipate each other's actions.

Alice Madison sat and waited; she hoped that she wouldn't need that much from Brown, or anybody else. Still, this was where she was and the rest mattered little when all she wanted to do was stare into the darkness ahead.

Brown had been right about the essential nature of stake-outs and yet Madison suspected that a part of her actually looked forward to the quiet waiting before the target appeared, when everything in the world stilled and there was nothing but the trap and the chase.

The Police Academy had taught her much, except what it feels like to run full tilt after a human being who means you harm – that she had to learn on the street. Detective Alice Madison settled into the worn leather seat. Spencer and Dunne might have been better company, but tonight she was exactly where she wanted to be.

The wind was blowing hard now; only a few blocks away the sea rose and fell, spraying the deserted piers, shaping puddles of black seawater. Stevens would not come home tonight; he would never come home again. He had probably already left the state, changed his name and started all over in some other campus. Madison did not dwell on that thought – she was still at a stage where she could remember every single red name on the Homicide board, and those gone from red to black, the all-important clearance rate.

'Good morning, Seattle, it's a balmy 30 degrees outside. And the time is . . .' Dunne's voice croaked from the walkie-talkie.

Brown picked it up from in between their seats.

'I make it about 4.15 a.m.'

'Same here. How long do you want us to stick around?'

'It's late enough.' Brown sighed. 'That's it, gentlemen – let's hit the road.'

Madison felt a twinge of disappointment. Even if they had gone out with no expectations, turning away wasn't any sweeter.

'I don't mind hanging around a little longer,' she said.

'There'll be other nights.'

'Not for Stevens.'

'Stevens has gone,' Brown said.

'He might not stay gone.'

'Us waiting here, it'll make him come back?'

'Probably not.'

'But—'

'It makes me feel better,' she said.

Brown turned to Madison. In the half light her eyes moved over the shadows in the street as if to conjure up their man.

'That and five bucks will get me a cup of coffee, I know,' she said.

'There'll be other nights.'

Dunne's voice came back. 'There's a twenty-four-hours place two streets away. We can meet up there.'

'Alright. We'll follow you.' Brown put the engine into gear and the car moved softly away. The street was left just as it had been found hours earlier.

A couple in their late twenties were wandering down the aisles of the Night & Day, picking up small boxes of MicrowaveWorld. They looked like they had been partying somewhere – they were a little giggly but not really drunk. They couldn't have been that much younger than she was.

Dunne had headed directly for coffee and donuts, Spencer for mineral water and Brown for a Diet Coke. They didn't say a word to each other; the hours in the car had become real as they had stepped into the convenience store. Dunne stretched and yawned.

Madison picked up a carton of milk and drifted by the video

rental shelf. It was mostly action and horror pictures with a few Disneys thrown in for the family. She had been on a diet of Billy Wilder for the last few weeks. Coming home after the graveyard shift, she had fallen asleep on the living room sofa listening to Josephine and Daphne. It took her mind off things because sometimes her mind was not a pleasant place to be. She paid and went to wait outside.

Madison leant against the car and drank the milk. It was still misty; maybe the morning light would get rid of it. The breeze from the sea was much stronger now, and brought the lone call of a fog siren. She hugged her heavy mountain jacket and thought about all the things that she wanted to cram into the next 24 hours, and that was when the girl came out of the mist.

Madison noticed her because she looked so young and out of place with her denim jacket and lightweight trousers. *She must be freezing.* Madison kept looking – the kid might need help. Her hair was baby blond and cut short. She looked 14, just about right for a runaway, small backpack included. She wore pink lipstick and heavy eyeliner, her cheeks flushed with the cold.

Leaning against the car with her coat and baseball cap on, Madison didn't look the obvious cop, which was good – she didn't want to spook the kid. Now she could see the dark shadows under her eyes.

'Hey.'

Her voice broke the girl's step; she turned toward her and nodded slightly. Madison gave her a half smile so that she wouldn't think she was some kind of creep, at once realizing that was exactly what she looked like. Experience told her that she was probably sleeping rough, eating not nearly enough, and possibly nursing the beginning of some infection of the respiratory system.

The girl paused, hands deep in her pockets, and with two strides was up the stairs and into the store. She was traveling light, Madison had noticed; the small bag on her shoulders couldn't hold much, and then there was the thing in the right-hand side of her jacket, the thing her hand had been clutching under the thin white fabric, and she had seen it as the kid was turning away. It had been a cold, sad waste of a night and it was getting worse: what Madison had seen looked like the tip of the butt of a gun. She was up the steps and behind the girl.

The kid was ten feet in front of her, looking at row after row of candy bars, her head swaying very slowly from side to side.

Brown was standing by the cashier and about to pay, four maybe five feet to her right; Spencer and Dunne were at the back of the store. The young couple had piled up their basket with boxes and cartons and were coming toward the cashier. Their chatter had died out and the only sound was the hum from the neon lights and the fridge.

In one movement Madison opened her jacket and unhooked the small leather strip that secured her gun to the holster on her right hip. It wasn't a good time to remember that the majority of Homicide detectives never even have to draw the damn thing. She took one step toward Brown and touched him on the shoulder, her eyes never leaving the girl. She nodded toward the kid and made a gun with her fingers. Brown raised his eyebrows and unhooked the strip on his holster.

In the pocket of the jacket the hand was clammy and the kid didn't like it, but she didn't want to take it out and wipe it against the side of her trousers – that would have been much worse. She hated the feel of the weight of the metal; it dragged her pocket down on that side. The hand clenched and unclenched around the butt of the gun, her eyes swept over Hershey bars, Mars bars, Reece's. Too many names.

The couple put their basket on the desk and an underpaid and overworked clerk started to ring up the items. Madison went up behind them, her voice so soft she could hardly hear it herself.

'Police. Leave the store.'

'What—' The young man opened his mouth and closed it when he saw the flash of the badge on the inside of her jacket.

'Now. Do not look around. Go.'

Mercifully, they did as they were told, but not without shooting a glance over their shoulders.

The clerk wasn't as accommodating.

'What is this—?'

The girl turned around, gun held with both hands at eye level.

'Nobody move.' Her voice was shaky but clear and the clerk dove under the bar.

The girl was facing Brown and Madison, the gun moving in jerks between one and the other. Spencer and Dunne had disappeared behind the racks. Madison knew as if she could see them that they both had their pieces out and were figuring out a way to get to the kid without getting either of them shot.

'You have our attention. What next?' Brown was calm and in control. Some part of Madison could actually appreciate the man at work.

'Do as I say. Lie on the ground. Do it.' The girl's voice went up and cracked.

Madison could see her breathing getting more labored; they needed to calm her down pretty quick or she'd give herself a heart attack.

'Do it!' She was losing it fast.

'It's not worth it,' Brown said. 'There's less than fifty bucks in the till. And you're pointing your piece at two cops.' He nodded toward his partner.

The girl's eyes went into 'Oh shit' for a fraction of a second. It was long enough.

'Put the gun on the ground and run like hell.'

The girl's mouth was hanging open and she was thinking very

hard. The four detectives knew all too well that anybody can be a tough guy with a gun in his hand, but some lucky ones could still hang on to their brains.

Madison struggled to keep vision, to still the hum and clear her mind. There was the girl's hand, pointing the revolver at Brown's head, and the girl's arm and the girl's heart. She knew she could clear leather and shoot and fell the kid in less than three seconds. She saw the muzzle tremble in line with Brown's eyes and the man not flinch and look straight back and still talk kindly. The girl wore glitter nail polish and her ears were pierced, twice on the left side, once on the right. There was worn sheepskin lining on the inside of her denim jacket and under the neon light her pale skin was translucent.

'Stop talking to me!' the girl screamed, and Madison did not see her anymore but only the gun, and steadied herself to move. In the space between heartbeats Madison felt everything that was good and true drain from her.

'It ain't worth it,' Brown said, Madison didn't know to whom.

'Alright. Alright.' The girl was nodding. 'I'm going to grab some things. You stay where you are.'

The moment had passed.

'Nobody's moving.' Brown smiled. 'We're just three people talking.'

She reached behind her with her left hand and found the candy bars, grabbed a couple and stuffed them in her jacket, grabbed another couple and put them in the back pocket of her trousers.

'I'm going to leave now. I'll leave the gun on the steps. Nobody follows me.'

'Wait a minute. Put the gun on the floor now. I give you my word me and my partner here won't move for three minutes after you leave.'

'Yeah, right.'

'My word.' Brown didn't want her out on the street with a piece in her hand.

'Do as he says. Nobody wants trouble. Put the gun down and get the hell out of here.'

'What if I don't?'

Brown looked her straight in the eye. 'Juvenile Court is closed for the weekend and you'll have to spend twenty-four hours in a cell with drunks and all kinds of violent offenders.' The girl blinked twice. 'I don't think you want that.'

The kid swallowed hard; it had been a bad night all round.

'Alright.'

She moved a couple of steps in the direction of the door, her eyes on the two cops in front of her. She bent down and put the gun on the ground, eyes still on them, poised to flee.

Spencer's arm got her around the neck and Dunne snapped his cuffs on the thin pale wrists. It was over in seconds. The girl yelped. She tried to fight them off, without energy or hope, tears already streaming down her cheeks. Spencer let go of her. Madison knew he had a boy her age. She breathed in deeply and fastened the leather strip back in its place on her holster, heart still drumming.

'It's not loaded.' Dunne said, shaking his head in disbelief. 'Jesus, Mary and Joseph!' The clerk popped his head up from behind the bar, evaluated the situation and put in his two cents' worth.

'Who's paying for the candy?'

Brown went over to the till and put a bill on the counter.

They walked the girl down the steps; she would ride with Brown and Madison, with Spencer to baby-sit her in the back; Dunne would drive the other car.

'Are you taking me to jail?' she asked nobody in particular.

'You're coming to the precinct, so we can talk about how you ended up in possession of this.' Spencer pointed at the gun.

The girl sort of flopped, as if all her energy had left her, and she hadn't had much to start with. Spencer and Madison held her up, not to restrain her but to make sure she would not collapse and split her head on the concrete.

The wind had brought some light rain, shaking the trees for all they were worth and washing over the street a thin layer of damp leaves. It was still pitch black all around them except for the few lamp posts glowing orange and the neon lights of the 'Night & Day'. As they were helping her inside the car, the girl looked up.

'Do you have like a newspaper or something?'

Her voice was less than a whisper.

Madison saw the dark patch on her trousers.

'I'll get a paper in the store.' She started up the steps. 'Would you like a hot drink?'

The kid thought about it for a second.

'Coffee. Black.'

The car heater made the sharp smell of urine almost unbearable and they rode with the windows down. The kid sat between two detectives, holding the cup with the tips of her fingers and drinking in small sips. They just couldn't shut her up. It was not an uncommon reaction: her name was Rose, no second name, 13 years old, no permanent address. She had seen a guy dropping a heavy brown paper bag in a bin in Pike Place Market, she had hoped for leftovers. The piece had been wrapped in a tea towel.

'You pointed an unloaded gun at two cops,' Spencer said. 'That's a full ten in the Dumb scale.'

'You *knew* it was unloaded,' Madison said.

'What do you think?' There was a one-second delay in the answer.

'Maybe and maybe not.' Brown drove quickly, with the odd glance in the rearview mirror. 'Either way we got ourselves a problem. We're Homicides. We can't keep you in our precinct since you didn't kill anybody.' He paused. 'You didn't kill anybody, did you?'

'No.'

'That's good. But we can't let you go either, 'cause you just waved your piece in my face and that put you right in my jurisdiction.'

If Brown had wanted to put the fear of God into the girl, he was doing it well. Madison gave her between two and four weeks since she had left wherever she was coming from.

'What we'll have to do is call somebody from Social Services to come pick you up,' Brown continued in a steady monotone. 'And they're going to be pissed off because it's five a.m. Sunday and they have already had a weekful of this crap. And one of us is going to have to stay on with you, call your family, write a report on how you got the gun and what happened. And wait for somebody to get you off our hands. You understand? You could be dead now, kid.'

'And your word is jackshit on a cracker,' the girl said to herself.

Forty-five minutes later Madison sat at her desk in the squad room, typing. The others had gone home with mumbled thanks as she had volunteered to stay on. The girl was wearing a pair of clean tracksuit bottoms Madison had in her locker and eating a chicken sandwich rescued from the fridge next door. Madison hoped the 'best before' date was merely a suggestion – it smelled okay.

A few phone calls had been made and Shawna Williams was on her way from Social Services.

Madison pulled the sheet of paper out of the printer and put it on the side of her desk. She stood up and stretched; the midnight-to-eight tour was all out and they were alone.

It was a grim room: desks, lamps, chairs, and a few filing cabinets, all in a charming shade of gunmetal gray. Brown's desk was opposite hers; he kept a paperback copy of *Moby-Dick* in the drawer as a sign of hope. One day, he had told her, people might stop killing each other long enough for him to read it. It hadn't happened so far.

Rose was oblivious to the room; she was concentrating on a donut and a mug of hot chocolate. A detective had brought the mug from home; on the side it read *I've walked Mt. Rainier*.

Exhausted as the girl was, Madison could see the food had done her good. A smart kid can travel a long way, but not in winter: if the street doesn't kill you, the cold and the rain will.

'Are you sure there's nobody you'd like to call? You can call long-distance, or I can find out the number for you if you have a name.'

The girl shook her head. Madison knew what she was seeing: an adult wearing good warm clothes, three meals a day and the keys to an apartment – maybe even a house. She didn't want to explain herself to her. Madison understood that better than she would ever know.

'I remember the first time I was in a police station,' Madison said as she picked up an apple from her desk and took a bite.

The girl was too tired to even pretend that she was interested.

'I was twelve years old. Ran away from home. County police picked me up near the Canada border, north of Anacortes. I was gone for one week before they found me.'

'Bullshit.'

'Nope. One week. It was August and very hot, not like now.' Madison was matter-of-fact. 'We were living on an island; one day I just took the ferry.'

'This is just something you are making up. I bet you tell this story to all the kids you pick up.'

The girl seemed very small just then and closed up like an angry little fist.

'What do *you* think?' Madison said.

'Morning, detective.' Shawna Williams walked into the room, an African-American woman in her early forties. They had met for the first time when Madison was still in uniform. She looked down at the blond girl.

'Who's this then? Can I borrow your interview room?'

'Be my guest. Help yourself to coffee.'

'Who made it?'

'I did.'

'You make coffee like it's the last cup you'll ever drink.'

'You say it like it's a bad thing.'

'Only if you want to live past forty.'

'I'll bear that in mind.'

'You do that,' she said and she poured herself a cup. 'Let's go.'

Madison and the girl nodded a sort of goodbye to each other; she extended her hand toward Rose.

'You find another gun . . .'

The girl put the card in her pocket and went off down the dimly lit corridor. Shawna's warm tones bounced off the walls but Madison could not hear the words anymore. Somebody somewhere would have to investigate how she had got the gun and whether it had been used for anything less than legal, but not till tomorrow.

Six a.m., Madison slips her jacket on, straightens the papers on her desk, turns off her lamp and leaves. Howard Jenner, the desk sergeant, waves with the receiver cradled on his shoulder. Two detectives walk up the steps with a drunken man in handcuffs; he looks at Madison as she walks past.

'Sweet dreams, honey.' His voice is like a broken bottle.

The rain has stopped and the sky is wide above them.

Alki Beach was deserted at this time of day. Madison parked in her usual spot and climbed into the backseat. She peeled off her trousers and pulled on sweatpants and a faded Sonics T-shirt. She had never liked the idea of leaving her weapon in the car, in case some bright spark decided her four-year-old Honda was worth stealing. She adjusted the holster under her sweatshirt and rolled her head from side to side. The muscles above her shoulder blades began to tighten;

it was cold and damp and she would need to warm up pretty quickly. She leant on the car with one hand, grabbed one foot and pulled it up high behind her, then did the same with the other.

She started toward the water's edge with a gentle jog and after a couple of minutes she put some speed into it and really dug into the ground. In a while the world would just be the water lapping and her feet hitting the sand.

In the near-complete darkness of the Hoh River trail, a three-hour drive from Seattle, a man races through the woods. He's a blur through the trees. It is the thirty-seventh time he has run that stretch, the twentieth in darkness. Fast enough to keep him alive for the time he will need, slow enough for his ultimate purpose. He reaches the bottom of the bank and checks his watch. *Twenty-three minutes.* He lifts his face to the open sky, shivering in the sudden breeze, and his colorless eyes find a smattering of stars. *How long does it take to be good?*

Chapter 2

Alice Madison drives into the first light of the morning. Her own car smells fresh – not perfumed, just very clean and slightly leathery – and Madison drives it to the legal speed limit. From the speakers Arcade Fire blasts 'No Cars Go' loud enough to knock any thoughts about what happened in the store right out of her.

When news of her transfer to Homicide had come through, Brown and Spencer had done the usual checks. It was an unofficial tradition: a few phone calls here and there and even Madison's college records could have been pulled from the University of Chicago. What they learnt was what they needed to know; the rest would take care of itself soon enough.

Alice Eleanor Madison was born in Los Angeles and had attended six different schools in six different cities before she arrived in Seattle at 13, and apparently decided to stay put. University of Chicago, Degree in Psychology and Criminology, magna cum laude. Sailed through the Police Academy and, Spencer was pleased to add, in the sixty-seconds hand strength test held an above-90 average for each hand, with a Model 19 Smith and Wesson.

'Just what we needed.' It was Brown's only comment.

She was single, drank little, didn't smoke and paid her bills on time. She socialized occasionally with other cops but mostly kept herself to herself.

Dunne's contribution to the checks was the fact that Madison had been asked out by at least seven of his acquaintances in other precincts and politely turned down every one of them, even the unmarried ones.

For the past four weeks Madison had been working flat out, keeping her eyes and ears open, her years in plainclothes only the foundation of the house she wanted to build. Between them Brown, Spencer and Dunne had 40 years on the job, 20 of them in Homicide. It was like being in school again.

Three Oaks is a green neighborhood on the south-western edge of the city limits. Two- and three-story houses can be seen through the Douglas firs, with their tended gardens and two-car garages. Behind the houses the lawns slope down to the still waters of the Puget Sound: there are boats and small neat piers, a narrow cobble beach runs along many properties, Vashon Island is a dark green strip across the water. It's quiet wealth, professionals bought in or inherited from their parents.

This early on a Sunday the streets were empty and only a few keen birds dared break the silence. Madison turned into Maplewood Avenue and some yards later into her driveway. For just one heart-beat there was someone at one of the first-floor windows, but she knew it was only the shadow of a tree.

She parked her car next to her grandparents' Mercedes. It had not been driven now for over a year and Madison didn't notice it any more than the trees around her or the rocks that lay under the leaves. It was landscape.

A large padded envelope was propped up against the door, nothing written on either side of it. Madison smiled; it felt soft and full to the touch. She let herself in and opened it from the little catch on the back. The note inside it said: 'Brunch is at 12, come when you can. See you later, Rachel.'

Madison dug into the envelope and took a bite off a chocolate chip cookie.

Shawna Williams had thanked her for waiting with the kid; given she had pointed a gun at her, she had said that she was a good guy.

Vague shapes were only beginning to form through the large windows onto the patio at the back. Madison sat down on the sofa and looked out at the lawn and the water. She leant her head against the back – nothing to do for the next 24 hours.

Her mind flashed back to the girl gripping the gun for dear life. Rose. Madison knew with complete certainty what she would have done if the kid had tried to take a shot at Brown. It didn't surprise her but filled her with a dull ache. What would Shawna Williams make of that? she wondered.

The run had used up the last of her energy, just as she had hoped it would; she closed her eyes, fell into the dream and Alice Madison, 12 years old, wakes up with a start in her bedroom in Friday Harbor.

The moon is high in the open window, as always, a warm breeze brushes her cotton sheets and her heart beats rabbit-fast. She knows what's coming. The Mickey Mouse clock on her bedside table reads 2.15 a.m., as always, and her eyes slowly focus in the gloom.

Her mother has died five months earlier and in her grief Alice can barely breathe. Her books stand in rows on the shelves, her clothes folded neatly on the chair, her bunny slippers by the bed. She knows what's coming. The floor in the hall creaks and her head whips around to her closed door. Someone is in the house. Her father works nights and she does not expect him back till dawn.

Her eyes blink and she forces herself to think. *It could be Dad.* No, the light in the hall is off, he would have turned on the light, he would have checked in on her. Dad would not creep around in the dark. Someone is moving from room to room and her nails press into her palm through the sheets, heavy steps trying to be light going into her parents' room.

Her baseball bat is under the bed and she reaches for it quick without taking her eyes off the door.

He's in the hall again. Alice is afraid to move and afraid to stay where she is. She is frozen with one bare foot on the cold floor and the rest of her still under the sheet, the bat gripped in both hands. The steps pause in front of her room and time stops: 2.18 a.m. Alice doesn't make a sound, doesn't blink, doesn't move, doesn't breathe. Then a dog barks nearby and Madison wakes up in her empty house, her holster digging into her side and her heart still drumming.

She was used to the dream like a scar when you roll up a sleeve: ugly, permanent and private. It didn't always end there; sometimes she would get to the point where the bat would swing and the crashing of glass would wake her, but not this time.

Less than half a mile away, James Sinclair has not moved for hours and cannot feel the first light across his body. Shadows form, lengthen and melt away. Silence, like smoke, has reached into the corners of the room.

Chapter 3

Miles and miles away from the city. The man closed his eyes and listened to the stream. The fly hit the water delicately, cast with a fluid motion of the wrist. His hands were cold but he did not like the feel of gloves against the skin when he was fishing. On the back of his right hand, three thin scars four inches long crossed and glistened white. The sky was turning into day and the quiet of the woods gave it their blessing.

He looked like a regular guy out for some camping and maybe a little fishing. A short neat haircut and good, expensive gear on the ground by his boots. Nothing an accidental hiker would look at twice, nobody anybody would remember for more than five minutes. Under the right trouser leg, the small revolver in his ankle holster was a familiar weight he hardly noticed anymore. The man knew little about blessings.

He cast the line in the water once more, eyes following the long slow arc, and knew then that that was very probably all the peace the world would ever grant him.

The shots of the hunters above him on the mountain did not startle him at all.

It was 12.45 p.m. when Madison stirred. She was a little stiff from falling asleep on the sofa – nothing a long hot shower and a strong cup of coffee couldn't take care of. She pulled on a pair of chinos, a dark denim shirt and a tan padded suede jacket. She set the sneakers she'd worn on the stake-out by the closet in her bedroom and picked up some black ankle boots instead. The holster with the gun went into a locked safe under the bed.

The deal was that if Alice was off duty she wouldn't carry her gun in Rachel's house. They had both agreed that it would not be healthy for the children to get used to the sight of an adult with a gun on her belt having coffee in their kitchen.

Madison walked to Rachel's in seven minutes. Over their twenty-year friendship their homes had never been further away than fifteen minutes on foot. It means everything when you are thirteen.

On Blueridge a few houses had already put up their Christmas decorations, lights blinked from behind curtains. Alice had never been much for that sort of thing – her grandparents though had decided that she should have the biggest tree in Seattle for their first Christmas together and she had loved it.

Rachel's house was crammed with relatives. Neal's brothers with their wives and kids, aunts and uncles, cousins whom Alice hadn't met for years. Several children were parked in front of the television playing video games. Adults sat on the sofas and stood by the buffet table. Ruth, Rachel's mother, made sure everyone was fed and watered to capacity.

Rachel had steered Alice through the room and they had ended up sitting on the stairs by the first-floor landing, holding their plates on their laps.

Once, when Madison was still in uniform, she had worked the case of a missing nine-year-old boy. The day they found him, buried under bushes in the playground, Rachel went and sat with her in the dark house for hours. Now that she was in Homicide Madison did not sit with the lights off anymore.

Rachel took a sip from her wine and looked at her friend.

'How are you doing?' she said.

'Fine. I slept like a rock. How was your week?'

'Okay. Term's over, no major dramas. I'll spend the holidays marking a pile of essays.'

Rachel taught classes twice a week at UW, in the Psychology Department. 'What about you? Any dreams?'

Rachel was the one person in the world who knew.

'Every few months. It's not too bad.'

'The woman I told you about is really good, if you want to talk to someone.'

'I'm okay. I'm used to it.'

'I don't think it does you any good just to live with it.'

'It's not a big deal anymore.'

'For Chrissake, girl, you do have a Psychology degree.'

'I know. Amazing, isn't it?'

'Yeah, right. By the way, Tommy wandered off in the super-market. Again. I found him sitting on the floor by the cereal aisle, playing with the boxes. It's the second time in a month. Did you catch your guy last night?'

'Nope. Just a thirteen-year-old girl, held up four cops in a corner store with an unloaded gun.'

'Jesus.'

'Almost got herself shot over a couple of Mars bars.'

'You were there?'

'Yes. She's with Social Services now.' Madison took a sip of wine. 'Her name is Rose.'

'Pretty,' Rachel said.

A couple of hours later Madison was on the sofa with Tommy, Rachel's six-year-old, reading one of his books. It was a collection of Native American myths written for children; Tommy knew it by heart but he liked to be read to.

The fire was crackling in the fireplace and they had Tommy's quilt on their lap. After five minutes without being interrupted by his little voice, she realized that he had fallen asleep.

Madison's eyes went to the wall above the fireplace. It was what they called 'the family wall'. Photographs of the Levers and the Abramowitzes going back generations. Alice had always had her favorites: Rachel's Russian grandparents on their wedding day, Rachel and herself on the steps of the apartment they shared in college, the black and white portrait of an unknown boy in his best Sunday suit.

Alice didn't have any photographs of her parents. She liked being on the wall with the rest of Rachel's folks.

Somebody was playing Bach next door, the beauty of the structure coming through in spite of the useless piano lessons.

Madison looked at the fire for a while longer, then got up slowly so as not to wake the child. Tommy didn't stir. After thank-yous and goodbyes she walked home, had a quick look inside her fridge and went into the bedroom. Before she even realized what she was doing, she put on her holster with the off-duty piece, closed the safe and left.

At the supermarket she picked up fruit and vegetables, cheese from the deli counter and fresh bread. The store was already in full Christmas swing and a tape of carols was playing around the clock.

She was standing by the chicken and turkey aisle when she noticed the man, a skinny white guy in a denim jacket. He was shifting his weight from one foot to the other and looking over his shoulder at the security guard who was talking with the young woman at the checkout.

His clothes looked alright and his hands were both in sight. He looked toward the exit again; the guard was still deep in conversation. At that moment the man was joined by a woman and a small child. Madison picked up some pieces of chicken and went to pay. The things we see in people . . . Madison didn't know a cop who didn't automatically keep an eye out for the guy with the long coat on a warm day.

Back home she pulled on sweatshirt and pants and ran for 45 minutes around the neighborhood. Brown was on her mind. Starched white shirts and raincoat. Her nose stung in the freezing cold. She would learn from him whether he liked it or not. She'd be right there where the job was.

She cooked with the news on and ate out of the pan, watching a *Sports Night* rerun. Just before going to bed, she took her gun out and cleaned it completely, dry-fired it a couple of times, reloaded it and put it under the bed. She fell asleep at 9.30 p.m. and dreamt no dreams till morning.

Chapter 4

The offices of Quinn, Locke & Associates occupy the ninth floor of Stern Tower between Pike and 6th. Nathan Quinn has been in his office since 7.30 a.m., reading a brief for King County vs Mallory and making notes. On his desk there is nothing except for the brief, his laptop, a lamp and black coffee in a white china cup and saucer. The rain traces fine lines across Puget Sound and the harbor, as they come slowly into sight in the corner window.

The quiet, elegant office and the beautiful view suited him well, as well as the dark suit and expensive shoes. But nothing suited Nathan Quinn better than the small pool of light over the mahogany table and the brief in his hand, preparing to go to battle. The view stayed unseen and the coffee untouched.

Carl Doyle, who managed the day-to-day running of the firm, brought him his mail at 8.30 a.m. with a list of the messages that had been left on the answering machine overnight and a reminder of the times he was due in court that day.

Quinn looked briefly over the envelopes and opened a couple. One was a thank-you and the other a thinly veiled threat from a witness he had subpoenaed. The third envelope was heavy cream paper and looked like an invitation. Quinn opened it and took out the simple card that matched it. There were only two words on it, printed in black ink. He turned the card around but there was nothing more. He read it again:

Thirteen Days

He put it to one side and went back to the rest of the mail. It was not the first, nor would it be the last, anonymous letter that he had received; this wasn't even particularly original. Later, much later on, he would think of that moment as a small death.

Chapter 5

Monday morning, 8.30 a.m. Maria Davis was late. She walked quickly up Blueridge, holding her umbrella tight against the wind. Monday was always the worst for traffic, yet she didn't mind coming to Three Oaks. She had worked for the Sinclairs for seven years, since their youngest was born. They were a nice young couple and the housework was light. Mrs. Davis was 43, her own two kids in high school; and she held another job with a family in the neighborhood.

She walked into the driveway and noticed that the curtains were still drawn on the first-floor windows. She rang the doorbell once and put her key in the door, turned it and stepped in.

'Good morning!' she called out. She closed the door behind her and listened out for voices. The only light in the hall came from the flashes of the Christmas tree.

'Hello!' She hung her coat on the rack by the door.

Tree branches brushed against the windows as she took two steps into the living room and paused. Everything in place, curtains drawn, the Christmas tree next to the French doors.

'Mrs. Anne . . .?'

She peeked into the kitchen; the dishwasher light was on, the cycle finished. Maria Davis looked around; no one had made coffee today. It was a tiny thing and she didn't know why it should upset her so much. *I should check the bedrooms.*

At the top of the stairs, under the wood polish, an ugly scent hit her hard and the small hairs on her arms rose against the fabric of her shirt.

The door was wide open: four bodies on the bed next to each other like flesh turned to stone, hands tied and blindfolded, spots on the pillows slick with blood and the boys between them. She didn't have the breath to scream; she stood and stared. When she found her way downstairs she called and the operator asked which service she wanted.

'The children . . .' she said and she had to hold the receiver with both hands. After they told her a patrol car was on its way Maria Davis opened the front door and sat on the step.

The first blue-and-white arrived at 8.47 a.m. Officers Giordano and Hall left Mrs. Davis in the back of the patrol car and went in. She leant back with her eyes closed.

This was no way to start a Monday morning, Giordano thought; his ulcer had already started to glow red.

Hall pointed to the stairs. Their pieces were out, the crime scene had not been cleared yet. They walked up, step after step, got to the landing together and saw what she had seen.

'Don't touch anything,' Giordano whispered.

'I know,' Hall snapped back.

Giordano had seen more bodies than he cared to remember, but every time children were involved he felt he had to speak softly in their presence. Hall stood, unable to move or look away.

A few minutes later, back in the car, Giordano's voice was clear.

'. . . Two adults, two kids. 1135, Blueridge, Three Oaks . . .'

He rubbed his face with the palms of his hands and went back in, took out his notebook and started writing.

*

Lieutenant Fynn took the call in his office at 8.58 a.m. He jotted down details and stood up to get his crew together. Madison knew him to be a heavyweight, a cop who'd rather stay on the floor and work with his men than get promoted and play golf.

'Everybody. We have four D.O.A.s in a private residence in Three Oaks.'

Madison looked up from her paperwork; she hoped her voice would come out steady.

'What's the address?'

'1135, Blueridge.' Fynn looked around the room. 'Let's have everybody down there. Brown, you're up?'

Brown already in his raincoat. 'This one's mine.'

Madison put her coat on. She didn't know anybody on Blueridge. She ought to have been relieved, but it doesn't always work that way. For the first time she was going to work on home ground. There was no relief in that.

Madison and Brown were riding with Chris Kelly, a veteran Homicide with a ratty temper whom nobody liked. He thought himself *a mean bastard* and liked that. Brown tolerated him, Madison just kept away.

'You know people there?' Brown asked her – the man didn't miss a thing.

'It's my neighborhood,' Madison replied.

She could almost see Kelly's ears pricking up, mentally calculating the price of real estate. The sirens cut through the steady hum of I–5 and Madison felt the initial rush of adrenaline.

'I don't know what we are going to find when we get there,' Brown said, 'but it's going to get a lot of coverage.'

You can take that to the bank, Madison thought.

A white helicopter from a news channel hovered like a beacon of tragedy above the wooded hills. A small crowd of onlookers was already forming at the end of the driveway; Brown slowed down and showed his badge to one of the three uniforms manning the road.

Four patrol cars were parked on the side, lights off and radios crackling. They were waved in. The ambulances arrived at the same time.

Brown walked up to a couple of young cops standing by the main door and flashed his badge.

'Brown, Homicide. Who's the first officer?'

Madison took out her notepad and glanced at the crowd. It would get bigger, you could bet on that. Nothing like free entertainment. She had left her coat in the car and was wearing a blazer over her shirt and trousers, her Homicide badge hooked over a breast pocket. One of the two uniforms eyed her up and down, she looked straight back and he looked away.

Giordano walked them all upstairs. 'It's pretty bad,' he said.

Yes, Madison thought as they filed into the room, *it is*.

'Spencer, can you go talk to Mrs. Davis?' Brown said. 'See if she needs a doctor.'

Spencer walked off and Madison knew that he would talk to the lady with that quiet voice of his and she'd calm down and tell him what she knew.

'Did she give you the names?' Brown asked Giordano.

'Yes. This here is the father. James Sinclair – late thirties, she thinks. That's the wife, Anne. Same age. These are their kids, John and David, nine and seven years old. Someone took out the whole family.' Giordano slapped his notebook shut. 'No sign of forced entry anywhere. All the lights were off except for the hall.'

'Thank you, Officer.'

Brown switched the central light on with the sharp end of a pencil. Giordano shifted on his feet; he wanted to do something for those poor folks and didn't know what.

'I'll make sure you guys can work in peace.'

Somebody had gone to great lengths to set the scene for them. Somebody had prepared tools and positioned bodies and thought the matter through very, very carefully. Though Madison did not know much about the crime yet, she knew this: whatever passion had sparked off such a horror, the hand that had brought it to completion was controlled, accurate and dead-cold steady. It was the evil stillness in the eye of the hurricane.

She took it all in, her eyes going over things, her hands deep in her pockets.

'Alright, tell me what you see,' Brown said. 'Let's start with the father.'

Madison crouched; she was balancing herself on her heels. Her sense of smell protested and she ignored it.

'Looks like at least twenty-four hours.'

'Yes. Why?'

'Lividity. I can't tell about rigor without moving him and we ought to wait for the ME people.'

'Go on.'

'He's blindfolded with a piece of black velvet. Not torn, cut. On the forehead, there is a sign like a cross. Drawn in blood. He's bound with ... looks like leather. Thin strip. Around his neck, hands and feet. Hands are tied behind his back. Makes it really difficult to move if you're lying down on them.'

Madison paused and breathed; it was not easy; she let the facts come to her.

'Deep red ligature marks where he's been tied. Some bruising. He put up a fight. I'm not going to take the blindfold off yet. No obvious wounds. It doesn't look like it's his blood there on the pillow. Cause of death, probably asphyxia. We'll have to check the eyes for spots.'

'What about the others?'

Madison was aware of the Crime Scene Unit men setting up on the landing; the pathologist had just arrived and was snapping his gloves on, a double layer. She focused back on the dark-haired woman and her children.

'All blindfolded. All with a cross on the forehead drawn in blood. Only the hands are tied. At the front. No ligature marks.'

'What does that tell you?'

'Post-mortem. They were tied up when they were already dead. Contact wounds to the head. You can see the tattooing. The shooter was less than two feet away. All of them, except the father. Just one shot. No bruises, no signs of struggle.'

She stood up. The room was cold, the door was open with people coming and going. The Sinclairs and their children were wearing pajamas. Brown gave her a brief nod. It was the most she had got from him in four weeks.

'How are you doing, old man?' The forensic pathologist gave Brown his usual salute.

'I was doing a hell of a lot better before I got here,' Brown said.

'I can see why.' Dr. Fellman took it in and knelt next to the father.

'James and Anne Sinclair.' Brown pointed. 'John and David Sinclair.'

The photographer joined them. Someone was already sketching out on a pad the position of the furniture.

Spencer came back. 'The maid's in shock. She's been with the family for seven years. Nice folks, never a problem. Man's a tax lawyer, wife does something part-time at a local primary school. No enemies that she knows of; never a cross word in the house.'

Madison looked away from the harshness of the camera flashes.

Brown filed the information somewhere in his mind. 'How are you doing with the photos? I want to take his blindfold off.'

'Give me another minute.'

Madison wanted to hear the pathologist's preliminary examination; she stood by and wrote on her notepad what she had just given Brown. From this moment on, the lives of James Sinclair and his family would be systematically stripped of all privacy. The camera flashed, snapped and reloaded, and somewhere above the house the helicopter waited patiently for a shot of the bodies being taken away.

Andrew Riley had heard about it on his police radio scanner. He had to think fast – an opportunity like this might not happen more than once in a lifetime. He surveyed his shabby studio apartment: four dead bodies in Blueridge might just be his way out of there.

He went to the closet and took out the Federal Express uniform that he had paid top dollar for three months earlier. It was a beaut. It came with clipboard, pad, baseball cap, boots and, best of all, a pristine Federal Express bag that he could carry slung on his shoulder. The day he got it he took it to a friend of his to get it customized. The lens of the micro-camera was hidden by a buckle on the side, a tiny remote that fit easily in his pocket controlled the shutter release button; it was sensitive enough to shoot indoors with no flash. Because that's where the bodies were.

He shaved quickly – appearances mattered – and cut himself slightly on the cheek. A reverse directory told him who lived at 1135 Blueridge: *Sinclair, James R.* Riley wrote the name on the FedEx envelope, together with the details of an imaginary sender, put in it a copy of yesterday's *Seattle Times* and pressed the envelope shut. If he managed just one good shot of the bodies – *four dead bodies* – inside the house, where nobody else was allowed, it could be worth thousands.

From the second he had heard it on the scanner, Andrew Riley was out and driving in 13 minutes.

*

The crime-scene photographer had covered every inch of the victims and the room they were in.

'Alright,' Dr. Fellman said. 'Let's see.'

He took out of his pocket a tape recorder, put it on the night table closest to the body of the man and pressed the record button.

'Sam, can you check the heating system? I need to know the exact time it comes on and goes off.'

Dr. Fellman's assistant, whom Madison had never heard utter a single word, went off. The pathologist placed the tips of his fingers on the side of the man's head and tested the rigidity of the neck muscles. He ran his fingers along the jaw.

'Rigor's complete. I'd say between 24 and 36.' He turned to Brown. 'Can you smell it?'

'What?'

He sniffed the air two inches from the dead man's face. He reached behind the head.

'Did you get a picture of the blindfold's knot?' he yelled to the photographer who was on the landing.

'Yeah. All of them.'

Dr. Fellman cut neatly through the blindfold near the knot and held it toward Brown and Madison with the tips of his fingers.

'Chloroform. Look at the blisters around his nose and mouth. It could have been enough to cause heart paralysis in a few minutes. We'll know for sure after the PM. It doesn't look like he suffocated, though.' He pushed up the eyelids in turn and looked into the eyes.

Madison had not smelled the chloroform and made a mental note not to make the same mistake again.

Dr. Fellman put the blindfold in a paper bag and tagged it. 'Let's roll him over.'

Brown helped the pathologist turn the body on his side and Dr. Fellman proceeded to snip the leather strip close to the knot and put it in another paper bag. It was encrusted with blood from the man's wrists. He tested elbows, wrists and fingers. He rolled him back and tried to bend the man's knees without taking off the ligature around his feet. Then he went around the bed and started all over, took off all the blindfolds by cutting near the knots and looked closely at the gunshot wounds.

'.22?' Brown asked.

'Looks like it. Very close range and she has no exit wound.'

'There's a couple of rounds in the wall by the children's bunk beds,' Dunne said, standing by the door.

'Any good?' Brown said.

'Pretty flattened out.'

'That's all I am going to do for now,' Dr. Fellman said and turned toward his assistant. 'Let's bag the hands and get them out of here.'

Brown was looking intently at the four naked faces, dark crosses above the eyes.

Officer Hall, not quite stepping into the room, half cleared his throat and half coughed.

'Yes?' Brown said quietly.

'There's a FedEx man downstairs, says he has an envelope for the victim – somebody's got to sign for it.'

'Madison, could you . . .'

'Yes.'

Hall turned around and pretty much bumped into the delivery man.

'Hey. I told you to wait downstairs.'

'Sorry, officer.' The man was short and stocky, with a crew cut under the baseball cap and bright eyes like a bird. 'I have to get this signed.'

Madison stepped right in front of him, between the man and the open door.

'I'll sign this for you downstairs. You can't be here.'

The man did not move. Madison stepped closer.

'Sorry but you can't be here. Let's go.' His eyes kept going past her to the room.

'You in charge?' Andrew Riley said, one hand holding the envelope out, the other in his pocket with his finger on the remote, trying to edge around the woman cop who was blocking his way, only half listening to her. 'I have to get this signed by the person in charge. Company rules.'

Madison saw his eyes and did not like what she found there. The news channel helicopter made a slow pass just above the house, and she knew.

'You. Downstairs. NOW.'

Riley backed off, his voice suddenly apologetic. 'Sorry, officer. I didn't mean to get in the way.' He started down the stairs, Madison and Hall by his side.

Her eyes on his hands, the envelope, the bag.

'Let me see your bag.' Madison said.

'No. It's this here you've got to . . .'

Madison put her hand out. 'Give me what you've got.'

Riley was pretty much surrounded; the two uniforms he had passed at the door were now standing behind him as he walked backwards and the woman cop was right in his face. He raised his hands. 'Hey.'

'"Hey"? Just give me the damn bag.' Her voice low and meaning it.

Riley took it off his shoulder and handed it to her. Madison held his eyes. She opened the large flap and the mechanism on the side was easy to see.

'You have anything else on you?'

'No.'

His belt had no buckle, no other hiding places.

'Any ID?'

Riley took out his driving license. No point in trying to show them a dud. Riley's eyes went to the bag. *You bitch*, he thought. *You bitch*.

Madison took his right arm above the elbow and started walking out, dragging him with her.

'If I were you I would keep a really low profile.' She could feel anger flapping in her chest. 'The people out there could get *very* upset if they knew what you were trying to do.'

They were going up the driveway toward the main road. Caring neighbors and curious passers-by alike were under dark umbrellas, the crowd now a few dozens. Bored news people started their cameras as the two of them left the house.

'I was just doing my job,' Riley hissed.

Madison's grip tightened. They got to the line of blue uniforms holding back the crowd. Madison had her back to the press; she leant forward and whispered, 'I ever see you again on a crime scene, you and I are going to have an abrupt disagreement. Have a nice day.'

She gave one look at the crowd and started back down, ignoring the calls from the reporters.

'Bitch!' Riley said to himself. He was getting soaked.

'Yo! Riley!' A familiar face from the wall of photographers and cameras beckoned him, more flashes went off.

Madison got back inside just as Andrew Riley started to tell his tale to a buddy, under a borrowed raincoat.

The bodies were carried out in bags; the little procession would be online news within minutes. The ambulances left, followed by the ME's car.

As the crowd closed in behind them some walked off back to their houses and others just stood around uncertain about what to do now that the principal players had gone. The rain just kept on, soft and steady over the detectives, Spencer and Dunne among them, who walked from person to person and from house to house gathering what information they could.

Brown gently poked at the hole where a bullet had been, by the top bunk of the boys' room.

Madison froze her anger out – no use for it. Someone had tried to tell them something with the murders: the message was cruel and twisted and ugly, it was time to find out about the messenger.

They moved through the house, becoming familiar with it, trying to get a sense of the life that had been lived in it. Brown paced back and forth between the master bedroom and the children's. On the white glossy door frame, about five feet from the ground, a smudge of blood and something else, probably hair.

Madison walked from room to room; no other place seemed to have been visited by the killer. The windows had not been disturbed, no broken glass swept under carpets or sofas. The kitchen on the ground floor was a long narrow room, windows to the garden on the left and white units on the right. It was spotless. Still wearing her gloves, Madison opened the door of the dishwasher; inside plates and glasses were clean. By the sink, a tall glass and a can of Coke. She looked in it – empty. One of the forensic technicians was dusting the bottom part of the window for prints.

'Will you pick this up?' she said, pointing at the can and the glass.

'Yeah,' he said without turning.

Madison made a note in her book to check whether the husband, the wife or one of the kids had been the last person walking around the house, for chronology's sake. Judging by how neat everything was, the dishwasher must have already started its cycle or the glass would have been put in it.

Upstairs, Madison was thinking her own thoughts and almost missed Brown's question.

'Why did he not shoot the father? If you come into the house to do your thing, what's the greatest threat?'

'The father,' Madison said. It had bothered her too.

'Did you see the bruise under the blindfold?'

'Yes. He put up a fight. So why not shoot him?'

'I don't know,' Brown said.

'I think he came at them and they never even knew it.' Madison looked around. 'He knew the lay of the place. He got in and just got on with it. So cocky he even let the father try to struggle his way out of it.'

Brown said nothing for so long she thought he had left the room. She turned toward him. He was transfixed, staring at the top of the door frame on the inside of the bedroom. Two words had been carved in the glossy white, the letters two inches tall, rough and angular but perfectly readable.

Thirteen Days

'We'd better get CSU to take a look at it,' Brown said.

The letters were carved with a kind of violent precision that was almost hard to look at. Someone had tried to give a little curl to the end of each one, to make them pretty.

'Have you ever seen anything like this?'

'No,' Brown replied.

'It could be a warning.'

'It could be many things. None of them good.'

Walking down the stairs, you could still smell the pine wax. The banisters were oak and recently polished. A lovely house, a nice family.

On the doorstep, Brown looked out at the crowd.

'Has someone taken pictures of the crowd? Somebody shoot us some video. The faces – I want to be able to see the faces.' He pointed at the wall of umbrellas as flashes started going and television cameras swung into action.

Chapter 6

Frank Lauren stood in the middle of the upstairs study in the Sinclairs' house and took it in. His partner, Mary Kay Joyce, snapped on a fresh pair of gloves. They had been collecting evidence. The window had been dusted and the powder had stained the glossy white windowsill. On the leather armchair in front of the desk a book lay open face down, a hardback edition of Isak Dinesen's *Letters from Africa*. Joyce picked it up, slid it, still open, in a plastic bag; sealed it and fixed the sides with two very small clamps, tagged it and signed the label, Lauren scribbling his signature under hers. They worked the room methodically and in complete silence.

Joyce was running her hand around the side of the chair behind the desk, to check whether there was anything trapped in the fold. Her fingers dislodged a thin strip of pale green paper. She picked it up with a pair of tweezers and held it against the light.

Madison was organizing her notes as Brown drove. They had found the name of the next of kin in Sinclair's wallet and – for the maid's benefit – on a pad on the kitchen wall. In this case more than others it was important to talk to them as soon as possible as the house was probably already on the news, with all its gory significance.

There had been a statement from Lieutenant Fynn about 'the swiftness of justice' but no details of the victims or the crime had yet been released. Madison wrote a note to remind herself to ask Dr. Fellman about the time of death of the father compared to the others.

'Something else is going to happen,' Madison said. 'Thirteen days from the victims' death will fall sometime in the night between the 23rd and the 24th. That's only twelve days from today.'

'Two hundred and eighty-eight hours and change, to be precise,' Brown said.

The car pulled up to the curb, the traffic slow and the crowd of shoppers a sluggish river around them. Madison saw a mother yank her five-year-old back to her side just as he was stepping in front of a car.

'Have you met him before?' Brown asked as they got into the Stern Tower elevator.

'No. I have seen him in court. He can make it pretty nasty for a witness.'

'Yeah, well, most cops would rather stick pins in their eyes.' Brown smoothed down his tie with the flat of his left hand.

They stepped out on the ninth floor and entered the offices of Quinn, Locke & Associates.

Brown asked to see Nathan Quinn. They were directed to a waiting area and asked if they wanted anything to drink, which they declined, and were told Nathan Quinn would see them in a few minutes. Madison looked around. There was art on the walls and she remembered pictures in the papers of charity events Quinn had attended.

They were shown to his office and Nathan Quinn stood to meet them. He was somewhere in his forties; his eyes were black and had the same grave quality she had noticed in court. Up close, he didn't have the manner of detached affluence one expected from a partner in a successful firm with corporate clients. He looked like a man who would take somebody apart with what the legal system had given him, and failing that he'd just use his bare hands.

'Sergeant Brown. Detective Madison. What can I do for you? Please sit.'

This was a man who was used to dealing with the police and Madison realized that he probably thought they were there because of a case he was working on.

'Mr. Quinn, is James Sinclair an associate in this firm?' Brown asked.

Quinn sat back in his chair.

'No. He has been a partner for the last four years.'

'How long have you known him?'

'What is this about?'

'I'm sorry,' Brown said. 'I have some very bad news.'

Quinn pulled himself back.

'There is no good way to say this. James Sinclair was found dead this morning in his home. His family . . .' Brown paused. 'His wife and children were with him.'

'Annie and the boys?'

'Yes.'

'What happened?'

'An intruder. We think sometime on Saturday night.'

Nathan Quinn leant his elbows on his desk and looked down at his hands. For maybe a minute the only sound was the clicking of a computer keyboard nearby. When his eyes finally came to rest on them he spoke and his voice was steady.

'Can I see them?'

'Yes. If you think you are up to it, we would like you to do a formal identification.'

'I understand.'

'There are some questions that we need to ask you – to ask the people who worked with him.'

'Whatever we can do.' Quinn hesitated. 'How did they—'

'We will know more later on,' Brown said, avoiding the word 'post-mortem'.

'Was it a burglary?'

'It's not clear yet.'

'If there are any questions you'd like to ask me—'

'I appreciate that,' Brown said. 'We'd like to find out enough to give us a picture of the family. You knew them well?'

'Yes.'

'When was the last time you saw them?'

'I saw James in the office on Friday. He left at about five, five thirty. I left a little after he did.'

'Did you notice anything strange, anything unusual in his behavior in the last few weeks? Did he seem worried or concerned about anything?'

'No. Everything was normal.'

'How well did you know Mrs. Sinclair?'

'I knew her very well.'

'Did you also meet outside work?'

'Yes.'

'Did you visit their home?'

'Yes.'

'As far as you know, did they have any enemies, someone who wanted to do them harm?'

'Absolutely not. James is a tax lawyer and Annie teaches in primary school. They are – they were – decent and kind and generous. They had no enemies.'

'Nobody from an old case?'

'No.'

'You understand, Mr. Quinn, these are questions we have to ask. Even if it's personal.'

'Go ahead.'

'Did James or Annie Sinclair ever have an affair? Somebody who might be angry enough to harm them?'

'No,' Quinn said.

'Would you know if they had?' Brown said gently.

Quinn's eyes held Brown's for a moment. He would tell the police things to help them do their job, Madison saw that in him, but Nathan Quinn would not unfold the lives of his friends and lay them open for strangers to take apart.

'They were devoted to each other.'

'This is it, for the moment. Thank you,' Brown said, standing up.

Quinn stood with him. 'Did the neighbors see or hear anything?'

'We are still canvassing.'

'Any signs of forced entry?'

'Not obvious ones, no. Of course, it is too early to say.'

'How many people do you think were involved?'

'We are still working the scene.'

Quinn rubbed his temples with his index fingers.

'Sergeant, the number of murders in Seattle last year was twenty, the year before that, nineteen. Compared to other metropolitan areas, it's a pretty safe place, with a high murder clearance rate. This was not a burglary.'

Quinn looked from one to the other, taking measure of them as they had done of him. 'I will meet you there in half an hour,' he said. 'I have to call Annie's sister in Chicago.'

As the doors of the elevator closed in front of them, Madison saw three or four people gather around Quinn and the expressions on their faces as they were being told. The dumb animal shock, the pain.

Back in the car, they checked the radio and found there was a message from Mary Kay Joyce. They were patched through and

Joyce's voice crackled on the line; she was calling from the unit van.

'We have found two halves of a check for $25,000. One half was in the study, the other in the kitchen bin. Do you receive clearly?'

'Yes, go ahead.'

'The signature is only half written; it stops in the middle, but it's very clear. The name is John Cameron. J–O–H–N C–A–M–E–R–O–N. You got that?'

'I got it.'

Madison looked up from her notebook. For a moment there was just the static crackle of the radio and the rain on the windshield.

'I've called in Payne,' Joyce continued. 'It's his day off and he was pretty pissed off. There are dozens of items to go through but I'll put the check on the top of the pile.'

Payne was the top man in Latents. If anybody or anything had touched the slip of paper he would find out.

Brown was not an expansive man and Madison liked how he wore his thoughts close to the chest. He wound down the window and took a couple of breaths as if the air in the car had suddenly turned foul.

'What do you know about John Cameron?' he asked her.

Madison had heard many things over the years – hard facts bulked up by speculation, hearsay and myth.

'I know about the *Nostromo*,' she replied.

'Then you know enough. If he is in any way involved in this thing, any piece of evidence we have is gold dust.'

'What do you mean?'

'There were five dead on the *Nostromo*. Two cops, three ex-cons. He slit their throats and let them bleed out.'

'I remember.' Madison had been barely out of the Academy and the case had been news for weeks. The boat and its cargo had been found in the waters near Orcas Island. They had never managed to get all the blood off the deck – the wood had been black with it. Nobody had ever been charged with the murders.

'We had nothing. No evidence, no eyewitness, no case. Snitches were afraid to even mention his name. But it was him alright.'

Madison remembered the pictures in the papers: standard ones for the cops and prison issue for the ex-cons. Brown drove toward the morgue.

'Two years later we had the body of a known dealer bobbing up in Lake Union. His hands had been cut off, his eyes were missing and he had been almost completely decapitated. A reliable informant said it was Cameron's work and we got a stampede of dealers leaving town. Next thing, the informant said he'd changed his mind and we are left with nothing.'

'How does someone like Cameron know the Sinclairs? What's the connection?' Madison said. 'Sinclair was an attorney. A *tax-attorney*. Very white collar, very safe.'

'Remember that we don't know for sure that it's *our* Cameron. It could just be the same name.'

'Maybe. Is there a file for him? Was he ever arrested?'

'We never got that close. But he was printed once, drunk driving, when he was a kid. After that, nothing. The only reason we have his prints today is that he had a couple of cold ones when he was eighteen.'

'Then we also have a picture.'

'For what it's worth, a twenty-year-old picture.'

'We can get it computer-altered. See what he might look like today. And show it to the neighbors.'

'Once we mention Cameron's name all hell will break loose, I want one definite link between them.'

'Let me get started on this. We need his file and prints. I'll catch up with you at the morgue.'

'Madison, be discreet.'

Brown had to stop at a busy corner. Madison left the car and disappeared into the crowd.

In the building that temporarily housed the office of the Medical Examiner and the Crime Lab, technicians came and went about their business. Brown waited in the hall. Quinn was a difficult man to read and Brown wanted to see how he would carry himself through the ordeal of the identification.

He hoped he would learn something about the kind of man Quinn was and maybe one day that knowledge would be a resource they could count on.

When the moment came Nathan Quinn stood by the window. Brown knocked on the glass and the blinds revealed four slain bodies. Quinn looked from face to face, then turned and nodded once.

In the parking lot, he sat in his car for minutes; after a while he drove off at speed. Brown looked at the space where the car had been and thought how Quinn's right hand had been shaking and he had put it in the pocket of his coat.

Brown took a glass of water from the cooler in the corridor and downed some Vitamin C with it. He cleared his mind, took out his notepad and walked into the sanitized chill of the autopsy room.

Chapter 7

Madison stood by the printer in the Communication Center and hoped that the quality of the picture that the Photo Unit was sending would be good enough for a first look. They would have to work from a copy of the original itself for the age alterations to be successful, if it ever came to that.

From the moment Cameron's name had been mentioned in the car, it had been in her thoughts like a low-level sound she could not get rid of. Her mind flashed back to the blindfolded bodies in Blueridge.

Like hunters of old, Madison felt her own need to see the eyes of the enemy to get a sense of him. She tried to remember the details of the *Nostromo* killings.

Little was known for sure about how the day went down. Every crook in every bar had a favorite version. Apparently the two cops, detectives from LAPD, had something nasty going on with the other three. Nobody knew how Cameron fit into that but somehow he did because the five men had decided that he would not be coming back from the trip.

It was a glorious day in August, the sun reflecting off the gleaming deck and a fresh breeze blowing in from the sea.

Whether he knew or not, when they started off, that they had decided to kill him, John Cameron did not run when he found out. The police recovered two 9mm Glocks and three revolvers near the bodies, all with a number of rounds spent, shell casings rolling with the swell. Yet no blood except for the dead men's, no physical evidence that anybody else had ever been on the boat and no explanation of how he had left it.

A fisherman on the dock had seen six men get onto the *Nostromo* but he could give no description. Some said Cameron drugged them, then killed them one by one; some said that he got them to shoot each other. The one known fact was that, in spite of all the ammunition gone, the men had each been killed by a single incised wound to the neck.

After that, Cameron disappeared. Very few knew what he looked like. For all you knew, the story went, he might be the guy at the end of the bar, or the guy you just bitched with about the game.

The machine started to hum.

A couple of patrol officers she knew were walking toward her in the corridor; Madison tore off the sheet of paper with the name and the picture and, without looking at it, left the building and found her car in the parking lot.

Sitting in her car, she turned the sheet over and looked at John Cameron, alleged murderer of six. It was the picture of a boy, a teenager who looked his age. A soft face with longish hair that would have been right 20 years ago. The charge had been drunk driving but he did not look under the influence. He looked somber and Madison held his gaze. Five eleven, dark and dark, the only distinctive marks the scars on his forearms and the back of his right hand. She put the photograph in an envelope with the set of fingerprints and drove off under the light rain to see James Sinclair and his family one last time.

In the four hours following the first item on television, the police switchboard received 27 calls confessing to the murders: 22 men, five women, the closest in Spokane, the farthest in Miami. All had to be dealt with and all had to be exonerated. It was a pointless task and a waste of man hours, and everybody knew it would get a lot worse.

The *Seattle Times* had given it the front page: a pretty photograph of the house and what little had been made public; it kept speculation to a minimum.

The *Washington Star* ran the headline 'Christmas Slaughter' with a picture of Madison holding Riley by the elbow. It speculated on the nature of the murders and gratuitously mentioned the homicide that had taken place on Blueridge some years before, when a little girl had accidentally shot her neighbor.

Under the spitting weather, people walked to the newsstands and went online: gradually, as if a storm was about to hit the city, windows were checked, back doors were locked and children were told they could not play outside.

Chapter 8

Madison walked in just as Dr. Fellman completed the Y-shaped incision on the body of the father.

They had already been through an extensive external examination and removed his pajamas. Livor mortis, the discoloration of the body by the settling of blood, had shown that it had not been moved after death. Blood, urine and hair samples had been collected, and oral and anal swabs taken. Nothing indicated that a sex crime had taken place but in this kind of homicide Dr. Fellman was too experienced not to cover all the bases.

Brown was leaning against the opposite wall with a view of the autopsy table. The doctor was dictating his notes into a hanging microphone and they would then take final shape in the report. His voice was a steady monotone of details and instructions to Sam, also in green scrubs and wearing a clear plastic eye-mask.

'. . . Organs will be congested and slightly cyanosed. Presence of an old appendectomy scar. We had found that the brain was swollen and engorged. The lungs appear similarly congested. Appearance consistent with prolonged inhalation. Toxicology will confirm. See blindfold.'

Madison tapped her envelope for Brown to see.

'I've got it,' she said.

'Any problems?'

'No. I have the picture, a comparison signature and prints. Have you seen the check?'

'Yeah, Documents has it upstairs. It's pretty creased up but workable. They will have to do the signature before it gets dipped for prints. They are waiting for you.'

'What have they found?'

'Chloroform.' Brown looked over at the notes he had taken as Dr. Fellman was talking. 'There was bruising on the zygomatic bone under his left eye, probably the butt of a gun. Enough strength to knock him out for a few minutes but no broken bones. I guess he then went on to do his business with the mother and the kids. When the father came to he was tied up, blindfolded and inhaling the poison.'

'He struggled.' Madison could see the deep red marks around his wrists and feet from where she was standing.

'It almost cut through to the bone. He struggled till his heart gave out.'

'Doctor,' Madison asked, 'how long was he conscious?'

It was something that had bothered her from the start, the difference in the manner in which the death sentences had been dealt out.

'It's difficult to say. It has been known to take up to fifteen minutes for chloroform to take effect. In this quantity and proximity, I'd say a few minutes definitely. With convulsions and severe pain.'

Madison turned to Brown.

'Few minutes of Sinclair thrashing around on the bed—' she said.

'And the covers were neatly turned under the bodies when they were found.' Brown nodded.

'The killer made the bed before he left.' She finished her thought.

Thus Madison saw him for the first time – the intruder, waiting for his victim to grow still, watching over him as his life ebbed away, then gently smoothing the sheets under the bodies, slightly moving this or that, until the tableau was complete. She did not recoil from the image. In her mind, she stood silent by the door and watched him work and tried to see his face. Dr. Fellman was starting on gastric contents as she left.

Fingerprint Identification and Disputed Documents were on the second floor of the drab concrete building. Madison had visited often during a stint in Robbery and was on good terms with the technicians.

Payne was in shirtsleeves and drinking rosehip tea. Madison had taken an extra course in Forensics and that gold star went a long way with him.

'How are you doing, Detective?'

'Very well. I have the signature.'

'Documents has a copy. I couldn't wait.'

Madison took out the set of fingerprints from the envelope and gave it to Payne. He looked at the name on the top of the page.

'I see. I'll run a parallel check for exclusion as with the family members. Points of entry, the usual.'

Madison remembered something. 'Did you work the *Nostromo*?'

'For what it was worth. It was clean as a whistle. It had been completely wiped down.'

Madison could smell the strong and unpleasant metallic odor of ninhydrin mixed with the overripe-bananas scent of amyl acetate. It was the best solution for dipping paper and would not cause the ink to run. She wasn't sorry to leave the room.

'When you see Brown, remind him this is my day off,' Payne called after her.

Wade Goodwin in Documents pushed his glasses back on his nose. 'Frankly, I'd be a lot happier if we had a number of genuine originals to compare it with. You're not giving us very much to work on here and this is a long way from standing up in court. Do you know about top of the letter and bottom of the letter comparisons?'

'I do,' Madison replied.

They were looking at two zigzag lines he had just drawn over the partial name.

'Well, having said all that, I think the check signature was forged.'

'Thank you,' Madison said. It was the beginning: five minutes ago they had nothing, now they had a possible motive. Someone had forged a check, someone had died.

In Blueridge the neighbors were cooperative and concerned but nobody remembered anything unusual about Saturday night or the days before it. Even though Brown knew that the King County Prosecutor's Office wouldn't hang a mad dog on eyewitness testimony, you had to have it on your side.

Payne and his people were dusting and comparing prints from dozens of items. The process took the time it took – snapping at their heels would not make them go any faster.

Dr. Fellman compared the angle of the entry wounds on the victims who had been shot and the bruising on the father's cheek.

'What do you think?' Brown asked as the doctor stepped away from the operating table.

'I know what I think, and it's too damn little to help.'

'Go on.'

'The victims were lying down when they were attacked; there was hair and blood on a door frame when he moved one of the children. I'd say he's about five eleven to six one, or near enough. Right-handed and physically strong.'

'Mr. Average. It fits. From the angle of the incision in the wood the words were probably carved with the right hand.'

'There was no sexual activity of any kind, so no body fluids either.'

The internal telephone rang and Dr. Fellman picked up. After a few words he replaced the receiver.

'I found a few hairs in the ligature knot on Sinclair's wrists.' He snapped off his gloves. 'I had them checked.'

'Whose are they?'

Fellman smiled. 'Unidentified adult male's.'

'We've got *his* DNA?'

'The hairs are beautiful. Roots and everything. Couldn't ask for more.'

Dr. Fellman was white and drained, almost ghostly in his green scrubs. Brown shook hands and left.

For hours he had tried to reach Nathan Quinn on his cellphone. He wanted to ask whether Sinclair had ever mentioned Cameron. As he sat in his car he tried again. No answer; the phone was still switched off.

Brown was tired and hungry. The rain had turned to thin snow and the air in the car was sharp.

On the way to the precinct, he stopped for a chicken sandwich and a cup of coffee and had both as he drove.

Chapter 9

Madison told Brown about the forged signature and then drove back to Stern Tower to interview some of Sinclair's colleagues. Nathan Quinn had left the office hours before. Carl Doyle set her up in a conference room with thick pale blue carpets and a table which could seat twenty. In the window, the gray slab of Puget Sound. There was a jug of water and glasses on a tray on the table.

'Anything I can do to help,' Doyle said as he ushered in a young associate. The woman tried her best not to cry. She had a tissue which she used to dab her eyes and the mascara left black marks on it.

'I wish there was something I could tell you but I just can't imagine anybody doing such a thing,' she said. 'This is so awful.'

After a few unproductive minutes Madison let her go. 'Thank you for your help. That's all I need for the moment,' she said.

She interviewed two more associates; they were all pretty much still in shock and had very little to contribute.

Carl Doyle sat down across from Madison; his eyes were red-rimmed but he looked under control. Madison liked how he had tried to comfort some of the others; under the slightly camp manner she sensed some real strength. He ran his hands through his hair and rubbed his eyes.

'What can I tell you, Detective?'

'First, how long have you been at Quinn Locke?'

'About ten years.'

'About the same as James Sinclair.'

'That's right. I started two months before he did.'

'Did you know him well?'

Doyle poured himself some water; he was giving the question some thought.

'I don't know if I can say I did. We did not go out for dinner or a beer, if that's what you mean, but I saw him every day. I knew when things were going badly with a case, when something good happened.'

Doyle's eyes were a sharp blue and fixed on Madison's.

'I remember when his first boy was born.'

Madison leant forward.

'What do you remember of these last weeks? How was he?'

'There's a complex lawsuit they wanted to sort out before the holidays; all was going well with that. James was tired but okay. He was talking about going away for a few days for New Year.'

'Was he in any way different from usual? Was there any change to his routine?'

'No.'

'Anybody came to see him who didn't look right to you?'

'No.'

Madison felt disappointment like a slow bitter drink she had to take over and over again.

'One last question: are you aware of a client or a friend of James Sinclair's called John Cameron?'

Doyle looked at her for a long moment, the pale eyelashes blinking.

'Of course,' he said. 'James has known him for years.'

'Excuse me?'

'They have known each other since they were kids.'

'How do you know that?'

'The Hoh River. They were the Hoh River boys.'

Madison hadn't heard the name for a long time but remembered instantly. How, years after the event, her grandmother had walked her to Rachel's house so that she wouldn't be on the street alone, not even for five minutes.

'Have you met John Cameron?' she asked.

'No, I haven't.'

'Thank you very much. That's it for now.'

Doyle left and closed the door. Madison punched in Brown's cell number and hoped to God he could be reached.

'Sinclair has known Cameron for years. They are *friends*. The Hoh River case,' Madison said.

Brown went quiet for a while, then his voice came back.

'We have DNA. There were hairs in a ligature knot. Preliminary tests indicate they don't belong to the victims.'

'Any possible characteristics yet?'

'Not really. About six foot, right-handed and strong. The hairs could be from a dark-haired man. It covers at least a quarter of the population.'

'We should talk to Quinn. He was that close to Sinclair, he must know he was friends with Cameron.'

'I've tried him all afternoon. His phone is switched off.'

'He's going to have to go home some time.'

'You're three hours past the end of your shift.'

'I know. I'll come in to write up the interviews. Will Records have the file for the Hoh River?'

'Not where you can find it this late. It's too old.'

'How late are you going to stay?'

'I still have to talk to VICAP.'

VICAP, the Violent Criminal Apprehension Program, is a database of offenders and crimes created by the FBI: if a murder in

Arkansas has the same characteristics as a homicide in Maryland, the investigating authorities can compare reports and find out if they have been committed by the same individual. It is an invaluable tool and Brown was the contact man in Seattle.

Madison got up to leave and switched off the overhead light. The view, which had been made invisible by the reflection on the window pane, revealed itself. From the pitch black where the sea was, the wind was carrying snowflakes out of the darkness and into the flickering lights of the city. Without thinking, Madison put her palm flat on the glass as if she could touch them. Beyond it, a Thing lived and breathed that had drawn crosses in blood. *I see you*, she thought.

Chapter 10

Andrew Riley sat on a stool at the bar, an empty shot glass by his hand and a bottle of Budweiser he was working his way through. He had been at the business of getting drunk for a while and had managed to dull the edge of his anger a little.

It still bit hard every time he thought of the camera in the FedEx bag he would never see again and the humiliation of having made the front page looking like a jerk. A copy of the *Washington Star* had been passed from hand to hand in the crowded bar and some of the regulars had bought him drinks and slapped his back.

Jordan's is a sports bar off Elliott Avenue; there are signed Mariners and Seahawks pictures on the walls and framed newspaper articles written by reporters who got drunk there from time to time.

After being dragged out of the house by Madison, he had stayed and bitched with a colleague. Standing on the balls of his feet he had seen the bodies being taken away and looked at the ME vans until they had disappeared in traffic.

Back home he had quickly changed out of the FedEx uniform, grabbed his bag with the Leica and the Olympus and their different lenses and practically run out of the house. He couldn't bear to be in it. Driving toward downtown he had called his agency and a friend at the *Star*.

Steamed up in his car, he had waited for hours to get a picture of a Hollywood actress who was shooting a movie in town. He saw her and snapped her and emailed the agency, and all the time he thought only of the three minutes he had spent inside 1135 Blueridge. Then he had gone to the bar.

The guy sitting on his right had been talking to him, his voice reaching him through the cheers of the crowd watching the game on cable and his own disordered thoughts.

'What it is, it's a hawk's game.'

What the hell is a hawk's game?

Riley rubbed his eyes with his fists like a child. His companion was a couple of decades older than he was, with a good suit and an expensive watch. He made a circling motion with his right index finger and the bartender nodded and brought them both fresh drinks.

Riley downed the shot in one, turned to the suit, his left elbow on the bar, and tried to concentrate on what the man was saying. *A whole load of nothing*, he thought.

He did not see the door open or the man walk in, find a way through the bodies, order a Coke and lean on the bar behind him, his eyes on the game.

More often than not it's what you don't know that keeps you safe. Andrew Riley would never be so close to the making of his own death as he was then, sad and frustrated, talking to a stranger in a noisy bar.

'Do you know who Weegee is?' Riley asked.

'Who?'

'Never mind.'

Alcohol made him melancholy and he'd rather be angry. He did not feel the eyes scanning the crowd and past him, resting back on the game. A loud cheer and clapping – somebody somewhere had done good work on the field.

The telephone behind the bar rang and the bartender picked up, the flat of his hand against his other ear.

'Riley,' he said and held the receiver to him.

He had occasionally got calls there.

'Riley here.'

Nothing. There was noise and crackle; he wasn't sure whether it came from the telephone or from the headache pushing against the inside of his eyes.

'Hello?'

The line went dead.

'Shit!' He replaced the receiver and finished his beer in one long draw. He could smell old sweat and cigarette smoke on the fleece top he was wearing and it almost made him gag.

'Nice talking to you, man,' he said and put a couple of bills on the bar. He had a heavy mountain jacket from REI with down-filled lining and Velcro straps on the wrists. He patted the inside pocket to check that his Olympus was still there. Like an off-duty police officer, he always carried a weapon.

He made his way through and a moment later was standing in the freezing cold. He had left his car in an alley on the side of the building, where staff parked. No more than three seconds away from a quick drive home and a long sleep.

'Riley.' The voice was in the darkness behind him.

'Yeah?' He started to turn and something hit him hard on the side of the face. A pain so sharp it knocked the breath out of him. And again, before he could put his hands up and fall to the ground on his knees. He couldn't breathe, he couldn't see. He put his arms around his head. He felt hands patting him down. His face was on the wet concrete, rough against his bloody cheek.

The man took the camera from his inside pocket, wrapped the strap around his own hand and hit it against the brick wall just above Riley's head.

Once, twice. A crunching sound and a shower of tiny fragments of plastic and metal shattering. Three times, until there was hardly anything left at the end of the strap.

Riley felt the man pause, standing over him as he fought for every breath.

This is it, he thought, and he passed out.

A waiter found him ten minutes later, called 911 and put a blanket around him to keep him warm until the medics arrived.

Chapter 11

Brown had three neat piles of paperwork on his desk and he referred to them as he was talking on the phone. His shirtsleeves were rolled up, his tie still tightly knotted.

'No. Thought not. The blood work isn't in yet.'

Madison came in the door with notebooks under her arm and a holder with two cups. They had taken over the third interview room. Members of the public came up to talk to detectives from time to time and the large open-plan room was an inappropriate location for their crime-scene photos.

Madison put a cup on the corner of Brown's desk and took out the pad with her interview notes.

'Thank you,' he said with a hand on the mouthpiece. 'It's Kamen.'

Fred Kamen was one of the bright lights of the Investigative Support Unit at the FBI Academy in Quantico, the section once called Behavioral Science. He had taught one of Madison's classes at the University of Chicago. It was at the time of the Goulden–McKee kidnapping, and she remembered he would always leave with another agent at the end of the sessions and spend the rest of his waking hours trying to get the teenager back to his family. It had given a sense of urgency to the classes and they had all felt somewhat felt involved. When the boy had been found safe and unharmed after four weeks of negotiations, Madison and her classmates had cheered.

'Yes, I know. It will be posted on the hotline. Tomorrow. Bye.'

Brown adjusted the reading glasses on the bridge of his nose. On top of the piles of interviews lay four pictures, one for each victim as they had been found. On the windowsill, unread and untouched, Brown's copy of *Moby-Dick*. For a second there Madison saw him as a clerk in some unearthly office.

'It will take a few hours to get an answer from VICAP but Kamen has never personally encountered this kind of staging before and he doesn't think *cult* either. He doesn't like the 'thirteen days' thing, though – there's a timeline here we know nothing about.'

'Any news from Prints?'

'Nothing unusual. Payne called half an hour ago – they were done for the day. They found a whole load of the family's, some of the maid's, some small ones in the kids' bedroom, friends probably. But no Cameron.'

Madison was talking and typing.

'If we did find any, a good attorney could argue he left them there on another occasion.'

She stopped typing and looked up.

'How many people know?'

'You, me, Fynn, Payne, Lauren and Joyce.'

'I mean, what are the chances of this being just a coincidence and the name on the check is actually a doctor in Tacoma whose taxes Sinclair was doing?'

'I'd say pretty close to zero.'

'I don't remember any message left on the *Nostromo* or the dealer's body.'

'No, that's a first.'

Madison went back to typing, the words coming out in a rush while her mind was somewhere else.

'You did good today,' he said.

She looked up but Brown was holding a blood-spatter chart against the light and did not meet her eyes.

'This case, whatever is going to happen with it, we are going to build it from the ground up. Piece by piece. The check is one brick. Don't let that close off all other possibilities,' he continued.

'What are you saying?'

'I'm saying keep an open mind.'

'I intend to.'

'I know, but cases have a momentum of their own. This one is going to start running very soon.' He was still looking at the chart. 'Don't let that affect your judgment.'

Somebody else might have found his tone condescending; Madison thought it over for a second. He was trying to teach her something – every other consideration was irrelevant. She finished the paperwork and added it to Brown's.

'First thing tomorrow we are going to dig up the Hoh River file,' he said. 'If that's how they knew each other, that's where we start.'

'I want to get going on that.' Madison put on her jacket. 'I'm going to the library.'

Brown looked out of the window. It was pitch black.

'I have a friend,' she said as she straightened a couple of pencils on her desk. 'The papers must have run the story at the time. I'll see what I can find.'

Madison, driving north toward 4th Avenue, pulls in by an all-night grocery store and punches a number in her cellphone.

'Mr. Burton, it's Alice Madison. Is it alright if I come by tonight?'

The store didn't have much in the way of patisserie, but manners dictated that you don't go visiting empty-handed. She remembered the last time and picked a rich chocolate cake. There was no traffic and, for no reason at all, she drove past the library and down 6th Avenue. The ninth floor of Stern Tower, the offices of Quinn Locke, lay in shadow. She looked up, drove around the block and then made a loop back to where she had come from. She parked only a few yards from the service entrance of the Public Library and pressed the buzzer lightly. The metal door sprang open almost immediately.

A few years before, Ernie Burton's sixteen-year-old daughter had got herself into some minor police trouble. Madison had made the trouble go away and that had bought her a lifetime all-hours pass at the downtown branch of the Seattle Public Library. Burton was the head night guy, as they called him, and he had wasted no time extending such privileges to her and making sure his colleagues did the same.

She found him and three others in the thick of a card game. They were all men who had come to security work after a life doing other jobs and who welcomed, as well as the salary, the opportunity to escape their retirement and their wives. Madison looked at the table for less than three seconds and knew who was winning, who was losing and who was glad of the interruption.

'Look who's here.'

'Jeez, Detective, I thought we'd never see you again. I was all heartbroken.'

'How's your wife, Ronnie?' Madison asked with a smile.

'Still alive. You married yet?'

'What, give up the chance to come down here and flirt with you guys?'

They cut the cake and ate it with some terrible instant coffee.

'I know you're here to do your work; we don't want to be holding you up,' Burton said.

'I'd better get going.'

The four men went back to their card game and Madison found

her way through the familiar building. It was never just about coming after hours to get something she needed.

When Burton had first given her the pass, it was the most he could do to repay a kindness; he couldn't have imagined that in Madison's eyes his gift far outweighed what she had done for him. It had taken her less than fifteen minutes to make things right with her boss and Social Services, in exchange for which she now had the keys to the toy store.

Most of the times she had come looking for something in particular, but after her grandfather passed on she would drop by once a month or so and spend a couple of hours reading in the vast room, after midnight, before the cleaners turned up.

Madison stopped by the Humanities Department on the first floor to check on a file card index the date on which the articles had appeared in the local papers. The reader-printers for the microfilm of the Newspapers Department were on the second floor and it took her fifty minutes to get together what she had come for.

The story had been covered extensively and she made photocopies of every single article. She organized the sheets roughly in date order, giving precedence to serious reporting over tabloid hacks. The large rectangular room was dimly lit; the sounds of the men playing cards downstairs didn't reach that far. There was a sign by the librarians' desk: No eating or drinking on the premises.

Shortly after 11 p.m. Madison sat at her usual table, took out of her bag a can of Coke and a yellow legal-size notepad, took a sip and started reading. The *Times* was the first: an unemotional piece, economical with the gory details. She read it twice.

On August 28, 1985 three boys had been kidnapped while they were fishing in a wooded park in Ballard. Their names were David Quinn, 13; James Sinclair, 13; John Cameron, 12.

David Quinn.

Four men in a blue van approached the boys at Jackson Pond.

They used chloroform on rags, bundled them into the van and left. There were no witnesses.

When the boys did not come home in the afternoon the parents started to worry and a search party was organized. Their bicycles were found at the bottom of the pond. The families started to panic. Relatives and friends searched every inch of the area surrounding Jackson Pond and knocked on every door of the neighborhood. Night came and brought no news. The boys had vanished.

At 5.30 a.m. on August 29, Carlton Gray was driving along the Upper Hoh Road. A boy, later identified as John Cameron, came out of the woods and almost got himself run over as he stopped his truck. The boy had difficulty explaining himself but Gray could see that he was in a highly emotional state and wanted to lead him somewhere.

At that point Gray had noticed that the boy's arms were covered in blood. The sleeves of his T-shirt had been repeatedly slashed. They walked in the woods for maybe 15 minutes and then reached a clearing.

There, tied to a Sitka spruce, Carlton Gray found James Sinclair, alive but in shock. He freed the boy and took both children back to his truck, from which he radioed for help. The State Police and the medics arrived quickly. They had mistakenly assumed that all three boys had been found safe and had alerted the parents.

What had happened in the previous 24 hours was not completely clear. The authorities were able to gather the following facts: the children had been driven there and each had been tied to a tree. Then things became confused: blindfolded, his friends had heard David Quinn gasp and choke. After a while, silence. A few minutes later the men had left and taken Quinn with them. The other two were abandoned in the forest.

David Quinn. Madison got up and went to the window. She finished her Coke and threw it into the librarian's wastepaper basket. She looked at her watch: Brown would want to know. She dialed his cellphone.

'The third boy. The one who died in the woods. It was Nathan Quinn's younger brother.'

'I guess we have our link.'

'Yup.'

'You're going home soon, right?'

'I'll just finish up here.'

Madison wanted a strong cup of coffee really badly but the stuff from the dispenser downstairs was like thin, bitter mud. Instead, she washed her face with freezing-cold water and went back to her desk.

The *Post-Intelligencer* had run pretty much the same story as the *Times*. The sad conclusion for both was that there had been no visible motive for the kidnapping and no one had ever been held accountable.

The tabloids didn't offer any further facts. However, they did have photographs. Madison held the page up to the lamp. It was school pictures, one for each of the boys. Her eyes went to Cameron's: he was the youngest and looked smaller than the others. James Sinclair was grinning and David Quinn was wearing a Mariners shirt, his hair was fair and curly and he had just combed it for the photograph.

Madison turned the pages. There was a picture of the families after David Quinn's memorial service, no doubt the work of an enterprising photographer who had sneaked into the cemetery like Andrew Riley into the crime scene.

He had caught up with them as they were leaving the grave. It was an outrageous breach of their privacy in the most painful moment. It was a stunning picture.

Black and white, it must have been overcast that day, no shadows from anything or anybody. In the foreground a man and a woman wearing black, surrounded by family and friends, their faces stunned beyond grief. A close group of maybe fifty people, mostly adults, some children.

All the men wore yarmulkes, the Jewish skullcap worn during prayers. A man had put his hand on the father's shoulder; he was saying something. Next to him the two surviving boys, Cameron's arm still in a sling. They looked lost. Standing by them, Nathan Quinn, a few years older, probably already in college. He was looking at his mother, raising his left hand as if to touch her.

A chill shook Madison as if the temperature had suddenly dropped, a wave of nausea and a sense of falling. She slapped the folder shut, put her palm on it.

She let a minute go by just sitting in the gloomy silence, then gathered her things and left.

She turned the engine on in her car and out of nowhere she smelled the sweet air of the day in March when her mother had been buried. There were cherry blossoms in the breeze. Madison wiped her eyes with the back of her wrist. Her father had stood behind her, the weight of his hands on her shoulders.

She let the engine turn over, closed her eyes, waiting for the car to warm up.

It was always the same funeral, over and over. Madison had gone to cop memorials, men and women she barely knew, and it was her mother's grave she would be standing by in dress uniform while the flag was being folded.

Her grandparents had arrived in Friday Harbor that morning and they would leave shortly after the service. She hadn't seen them in years. In their anguish they kept looking at this young girl who was so much like their dead daughter yet was a stranger to them.

Five months later, Alice woke up in the middle of the night. Her Mickey Mouse clock read 2.15 a.m. and the full moon shone in her open window. Her room looked neat in the pale light, the efforts of a twelve-year-old girl who had a stack of school counselors' telephone numbers and bereavement support groups' notices pinned to her board, and had not talked to either.

Alice made her own lunches and got good grades. *She's a fighter*, her year tutor had said. *She'll pull through*. So she covered her school books in plain brown paper and lined up her bunny slippers when she went to bed, and that somehow got her through the days; inside, though, she was drowning.

Alice heard the steps in the hall and knew it couldn't be her dad, who wouldn't be home till morning. She grabbed her baseball bat and waited, the adrenaline making her chest hurt.

When the intruder's steps had receded into the hall and out of the house, her relief tasted like copper from a bite on her lip. She waited for a minute, then slid out of bed and peeked out of the window to make sure the man had really left: way down the road, half in gloom, she saw him, walking fast and away from her. He passed under a street lamp and, even at that distance, Alice knew it was her father. She dropped her baseball bat and stood there feeling stupid. *Sugar! Why didn't he turn the darn light on?* She'd almost had a heart attack.

Turning the lights on as she went, Alice padded into the kitchen. Still unsettled and a little out of herself, she ran the water from the tap and into a glass. As she was walking back, the door to her parents' room – her father's room – was ajar and she saw that the top right-hand drawer of the dresser was sticking out a couple of inches. Her mother's drawer. They hardly ever opened it; it contained her mom's jewel box and Alice allowed herself to hold her things only very rarely, every one of them a memory too sharp and sweet.

She stood by the dresser now and everything in her soul told her to close the drawer and go back to bed. Nothing good could possibly come of it, that pinprick of doubt that would make her feel too guilty to look her father in the eye for days. She rested her forehead against the dresser; she had to look, and she knew it.

She pulled the drawer open and lifted the black velvet jewel box; the small latch in the shape of a hook was undone. The inside was lined in red silk, Alice ran her fingers over the smooth fabric: her mother's rings were gone, her pendant earrings, the necklace with the S-shaped clasp and the diamond butterfly.

Alice did not know how much they were worth but she knew they were gone and her father had not turned on the lights. She stood there for a minute, then gently replaced the box where she had found it, went back to her bedroom and picked up the baseball bat.

She had never felt such clarity before – it was dazzling. The first blow hit the bookshelf; she swung hard and it came off the wall. The desk was next. Alice worked her way methodically around her room until her arm ached too much to lift the bat; by then she had cut herself on the glass from her bathroom mirror and she was out of breath. Her father would be home before dawn. She picked her way carefully back to her bed and lay on top of it, still gripping the bat. She was going to close her eyes for just a moment, she would rest for just a second, and when he got home she would make him take her to whoever had her mother's things now. She fell asleep with a streak of dry tears on her cheeks.

Her eyes snapped open and the Mickey Mouse clock read 6.47 a.m. She looked around the room and shivered. Everything broken, everything torn. She slipped her bare feet in her sneakers and padded to the door, opened it a little. She could hear her father's deep breathing in his room.

He lay on his front under the sheets, his clothes in a pile by the bed. Alice knelt by the shirt and the jeans as she went through his pockets. She found $12 in small bills and a switchblade knife with an ivory handle she had not seen before. She put them back.

His breathing was slow and steady. She went back to the dresser and checked the jewel box. For a moment, as her hand was reaching for it, she allowed herself to hope. Nothing happened this time, no tears, no rage, no pain. In the cold light of day she knew enough about the world to know that what had been lost would stay lost and that was all there was to it. She sat on the wicker chair and watched his back rise and fall; she sat and watched him until every good memory of him had drained away; it didn't take long.

The tip of the handle of the switchblade knife stuck out of the jeans back pocket. Alice reached for it and the blade came to life. She stood over him. It seemed as if there was nothing at all between his back and the blade in her hand. She was empty and the one thing that made any sense was that he should not draw another breath. Nothing else mattered much, not the brown paper on her books or her solid grades. *Let's see the counselors get me out of this one*, a thin dark voice said inside her.

Then, gunshot loud, the dog in the yard next door barked twice and Alice saw the room and herself in it, every detail so sharp it felt drawn on her skin.

Her father would wake up late on a heavy August morning, the house empty and his daughter gone, the switchblade knife buried two inches deep into his bedside table.

One week later, when the state troopers found a little girl hiking north of Anacortes, they were surprised the father didn't seem to be in a rush to get her back home. In fact, he looked downright relieved when the grandfather took her off his hands. 'She looked like a nice kid,' one trooper said to the other afterwards, 'but you never know.'

Her grandparents watched her from the kitchen window as she sat for hours looking at the water and Vashon Island; they watched her on their quiet hikes up Mount Rainier.

'Let the girl be,' her grandfather said. 'The only thing that matters is that she's finally home, and she knows it.'

Madison didn't know whether she had adopted the city or the other way round; all she knew was that the dark woods around it had accepted her as their own. It didn't bother the mountains and the rivers that she had almost killed her father – they granted her safe passage and whatever peace she would allow herself.

Detective Alice Madison put the file on the passenger seat and the engine into gear, and she drove home. The answering machine was flashing red. 'Hey, Alice, it's Marlene. You're not ducking out of the reunion dinner this time. We should be celebrating your gold shield and that Judy made it out of Traffic, if you can believe it. Call me, before I put out an APB on you.'

Fifteen minutes later Madison was asleep on the sofa, wrapped in the white comforter from her bedroom, a half-eaten tuna sandwich on the coffee table and *Some Like It Hot* in the DVD player.

Chapter 12

Fred Tully's career had been less than shining for a long time. He sat at his desk in the offices of the *Washington Star*, a page of copy to proofread in one hand and a slice of congealed pizza in the other. He looked at the round clock hanging on the far wall. Midnight. He'd rather be somewhere else, anywhere rather than here, where he felt his life getting dimmer by the day. He thought of his wife at home, watching cable and not missing him.

The intern dropped the envelope on his desk, startling Tully almost off his chair.

'Wear shoes people can hear, will ya?' he snapped without turning.

It was a white envelope with a rigid back. His name was printed on a small label – there was no other writing. Tully looked around the room; he wasn't the kind of guy who got hand-delivered mail in the middle of the night – hadn't been for a while.

He tore the side flap with his index finger. Some son of a gun was going to get his butt kicked if this was a joke. Inside there was a sheet of paper and a smaller envelope.

Tully read the short paragraph once. He bit into what was left of the pizza and held it in his mouth as he undid the catch and took out a photograph.

It was color, taken indoors with a flash. A lamp in the foreground and what looked like part of the headboard of a bed. Tully didn't know what he was looking at. He read the paragraph, he stared at the picture, he read the paragraph, he stared at the picture.

Greg Salomon, editor of the *Star*, didn't look up when Tully strode into his office.

'What's up?'

Tully closed the door. He put the photograph on the desk. Salomon pushed up his glasses and picked it up.

'What am I looking at?'

'The Blueridge crime scene.'

There was a beat of silence between them.

'How did you get this?'

Tully smiled.

'I mean it, *how* did you get this?'

'Somebody out there loves me. I just got it.'

'Did you have to pay for it?'

'Not dollar one.'

There was a magnifier under a stack of papers, Salomon found it and examined the picture.

'You can't see too much, but enough to know what you're looking at. The real thing?'

'You bet. This came with it.' Tully handed him the sheet of paper.

I'll be in touch.

'What do you think?'

'It's not for publication – we'd get our butt chewed by the police and the DA's office. It's something to tell us he's close to it. I think *cop*,' Tully said.

'Yeah, he's just getting us interested. The next time he's going to want money. Thank God for government salaries.'

'Amen to that.' Tully scribbled on his pad. 'I'm calling the primary. We can confirm the positioning of the bodies, the blindfolds . . .'

He looked over at the picture. The dark crosses were out of focus but perfectly visible. That was all he could see – heads on pillows from the side.

'Could this be one of your regular guys?' Salomon asked.

'I don't think so.'

'I'm going to have to call Kramer; he's working the story.'

'This is *mine*, Greg.'

'I know. We'll sort something out.'

We'd better, Tully thought.

5.45 a.m., Madison was suddenly awake. The digital clock glowed on her bedside table. Only three hours earlier she had awoken on the sofa downstairs. The film had finished and, in a daze, she had switched the television off and dragged herself upstairs and into bed.

5.46 a.m., Madison got up and walked to the kitchen in her bare feet, turning on lights as she went. She poured water in the bottom half of the Italian stove-top percolator, measured coffee for the middle filter, screwed the top back on and put it on the ring.

She could perform those actions automatically and without being fully conscious; indeed she had done so many times getting up for a day tour after two hours' sleep. By 6.30 a.m. Madison had left the house.

She drove past Blueridge and pulled in next to the blue-and-white parked by the front door.

The two uniforms looked up, the long cold hours all over their faces. She had never seen them before. Madison wound down her window and showed her badge.

'Madison, Homicide. How are you doing?'

The older of the two just nodded.

'Quiet night?'

'A couple of jerks tried to steal some crime-scene tape.' He pointed at the yellow ribbon on the ground by the side door.

The house already had an empty feel to it, as if people hadn't slept and cooked and walked around inside it for a long time.

Madison hit the commuter traffic driving into town; in the thin sunlight, glass, metal and water shimmered in the distance.

She turned the car radio on, instantly regretted it and turned it off. It hadn't been such a good idea to stop by the house. She had felt almost compelled to go in right then and make her way through it, top to bottom, attic to basement. Now that search would have to wait for hours. The killer had chosen the house to set his work; the work was how he would reveal himself to them.

Nathan Quinn would not be pleased: they were going to need a warrant to sieve through Sinclair's financial affairs, work files, cases. He probably took work home – the check had been found in the study.

There it was: a paltry $25,000 had cost four people their lives and was going to bring down, once and for all, a pretty nasty piece of work who should have known better.

The rec room was cramped but it was the only private space that would contain all of them at the same time. The detectives sat around the table. The case file, between the polystyrene cups and notebooks, was already inches thick.

Brown was running the briefing, with Madison to back him up. He checked his watch. Spencer and Dunne had brought in the blackboard with floor plans of the Sinclairs' house. Lieutenant Fynn had come in with copies of the morning papers wedged under his arm: in two hours he was going to meet a woman from the department's Public Affairs Office. He'd rather have root canal.

They had Spencer, Dunne and Kelly for another 48 hours. After that, Brown and Madison would be on their own – the others would move to new cases and help with the legwork whenever they could.

Madison noticed Kelly was wearing his dark blue suit, tight across his ex-line backer shoulders but still smart, and a garish purple tie. It was his court outfit – they were going to lose him in the afternoon to a year-old robbery–murder just come to trial.

They had all been at the crime scene, smelled the 36 hours dead on their clothes. Brown went straight to the point.

'We have the ME's preliminary autopsy notes, I'll get to those in a minute. While you gentlemen were getting trench foot on the canvass Lauren and Joyce found half of a torn check in the folds of a chair in the study, the other half in the kitchen bin.'

Madison, her legs stretched long under the table, sipped her coffee and waited for Brown to drop the bomb. Fynn had already been told.

'The check is a dud,' Brown continued. 'The signature is a forgery, the prints on it are Sinclair's, the forged signature name is *John Cameron.*'

Any rustling of paper, feet-shuffling or note-taking stopped dead right then. Kelly put down his pen.

Dunne smiled wide. 'I guess this is what some people might call a "lead".'

Brown checked his watch again. 'So far, so good. Sinclair and Cameron go way back – they were the Hoh River boys.' There were flashes of recognition around the room. 'We know they knew each other. If Sinclair stole from him, anything's possible.'

'For years I've been waiting for that piece of shit to resurface. I swear to God, I knew he would,' Kelly said as he played with the knot on his tie.

'What have we got?' Lieutenant Fynn asked.

'We have hairs from the ligature knot around Sinclair's hands. Fellman is working on them; he says he can get DNA. It looks like they might belong to the intruder,' Brown said. 'Toxicology confirmed chloroform on the father's blindfold.'

Madison felt the shift in perception around the room like an icy draft: five minutes ago James Sinclair was the victim of a brutal murder, now he was quite possibly a greedy sonofabitch who got his family killed.

Brown took his glasses off and rubbed his eyes.

'Let's all hang on a minute here. One, we do not have a murder weapon – and, by the way, Ballistics says it was a .22. Two, we don't even have an entry point yet.'

'Doors and windows?' Spencer asked.

'Locked and clean. No footprints around the outside and no forced entry marks.'

'What, he beamed in?' Dunne said.

'Looks like it.'

'What about "thirteen days"?' Spencer asked.

'Nothing solid. If it's a message we don't even know who the message is for. We can presume it was for us to see but as for meaning, nothing yet.'

The telephone rang and Brown picked up. It was Bob Payne. They talked for less than one minute. When he hung up, he stared at the receiver for almost as long.

Around him, Dunne was asking Madison about the meeting with Quinn, while Lieutenant Fynn and Spencer went over the newspapers' headlines.

Madison's eyes met Brown's across the room. He looked as if he had just been told that the sun would rise from the west from now on.

'What?' she mouthed to him.

Brown blinked twice and came back to himself.

'It was Payne. There was a glass found in the kitchen by the sink. He made a match. John Cameron's prints are on it. Three prints, twelve points of similarity.'

Juries had convicted with less. There was a moment of silence in the room. Madison, who had been to countless Sonics games, when there were games, thought they collectively looked like the guy out of the audience who's just been told he's going to shoot the basket at half time. It's a great opportunity and, sure, he could win some serious goodies, but he is shooting from the middle of the court, everybody he knows in the world is watching, and nobody will ever forget he missed.

Lieutenant Fynn had enough to help him survive his meeting with the PA person. He stood up, said a few private words to Brown and left everyone to get on with their job, which in this instance, as Dunne put it, was pretty much like nailing jello to the wall.

There was much to do. Madison vaguely remembered that they still had not interviewed Annie Sinclair's colleagues at the primary school. It was strange: from the first moment she had stepped into the crime scene, it had felt as if the energy of the intruder had been centered on the father. Twenty-four hours on, given the evidence they had, nothing had yet contradicted that first impression.

'Have you seen Klein?' Brown asked her.

'She's in the building; I saw her earlier.'

'I'll page her.'

Sarah Klein was the Assistant County Prosecutor on call. Not exactly Madison's favorite – that was Georgia Wolf, a litigious attorney in her mid-thirties with an attitude to match her name.

Madison started a search on the system for all the DMV records she could dredge up on Cameron: all the vehicles he'd ever owned, all the addresses he'd ever lived at. Her right hand bet five dollars with her left that they would find nothing more recent than what they had on that 20-year-old arrest sheet. *Say what you like*, Madison considered, *you got to hand it to him, the creep had been careful.*

*

Sarah Klein leant on Madison's desk. She had dark, shiny hair in a boyish cut and a sharp gray suit with a silk shirt. Madison always expected her to wipe the desk before leaning on it, but Klein never had.

'I heard you picked a real winner,' she said.

Madison brought her up to speed and Klein listened in silence.

'The hairs are good only if Fellman can get DNA from them,' Klein said finally.

'He said he can,' Madison replied.

'I trust him. The check and the glass together – you've got something there, but you're on thin ice.'

'Meaning?'

'The glass gives you a name. The check links the name to a motive. Forget the personal relationship between them and follow the money. You have probable cause to believe there was financial impropriety.'

'I'm calling the IRS next.'

'It's a start. If Sinclair was Cameron's tax lawyer you can probably get a warrant to go through the file. But only if he was. His firm is not going to make it easy for you.'

'Brown is working on the affidavit right now.'

'Which judge?'

'Hugo.'

'Not today. I spoke with him earlier; he's in a foul mood.'

'Then Martin.'

'Okay, what else?'

'Once we find Cameron,' Madison let herself be optimistic about it, 'what are our chances to get a court order for a DNA comparison with the hairs from the scene?'

'With what you have right now, short of getting him to bite you or spit on you, pretty much nil.'

'Great. Next, the house.'

'What about it?'

'We need the whole structure considered "crime scene". We don't know where the intruder might have been. We need access to every scrap of paper in every drawer in every room.'

'Shouldn't be a problem.'

'Every nail in the garage, every box in the attic.'

'Shouldn't be a problem.'

'Every file in Sinclair's computer in the study.'

'Everything but his work files.'

'That is less than helpful.'

'I don't make the rules.'

'Something else: the next of kin, possibly the executor of the will, is Nathan Quinn.'

Klein sighed.

'Tell Brown to make that warrant tighter than airtight. So tight it practically squeaks. Quinn is not going to be delighted to find out one of his tax attorneys committed embezzlement. Clients tend to resent that.'

'They were old friends.'

'Whatever. It's what brought down Capone.'

'Taxes?'

'Taxes.'

Klein turned as she was leaving. Madison had already picked up the receiver to dial out. The attorney held out her right thumb and index finger a fraction of an inch apart.

'Thin ice,' she said.

'I know,' Madison replied.

Neither of them was thinking about warrants.

Ten minutes later Madison returned to her desk with the printout from the DMV. Her eyes went to the photograph first: as old as the one on the arrest sheet – a serious-looking young man in a sheepskin coat.

There was an address, the same they had. How good that was going to be 20 years later, they would soon find out. Apparently John Cameron had owned a series of identical black Ford pick-up trucks. Brownie points for loyalty there.

Madison dropped the pages on Brown's desk – he was on the phone. Before him, the affidavit was almost complete.

The clerk from the IRS called Madison back. By the time they finished talking she realized she had filled three pages of her notebook.

'Things are a tad more complicated than we thought,' Madison said.

'Did the IRS come through?'

'It sure did. Except that now we have more questions than answers.'

'Go on.'

'Sinclair was Cameron's tax attorney. And quite scrupulous too. He filed a tax return for him every year since forever.'

'How very proper of him. Where exactly is Cameron's income coming from?'

'That's the kicker. Their fathers owned a restaurant, The Rock, on Alki Beach, and some real estate around it, and they left it to them.'

'Left it to Cameron and Sinclair.'

'Nope. To Cameron, Sinclair *and* Quinn. Their fathers started the restaurant together in the early 1960s. I checked with the State Licensing Board; they hold the license. Somebody runs it for them but they still own it.'

'And pay taxes on it.'

'Like clockwork. They're going to send us a copy of the file.'

'Well, what do you know.' Brown stood up and picked up the affidavit. 'Judge Martin is in chambers now; let's go ruin her day. Where's Quinn?'

'In court all morning.'

As they walked past the desk sergeant downstairs, he motioned Brown with his hand covering the receiver.

'Fred Tully from the *Star*,' he said.

Brown shook his head.

'Sorry Fred, he's not in the building.' Jenner rolled his eyes. 'No, I don't think so.'

'Third time today,' Brown said.

Outside, the sunlight was unsure of itself. A photographer, waiting on the steps for somebody else, recognized Brown and Madison from the television footage and snapped them once, the flash so much brighter than the sun.

Chapter 13

Judge Claire Martin signed the warrant for Sinclair's tax files with a flourish and a look that said *Don't mess this one up.*

They were waiting for the elevator when Brown stuck his hands deep in the pockets of his raincoat and looked at Madison.

'Something came up at the lab. That's what the call was before. It might be nothing, it might be something. Fellman is checking it out.'

'Please tell me it's not the DNA.'

'It's the ligature, the leather strip where the knot was. We found it tight around the man's wrists.'

'He had deep cuts and bruising.'

A couple of lawyers were lingering by the water cooler. Brown waited until they walked past, their heels clicking on the tiles.

'That's the problem. The blood and cells on it are not consistent with Sinclair's injuries.'

The elevator arrived and they stepped in, grateful that they had no company on the ride down.

'In what way?'

'The cuts went deep into muscle tissue but there's relatively little blood on the ligature. Not enough for the fight Sinclair put up.'

'We found him tightly bound. Hands behind his back.'

'I know. Even so, given the friction, there should have been more wearing of the leather.'

They came out of the King County Courthouse on 4th and James. The drizzle carried the roar of I-5, more like a veil of dampness they breathed through than real rain.

Madison leant her elbows on the roof of their Ford sedan.

'Are we actually saying he replaced the ligature *after* Sinclair died?'

'I don't know what we're saying yet. But that's what it looks like.'

Madison got into the passenger seat; nobody ever drove Brown around.

'He changed the ligature,' she repeated.

'Lucky for us. If he hadn't we wouldn't have his DNA.'

'After,' she said, more to herself than to Brown. It was a half-remembered thought, not even a question yet. Somewhere in Madison's mind a small round pebble dropped into a pool.

There was a coffee place on Cherry Street; they pulled up.

Brown had been watching Madison for weeks: how she had walked into the squad room the very first day, the way she had handled herself at the different crime scenes. Two nights ago, the kid in the grocery store, Brown knew she had had to decide quickly whether the girl was going to take a shot at him or not. Her judgment had been sound and they were all still alive and well.

Madison sipped her coffee without the apparent need of a conversation. Brown liked that about her. Whatever had happened in the four weeks since she had joined Homicide, it was just a prelude to this: driving in the slow Christmas traffic, their Kevlar vests in the boot, on their way to John Cameron's house.

*

They drove north on Fourth Avenue and east on University Street, got stuck like everybody else at the Convention Center and finally joined I–5. They sped past Lake Union and Capitol Hill, through Eastlake new commercial developments and into the university district.

Madison saw nothing and heard nothing. She was in Blueridge, trying to fathom the mind of a man who had thought it necessary to change the ligature on a dead human being, who had dipped his finger in his victim's blood to draw a cross with it.

There was a straight line that connected the victims to the motive and the evidence to the suspect. It was simple enough. However, walking into their bedroom and seeing the slain children between their parents, that was beyond description.

It wasn't just payback, it was vengeance of inhuman proportions. The sins of the fathers visited upon the children, an example to fear and remember for all those who will ever deal with the man.

Madison knew that the address they were going to visit in Laurelhurst was on Cameron's driver's license and his tax returns. It was the house where they had moved after he had been kidnapped as a boy and that, years later, he had inherited from his parents.

It was Cameron's only legal address. Madison had no doubt in her mind that he did not live there any more than he actually drove the black pick-up truck that was registered to him. But it was *his* house nevertheless, the place where they would pick up the scent. Of course, they didn't have a warrant to enter the premises as yet.

When she was in uniform Madison had apprehended many suspects climbing out of the back window while her partner was knocking on the front door. This was not going to be one of those.

Laurelhurst is a wealthy neighborhood with well-kept houses and tended lawns. The Parent Teacher Association meetings are as wild as it ever gets in their community, and that's just how they like it.

They turned into one of the smaller streets, trees lining both sides. The houses not as big and as far from each other. Christmas decorations were discreet and there were a fair number of cars in the driveways. Not everybody was at work.

Cameron's house stood halfway down the street: wood and brick, a sloped roof which probably concealed an attic with a skylight window in the back. There was no car parked on the driveway; Brown pulled up by the curb.

The curtains were drawn and there was no light from behind the glass panel on the front door. Brown turned off the engine and for a minute they both sat there, still and quiet. It wasn't that different from her grandparents' house, Madison thought, and in spite of herself she was glad of the weight of the holster on her right hip.

'If we sit here any longer someone's bound to call the cops on us,' Brown said, and got out of the car.

Madison stepped on the lawn and felt the frosted earth crack slightly under her feet. She inhaled deeply – the air was cold and clean. Thin smoke from some of the chimneys twisted up the pale sky. Pretty as a picture, and her fingers brushed the speed-loader on her belt.

They walked up the concrete driveway. The garage was wide, enough to accommodate a pick-up truck and one other vehicle, if necessary.

They got to the door and looked at each other – for one crazy second Madison expected it to open. Brown rang the bell, just as if he had been dropping in on any old friend. They waited. No sound or movement at all from inside. After about one minute, Brown rang the bell again. Nothing.

'I'm going to look around,' Madison said. She stepped back and examined the front of the house. There were three windows on the second floor and not a flicker from the cream-colored curtains. On the right side of the house the garage extended out, flanked by red maples. On the left, a six-foot wooden fence with a door to the garden. She took the right side.

Hours before, driving past it, the Sinclairs' place, empty for less than four days, had felt desolate. Here, before the arrest, before the *Nostromo*, before all the other unthinkable deeds, John Cameron had come back after a day at school, sat down and done his homework, like any other kid in the street. Madison felt his presence like a trick of the light.

The bushes, about shoulder height and barren, grew quite close to the garage side walls. She squeezed by them and stood on tiptoe to look inside the narrow window – it was safely shut and obscured. Madison kept walking, close to the wall. Her jacket got caught on a branch, which snapped off sharply.

Suddenly, there was a shuffle above her and to the side, behind a maple. Madison froze. The smell hit her and she knew instantly what it was.

She stepped forward. The bushes were behind her and she was standing by the long side of the house. There were no windows; on the far corner the fence started and carried on till the bottom of the garden. There was about ten feet between the brick wall and the trees.

The putrid smell was made worse by the winter chill. Madison saw the wing of the gull behind the roots; it shuffled out of sight and the feathers rustled against dry leaves. She walked around the tree and saw it. The gull squawked. The cat was dead – it must have crawled there after being hit by a car, or maybe it had just been old or sick. She couldn't tell. The gull had been feeding on it for a while – the fur had once been gray and black.

'Damn!' she said, not loud enough for even the bird to hear. She stepped closer and the gull hopped backwards, not yet ready to leave his find.

Madison sat on her heels and lifted the branches under which the cat had sought refuge. There was a deep cut on one of his hind legs. It was still curled up. The gull had done a lot of damage to the soft tissue around the face. Madison picked up a small stick and ran it gently along the side of the neck. No collar.

She picked up a handful of leaves and bits of wood and placed them on top of the small body, covering it up completely. The gull stood by.

Madison straightened up and took a quick step toward it and the bird flew off.

The fence was tall enough to say *Go away* without being too unfriendly toward the neighbors. The Camerons had wanted safety and privacy for their boy while he was recovering from the ordeal on the Hoh River Trail.

Madison looked left and right: nobody around and completely out of sight from the street. She gripped the top of the fence with both hands and kicked up, straightening her arms at the same time. She leant forward for balance, half of her over the fence, her hips taking her weight against the wood.

The backyard was large, a patio behind the conservatory, a brick barbecue to the side. It was bare, the grass burnt by the frost. Dry leaves carried by the wind had come to rest against the glass door – nobody had pushed it open for some time.

Sometimes places carry a kind of memory of what happened within their walls: this house was a blank space.

The gull flew above her and perched on the roof, keeping an eye on Madison. She let go and hit the ground easily on the outside of the fence.

'See ya,' she whispered and walked back to the front of the house.

Brown was coming out at the same time from the opposite corner.

'Nothing.'

'Nope,' she said.

'May I help you?' The voice was behind them. Brown and Madison swung around just a touch too quickly.

It was a man in his seventies, short white hair and a nice red Gore-Tex jacket, a bag of groceries in one arm. The front door of the house across the street was open and a woman with a matching jacket was carrying in more shopping bags.

'Hello,' Madison said. 'We are from the Seattle Police Department.' They showed their badges.

'Clyde Phillips.' The man smiled. 'I'm a neighbor. If you're looking for Jack, he's not at home.'

'Mr. Cameron,' Brown said.

'Yes. He's out of town on business. Is it about the burglaries on Surber Drive?'

'No, it's a personal matter. Do you have a couple of minutes?'

'Sure.' He put the bag on the ground by his feet. He was in good shape for his age; his walking boots looked like he had put some miles on them.

'What exactly do you need with Jack?' Although Brown was clearly the senior officer, Clyde Phillips had turned very slightly toward Madison as he was asking. 'Is everything alright?'

She picked up the ball.

'We need to talk to him very urgently. Do you know where he is or when he is coming back?'

'And you are?'

She gave him a reassuring smile.

'Detective Sergeant Brown and Detective Madison, Seattle Homicide.'

Phillips moved his head back one inch. It was not a polite word in Laurelhurst.

'Oh,' he said, then it registered. 'Is it about the family in Three Oaks?'

The media were still feasting on it; the same footage was being played over and over again.

'Yes, they were acquaintances of Mr. Cameron's. That's why it's important that we talk to him as soon as possible.'

'Is Jack in some kind of danger?'

Jack.

What would be more helpful? Telling the man that they suspected his neighbor of at least four brutal murders, would that get them his cooperation?

'He might be in danger; we don't know yet.'

Score one for the pants-on-fire team.

'He comes and goes but . . . I tell you what, I have a telephone number for a friend of his in case of emergency, for the house. He would know where Jack is. Let me get it for you.'

He came back with a piece of paper. His writing was neat.

'I hope this helps. I hope Jack is going to be alright.'

'I'm sure he will be.'

'Please tell him we're sending him our best wishes.'

'I will as soon as I see him.' Madison shook his hand, feeling like a thief. 'Thank you.'

She turned and started toward the car. Brown was already inside, talking on the radio. She looked at the piece of paper. In red ink and well-spaced letters, it was Nathan Quinn's work number.

They wove in and out of the traffic, driving south on I-5.

'So, say the house is on fire, Phillips's second call would be to Nathan Quinn,' Brown said.

'Yes.'

'And Quinn always knows how to reach Cameron.'

'Yes.' Madison drummed her fingers on the dashboard. 'Is Quinn dirty? Has there ever been any talk?'

'It would be easier if he was, wouldn't it? He's a pain in the neck but as far as I know he's clean.'

'By the way, just for the hell of it I've run a check on both Sinclairs. Neither of them has ever had any convictions.' Madison flipped through her notebook, the notes she had taken in the library about the Hoh River kidnap. 'In one of the papers from the library, last night, there was a picture of David Quinn's funeral. They were all there.'

'It was a disaster,' he said. 'There were no leads. The boys wouldn't talk about it. There was absolutely nothing to go on. They never even recovered the body. A total mess.'

'I remember. A lot of parents thought it was the start of a wave of kidnaps.'

'No.' Brown tapped the steering wheel. 'It wasn't about that. It was personal to those three boys and their families. Except, of course, nobody was saying diddly squat to us. Also, we didn't have the forensics we have today. The crime scene was no good to anybody.'

'Quinn is Jewish,' Madison said after a pause. 'The custom is to hold the funeral as soon as possible after a death.'

The flat, gray waters of Lake Union were a blur past Madison's eyes.

'They buried some of the earth from the place where they think he had died,' she said.

'Hell.'

Madison didn't know whether Brown meant it as a comment or a state of mind but it didn't matter, it fit too well one way or the other.

'The thing with Quinn,' he said, 'either he doesn't know what Cameron has been up to all these years, which is unlikely, or he does know and is involved.'

'There's another possibility. He does know and he's not involved.'

'He is an attorney, an officer of the court. Knowledge of a criminal act implies involvement.'

'Cameron doesn't have any known associates. He's never had a crew. He's never had *people*.'

'A smart man.' Brown put his foot down hard on the gas. 'It's time for Mr. Quinn to make a phone call.'

The first drops of rain hit the windshield as they flew back toward Elliott Bay and downtown Seattle, surrounded by water and defined by it. Cameron's house was on fire.

Chapter 14

It was only 24 hours since Brown and Madison had stood in the offices of Quinn, Locke & Associates, waiting to meet Nathan Quinn for the first time. Paralegals were rushing around, envelopes were being delivered by couriers and art was on the walls. Still, nothing was the same, nor would it ever be. Flowers had replaced the Christmas decorations, every client and every business in the building had sent their condolences. There were looks when the detectives walked in.

Downstairs, they had met Tommy Saltzman, on loan from Treasury, who would be going over the tax returns Sinclair had filed for Cameron.

Saltzman, a tall, pale forty-something who looked like a stiff breeze would blow him over, was enjoying this diversion from his routine. All he had been told was that one of the victims was a tax attorney, and would he run a check on some work he'd done? He'd jumped at the chance.

Carl Doyle walked over to them, immaculate in a charcoal suit and black silk tie. He looked like he'd had maybe three hours' sleep. Brown shook hands with him, his eyes found Madison's and they nodded hello.

The first time they'd met they had brought unbearable news; today they had come with a legal crowbar.

During the elevator ride Brown had left it to Madison to answer Saltzman's many questions. He knew all too well that a warrant was only a blunt tool if they didn't get Quinn on their side: fraud was small potatoes when the top prize was murder in the first.

Quinn waved them into his office and closed the door behind them. His attention was focused on Brown and he barely registered the others. They were not asked to sit.

'What do you have?' Quinn said.

'We have a lead.' Brown went straight to the point. 'Evidence was found on the crime scene that links the murders with one of James Sinclair's clients.'

'Who?'

Brown ignored the question.

'The implication is that there might have been financial impropriety on Mr. Sinclair's side,' he said.

'Impossible.' Quinn's tone was contained but unequivocal, his reaction strong enough that Madison felt Saltzman shrink a little.

'We have a warrant.' Brown offered it to him. Quinn took it without looking.

'Understand this, James has never been less than completely straight in everything he's ever done. If that's your lead, you're wasting your time. Who's the client?'

'What I understand is that we have evidence we have to pursue. This is a warrant. Help us to clear this up now and things will go a hell of a lot faster. Mr. Saltzman here is going to look at the file.'

Quinn's eyes did not acknowledge anybody but Brown.

'The evidence,' he said.

'We would like for you to come with us to the precinct. We'll talk about it there. It's the best thing you can do for them.'

Quinn had spent years in front of juries, judges and opposing counsel. He scanned the warrant for less than a second, called Doyle on the intercom and set up an associate to help Saltzman find the files he needed.

Doyle unlocked the door to Sinclair's office and turned on the light. It was a space suitable for a partner in a successful firm. His vast desk, larger than Quinn's, was covered in well-organized piles of papers. To the left of the door a whole wall was occupied by a bookcase; legal reference tomes lined every shelf.

Behind the desk, on the right of the leather chair, there was a small antique table. On it, three framed pictures of his wife and children: one of the whole family, two school pictures. A flower vase, the white freesias doing their best. Madison noticed the pale blue carpet and footprints around the desk, maybe the overnight cleaner's, maybe Sinclair's own.

There was a conference table by the windows. Doyle asked Saltzman if he needed anything, his voice as polite as if he had been talking to a guest in his own home. Polite, and as warm as a January shower. Madison liked him a lot.

'Let's go,' Brown said.

They went to wait for Quinn outside the glass doors, by the elevator.

When Doyle had shown them in, Quinn had not stepped or looked into his friend's office; Madison had a feeling he still hadn't.

'He didn't really look at the warrant,' she said quietly.

'No.'

It was a bad sign: it meant that Nathan Quinn truly believed that there was nothing for them to find. If Sinclair's conscience had been lily-white, then it followed that so was Cameron's. And that, they knew, was impossible.

'Hungry?' Brown asked.

'Starving,' Madison replied.

They had twenty minutes. Quinn needed the time to brief the partner who would take over his afternoon meetings. There was a deli on Fourth just past Seneca – they had long enough for a quick bite.

Madison couldn't remember whether she had had any breakfast. She loaded a plastic salad box with everything minus sliced cucumber and beet, which she didn't like, grabbed a bread roll and took a seat in a booth by the window.

Brown was working quickly through a smoked salmon and cream-cheese bagel.

Neither of them said a word; they ate their lunch and drank juices from the bar. They had eaten lunch together most days since Madison had joined Homicide. She knew he liked chicken but not beef, fish but not shellfish, and drank at least as much coffee as she did. On the other hand, before yesterday, she wasn't sure he could have picked her out of a line-up.

Brown wiped his fingers on a napkin. Lieutenant Fynn had called him into his office earlier that morning, before the briefing, and closed the door. He had asked him if he thought Madison would do okay on the case or whether he wanted a more experienced partner to back him up. It was a straight-up question: there was no time for on-the-job training on this one. Madison would just take a less prominent position, that was all.

Brown balled up his napkin and put it on his plate.

She'll be fine, he had said.

Forty-five minutes later they walked into the precinct together. Madison picked up a small pile of messages from the desk sergeant, handed a few to Brown. In the car Madison had asked him how he wanted to run the interview, if he thought they could get to him first time round. Brown's reply was terse.

'I want him to forget what he thinks he knows.'

When it came down to it, it was a question of turf: they could have questioned Quinn in his office but that was not appropriate. In any other situation, a witness would have been brought into the precinct so that he would feel the importance of the proceedings and the formality of the occasion. A trick of the trade, so to speak. No such luck with Quinn: he was not likely to be intimidated by a drab room with a one-way mirror. They didn't think his answers would change with the change of location. It was just the way the game was played and they all knew the rules.

Standing by the desk sergeant's raised position, two detectives stared long and hard at Nathan Quinn when he came in, their eyes on his back as he walked past. He didn't have many friends there. He didn't exactly ignore them – they weren't even blips on his radar.

They found an empty interview room on the second floor. Madison turned the door handle.

'We can go in here,' she said.

Quinn looked in. A square room, a table with some chairs around it and a one-way mirror concealing an observation box for officers and DAs. He turned to Madison.

'How many people will I be talking to today?' he said, nodding to the mirror.

'Just the two of us,' Madison replied.

'That's good. I like that,' he said. 'Let's find somewhere else.'

He was there at his own discretion – plenty of time to get him cranky later on. They took over the rec room.

Brown excused himself for a couple of minutes with the pretext of checking up on a message. He went to Lieutenant Fynn to get him up to speed.

'I don't like this one bit,' Fynn said. 'What is he? A material witness, next of kin of the victims *and* of the prime suspect?'

'He doesn't know. Right now he's sitting on the fence. He's going to have to jump one way or the other. Where he lands will tell us a lot.'

'You think?'

'I hope.'

For the first time Madison was alone with Quinn, and it suddenly struck her that she had probably said no more than five words to him since they had met yesterday, maybe not even that.

He sat across the table from her, his coat neatly folded on the back of his chair, a glass of water by his right hand. He flicked an invisible speck of dust off his sleeve. Nathan Quinn's eyes glow without warmth as he considers Madison.

She knew he would be familiar with most senior detectives of the Seattle PD; the fact that he had never met Madison meant only that she hadn't had her gold shield very long.

'Let's get this over with,' he said.

Madison flipped open her notebook. Brown came in with a folder, closed the door, sat down next to her and put the folder on the table. The rules of the game.

'The evidence,' Quinn said.

'Enough to get us a warrant,' Brown replied.

'You're going to have to be a little more specific.'

Brown's right hand was palm down on the file.

'Let's put that to one side for a moment. We have a pretty good idea of the sequence of events on Saturday night. Do you want to know?'

Madison knew in that instant that the folder contained the pictures of the bodies at the crime scene. Now they were bait.

'Go on,' Quinn said.

'It's not going to be dainty.'

'Go on.'

'Alright. Sometime during Saturday night and the early hours of Sunday morning, a man let himself into the Sinclairs' house.

I'm saying "let himself in" because there is no sign of forced entry. Doors and windows, they all check out. We think he might have had a key.'

Quinn sat slightly forward in his chair, didn't even blink. Brown had paused for a second, let him absorb the information.

'The intruder went to the master bedroom, where he hit James Sinclair on the side of his face with the butt of a gun. He had been asleep at the time, probably passed out for a few moments. Then he put his gun to the head of Annie Sinclair and shot her. Once. After that, he went into the children's room. He put his gun to their heads and shot them – the boy in the top bunk first, then the boy in the bottom one. Both once. From the hole in the blankets it looks like the second kid was trying to hide.'

Brown paused again.

'Then he went back to James Sinclair, blindfolded him and tied him up with strips of leather. Neck, hands, feet. When he came to, he couldn't have moved if he tried. And he did. Sinclair knew his family had been attacked and he fought like hell. The ligatures cut right through his skin.'

Quinn was completely still.

'The intruder carried the bodies of the children and placed them between Sinclair and his wife. Sinclair is still trying to get himself free, can't do it. Finally, the man pours a few drops of chloroform on his blindfold, waits for a few minutes for it to work. James Sinclair dies of cardiac arrest. The intruder leaves.'

Quinn looked at the folder.

'Are those the pictures?'

'Yes.' Brown pushed the file halfway toward him. Quinn reached for it.

The first photograph was a wide shot of the bed and the four bodies. His face didn't change. He looked at it for a long time, then turned the page. The second was a close-up of Sinclair blindfolded.

The third was Sinclair's wife. The fourth was a little boy. Quinn closed the folder and moved his hands away from it.

'That was what we *know*,' Brown continued. 'This is what we *have*: we recovered a glass in the kitchen by the sink – the prints on it don't match any of the victims'. Maybe the killer got himself a drink before he left. Also, in the study, we found a check; the signature on it had been forged.'

'Someone forged James's signature?'

'No. Sinclair signed for somebody else. His prints are on it,' Brown replied.

'No.'

'We matched the name on the check to the prints on the glass,' Brown continued. 'The prints are a match with a twenty-year-old drunk-driving arrest. John Cameron's.'

Quinn sat back in the chair, holding both of them in his level gaze.

'No,' he said slowly and clearly. 'James would have never done anything like that.'

'How do you know?' Madison asked. 'How do you know what someone is doing twenty-four hours a day?'

'I know the man.'

'Sure, but you have to admit he *could* have done it. He had the opportunity, he handled Cameron's affairs. Does John Cameron have a key to the house?'

Quinn didn't reply; his eyes went to the closed folder.

'You don't have to believe me,' Brown said. 'You just have to believe the evidence.'

'Prints mean nothing. He has been inside the house dozens of times. Can you prove they are from the time of the murders?'

'How well do you know John Cameron?' Brown flipped the folder open to the first page, the first photograph.

Quinn reached for it, without looking, and closed it.

'"Cheap" doesn't suit you, Detective,' he said.

'When was the last time you saw him?'

Quinn didn't answer.

'Yesterday,' Madison said. It had just occurred to her. 'You saw him yesterday, when you told him.'

Both men turned to her.

'You didn't want him to find out on the news.' She knew she was right and she drove it all the way in. 'How did he take it?'

Quinn's eyes held Madison whole, the silence a tangible shape stretching between them.

Abruptly Quinn got up and walked to the window. It looked out on the parking lot, just a lot of cars and thin rain. He stood with his back to them and when he spoke the words held no emotion.

'I am John Cameron's attorney. Anything he has said to me has been said in privilege. You may not ask me about it or about anything else regarding our relationship.'

He took out his cellphone. 'I'll prepare an affidavit and pass on all the duties of the Sinclairs' estate to Bob Greenhut, at Greenhut Lowell. He will be the executor until deemed by a judge that there is no further conflict of interest. Then, and only then, it will revert to me. Is that acceptable to you?'

'If that's what you want,' Brown said.

'I assure you, none of this is what I want. I'll call Bob right now and start on the paperwork. Then we can talk about what you want from my client.'

Quinn dialed the call and Brown and Madison left the room.

'So much for friendship,' Madison said. 'Why are you not upset about this?'

Brown shrugged. 'He made his choice. We need to get Klein in for the rest of the interview. By the way, how did you know he'd seen him?'

'I don't know. That's what I would have done.'

'Quinn didn't tell us how Cameron took it, but you got him thinking about it.'

Lieutenant Fynn took it less than well. 'We haven't picked up the guy yet and you got him lawyered up already?'

Twenty minutes later Bob Greenhut was on board, papers had been filed quickly and efficiently and copies sent to the precinct, the hard copy was being couriered presently. In short, if Nathan Quinn wanted to so much as look in the direction of the Sinclairs' house, he needed Greenhut's permission.

The four of them sat around the table, one on each side.

'I'm only sitting in to make sure you all play nice.' Sarah Klein, the Assistant County Prosecutor, leaned back in her chair.

'You don't have enough to indict my client; you don't have enough to pick up my client. You try to sneak into his house again,' he looked straight at Madison, 'you'll get slapped with a police harassment suit. This is me being nice, Sarah.'

Thank you very much, Mr. Phillips.

'He needs to come in,' Brown said. 'I mean today. We have DNA from one of the ligatures. He gives us a blood sample and we can all go home. If you are so sure of yourself, you'll get on the phone to him right now.'

There was a knock on the door. The department PA passed a message to Madison. It was from Spencer. She read it and passed it to Brown. She must remember to buy him a drink tonight – his timing had been perfect.

Brown read the message and put it to one side.

'We have a witness. A neighbor saw a black Ford pick-up truck parked by the Sinclairs' house in the early hours of Sunday morning. What does Cameron drive, Counselor?' Brown turned to Klein. 'Enough?'

She nodded.

That was all they needed to proceed and Quinn knew it.

'We're done here.' He stood up and gathered his papers.

'Nathan.' Klein was also standing now. 'He's going to be arrested, and you know the grand jury will indict. If you are withholding information, if you know where he is—'

They were both aware of the legal consequences.

'I don't know where he is.'

'And if you knew—' Brown continued.

'You'd be my first phone call, of course.'

'Where did you meet him yesterday?' Madison asked.

Quinn stopped with one hand on the door handle. 'You put a tail on me or tap my phones and we're going to have us a fun day in court. Good to see you, Sarah.'

He left.

It was nowhere near good enough for Madison. She followed and caught up with him on the stairs.

'Mr. Quinn.'

One plainclothes and one uniformed officer were coming up; she let them pass.

'You were in the Prosecuting Attorney's Office once. You were a prosecutor.'

'A long time ago.'

'I'm interested. With the evidence you know we have, how would *you* investigate and prosecute this case?'

'Why do you ask?'

'I think there is a world of things about it you are not willing to share with us. It's a shame, but there you have it. Still, you do have a personal interest to see the killer caught.'

She wasn't sure why she had come right out and said it but it was the truth; maybe it was worth saying just for that.

'Impossible as it might seem to you now, there is one thing much, much worse than finding out John Cameron did this,' he said.

'What's that?'

'Knowing that he didn't. As for my personal interest in this case, Detective, I do what I have to. My reasons are not for your files.'

His car was parked not far from the entrance to the precinct. As he drove past, Madison couldn't tell whether he was already speaking on his cellphone. Her instincts told her that between legal wrangles and the wall of silence lay a half-truth, and she would rather find it than let it disappear with the fading daylight.

Brown and Klein were in Lieutenant Fynn's office. Madison joined them. They needed a judge to sign off a warrant to arrest Cameron and one to search his house.

Klein was very keen to go absolutely by the book on this one. In her words, if you get screwed in front of a jury by inadmissible evidence, it's not pretty to see and they never forget it.

'Then there's the question of Quinn,' Brown said to Lieutenant Fynn.

'What's that?'

'Well, he might very well have information that would get us our guy; he's just not telling. There might be things that fall outside attorney–client privilege.'

'What do you mean?' Klein asked.

'You know what I mean.'

'You mean *subpoena* Quinn?' Klein said.

'Yes.'

'And you think a judge is going to go for that?'

'If you push for it, explain the circumstances, maybe.'

'Black-letter law is pretty clear on privilege,' Madison said. 'No judge is going to jump at the chance to make history with this.'

'I know. But what else have we got? A house he doesn't go to and a car he doesn't drive. Quinn met with him yesterday, and I'm betting the house he's on the phone to him as we speak.'

'Point taken. As long as we all know that it will never work, and the judge will throw me out just for trying, I'll run it by my boss,' Klein said. 'About Cameron's house, make sure you're clear about what you want. You're looking for a telephone bill, specify small spaces, drawers, shoeboxes. Whatever.'

'A murder weapon would be nice,' Lieutenant Fynn said to no one in particular.

'I'm on that.' Madison knew what she meant: they were looking for anything that might give them a clue about Cameron's life. If they didn't specifically mention the smallest item on their wanted list, their search warrant might be limited to what was in plain view. Which, if his house was as tidy as the crime scene, might be nothing.

Somehow, held between hearsay and myth, that was how Madison imagined Cameron's life – tidy and out of sight.

Chapter 15

The uniformed police officer pressed the boy's right index finger on the ink pad, careful not to brush his own shirt cuff against it. He got him to roll the finger gently left to right on the index card, leaving a perfect imprint.

He felt a little sorry for the boy; he hadn't been completely innocent of driving with a cold one by the seat himself, when he was his age. Most other drunk teenagers would give him a certain amount of lip while they were being printed, just to prop up their failing courage, but this one had been polite and courteous. Hard to believe he had been found half soaked in bourbon, with an empty bottle in his hand and a car that wouldn't start.

'You got your phone call?' he asked the kid.

'Yes, thank you,' John Cameron, 18, replied.

The officer saw the scars on the back of his hand. He knew what a sharp blade could do and somebody had really gone to work there. They looked years old.

'Ever been in trouble before?'

'No, sir.'

John Cameron took a tissue and slowly rubbed each finger in turn. It didn't do much good. He looked around and took in the room. Four-thirty in the morning, four officers. Two picking at slices from a pizza in a carton, another by the door, one on the phone. A man sitting up on a bench, cuffed and asleep.

There were chemical smells beyond the alcohol that hung on him like a cloud; there was a flash from the camera ten feet to his left. He could still feel the white light on his face when they had snapped his picture.

He let them take him to the holding cell. Bleach had been used recently; a bucket and a mop had been left in a corner at the end of the corridor. A light bulb flickered through the glass of a closed door as the whole building struggled to keep awake.

The holding cell was square and had bars on two sides; the floor was concrete. Two men were sleeping on the bunk beds; they had covered themselves with their coats and snored softly. Another was sitting on a chair, leaning back against the wall.

'You be good now, Larry,' the guard said, pointing his finger at him.

When the metal door slammed shut behind the boy, Larry straightened the chair and took a long measured look at the kid in the sheepskin jacket. The man was about six foot and heavy, not much muscle there but a lot of extra weight. Cameron could smell him from where he was. His eyes were glazed from the drink as he decided what to do about the boy.

Cameron walked across the cell and leant against the bars on the opposite side, crossed his arms and looked at the round wall clock. Minutes inched forward.

Larry stood uncertainly and staggered close enough to slap his mitten on the boy's shoulder, should the need arise.

'Hey,' he croaked.

Cameron looked up: it had been the second-longest night of his life and whatever it had left in his eyes, the man didn't like what he saw. He rubbed his chin with the back of his hand.

'Hey,' Cameron said.

The man's mouth moved but nothing came out. No, he didn't like this kid at all. Something fluttered in his throat.

Larry wiped his hands against the sides of his jeans and took one step back. He found his chair, never turning his back on Cameron, and sat down. He was suddenly sober and thirsty, the worst combination.

'Jack.'

The guard opened the metal door. Nathan Quinn stood there, his coat open over the clothes he'd thrown on after the phone call, a couple of snowflakes melting on the bill of his baseball cap.

Cameron walked out of the holding cell, Quinn grabbed him in a quick hug.

'What the hell!' He led him to a table in the corner where they could talk. 'Thanks, Jeff,' Quinn said to the guard.

'No problem.'

They were left alone.

'Are you alright?' Quinn took off his coat and put it on the table. Cameron noticed he would need to shave again soon and his curly hair was getting too long for the County Prosecutor's Office.

Quinn was talking to him but John Cameron breathed in the icy air from the car, waiting for the patrol officers to pick him up, on the side of the road. It burned in his chest. Blurred lights from the traffic washed over the windshield and his hands were so cold he couldn't grip the steering wheel. He twisted the top off the bottle, took a long swig and spat it out. Spilled some on the front of his mountain jacket and a few drops on the empty passenger seat. He pulled the choke and flooded the engine.

The beam of the policeman found him as he was trying to start the car for the hundredth time. Finally.

'What happened?' Quinn looked concerned. Then again he always did, Cameron thought. 'You are going to be arraigned at night court. Bernie Rhodes from the Public Defender's Office is coming over – he owes me one. You'll plead "not guilty" and I'll bail you out.'

Quinn's kind dark eyes swept over the boy. He was going to take him home to get him straightened up or his mom would have a fit.

'What happened?'

'It's done now.'

'How much have you had to drink?'

'Enough,' Cameron said. 'It's done, Nathan. It's over.'

'You're going to be alright.'

Bernie Rhodes came into the room, the guard holding a cup of coffee, both laughing at the end of a knock-knock joke.

Cameron leaned toward Quinn, his voice hollow and cracked.

'It's done.'

Quinn put his hand on Cameron's shoulder.

'It's okay. Let's go.'

Larry's eyes followed him out of the room.

It took a few months for Quinn to understand what Cameron had meant. By then spring had gone to work on the winter snow and it was too late for everybody.

Chapter 16

They rode in two cars. Brown and Madison first, already wearing their vests, the warrants in Brown's jacket pocket. Spencer and Dunne followed.

By the time they got there it was early evening and Laurelhurst was getting ready for dinner. Brown stole a sideways glance at Madison: she wore the Kevlar over her shirt and under her blazer. The vest's outside layer was midnight blue, the texture coarse. Madison rubbed the side of her thumb against it, the rest of her utterly still.

Windows were lit in Clyde Phillips's place. Across the street, Cameron's house sat in complete darkness. They left the cars by the curb before the turn into the driveway; a few trees stood between them and the house. A patrol car was parked, lights off, fifty yards away. When they saw them, two uniformed officers approached on foot.

'No one went in or came out in the last hour.' Officer Buchman was short and wide, all shoulders and cropped hair. His partner, Officer Glaiser, nodded Dunne hello. There were maybe five people in the whole of the Seattle Police Department Dunne didn't know well enough to say 'hey' to.

'There is no sign of life in the house,' Brown said. 'But I want standard operating procedure anyway. We're going in "as if".'

'I'll cover the back,' Madison said. 'I've been there earlier today. Give us three minutes to get into place.'

Madison was glad she had seen the house in daylight. Followed by Spencer, she walked into the deeper shadows under the trees and quickly found herself by the small heap of leaves. Spencer sniffed the air.

'What in the name of—' Spencer whispered.

'Dead cat,' Madison replied, and unholstered her weapon.

They reached the side of the fence. She peeked. The yard was as she had left it, doors and windows shut and dark. It was much quieter now that they had left the main road. Her heart was drumming a little, but it was normal.

She was going to need both hands to get over the fence. She put her piece back in the holster and automatically secured the thin leather safety strip on it.

Madison and Spencer exchanged a look and, without a word, both of them vaulted over the fence and landed quietly on the inside of Cameron's yard. Weapon in hand and pointed at the ground, Madison crossed it, keeping close to the edges. In five seconds they had all the entrances and exits covered.

Now, she said to herself.

Brown was about to step onto the driveway. A car came down the street. He wanted to wait for it to pass. When the car had almost reached them, Brown heard the brakes come on and he turned toward it. The car stopped.

A young man in suit and tie rolled down the window. 'Detective Brown?'

That was really not what he wanted to hear and he sensed that things were about to go south from then on.

'My name is Benny Craig. I'm from Quinn Locke. Nathan Quinn sent me. You are about to execute a search warrant on this address. He thought you might want to have these.'

Benny Craig stepped out of the car and extended his right hand to Brown. A small key ring with three keys twinkled in the dim light.

'He said this way you won't have to break down the door and he won't have to fix it.'

If Benny was smiling at all Brown couldn't really tell.

'Could I see your warrant?'

Brown took the keys and started walking briskly up the drive.

'Let's go.'

Benny wasn't finished.

'There is no alarm and I am to have the keys back when you are done.'

Without pausing, Brown fished out the search warrant from his inside pocket and passed it to Benny Craig. Officers Buchman and Glaiser were not quite sure what was going on or why Brown looked like he was passing razor blades, but they were not altogether unhappy they wouldn't have to force the door open.

'Stay back.' Dunne put his open hand over Benny's chest and gently pushed him out of the way. He pointed about 20 feet to the left and toward the road. Benny retreated.

The four police officers all unholstered their weapons. Brown inserted a key in the bottom lock. It turned easily. He tried the top one and felt the door coming open.

The room was barely lit by the outside glow of the lamp posts. They paused.

'This is the Seattle Police Department . . .' Brown heard all the right words coming out of his mouth.

They turned on lights, walked from room to room calling 'Clear!' to each other, checked every space where a man could hide.

Dunne opened the garden door, let in Madison and Spencer.

'We've just been dissed,' he said.

Benny was standing by the front door, unsure what to do with himself. Dunne pointed at a bench by the coat rack.

'Sit. Don't touch anything.'

Benny did as he was told.

Madison snapped her latex gloves on and rested her back against the front door. They were inside.

Madison had done searches in more places than she could remember: from large houses to one-room shacks to cars people drove around in the day and slept in at night. Every time she had felt she would know more about the person after ten minutes of looking at how they lived than after one hour in the box.

She had had good teachers, John Douglas at the Academy and Dave Carbone in uniform. She knew the moves and what they wanted out of that warrant. The .22 which shot the victims would be nice, and any part of the ligatures which had been used to tie them would be pretty welcome too. Also, any paperwork that could connect Cameron, Sinclair and the embezzlement funds would be gold for the prosecution's case.

A search, Douglas used to say, is always about more than what is tangible. It's not about the one book on the shelf that's been put back sideways, it's about the last thing a man read before he went out to kill somebody.

Madison stood stock still. She was aware of the others talking and working out who was going where and wished they would just shut up for one second.

'What's up?' Brown asked.

'I'm trying to see the room without us in it.'

John Cameron comes home, puts the key in the lock, turns it and steps in. This is what he sees. This is where he is. He would put his jacket on the coat rack. She ignored Benny Craig. There was a small table with a handsome porcelain dish on it. The keys would go in it. It was empty. The hall opened into a wide and long living room. It had been decorated by Cameron's parents, quite probably. There were two large sofas and two chairs, upholstered with a discreet flowered pattern that felt both old-fashioned and pleasant. Something her grandparents might have chosen.

A couple of ceiling-high bookcases stacked with hardbacks and paperbacks. There were small objects in the spaces in front of the books: someone had collected tobacco tins.

Spencer and Dunne were already at work on the bookcase and the antique roll-top table in the corner. Madison stood back: the cushions on the sofa and the chairs were puffed and in place. She ran a finger along the table: no dust.

There was a fireplace at the end of the room, on the mantel-piece only one photograph: a couple in their sixties smiling at the camera. Cameron's parents. The picture frame was centered. There was a basket on the right side of the fireplace, four pieces of wood neatly stacked in it. A scent of vanilla from dried petals in a dish on the coffee table.

Madison had a feeling that if she opened the fridge she would find fresh milk. In a house where nobody lived.

'Guys,' she said.

They all turned and she pointed. On a corner table, a tall glass vase. In the vase, a bunch of white lilies. There were tiny drops of water on the leaves. At the bottom of the vase the powdery residue of flower food had not yet dispersed. He had been there, not even hours before them.

'Sweet,' Spencer said.

'Tell me about the witness,' Brown asked him.

'Neighbor in the opposite house, came home from a party about 2.30 a.m. An office party by the way, but he was the designated driver—'

'Thank you, God.'

'He happened to glance at the Sinclairs' house and noticed the pick-up parked at the top of the drive. Nothing else, just the truck.'

'What does he look like?'

'Solid witness. He'll be fine in court.'

Madison found the kitchen. Cameron's father had been the chef of the restaurant and the kitchen reflected the taste of people who knew about food.

It was larger than average: cupboards and glass-fronted cabinets along two walls and a vast preparing surface in the middle. Saucepans hung from hooks on one side and on the other stood a professional metal cooker with two ovens and six hobs.

Madison could not resist and opened the fridge. It was clean and empty. No milk, no eggs, no leftovers of any kind. She opened the freezer and there it was: a single carton of Ben & Jerry's Chunky Monkey. She smiled for no real reason. Maybe it was just that the ice cream brought Cameron a little closer to human. Madison closed the freezer door and looked around the surfaces: there were ladles and spoons in tall, slim pots.

She heard Brown behind her.

'There are no knives,' she said without turning.

Madison opened and closed drawers until she found what she was looking for: cutlery.

'Cameron's father was the chef of The Rock. Knives are pretty important to a chef but there's only one photograph on the mantelpiece and no chef's knives in the kitchen.'

She slid the drawer shut with a rattle of the metal inside.

'We are not going to find anything personal here,' she said. 'He emptied the place when he moved out. Whenever that was. There's a house somewhere with all the stuff that should be here but isn't. Family photographs and his father's knives.'

'You pick me right up.'

'Sorry.' She said as she checked every cupboard and cabinet.

'Saltzman called. He found nothing in the lawyer's files. He's going back tomorrow.'

Brown delivered good news and bad news in the same steady voice. Madison saw his pale blue eyes drift unfocused over the room.

'Oh, and the truck is not in the garage.'

'What's in the garage?' Madison asked.

'Absolutely nothing. I'm going upstairs.'

Just as he was leaving the room, the first unmistakable bars of The Clash's 'Should I Stay or Should I Go' filled the air.

'Dunne's "get to know your perp" theory,' he said.

Madison peeked into the living room: Spencer was running his hands around the sofa cushions and Dunne was shining a slim torch at the space between the bookcase and the wall. Both of them were engrossed in their work.

From the outside it was some kind of party, lights blazing and The Clash blasting through the speakers. Benny Craig shifted uncomfortably on the bench and, for the first time, looked seriously concerned.

Madison finished in the kitchen. Her steps creaked on the stairs. The landing opened on three rooms and a bathroom. Brown was in what seemed to be the study. He sat behind the desk and was cleaning his glasses with his handkerchief.

'Your folks have your graduation picture on the wall?'

'Sure,' Madison said.

'Well, looks like our boy is pretty touchy about getting snapped.'

The walls were bare except for three mountain landscapes. Madison thought of David Quinn's funeral pictures.

As the music found its way to them, they worked the room together. The Camerons' life was summed up in utility bills and receipts and fifteen-year-old correspondence with relatives in Scotland.

By the time they were done, the others were in the parents' bedroom, where the shoeboxes in the closet contained only shoes.

The door to Cameron's room was shut. Madison put her hand on the handle. Brown, Spencer and Dunne were behind her, as if one of the uniformed officers hadn't already checked and cleared it.

She pushed the door open. Slowly, the hairs on the back of her neck stood up.

Bright red blankets covered the bunk beds; Mariners and Sonics banners were pinned to the walls, clashing against the delicate pattern of the wallpaper. In the bookcase, sci-fi paperbacks and encyclopedias. A pile of school books lay in disarray on the desk and a green windbreaker was draped on the back of the chair. Hung from the ceiling, a model airplane swayed gently. A terrycloth robe was on a hook behind the door. A pair of worn sneakers were half visible under the bed, their laces all tangled and mud on the white leather sides. A boy's room.

Dunne exhaled.

'Okay,' Brown said.

'Okay,' Madison replied, and they walked in.

They stood for a moment in the middle of the room. Brown ducked to avoid the airplane.

'Closet.' Madison started on the top shelf, keen to get busy.

Brown went to the desk and flipped through the pages of every book in the pile. Their eyes met and they knew with complete and utter certainty that it was not a room they were standing in but some kind of madness made visible.

There weren't many clothes hanging in the closet but those present couldn't have been worn by an adult. Madison ran her hands over the denim jackets and the shirts, with an obvious preference for the color blue, and considered that, at most, Cameron had stopped wearing them in his late teens. There was a red high school warm-up jacket with yellow sleeves, a smaller size than most of the other items. Perhaps he had stopped caring about school games after that. Madison didn't know whether he'd gone to college, or whether that mattered anyway.

A baseball bat with a leather mitt, the ball still cradled in the pouch, was in the corner behind the clothes. Madison picked up the bat and held it with two hands like a batter would; she angled it and looked at its clean lines. It never ceased to amaze her how good the weight of it felt in her arms, the swing almost slipping off her, right to left.

Something caught her eye: the wood was unblemished and well taken care of except for a small mark. A sliver of something no thicker than a human nail was embedded pretty much dead on the spot where you would expect to hit the ball. She ran her finger over it; even through her glove she could feel the smoothness of the wood. Whatever it was, it was in so deep you wouldn't know it was there unless you were looking for it.

'Can you see a magnifying lens anywhere?' she asked Brown.

It was standard equipment for any kid who, at some point or other, would try to use it to burn a hole in something. There had to be one somewhere.

'Here.' It was in the china mug with an assortment of pens and pencils. Brown handed it to her. 'What have you got?'

'I don't know yet.'

Madison turned on the Anglepoise lamp on the desk and moved it so that it shone straight onto the bat. The lens was not as good as the one in the police lab, just good enough for her to see what she needed to see.

When she was in little league, a boy her age but twice her weight had the great idea to try to stop her from batting by grabbing the bat from behind while she was in full swing. The boy got his hand broken and Madison learned what a bone splinter looks like when it's embedded in a baseball bat.

'It's old,' she said.

'It's very old,' Brown replied.

'Still, it's worth having it checked.'

'Yup.'

Madison stood the bat by the door. The room wasn't any less eerie than it had been at first; if anything she was expecting that locker-room smell which seems to hang over every teenager's room.

'I'm calling him.' Brown sat back in the chair and dialed his cellphone. After getting transferred a couple of times he reached Fred Kamen at Quantico.

'I'm in a place that doesn't make any sense,' he said. 'No, I mean that literally. Do you have five minutes?'

You have a golden time at the beginning of an investigation: after those first precious 48 hours everything begins to fade. With each new day witnesses forget details and the pencil line between victim and killer becomes a little less clearly drawn.

Before the check had been found, Kamen might have helped to build a profile of the killer. With Cameron in the picture, he might help them to understand him and find him. The call was not to the FBI, it was from Brown to Kamen. One hand held the phone, the other went through the drawers in the desk.

Madison tuned him out. If you are a boy and you have bunk beds, where would you normally sleep? Top bunk, no question. Madison lifted a corner of the pillow with two fingers. No pajamas. She didn't really expect to find them there, then again she didn't really know what to expect.

She leant against the beds, stretching her arm over the top one until her fingertip brushed the triangular Sonics banner over it. It was fabric and raised lettering, the kind they don't make anymore.

Cameron had left the room as he had once had it, not for them to find it – he couldn't have known they'd come – but because he needed to. Madison took off her glove and traced the lettering with her finger. As surely as the dark line around the bone splinter was somebody's blood, that room, whatever it meant to him, would eventually bring him down. Madison knew it then like a hound that has just caught the scent. She wished that knowledge would make her feel better about being there but it didn't. She put her glove back on.

They finished their job, each to his own thoughts, and were glad to leave, having found little and taking with them a chill they wouldn't shake off for hours.

Chapter 17

'What did Kamen say?' Madison asked Brown.

They had just left Laurelhurst and the baseball bat was on the backseat, rolling with every turn.

'He said Cameron has been smart all these years and $25,000 turned him into a shmuck.'

'Go on.'

'That was the gist of it.'

Madison kept quiet and let Brown come out with the rest in his own time.

'What would you say is the difference between "posing" and "staging"?'

'Are you giving me a pop quiz?'

'You asked me what Kamen said.'

'Okay.' Madison shifted in her seat. "Staging" is when something is arranged to look like something else, like a hit is made to look like a robbery. "Posing" treats the victim like an object, which is put in a particular position to make a point, to leave some kind of message.'

'Yes. How many cases of posing have you worked?'

'None. It's extremely rare.'

'What is the perpetrator's reason for it?'

'It gives him a high – not only the kill but the complete control of the scene.'

'Yes. In the Sinclairs' homicides the victims were posed, bound and blindfolded. The signature, the thing the killer had to have, was not just their deaths but complete power over them after their deaths.'

'Agreed.'

'This is what Kamen asked me: was there any posing in the *Nostromo* killings? Was any physical evidence recovered afterwards? Was there any posing in the drug dealer murder in Lake Washington? Was any physical evidence recovered afterwards?'

'No and none, for both.'

'There is the likelihood that Cameron might have committed other murders that we don't know of because we couldn't link them to him. Still, no posing, no evidence, and no warning or message left on the scene.'

'What you're saying—'

'Cameron's changed. Suddenly, the wife and children are included in the kill and he needs to show off.'

'This time it was very personal: a friend stole from him. He made sure Sinclair knew what was happening to his family by killing him last. He had to, I don't know, erase the insult.'

'That was the point. The knowing.'

'What do you mean?'

'You just answered the question you asked yesterday. Why the different mode of death for the father? Why the chloroform? Why tie him up before he died and not after like the others?'

It was so simple.

'Because he wanted him to know,' she said. 'He wanted him to know what was happening to his family – that was the punishment.'

'A shot in the back of the head in a dark alley wouldn't have achieved the same goal.'

'Does Kamen have a problem with this scenario?' Madison asked.

'He doesn't like it when people change their habits, that's all. It worries him.'

'Does it worry you?'

Brown shrugged.

'Did Kamen have any idea about *Thirteen Days*?'

'No.'

'This morning, when Payne told you the prints on the glass were Cameron's, you were surprised, like it was bad news for us somehow.'

'I was surprised,' Brown conceded.

'Why?'

'I don't know. Maybe I just didn't expect him to be able to leave any.'

Carl Doyle knocked softly on Nathan Quinn's door and walked in.

'He's here,' he said.

'Show him in.'

'Do you need anything else?'

'No, Carl. Thank you for staying. You should go home.'

It was too late to discuss the situation with Sinclair's files or why Bob Greenhut was now the executor of Jimmy's will. At the best of times, Nathan Quinn was not a man who would encourage questions about his private life, and this was far from being the best of times. All Doyle could offer was his support and his kindness, and he would do just that.

'I'll see you tomorrow.'

Doyle didn't mind staying late – it gave him a chance to catch up with things. He did, however, mind seeing Tod Hollis, the firm's chief investigator, coming in at that hour in the evening. Nothing good ever started that way.

As always, Hollis wore a dark suit and tie, more a federal agent than the cop he once was, close-cropped hair and a mustache that had more gray in it than black. He had been shot after 25 years on the job and the resulting limp, however slight, had put him into the private investigation business. Quinn Locke was his main client.

Hollis gripped Quinn's hand and shook it hard once.

'I'm very sorry about James and his family.'

'Thank you.'

Hollis had dealt with many relatives of victims through the years. He looked at Quinn to see how far along he was on that ugly road.

'Have a seat. Would you like a drink?' Quinn gestured to a couple of chairs opposite his desk. He had poured himself a shot of bourbon half an hour ago and it was still untouched.

'No, thank you.'

Quinn sat down on the companion chair.

'How are you doing?' Hollis said.

'I'm fine,' Quinn replied. 'I'm sorry to have called on you so late—'

'Don't worry about it.'

'I need your help.'

'Anything I can do.'

'This is going to be different.'

'What is it?'

Hollis saw the line of darkness around Quinn's eyes and hoped it was mere tiredness.

'I want to put a reward out for information that will lead to the arrest of the man who murdered James and his family. $250,000. I would like you to be in charge of that.'

'It's a lot of money.'

'It's worth it.'

'I know. What I mean is, an amount like that, every creep from here to Miami is going to crawl out from under a rock and tell on his mama.'

'What do you think would be appropriate?'

'$100,000, and we are still going to have a tough time sifting through all the calls.'

'The checkbook is open.'

'I know.'

'Something else. I would like you to investigate the murders yourself.'

The police investigation was hardly two days old and Hollis knew the department – all good people who would put in the hours 'until'.

'What's going on?' he asked.

'The police say that they have found evidence that James might have been embezzling funds from one of his tax clients. They say it could be a revenge killing. They were here today going through his files. Of course, they found nothing to support their theory.'

'What do you think?'

'I don't believe it for a second.'

'What about the evidence they have?' Hollis would always think like a cop.

'I'll come to that. There's more: they are already looking for someone.'

'Who?'

'The wrong man.'

'Okay.'

'And I am his attorney.'

Hollis waited.

'John Cameron.'

Hollis sat back in his chair.

'I think I'll have that drink now,' he said.

Quinn poured him a shot. Hollis held the glass without drinking.

'If I'm taking this on, and I want to, you are going to have to tell me all you know. I can't go into this half-cocked.'

'I'm going to tell you everything the police told me. Everything that's relevant to the case. After that you make your own moves.'

Hollis took out his pad.

'You do realize they might be right?' he said.

'I don't think so,' Quinn replied.

'Is it like something you have a feeling about or something you know absolutely, without the shadow of a doubt?'

'I know this absolutely.'

'Nathan, this is an open case. Two days old. No one is going to welcome us with open arms while the police are still on it. What happens if whatever I dig up confirms their theory?'

'It won't,' Quinn said. 'Find out what you can about the detectives. I want to know who I'm dealing with. And I couldn't care less for their welcome.'

The patrol car was parked in front of the Sinclairs' home. During the evening the uniformed officers had regularly walked around the outside of the property. There had been a problem in the last few years with the sale online of items from crime scenes. For a considerable price, an object from Blueridge would be out of the house, the city and the state before their shift was over.

Brock and McDowell turned off their torches as they reached the car. They were about to run out of coffee and that thought held McDowell's attention as much as securing the house. Neither of them knew the neighborhood very well. They had driven around on patrols, sure, but they were not familiar with its secrets. They were not aware of a path three hundred yards past the house. From Blueridge, through the trees and between the houses, it led down to the narrow cobble beach and the water. They couldn't have known about it, but John Cameron did.

He moved through the pitch-black darkness without hesitation, a shadow deeper than the rest. He made no sound on the dirt path and in seconds reached the water. Puget Sound glimmered for a moment before him, then a cloud passed over the moon and John Cameron stepped onto the beach.

Tiny lights blinked from Vashon Island. James Sinclair's house stood empty on the right. Cameron started walking.

He had observed the patrol officers, seen the beams of their torches. He had waited till he was sure they were back in their car and then moved down the path.

Cameron climbed the wooden steps up to the lawn, crossed it and reached the patio door. The key was already in his hand and he let himself in. He closed the glass door behind him, locked it and pulled the curtains shut as he had found them.

John Cameron stands still and hears himself breathe the stale air in the living room. He knows the position of every piece of furniture and every object as if he can see them. His eyes adjust to the inside. From the right-hand pocket on his trouser leg he takes out a small torch and turns it on. The circle of light is strong, Cameron sweeps the floor with it to make sure nothing has changed from his last visit.

He raises the beam slightly and notices the smudges of black powder used by the crime-scene unit to dust for fingerprints. They are everywhere. He takes in the powder, the dank smell and the changes around him. He sees the room whole, in daylight now, police officers busy with their trade or standing around. Someone has moved a pile of magazines from its usual place. Scuff marks on the wooden floor from the number of people who walked back and forth. Small intrusions into the life of the house.

Less than 30 feet away, two police officers are shooting the breeze. John Cameron is both aware of their presence and unconcerned by it.

Whatever his thoughts or his memories of what happened in the house, they do not spill over the present and the job in hand.

He points the torch to the ground and takes the stairs to the master bedroom. Halfway up, the air changes into a heavier scent like a warm day in a butcher's.

From many visits, he remembers which steps will creak where, and he's light on his feet. A man standing on the landing wouldn't know he was there.

He reaches the bedroom. The beam of the torch finds the bedstead and lingers there for a long time. He follows the trail of the detectives' work in every mark circled on the wall and every powder stain around the window. He notices that the top of the inside doorframe has been removed; the blood smudge on the door leads him to the children's room and the bullet holes in the wall.

In a place where awful violence has been committed, John Cameron walks from room to room, observing without hurry. In the study, he sits back on the leather sofa and turns off the torch. There is a lot of sky in the window but no stars.

Madison, tired and restless, drove as fast as the law would allow toward Three Oaks. She dialed Brown's number.

'I'm not done with the day yet,' she said. 'I'm thinking of going to the crime scene for a walk-around, see if anything overlaps with Cameron's house.'

'If you find something—'

'I know. I'll get one of the officers to co-sign the slip.'

'By the way, the keys are here. How are you going to get in?'

'Well, I'll have to improvise. I'm counting on a spare key under the mat.'

'I don't want to hear someone broke a back window to get in.'

'Don't worry. If I don't find it in five minutes I'll just go home and not sleep.'

By the time she pulled in alongside the patrol car, Madison was reasonably annoyed with herself. She showed them her badge, explained who she was and what she was going to do. Brock and McDowell exchanged a look; there might have been some eye-rolling involved – Madison couldn't be sure.

It took her ten minutes to find the small plastic bag, the kind that seals up, inside the hollow of a stump a few yards up the driveway, in it a key ring and two keys.

Five minutes past midnight, Madison crossed the threshold. She turned on the lights in the hall and in the living room. Everything was as she remembered it. She didn't have a plan exactly, it was more a case of knowing what she was looking for after she had found it. However, there was one thing she had to do first.

She flicked the stairs light on and looked up. Nobody had bothered to change the central heating setting and the system was just turning itself off for the night, soft clicks rumbling from the pipes.

Madison reached the master bedroom and turned the light on but did not enter. In terms of blood and sheer destruction, it was not the worst crime scene she had visited, not by a long shot. But what her mind saw was rage, blind and overwhelming and yet contained in the neat turnout of the bedcovers.

Rage implied more than revealed. If that thing made a sound, Madison considered, it was not something she ever wanted to hear.

She did not need to hold those thoughts for long; it was late and she was rattling around in an empty house. She knew very well that there was a reason why she had gone upstairs: if she was going to search their house and get into their things, it was a way of asking their permission. Certain things cannot be taken; maybe the house would be willing to give her what she needed.

Her steps creaked as she passed the study. She didn't go in and that was a good thing, the best thing she'd done all day.

Madison turns the lights out on the stairs and John Cameron

puts his knife back in its sheath and leans against the inside of the door.

He could tell from the weight behind the steps that it was a woman. She had to be a cop, a detective too. The officers in the car have not set foot in the house since he has been watching them. It is an intrusion into his private time and he resents it deeply. Still, she is there now and if someone is looking for something in the middle of the night, it might be worth knowing what exactly they have come to seek.

For less than a second Cameron balances curiosity against caution; head cocked like a bird he listens to the small sounds from the living room, then he starts moving. See him, not see him – he honestly doesn't care one way or the other. His work has been interrupted and tonight he's not in a forgiving mood.

Madison looked around. The Sinclairs had lived well but not extravagantly. There were two cars in the garage and the usual trappings of an affluent lifestyle scattered around the house. A widescreen television in the living room and a DVD player. Madison remembered seeing an Olympus and a Sony digital video camera in the study, both collected by Lauren and Joyce.

The furniture was nice, mostly modern, with some antique pieces. It all added up to a comfortable life and yet it didn't answer Madison's question: why would James Sinclair need to steal money from the one person he knew he shouldn't mess with? How could he be that dumb?

Gambling, debts nobody knew about, blackmail, a woman on the side – it was all possible. Madison knelt in front of a couple of low bookshelves of DVDs. Possible, but not very likely. If James Sinclair had a secret life it was so well hidden they might never find it.

The films were children's films, mostly Disney classics she had once owned herself. Some Scorsese and a few Spielbergs. All pretty standard stuff.

Madison stopped reading. *Christmas concert and party*. The handwriting was neat and clear. Home movies. She reached for the disk, put it in the player and pressed 'play'.

A school hall, Christmas decorations hanging from the walls. A stage with empty chairs. Whoever was shooting it was doing a good job, carefully pulling out of a golden star and widening the framing to the back of the audience; adults whispered in the dim auditorium.

'Here they are.' A male voice speaking on the left of the camera.

'I see him.' A female voice.

Annie Sinclair pointed the camera at a group of thirty or so children who trooped out from the wings and took their seats with their instruments.

'Where is he?' A boy's voice. A rustle of clothes close to the mike.

Without seeing it, Madison imagined James Sinclair lifting one of the boys on to his shoulders so that he could see his brother play. They started. Madison smiled in spite of herself: teachers never changed. It was Pachelbel's 'Canon'.

The first bars would have covered Cameron's steps on the stairs, had he made any sound. He comes halfway down and pauses; the house is dark except for a table lamp in the living room.

In the pool of light, a woman sits with her back to the door, the television throwing blue shadows on the walls.

Cameron sees her profile against the screen as she turns to pick up the remote. A black and white photograph taken by a bored reporter is enough for him to recognize Madison as the detective who had marched the fake FedEx man out of the crime scene. He files that information away. Whatever Detective Madison is looking for, she is looking for it in a Christmas recital.

He'd rather have found her going through the bookshelves and emptying the drawers; instead she sits, stock still in the changing lights. Cameron watches her and the screen in front of her. She doesn't move and neither does he.

The music was awkward and frail, John Sinclair's face half hidden by the recorder. Madison, with her back against the sofa, was hardly breathing.

The piece came to its end and another one started; this time it was Bach's 'Jesus, Joy of Man's Desiring'. Sometimes the shot changed to show the whole stage but mostly it stayed on the Sinclair boy.

When the audience started clapping Madison paused the video. She got up and went to the kitchen. It was off the living room to the right.

Cameron heard cupboards being opened and a tap turned on. Had he been a sensible man he would have left then – the study had a window. He could have dropped to the ground and crossed the back lawn in seconds. But John Cameron doesn't feel sensible at that point of the evening. He leans back against the banister and crosses his arms: time is all he has. To his immense relief, he feels nothing at all.

Madison drank a glass of water from the tap, refilled it and drank another. Those films were all that there would ever be of the Sinclairs on this earth.

After she washed and dried the highball, she put it back and sat down with the video again. She pressed 'play'. The film continued into the after-performance party: children ran around and parents stood in groups and chatted. James Sinclair wore a navy blue shirt and jeans; he had an easy smile and looked nothing like the dead man Madison had seen upstairs. She was glad there wasn't any more music.

Madison ignored the boys and concentrated on the parents: when the husband took over the camera, she saw that Annie Sinclair was tall with an angular face and intelligent eyes. She wore no jewelry that she could see aside from her wedding band.

Madison played the video till the end. She puffed her cheeks and exhaled slowly and went on to the next. There were at least a dozen. They must have shot the films on the digital camera she had seen upstairs and then transferred them.

She ran through a school recital and a birthday party with the fast-forward button pressed and wished that she could make herself a cup of coffee. Strangely enough that seemed inappropriate.

She was changing disks when her phone rang. It startled her and she automatically looked at her wristwatch.

'You're still there.' It was Brown.

'I'm going through the home movies.'

'Anything good?'

'A lot of regular life stuff. School plays, birthday parties.'

'No jackpot yet?'

'No. I guess he's not a kiddie party kind of guy.'

'Probably not.'

'I'm going to watch another couple of films and then I'll clock off.'

'Half day.'

'You got that right.' She smiled. 'Brown—'

'Yes.'

It sounded as if he was in his car.

'What did he do with the money? I'm looking around here and I see nothing that he couldn't get with his salary.'

'Which, as it happens, is far higher than either yours or mine.'

'Exactly. So?'

Cameron wished he could hear the whole conversation and not just Madison's half. It was certainly a very interesting subject for him. He would have been able to give them one or two illuminating facts but this was neither the time nor the place.

Suddenly, Madison stood up and stretched. Cameron's eyes followed her every movement.

'I don't know,' Brown said.

'Well, we'd better find out.'

'We'll talk to the bank in the morning.'

'See you tomorrow.'

Madison slipped a new disk in the video; it was the youngest child's birthday – David. His seventh, his last. She let it run at normal speed, listening to the now familiar voices and keeping an eye on it while she looked at the pictures on the mantelpiece over the fireplace. It was the normal assortment of formal occasions and candid shots. A nice group wedding picture taken at the reception. Her eyes found Nathan Quinn, paused for a second and moved on. She scanned all the faces. No Cameron.

David Sinclair's voice screamed in delight from the television. His mother laughed.

'What do you say, David?' she said.

'Thank you, Uncle Jack.'

Madison froze. Cameron exhaled slowly. Madison rewound the film a few seconds and pressed 'play'.

The family was inside the house. A big table was covered in paper plates and decorations and discarded wrapping paper, flashes from the cameras. Madison found the mother, the father, the elder brother, the birthday boy. Quinn was there too, a dozen other children of roughly the same age and more unidentified adults. Once she had eliminated the women, there were only six unknown men. Two were too old, one was Japanese, three were just plain wrong.

'Thank you, Uncle Jack,' David said, looking at the camera.

Damn, he's shooting the film.

She went back to the beginning of the tape and watched every last frame. She did that three times and got absolutely nowhere. Uncle Jack was never on camera and if he had spoken at all, which at some point he must have done, he had done so away from the mike. There was no way to identify his voice in that mess of sounds.

Madison freeze-framed the shot of the child looking at the camera. She drummed her fingers on the remote. To be so close was maddening.

John Cameron is also looking at the screen, his eyes narrow at the memory of that day, and he blinks at a camera flash. For a moment he doesn't even notice Madison getting up.

Madison opens the cupboard doors under the bookcase, closes them, opens the next ones. No good. She opens the last set of doors: on the bottom shelf, a small pile of photographs. They were in the fourth envelope: David Sinclair's birthday pictures.

John Cameron takes a step down on the staircase.

Madison stood under the lamp. She looked at each picture intently for a few seconds and then put it to one side. She was halfway down the pack when she found it. He was not in the picture but his reflection was, caught in the glass of the garden door: a dark-haired man holding a camera against a blue sky.

'Hello, Jack,' Madison said quietly.

In the near-darkness, Cameron's right hand twitched.

She held the photo under the light; it was like looking at someone under water. A loud knock on the front door brought her back. Madison turned and walked out of the living room, through the hall and to the front door. She didn't look back. She didn't turn on the light. She opened the door and Officer McDowell was stomping his feet on the ground to get some circulation going down there.

'Just wanted to say we're being relieved.'

There was another patrol car parked next to theirs; a couple of uniformed officers looked rosy-cheeked and rested at the beginning of their shift.

'Thanks for helping me with the keys.'

'I told the guys you're still in here.'

Madison glanced at the relief shift; they nodded but she could see they were mildly suspicious of anybody who chose to be there at 2 a.m.

Hell, I'd be suspicious myself, she thought, and closed the door. She was still holding the photograph and, for the first time that night, she was completely alone in the house.

Madison went through the other packs and found nothing. She put them back as she had found them and finally decided that she was done for the day.

When she got home, she could still smell the crime scene in her hair. She showered and shampooed, put on her red flannel pajamas and climbed into bed.

Out of Three Oaks heading north, John Cameron drives fast with the windows rolled down.

Chapter 18

Fred Tully had barely left the offices of the *Star* in the last 24 hours. He'd gone home to change his clothes and managed a one-hour nap on the sofa. In spite of that, he hadn't felt that good in ages.

It was 4 a.m. and he was sitting at his desk, in his hands a proof of the front page which was about to hit the newsstands. Tully was smiling.

The intern had dropped the envelope on his desk around 8 p.m.

'Did you see who brought this?'

The kid just raised his eyebrows.

In the last 36 hours, since the identities of the victims have been made public, a steady stream of visitors has come to Lincoln Elementary in Three Oaks, the school attended by John and David Sinclair. It started with a couple of bunches of flowers by the main gates, brought by mothers who had known the boys. It has now become a shrine with candles, small gifts and messages taped to the flowers.

KING and KOMO-TV reporters use it as a background when they shoot their updates and a couple of volunteers from the school make sure the children are careful with the candles' flames near the cards and the soft toys.

Harry Salinger got out of the van with the camera already on his shoulder. The van, white with Oregon plates, had darkened windows and the letters KTVX printed on its side.

Harry Salinger is six foot one, built for high jump rather than heavy weights. He's been wearing his sandy hair in a buzz cut ever since he started losing it in his early twenties. Today, under timid rain, he wears a fleece cap with flaps that cover his ears and a heavily lined jacket.

Salinger moved through the group of reporters as if he belonged with them. He shot a few minutes of the makeshift shrine and looked suitably somber as he did so. In truth, being around children made him uncomfortable and he left as soon as he could.

As he turned to go, a mother holding a toddler bumped into him. She apologized with a smile to the man with the kind doctor's face and went on her way.

Salinger reached his van, unlocked the door and climbed in. He slid the door shut behind him and pulled off his hat. Inside, the van smelled clean: Salinger had laid a new carpet in it only the previous week.

Crowds usually unnerved him – the voices, the physical contact. The camera had given him a safe distance from which to observe and record without getting caught up in the unpleasantness of all that human proximity.

The shrine was lovely; he was glad he got a few shots of it. He especially liked the muted colors of the cards and the way the candles looked blurred in the viewfinder.

He backed out of his parking spot and drove off. He found KEZX on 1150-AM and waited for the news to come on. When it did, he knew what the first item would be. In his eyes, as colorless as rainwater, a light flickered briefly. He got onto Highway 99 and headed north, past Greenwood and Mountlake Terrace. He came off 99 in Lynnwood.

His house sat on a drive two hundred yards back from the road, behind a group of firs bunched together in the middle of a field. He had no neighbors in the immediate vicinity and the house was closer to Everett than Seattle.

He parked the van in the garage, next to his Accord. The house had been built in the 1920s, with parts added to it as it became necessary: three small bedrooms upstairs and living room, dining room and kitchen on the ground floor.

Salinger usually ate in the kitchen and no one had sat on the upholstered sofa since his grandparents' notary, who had given him papers to sign and slapped him on the shoulder. Salinger had said all the right words and the man was out of the house quickly. *His* house now.

Salinger had closed the door behind him and looked at the spot on his blazer where the notary had touched him; he rubbed it lightly. Then he had opened all the windows to get rid of the man's cologne.

The garage could barely accommodate two vehicles but Salinger was as careful in his driving as in everything he did.

There was no communicating door with the inside; he locked the garage with a padlock and walked to the small porch that led to the entrance. The house had been painted white years before and it would soon need seeing to again; he put it in a mental checklist of 'to dos' for the new year and then realized that, all being well, he wouldn't be there to do it anyway, and he smiled. It was an immense relief to know that things were on their way and soon all this would be behind him.

Salinger lived alone. He still loved the feeling of walking into his own home, shutting out the distant sound of traffic and being almost absorbed by the complete silence. Others might have found it unsettling but for a man who had been in the places he had been, it was more than his heart had ever dared to wish. He would eat a bite while he worked, he thought.

He made himself a ham sandwich, pink and white, wrapped the end in a triangle of kitchen paper and took it downstairs, where his work was done.

The basement was vast and ran the length and breadth of the house, completely open. He used a quarter for storage and the rest had been swept clean, extra lights hung from the beams and spotlights clipped to the plain wooden shelves on the brick walls. Dozens of pencil sketches have been tacked on the glossy white, some are floor plans and others show the development of a metal and glass object. Salinger has never taken any art class but his efforts would be first puzzling then shocking to any visitor.

Metalwork and welding tools had been lined up on a bench in the corner and two large desks, next to each other, took up most of the space in the middle. On each desk sat three television monitors, the kind that comes with a video player/recorder. Next to a row of pencils, a seashell caught his eye for a moment, its delicate spiral no bigger than his fingernail.

He bent down by the table on the left and found another switch among the many cables and wires: two monitors came to life, the sound muted. Morning television.

His eyes drifted from one to the next, his skin prickling. Cooking shows, chat shows, quiz shows. It was a language he did not speak from a world he did not understand. He checked his wristwatch: the news would be on soon.

On a smaller table at the side he had set up a sound system; he pressed a couple of keys and a crackling sound came through the speakers.

It was definitely a home-made job, nothing high-tech, nothing that anybody with time on their hands couldn't put together. Still, Salinger was very proud of it, and so he should be. He fast-forwarded until the numbers on the counter told him that he was where he wanted to be, then he let it play. Alice Madison's voice filled the basement.

'He's blindfolded with a piece of black velvet. Not torn, cut. On the fore-head, there is a sign like a cross. Drawn in blood. He's bound with ... looks like leather. Thin strip. Around his neck, hands and feet. Hands are tied behind his back. Makes it really difficult to move if you're lying down on them.'

A pause.

The screen flickered on the third monitor and when the picture came into focus, it was the Sinclairs' bedroom. In the grainy darkness, a figure moves before the lens. Behind it, on the bed, three bodies are visible, completely still; the fourth body, closest to the camera, is struggling, thrashing around, almost coming off the bed in an effort to break free.

Salinger turned down the volume; the muffled sounds from under the blindfold were a distraction.

'Deep red ligature marks where he's been tied. Some bruising. He put up a fight.'

Harry Salinger narrowed his eyes as he looked at the screen and started on his sandwich. He has listened to it many times. In fact, he has transferred the whole thing onto a cassette so that he can listen to it anywhere in his house, on a cheap Walkman he can hook onto his belt.

When he had left a voice-activated microphone on the crime scene, one he could easily monitor from the crowd of reporters, it had been a purely functional decision. He had wanted to have an idea of what they were talking about, their first impressions of the case, his work. He knew part of it was vanity – he had to admit that much. However, he honestly needed that little advantage and that was all.

He had seen Madison drag out the photographer. A display of intuition and strength that he had watched over and over: most of the reporters had pointed their cameras at Riley, not Salinger; he had followed Madison down the drive, caught her look at the crowd, and stayed on her until she went back inside the house, which he knew as well as his own.

That first night, after his work in the basement was done, for hours he had walked from room to room in headphones.

'*Contact wounds to the head. You can see the tattooing. The shooter was less than two feet away. All of them, except the father. Just one shot. No bruises, no signs of struggle.*' Salinger closed his eyes and each word revealed its true color, a blaze of scarlet and blue that burned right through him. Best of all though, something he would never have expected: Madison's voice was indigo. In the deep hollow of the house, it is the only human sound.

Chapter 19

Alice Madison, 10 years old, leant her bike against the warm concrete wall and knocked on the rusty screen door of the bungalow. She had told her mom she would be back in one hour and she had ridden fast in the midday wind. The sky above the Nevada desert was blazing but she knew the house would be soothingly dark and air-conditioned.

The men in the basement had been playing for 12 hours straight and nobody cared the basement had no windows. It did not have a famous Vegas name either but that didn't seem to matter much – the game was just as real and the money just as hard.

A $500 entry fee bought you a chair in Joey Cavizzi's basement; the rest was down to them.

A soft knock and a stocky man pushed the door ajar. The girl walked in.

'Hey, honey,' one of the players said.

'Hey, Dad,' Alice replied.

She went around the table and climbed on a tall stool next to a bar in the corner; the room was a combination of ashtray and monkey cage. Joey's nephew was in charge of drinks.

'The usual?' he asked her.

She nodded. From a small refrigerator he got out a ginger ale, scooped some ice cubes out of a bucket and into a tumbler, poured the drink with a flourish and wrapped a folded napkin around the glass. He handed it to her and slid a fresh bowl of pretzels to where she could reach it.

'Honey,' her father said, 'ten minutes ago, Richard here was dealt a straight flush. What are the chances of that happening?' His eyes glinted.

'Seventy-two thousand one hundred and ninety-two to one,' Alice replied without hesitation. All the men laughed. Alice Madison had been to countless games of theirs. The players didn't mind – in fact they got a kick out of it. She was their mascot: the ten-year-old who understood the joys and mysteries of their religion.

She sat quite still but her eyes followed the cards and the men's hands. Her father watched her and she watched Richard O'Malley, sitting on his left. Father O'Malley, that is, weekdays at 5 p.m. and twice on Sundays. Alice knew he held enough to take the plate and was ready to make his move. Her father smiled.

Wednesday morning. Madison walked into the precinct at 7.45 a.m., a quarter of an hour before the beginning of her shift. A couple of reporters saw her from the opposite side of the parking lot and tried and failed to catch up with her on the steps.

The alarm had woken her from a heavy sleep. She felt like she had been chasing things and doing things and generally running around without a break even in her dreams.

As she walked upstairs, a couple of detectives from Vice were coming down. A look passed between them when they saw her. The woman half turned to Madison as they passed each other and said: 'Fasten your seat belt.'

It could only mean one thing: OPR was on the floor – the Office of Personal Responsibility; the change of name from Internal Affairs had not made it any nicer. Madison rolled her eyes.

One man and one woman were in Lieutenant Fynn's office. The door was closed, the slats from the blinds were open enough that she knew she hadn't met them before.

Brown was standing at his desk, holding a newspaper.

'Coming in today, you didn't listen to the radio?'

'No. Why?'

She had wanted to and had done the usual little dance of switching it on, regretting the chatting voices and turning it off.

'Have a read. It's a charming piece of investigative journalism.' He passed her the copy of the *Washington Star*.

Blueridge killer slew family for revenge. It went downhill from there. Madison sat on the edge of her desk and read on. Her eyes caught the name of the reporter, Fred Tully. The article went into sufficient detail about the manner of the deaths that any crank with fourth-grade literacy would be able to bluff his way into a confession. It mentioned evidence, documents and motives. And finally, to crown it all, there it was: John Cameron's name.

Tully wrote about his relationship to the dead family, to Quinn, Locke & Associates; he listed all the myths, the rumors and the half-truths that came with Cameron's name.

'Sonovabitch,' Madison whispered under her breath.

Brown looked darkly at the paper. 'They've started a thirteen-days countdown.'

'How did he find out?'

'We'll know soon enough.' Brown's voice was dead flat.

The implication was that someone had talked. It was not entirely unheard of, reporters arriving at a crime scene at the same time as the detectives. It happened: a small exchange of information for some green. It was bad but it happened.

Madison thought of the message slip in the bin downstairs: this was not about a couple of guys with a camera turning up unexpectedly. It was unthinkable to her that anybody who had looked at dead children would pawn them for an easy buck. It was as simple as that.

She read the article once more. She realized that she was standing up. Her first instinct was to get into her car and go find the little worm.

'Later,' Brown said, snapping her back from that line of thought.

Lieutenant Fynn's door opened and he motioned for them to go in. Introductions were made: Detectives Julianne Casey and Bobby Carr from OPR were there to investigate how the case had sprung such a monumental leak. Nobody shook hands.

Casey and Carr were both in their early forties and Madison judged they probably hadn't soiled their loafers on a crime scene for quite some time. On the other hand, they seemed smart and they had both made eye contact when introduced.

'Tully is a hack,' Casey started. 'And to be honest, I'm surprised he even knows that the past tense of "slay" is "slew". The point though is that this is an embarrassment we don't need. It hurts the case, it hurts the department.'

Good work, Madison thought. She was going for the 'we are all one team' approach.

'As soon as possible, we are going to need to interview all the detectives involved,' Carr said, clearly not feeling they were all one team after all. His eyes were dull and his tie too bright.

'I would like to make one thing absolutely clear,' Lieutenant Fynn said. 'You find a leak, it's not going to be from this room. If this situation is going to be taken care of in the middle of a multiple murder investigation, I don't want anybody's time to be wasted. If you want to start talking to my detectives, do it now. We've all got jobs to get on with. But, my advice to you is to look elsewhere.'

Casey and Carr turned to Brown and Madison.

'Okay if we start with you two?' Casey said.

*

Madison poured herself some water from the cooler. The interview had been predictably pointless. Anger and frustration were not going to make her thinking any clearer; she needed to get on with something and put the *Star* on the back burner for a while.

Chapter 20

Nathan Quinn stood by the window in his office, looking out and seeing nothing. He had spent most of the night talking with Tod Hollis and arranging the notice of the reward with the offices of the *Times* and the *Post Intelligencer*.

He had been the last person to leave the office in the early hours of the morning, and the first back in. The darkness in the window hadn't changed.

When the detectives had come in to give him the news, he knew what would happen. He knew that the bitter taste in his mouth was adrenaline; he remembered it from when they called him and told him about David. His father had come to pick him up at the airport and explained. All those years ago, and that taste was the first thing that came back to him. He couldn't get rid of it now and genuinely thought he never would.

He kept thinking of his father, dead for years, and how he used to sing to David when he was a baby in his heavy Scottish brogue: 'Now the summer's in its prime with the flowers sweetly bloomin''. His father's favorite song. Quinn hadn't thought of those words for so long and here they were, squatting in his mind when all he wanted was blessed silence.

Carl Doyle knocked on the door and came in with his mail.

'Nathan,' he said, 'you should read this.'

Doyle put the pile of envelopes on Quinn's desk and gave him a copy of the *Star*.

'Thank you, Carl.'

'You're meeting Victor about Redmond vs. Woodleigh in five minutes. And Judge Martin expects you in chambers at 11.'

'Give me ten minutes and then bring him in.'

'Okay.'

Doyle left. He needed to tell Quinn about the interview with Madison, even if it mattered nothing to anybody but himself. He had been the one who had connected the first dots, wherever they would lead. Doyle sat at his desk and tried to busy himself with the appointment book.

Nathan Quinn read the article where he was standing. He read it twice to make sure he understood exactly all the connections that Tully had made. The background work he had done on the relationship between the men was sketchy, but every newspaper in the state would pick up the story and the later editions today would carry the Hoh River kidnapping and their common past. Quinn was not surprised: 48 hours from the discovery of the bodies, that was exactly what he would have expected. The *bodies* . . .

Quinn dialed Hollis's number. Hollis picked up on the second ring.

'It's started,' Quinn said.

In the pile of mail, among the holiday wishes and the condolences, sits a cream envelope, waiting to deliver neither blessings nor sympathies.

Billy Rain worked in his brother-in-law's garage off Eastlake Avenue. He was an okay mechanic who understood cars and knew how to deal quickly and accurately with most problems.

He was working on the engine of a Pontiac when he felt Tom

Crane's eyes on his back. He kept his head down; he knew his brother-in-law despised him and disliked him in equal measure and didn't even hold it against him.

The problem with Billy Rain was that there was only one thing he was truly great at: Billy was the guy you go to if you need something opened, like a steel door, a multiple lock, a bank safe. Billy had a gift. Some people find early in their lives an aptitude for a musical instrument or maybe Math. Billy Rain knew that he could get into anything or anywhere. Older boys found him soon enough and never really let him go.

Billy straightened up and saw that Tom was talking to another mechanic, both of them looking at him every so often. In spite of the looks, no one there had ever given him any real trouble: he stood six foot four and they all knew he had been in and out of jail all his life. The myth of the tough ex-con suited him just fine.

Billy Rain had never been in a fight or looked for one: while in jail he had been left alone, protected by people who might need his skills on the outside. His hands, now smeared with grease and oil, were a valuable commodity. He wiped them on the sides of his blue overalls.

Tom Crane had told his sister that her jailbird husband could work for him when he was paroled. A once-only concession, Billy thought, that would allow Tom Crane to look down every day on someone more miserable than himself. Billy didn't care. He had a wife who deserved better, a 15-year-old son who detested him and a nine-year-old daughter who adored him.

He had no idea what to do with himself. One day soon Tom would find a reason to fire him and the only life he had ever felt comfortable in would claim him again.

'I'm going on a break,' he said.

He grabbed a cup of coffee from the pot in Tom's office and took it to the yard. It was cold and the sky was sheet-metal gray but there was a small bench by the chain-link fence, away from the radio and the unremitting chat.

He balanced the cup on the slat by his side and glanced at the paper he had picked up that morning. It was the *Washington Star*. He started reading Tully's piece.

Billy had never been a violent offender. He wasn't even a thief really – he only ever got the other guys in. The business in Blueridge was upsetting; one of the boys had been the same age as his girl.

Billy Rain read the description of the killings and slowly, gradually, the banging and the radio fell away and a heavy clammy silence pressed on him from the inside. In his sordid way, Fred Tully had been as revealing as the photograph he had been sent.

Somehow Billy Rain found the toilet on the left of the yard and locked himself in. It was a one-man job with a mirror and a gray little soap bar on the sink. His face in the mirror was as white as the tiles on the wall. He felt a dry heave coming and threw up in the toilet.

About three years ago, doing time upstate, on a morning as cold as this one. He threw up again.

Billy Rain was finishing up in the prison laundry; nobody else was there during the shift change. He turned a corner and was suddenly aware of two men locked in a silent fight. He pulled himself back and out of sight, waiting for them to get it over with and leave. There was a wet, choking gasp and someone trying to kick his way out of trouble. Leaning with his back against a tall cart, Billy was frozen.

Then, one minute of quiet rustling and one man's steps walking away. The body laid straight on the concrete floor, the hands tied at the front. Billy recognized a young firebug called George Pathune; he'd been blindfolded with a strip of dark prison denim. He was dead. On his brow, what looked like a cross had been smudged in blood.

Billy Rain looked at him only for a few seconds and left in a hurry. He told no one and when the body was discovered, he didn't talk about it with the other cons. He kept his head down and waited for his parole hearing.

In the garage toilet, Billy rubs his soapy hands on his face and splashes water on it. The work on the Pontiac and the rest of the day are little more than a blur.

Shortly before 11 a.m., Nathan Quinn left his office and took the elevator to Stern Tower's underground parking level. He got into the Jeep and started the engine for the short journey to the court-house on Sixth and Spring. He wasn't anxious, he wasn't afraid. Sarah Klein, a prosecutor who could sense a weak argument from further away than a cheetah could spot a limp, couldn't possibly fathom his real concerns, not in a thousand years.

The sky was low and dazzling over the city, waiting to snow and heavy with it. Nathan Quinn blinked into the light as the car left the building. Under a sheet of frost the ground would be hard, he thought; the gravediggers would have to start early and finish late.

'I was having a good week, Miss Klein. And we all know how rare that is. Then your request landed in my docket.'

Nathan Quinn and Sarah Klein sat in silence opposite the Honorable Claire Martin. They had both spent enough hours in her courtroom to know better than to interrupt. They waited as the judge took off her robes and hung them on a coat rack. As always, her long salt-and-pepper hair was in a bun and her bifocals on the tip of her nose.

In over two decades on the bench the Honorable Claire Martin had surprised many an unprepared attorney: no one could, on any given day, make any assumptions about how she would rule, only that her rulings stuck and had never been reversed by a superior court.

'Attorney-client privilege,' she said as she sat down. 'Alright then, Miss Klein, pretend, if you will, that I live in a paper bag and haven't read the papers or seen the news. Give me the details. Be brief.'

Sarah Klein had rehearsed that opening in her mind over and over. Four counts of murder, the manner in which the crime had been planned and executed, the young age of the children – these factors would lie heavily on the judge's mind when it came to rule.

She was indeed brief and still managed to spare no detail. Judge Martin listened and took notes.

'At present the Seattle Police Department and the County Prosecutor are doing what they can to locate Mr. Cameron, who has an outstanding arrest warrant on his head. Meanwhile Mr. Quinn here has been in contact with him from the very start of this and knows exactly how and where to contact his client.'

'Your Honor—' Quinn started speaking but Judge Martin raised her left hand.

'Not yet,' she said. 'What do you want from me, Sarah?'

'The privilege protects the communications between an attorney and his client but not the fact that they occurred or the manner in which they took place or the location where they happened. Not when, on balance, the interests of justice override the purposes of the privilege.'

'It took you ten minutes to get to *the interests of justice*,' Quinn said pleasantly.

'I think society's interests would be best served should Mr. Quinn be required to reveal the whereabouts of his client and the means he uses to get in touch with him. Your Honor, Mr. Quinn can pick up a phone or send a message in a bottle for all I care, but if he is protecting the murderer of at least four people, that does not fall within the privilege.'

'"At least four people"? We're not dealing with anything but the case on the table.'

Klein nodded.

'The People have the right to ask these questions,' she said. 'A dangerous man is hiding behind the Right to Counsel. This is not what the Sixth Amendment was created for.'

Judge Martin turned to Nathan Quinn. 'Nathan—'

It was his turn to speak. He looked from one to the other.

'No one in this room wants the man who committed the murders more than I do, I assure you. The arrest warrant is based purely on circumstantial evidence and that the eyewitness, in the middle of the night, across a dark street, saw a truck "similar" to my client's. He couldn't put my client at the scene or anywhere near it.'

'I signed the warrant myself; I know what it says,' the judge said.

'Let's put the prosecutor's wishful thinking to one side for a moment. Nothing in the case as presented challenges the principle of the privilege: any question asked by Miss Klein is still improper and any disclosure would be a violation of the canons of professional ethics. Before the privileged status of those communications can be lifted, the Prosecutor has to show that they were in aid of an intended or present illegality, and that I, as my client's attorney, was party to that.'

'Come on, Nathan, that's beside the point,' Klein said.

'That is precisely the point.'

'The privilege does not extend to facts which are not part of the communication. You know where Cameron is because your relationship is personal. That is why you exonerated yourself from your duties as executor of Sinclair's will.'

'Is that true?' Judge Martin asked.

'Yes.'

The Honorable Claire Martin sat back in her chair and took her glasses off. Quinn did not like where they were going with it, not one bit. He realized in that second that there was indeed one door slightly ajar, and he hoped to God that Sarah Klein wouldn't see it. He needed to get her away from that angle.

'Sarah, I am both an advocate for my client and an officer of the court, with all the obligations that entails. I couldn't sit here and make an argument for confidentiality if I had any knowledge or evidence that my client committed the murders.'

'I don't believe it. You are giving me Drinker? Good faith, honorable dealing and a minister in the temple of justice?'

'Both of you,' Judge Martin interrupted, 'remember where you are and check your voices.'

'Your Honor, it's amusing Mr. Quinn would mention that he is an officer of the court, when his refusal to disclose is clearly a hindrance to the court's efforts to get his client to come in and be interviewed. That's all we're asking.'

'I'd say this is a mess, Miss Klein,' the judge said and turned to Quinn. 'Are you familiar with Heidebrink vs. Moriwaki?'

'Client's intent?'

'That's right. The crucial point in the attorney–client privilege is the intent of the client when the communication was made.'

Quinn continued: 'If there is a belief by the client that he is seeking professional legal advice and the lawyer is consulted in his legal capacity, then the communication is protected.'

'Miss Klein, the client's intent here is not in doubt. What else do you have?'

Quinn knew her answer before she spoke.

'What about the attorney's intent?' she said. She had seen the door and walked right through it.

'Go on,' the judge said.

'When Mr. Quinn was interviewed by Detectives Brown and Madison, it was put to him that he had given Mr. Cameron the news of the deaths *in person* because he wouldn't want him to learn about them in the news. My point is that Mr. Quinn's intent at the time was not to offer legal advice but to spare a friend the shock of finding out on television. And *that* is not covered by the attorney–client privilege.'

Judge Martin thought about it.

'Did you initiate that communication?' she asked Quinn.

'I believe that to be privileged,' he answered.

There was a long silence in the chambers. Judge Martin looked at the two attorneys on the other side of her desk; she picked up her fountain pen and signed the top sheet of the subpoena.

Chapter 21

'Tomorrow morning. Eleven a.m. God bless the Honorable Claire Martin.' Klein's voice crackled through her cell.

Madison smiled: they could all do with some good news. The OPR detectives had been hard at work all morning. They had gone through everybody and kept Lieutenant Fynn till last. When they were done, they left and the squad room went back to its normal noise level.

The investigation was now in its third day. There had been a lot of curiosity: even detectives who had no good reason to visit had somehow wandered in. Madison was glad they had set up out of everybody's way.

There were crime-scene photos on the wall, next to pictures of the Sinclairs cut from newspaper articles. The victims' photos were in color, with close-ups of entry and exit wounds. The newspapers' were black and white. The Crime Scene Unit had carefully removed the top of the doorframe to analyse it at the lab, Madison had tacked a picture of it still in situ on the board.

Pages of items removed from the crime scene were tacked on top of each other, jostling for space with floor plans of the house and a diagram of which detectives had interviewed which neighbors.

Above her desk, Madison had pinned the birthday party photo she had found at the Sinclairs'. Next to it, she had copied and enlarged Cameron's fingerprint card. A current photograph would have been nice but at least the whorls and the arches, black on white, reassured her it was a real person that they were looking for. Flesh and blood and mortal.

Madison's table was covered with papers. There was a kind of order in the layers: the first was her notes from the library about the Hoh River kidnapping, then the *Nostromo* file and the relevant press clippings; finally, on the top, James and Annie Sinclair's bank records.

'This one.' Madison picked up the sheet from Seattle First Savings & Loans. 'James Sinclair opened this account six months ago. The other one, both he and his wife have signatures. But this one is only in his name.'

She scanned the page; there was not much to read.

'He put $500 in when he opened it. Then, a deposit for $25,000 every month for four months. It goes in one day and out the next. Withdrawn in cash. It's the same amount on the forged check.'

'I guess we found where the money went, if not why,' Brown said.

'He took out the cash. That's $100,000 overall.'

Brown sat back in his chair, took off his glasses and started cleaning them with his white handkerchief.

'How much is Quinn's reward?'

Madison knew he didn't need to ask; he was not a man who forgot details.

'$100,000.'

They had both thought the same thing: in the end, it all evens out.

Quinn's reward was, first and foremost, a pain in the neck. Everybody agreed on that; news of it had been greeted in the squad room by a general groan. No workable information on Cameron was ever going to come out of it, just a whole load of nuts with phone cards and time to spare. It was an attorney's attempt to muddy the waters, no more, no less.

Brown went back to compiling a list of Cameron's known associates. It was a very short list. Cameron did not have associates as such. The list contained all the names that had been mentioned over the years in connection with the cases Cameron had *not* been charged with.

'Harry Cueron,' Brown started.

Madison looked up. 'Little guy. Low-level weapons dealer?'

'Yes.'

'ATF got him last year. He's doing time upstate.'

'Bobby Hooper, drugs and prostitution.'

'Moved to Miami.'

Brown drew a line through the names.

'John Keane,' Madison tried. 'Two times loser; his brother died on the *Nostromo*.'

'Killed in jail three months ago.'

'Eddy Cheung. Mid-level docks and distribution.'

'Maybe but not likely. Eddy keeps his head down.'

A small silence.

'This is not going to work,' Brown said.

The squad PA knocked and came in. 'This came in from Records and ID; it's the hard copy.'

She handed Brown an envelope, made a point of ignoring the photographs on the walls and left.

A computer program was developed in the 1980s to aid the search for children who had been missing for a long time: starting from the most recent photograph, the software could project what that child might look like in five, ten, twenty years.

Brown took out a six by four color picture.

'There he is,' he said and passed it to Madison.

Records had done some nice work: they had taken the mugshot of a teenager and turned it into a man. Even if something had been lost in translation Madison felt a cold shiver, not of fear but of recognition. There he was.

'We should ask Quinn if it's a good likeness.'

'That's probably privileged,' Brown replied.

Lieutenant Fynn put his head in the door. 'The chief is calling me every fifteen minutes. Where are we at?'

'I was on the phone with Gertz,' Brown said. 'Patrol is going to get the picture, as well as State, County, Port Authority and Airport Police. I'm going to make sure all the little runways who charter to the islands have them too. The photo and the details will be passed on to VICAP and the FBI. The truck we're not going to get – he's probably already ditched it in the woods. And tomorrow morning, which is not coming one minute too soon, Klein has Quinn in front of a judge.'

'We should sell tickets,' Fynn said and then paused for a moment. 'Cameron has been out there doing his thing for years: now I want him *visible*. I want his picture on the news. I want his face on the front page. They want him, let them have him. He shouldn't be able to buy a pack of smokes without being spotted by twenty-five people.'

A beat of silence as Fynn looked from one to the other.

'I don't know,' Madison said. 'The public should be aware, sure, and they are. But this is a woods and mountains state and the citizens have the right to bear arms. You just know some bright spark is going to start something ugly in the 7-Eleven.'

Fynn turned to Brown.

'Let's hold it back,' Brown said. 'Until we know what Quinn is going to give us.'

'It's another twenty-four hours he can move around as he pleases.'

'Not exactly. Every law enforcement agency in the state is looking for him. He won't be able to rent a car or buy a ticket anywhere. All he can do is stay put.'

'After Quinn, he's on the lunchtime news.' Fynn took a bite from an apple. 'Any luck with our regulars?'

'No.' Brown shook his head. 'Every snitch in Seattle has gone out of town for the holidays.'

'Wish I could do the same,' Fynn said, and left.

'We're working on the assumption he's still in Seattle,' Madison said. 'He could have left after seeing Quinn on Monday.'

'Maybe, but I don't think so.'

'I don't either. Be nice to know how he took the news, though.'

'I know a place on Alki Beach.' Brown got up and shrugged on his jacket. 'Let's go get some lunch.'

When you hit a wall, give it a couple of kicks, just to see if anything shakes loose. Madison was a great believer in that truth.

Alki Beach. The Rock was built on a pier out of wood and glass; it hovered above the water as if trying to get away from the beach. The long windows shimmered in the December gray and caught the clouds in the sky and every flicker of light they let through.

Madison stepped out of the car, glad for the salt in the air and how it felt in her lungs. The ferry to Bremerton had just gone past; seagulls followed in its wake, a thin white line in the still waters, and at the end of it, across Elliott Bay, the skyline of downtown Seattle.

Madison didn't know whether John Cameron ever visited the restaurant, but in any kitchen at any time two things will be happening: cooking and yakking. Who did what to whom and what they said when. If Cameron had been by, there had to be talk. And maybe someone might have noticed what car he was driving. Madison hoped that the people here would feel some kind of loyalty toward James Sinclair and his family. She hoped they would remember his children.

The manager came over and took them to his office. Jacques Silano, French-Canadian, mid-thirties, five foot nine, stocky with dark Mediterranean looks. He spoke with a slight accent and was dressed immaculately in a pinstripe suit and burgundy tie. The office, small and cramped with files, invoices and three different calendars on the walls – deliveries, staff holidays and block bookings – was just as neat and scrupulously tidy. They sat down.

'What can I do for you?' he asked them.

Madison had the feeling they wouldn't get much small talk out of him. None of the 'I still can't believe it' and 'It's so awful' they'd had from other acquaintances. Jacques Silano was all business.

So was Brown. 'John Cameron is one of the owners of the The Rock. We'd like to know about any dealings you might have had with him since you've worked here. Starting from when you last saw him.'

It took them only two minutes of back and forth to get him there.

'The last Friday of the month,' he said. 'Quinn, Sinclair and Cameron. They come late, after the kitchen has closed. There's a private room at the back. The kitchen and the floor staff would have left by then.' Silano smiled briefly. 'Poker night.'

'Go on,' Brown said.

'They've been playing since before I came here. I was invited to join them maybe three years ago. We'd start late and play till dawn. Then I'd go home, but often they'd stay on and have breakfast.'

'And Cameron would be there?'

Silano nodded.

'Every time?'

He nodded again.

'What can you tell us about John Cameron?'

'I don't know,' he said. 'The first time I met him, I'd had the job for one week. He had dinner here with Sinclair and Quinn. We were introduced; I didn't know *who* he was. Months later I heard two of the chefs talking about him. Just gossip of things he was supposed to have done. I told them I didn't want to hear that kind of talk in the kitchen and the head chef backed me up. Donny's been here longer than me. Donny O'Keefe. Quinn and Sinclair come every couple of weeks for lunch or dinner, but Cameron always comes late in the evening. After a couple of years or so, they asked me to join the card game. Donny was already in it. It was a private thing and I was glad to be asked.'

'Was it a good game?' Brown asked him.

'Oh yeah.'

'What do you talk about?'

'Nothing. Everything. Nothing personal.'

'And Cameron?'

'Same as everyone else.'

'How much money are we talking about here?'

Silano smiled. 'If I had a really good night I might win three hundred bucks; I might lose the same if I had a bad one. Nobody ever got rich or poor here.'

'Was Sinclair into it? Do you know if he gambled anywhere else?'

'Gambling? He never even bluffed.'

'When was the last game?' Madison asked him.

'The last Friday in November.'

By then Sinclair had been scamming Cameron for months, she thought.

'Was anything different?'

'No.'

'What time did the game start that night?'

Madison felt reasonably confident that a guy with that kind of order in his work life would have a pretty good memory for detail.

'After midnight, as usual,' he replied.

'Who got here first?'

Silano got his memories together for a second.

'Quinn and Cameron had dinner here. James arrived a little later.'

'What's the routine?'

'The routine is everybody else is gone for the night. We get set up in the private room and we play till sunup. That's all that ever happens.'

'Anybody else joined the game?' Brown asked.

'No.'

'No one dropped in to say "hi", grab a beer, that kind of thing?'

'No. It was always just the five of us.'

'Did you ever argue? Anybody ever cheated?'

'With those guys? You've got to be kidding me.' Silano smiled. 'No. Nobody ever cheated. We teased Sinclair a lot because you could see his hand in his face, like the time he got dealt a full house. You know what are the chances of that?'

'Six hundred and ninety-three to one,' Madison replied without thinking.

'Right. Well, he managed to make maybe ten bucks out of it. That was Sinclair. Quinn and Cameron you just wouldn't know. And Donny? I heard he put one of his kids through college playing poker.'

'Let's go back to Cameron. I would like you to think very carefully about the last game,' Brown said.

'It was a good night.' He closed his eyes. 'Quinn had brought some very expensive cigars for us to try. I won ninety bucks.' He opened his eyes.

'Was there any tension between Sinclair and Cameron? A look? Anything different in the mood.'

'No.'

'What did you all talk about?'

'The usual. All the games kind of blend together, if you know what I mean. There was nothing unusual that night.' Silano sat back in his chair. 'I read the paper this morning and I know what you are asking me, but no, there was nothing weird going on and there has never been any kind of argument. Not ever. Not about anything.'

After they were done, Brown stood up. 'We'd like a complete list of your employees, going back one year, if you have one handy, with addresses and numbers.'

'I have one here,' he said, and produced some typewritten pages from one of the files.

'We're going to ask the staff a few questions now.'

He nodded. There wasn't much else to say.

'Ever noticed what he drives?' Madison asked as she stood up, knowing in her blood what the answer would be.

'A black Ford pick-up,' Silano answered without hesitation.

'Of course,' she said.

Brown put his hand on the door handle. 'Why did you decide to tell us about the game?'

'One night, months ago, we were in the kitchen getting the food together and, behind me, I hear a crash like something's fallen and Donny starts swearing. I turned around. There was blood every-where. One of the kitchen knives had slipped, I don't know how, and Cameron's hand is pumping blood all over the floor. Sinclair and Quinn come in and start getting towels to wrap around it. Cameron just looks at it; he even opens his hand to see. Everyone else is trying to help out, slipping on the wet floor. He didn't want stitches, he wrapped it tight and let it be.' Silano paused. 'With all the shouting and the yelling, Cameron, he never made a sound.'

Silano shook his head. 'I don't know,' he said finally.

*

They found Donny O'Keefe having a cigarette on the deck. The kitchen's back door opened on a small platform with stairs to the beach. He leaned on the wooden railings with his back to them. There was a stiff breeze coming in from the sea and the sky was already darkening. O'Keefe was wearing only chef's whites: if he was cold, he didn't show it.

'Mr. O'Keefe,' Brown said.

He turned around. A wiry man in his late forties, his hair gone white and cut short. No taller than five foot six but with enough going on in his eyes that no one had ever picked on him.

After introductions were made, he regarded Brown and Madison for a moment. His sleeves were rolled up and they saw the old prison tattoo on his right forearm: an eagle surrounded by barbed wire. He looked down at it.

'Upstate, twenty-three years ago. I kept it to remind myself I was once young, cute and as dumb as dirt.'

He took one last puff and killed the butt against a small ashtray he balanced on the railing.

'How can I help you?'

'You know why we're here?' Brown said.

'I heard the news this morning. I figured sooner or later you'd come by.'

'How long have you worked at The Rock?'

'Three years sous-chef. Seven years head chef.'

'That's a lot of poker nights.'

O'Keefe smiled.

'A lot of chat over the table.'

'Yes.'

'You don't sit across the table from a man for ten years without knowing a little about him,' Brown said as he put his hands on the railings and looked out at the beach. A couple was walking a small dog.

'Sometimes you do. Sometimes the more you see someone, the less you know them.'

'What the paper wrote, you don't think he did it?' Madison said.

'No, I don't.'

'You don't think he could do it.'

'I don't think he *would* do it.'

O'Keefe stuck his hands in the pockets of his apron.

'You asked me about him and I'm telling you. Do you think we all gathered around, over chips and beer, and asked him how he did the guys on the boat?'

'We think he killed a man and his family,' Madison said, her voice soft against the noises from the kitchen, metal on metal. 'A man who had been in your life for a very long time. You might know things that will help us find his killer.'

'You think I wouldn't want to find the piece of shit who did this?'

'Talk to us.'

'You don't understand. Cameron turns up for the game once a month: *that* is all we know about him. What he does in between? Nobody asks. Where he lives? Nobody asks.'

He took a pack of Marlboros out of his chest pocket, shook one out – no takers. He lit it and drew on it deeply.

'In there, I have a chowder that would make a grown man cry. Anything beyond that, I just don't know.'

Brown took out one of Cameron's photos from Records and showed it to him.

'Does he look anything like this?'

'Sure,' he said, which sounded more like 'Not really'.

Brown pointed at the kitchen. 'We're going to ask around, in case anyone remembers anything worth the trip here.'

'Be my guest. Would you guys like a bite to eat?' O'Keefe crossed his arms and leaned back, squinting slightly.

'Maybe some other time,' Madison replied. 'By the way, twenty-three years ago, what did you do time for?'

'I thought you'd never ask.' He pulled on the cigarette until the end glowed bright. 'Grand theft auto. The car belonged to a cop. They found me in three hours.'

He seemed to find it amusing, as if it had happened to someone else.

'Smart move,' Madison said.

'Dumb as dirt,' O'Keefe replied.

They left him out there.

Five men – three Hispanic, two Caucasian – also in chef's whites worked in a long, narrow, spotless kitchen. They stood at their stations, chopping, slicing, cleaning and getting ready for the evening rush and the Christmas bookings. Brown and Madison walked in and the chat stopped dead.

Everybody knew who they were and what they wanted. It took Brown and Madison 45 minutes to interview them one by one. The waiters and busboys had already gone home at the end of their shift.

When they came out, cars were driving past with their headlights on. It wouldn't be long before dark. Brown ticked the names off the list Silano had given them. Madison just wanted to get moving and call the precinct: patrol officers had been checking with car rental places in case Cameron had ditched the pick-up and stopped by his nearest Hertz.

What she would have done, she thought, was have a clean car ready. One with local plates, paid in cash and unconnected to her. And she would have done that *days* before the murders.

There were also the security cameras at the airport: someone ought to go down to Sea-Tac with the photo from Records and check at least the first twenty-four hours after the crime. A slim chance, assuming he had not altered his looks too much. Madison used the standard black police notepad with the rubber band around it. She took it out of her jacket's inside pocket, leant against the roof of their car and wrote two words: *Poker night*. She closed her eyes and for a moment she was sitting high, looking at her father's hand over his shoulder. She could have learnt a lot about Cameron if she had watched him play even once.

Brown was a few steps behind her, already on the phone. It was the middle of the afternoon, Madison was hungry and that chowder had looked pretty damn good.

'That was Kelly,' Brown said, after he snapped his phone shut. 'He's at a crime scene up on Genesee Hill. He said we should go over.'

'What's he got?'

'White male, knife wound to the neck.'

Madison nodded. Kelly was far from being one of her favorite people and she knew from experience that he would be even less adorable if he was the primary on a case.

'You play poker?' Brown asked her out of the blue.

'I used to know people who did.'

Brown drummed his fingers on the roof of the car. 'Right,' he said. 'We could go via Husky's.'

Husky Deli. Now, that was a happy thought.

The press was already there. They had followed the scent and stood in groups, cameras poised, ready and waiting.

'They always know,' Brown muttered under his breath.

Three blue-and-whites blocked the entrance to the drive. Camera flashes started as they approached, Brown showed his badge and they were waved through.

The house was large, built on the most expensive part of Genesee Hill. The front lawn had been fenced and Madison spotted a small security camera mounted by the top of the gate. The Crime Scene Unit van was parked next to an ambulance by the main door.

Chris Kelly came out just as Brown and Madison stepped out of their car.

'Just in time,' he said. 'I wanted you to see him before he's moved.'

Kelly's partner, a skinny malcontent called Tony Rosario, was just back from sick leave. He nodded hello and went to his car. Of course, Madison thought, it was perfectly possible that Rosario was really the nicest guy: you spend 12 hours a day with Kelly, it's got to do something to you.

Kelly walked them through to the living room. Forensics people were already deep into the scene. It was a modern house, the inside matching the outside in a vague attempt of style through minimalism that Madison deeply disliked. The living room was furnished in black and white. A massive black suede sofa and a knee-high glass table dominated the space; the rest was sharp edges and hardwood floors.

Madison registered the blood on the walls as a disturbance in the patterns even before she realized what she was looking at. She saw it and knew it and felt the adrenaline spike kick in. Her eyes followed the red spray as it rose and fell, a fine mist covered the white cushions. No one could lose that much blood and live.

The man was slumped with his back against the back of the sofa; you wouldn't have seen him unless you'd gone around it. You wouldn't have seen him from the door unless you had noticed the blood.

Madison couldn't tell what color his shirt had been – maybe pale blue, maybe white. Blood had drenched it and his denim trousers. It had pooled in the creases of his clothes and around him on the wooden floor. His hands were lying at his sides, already bagged up, slick with red.

He had been a big man: around six foot six and wide to match, his hair dirty blond with a receding hairline he had tried to hide.

He looked fit and, if there had been a struggle, he would have been a dangerous opponent. But he lay there now, with a deep gash under his throat that ran almost from ear to ear and his mouth open as if in surprise.

'The girlfriend found him; the paramedics had to sedate her,' Kelly said. 'The main door has four locks, what with my man here being so keen on security and all. When the girlfriend opened the door with her keys, all four locks were in place. The windows haven't been touched and the backdoor has another three locks to get through before you can come in. All were in place. No signs of forced entry anywhere. And here's the kicker: in the main bedroom there's a safe you can actually take a walk in. Wide open. And enough white in it to build a snowman.'

'A dealer,' Brown said.

'Erroll Sanders.'

The name rang a distant bell with Madison.

Brown sat on his heels and peered into the wound.

'Mr. Sanders. Long time no see.'

'You know him?' Madison asked.

'He's been as quiet as a mouse for a few years.' Brown straightened up. 'Roughly since one of his boys bobbed up in Lake Washington minus eyes and hands.'

'Cameron's work?'

'In all probability.'

There were French doors on one side; the other three walls had been painted in dazzling white. Madison looked around: aside from the dark spots of blood in rising arches, there seemed to be no immediate evidence of struggle. There were a couple of vases on a mantelpiece near the door and lamps on two smaller tables by the sides of the sofa. Nothing had been disturbed.

'He got him from the front,' Kelly said, looking down at the body.

'Yes.' Brown examined blood spatter on the right-hand side wall. He pointed. 'This here came from the knife as it moved away, after the cut.'

His finger traced a fine straight line of droplets, their tail indicating the direction they had come from. His arm moving slowly, as he worked out where the killer had stood.

The wound was very deep and, given Erroll Sanders's height, it was unlikely that his killer could get him in a lock from behind and cut his throat in that manner.

Madison sat on her heels: the wound was deeper on the right side and slightly slanted up toward the left. He had been fast and incredibly strong; one quick slash and Sanders would have had only seconds before he lost consciousness from blood loss.

'He cut him right to left,' Brown said. 'He's right-handed.'

'CSU has been dusting for prints for hours.' Kelly seemed strangely pleased with himself. 'They've found diddly. He had a piece in an ankle holster, for all the good it did him, and a .45 on his nightstand – looks like he had just taken that off. It's still there untouched. There is about $5,000 cash next to the white. This wasn't about drugs, this wasn't about money. I think we have a *Nostromo*-type situation here.'

'We don't know that for sure,' Brown said. 'How about the security camera outside?'

'I've checked: the tape is missing. There's a couple of glasses in the kitchen sink, washed up. This doesn't mean that Sanders had a drink with our man, but if he did, the killer cleaned up after himself.'

The glass table would have been a perfect surface to retain prints and that's where they could have put their drinks.

'Nothing there,' Kelly said. It had already been dusted and found spotless.

The violence had started and ended with Erroll Sanders. Nothing else in his life had interested his killer aside from the taking of it in one quick, devastating blow.

'What about time of death?' Madison asked.

'Probably between four and six this morning.'

It was one of the pleasant quirks of their relationship. If Madison asked Kelly a question, he usually gave his answer to Brown. For a second there Madison wondered if it was worth her time and effort to have a word with him in private one of these days and put him straight. *Not now*, she thought. *Not here.*

'Can we take him?' A paramedic had been standing behind them.

'Go ahead,' Kelly said and Erroll Sanders was carefully lifted off the ground, zipped up into a body bag and carried away.

For a few moments the only sound was the Crime Scene Unit officers collecting and preserving.

'We don't know if he found the intruder already in the house when he got back. Whether the man followed him in. We don't know why and we barely know when,' Brown said.

'What do you mean?'

It was suddenly clear to Madison that Kelly would be pretty pleased if Cameron turned out to be the doer.

'I'd love to know how he got in,' Kelly said.

'You might want to make sure they dust the victim's car for prints. Maybe it was a Trojan horse. Mind if we have a look around?'

Kelly thought about it for a second, not a Homer reader but definitely familiar with the idea.

'Go right ahead,' he said and went to find Rosario.

Brown glanced at Madison, who was trying to work out the sequence of events by the blood-spatter patterns on the walls. Ultimately, the way she dealt with people like Kelly would be as important in being a cop as her gifts as an investigator. It was something she would have to find out by herself. That day Kelly would wish he hadn't gotten out of bed.

'We have little but we do have something,' Madison said. 'We have Sanders and we have the bodies on the *Nostromo*. I want to check the post-mortem reports and the description of the wounds.'

'Kelly's the primary.'

'I know. But Cameron has been lying low for years and now, within four days, we have five murders.'

'And you're looking for a connection?'

'Aren't we?'

Brown rubbed his eyes with the heel of his hand. 'All five men on the *Nostromo* had their throats cut by a right-handed man. Three from behind, cut left to right. Two from the front, right to left. Judging from Sanders's height and the high angle of incision of his wound, that puts his killer at about five eleven. The blade on the *Nostromo* was a non-serrated razor type, sharp enough to cut your breath in two. Same as what did this.' He pointed at the dark spots on the walls.

'The knife is a close-up weapon,' Madison interjected. 'And it's dangerous because you have to get that much closer. Kelly was right: someone was so ticked off with Sanders, he didn't care. He was so angry, he had to get him up close and personal.'

Madison was struck by it.

'With all the blood on Sanders and around, the killer would have been covered in it when he got out.'

Brown nodded. 'I'm sure Kelly has got them checking the garbage in the street.'

'No, he's too smart for that.' Madison started looking on the floor by the sofa, close to where the body had been found.

'He knew that once Sanders was hit he would be going down,' she continued. 'The danger for the killer is over. He can just relax and enjoy the show.'

She found what she was looking for.

'Look.'

On the hardwood floor, three feet from where Sanders had fallen, there was a slightly curved line of blood drops. The drops were large and round and had fallen perpendicularly to the ground. They didn't come from the spray that had hit the wall.

'He wore a long coat. A rain slicker. The blood hit it and slid to the ground. Once Sanders is dead, he takes the coat off – and whatever he had put over his shoes – and that's all. Stuffs it in a bag and goes home. Clean.'

'What about the bag?'

'A thin rain slicker burns easily; you don't want to leave that kind of thing around.'

'A rain slicker.'

'One of those clear plastic ones.'

'Exactly.'

'Neat.'

'I'd say.'

They walked through the hallway and the kitchen and the pool room and the bedroom with the vast open safe – the drugs and the gun gone by now – just to get a sense of the victim and possibly a reason for his death.

The house told them nothing except that Erroll Sanders had lived with poor taste and little judgment, and one early December morning either one or the other had caught up with him.

Back at the precinct, the *Nostromo* file, thick as it was, offered little help. It confirmed all the details Brown had remembered earlier, and nothing more.

Erroll Sanders's employee, the late Joe Navasky, had been in Lake Washington for days before they found him. By then it was difficult to judge whether the near-decapitation and the mutilation of his eyes and hands had been post-mortem or not.

Madison liked consistency: the *Nostromo*, Navasky, Sanders. She could see the similarities there: the manner of death and the obliteration of trace evidence and prints. She went back to her own notes on the Blueridge murders.

The weapon of choice, the mode of death, the use of chloroform on the blindfold, the involvement of the wife and children and even the evidence recovered on the scene: nothing matched.

She thought of the boy's room in Cameron's house and the baseball bat in the closet. The lab had told her that the blood and bone splinter were at least 15 years old.

Brown had hardly said a word to her since they had got back from the Sanders crime scene. Madison had learnt to negotiate her course around his silences but this time Brown had been reading the same page for half an hour. Assistant County Prosecutor Sarah Klein arrived to prepare for Quinn's hearing and the moment passed.

Just as Klein left, Kelly put his head in the door.

'Sanders's car was spotless, almost. They found the partial of a thumb on the axle.' Kelly twinkled. 'He half wiped it off but there's nearly enough points of similarity to stand up in court. What time is the hearing tomorrow?'

It was good. Good that Cameron was still in town and had gotten a little sloppy. Good that there was a lead in the Sanders case. Good and bad for Madison, who sat reading the Hoh River clippings for an hour until Brown stood up and put his jacket on.

'Go home,' he said. 'We're done with the day.'

'Quinn's younger brother,' Madison said. 'Why did they take the body if he was dead?'

'At the time it was impossible to prosecute a case without a body. The other two boys were blindfolded all the time, couldn't testify to anything.'

After Brown left, Madison looked for things to do and interviews to read but her concentration was off. She wasn't quite ready to go home yet and wandered into the main squad room. The usual comings and goings and the usual smells of take-out.

Someone had left a copy of the *Seattle Times* on a table. Madison picked it up and turned to the second page to avoid reading about the case. A few lines near the bottom caught her eye: the photographer she had ejected from the Blueridge crime scene had been attacked and left unconscious in an alley. In his statement Andrew Riley had said that somehow the police might be behind it – that some officer, meaning herself, might have it in for him after what had happened at the Sinclairs'.

Madison blinked. She had completely forgotten about him. It took her two phone calls to find the detective who had the case.

'He's a weedy little shit but he was knocked around some,' Detective Nolan said. 'Now he's locked up in his apartment like someone's out to get him. Actually he mentioned you.'

'I'm sure he did.'

'We're not taking that seriously. Still, he must have pissed off somebody somewhere.'

'It was not a robbery?'

'No, nothing was taken. He thinks he was attacked because he came to the house. He was in Jordan's, off Elliott Avenue, got a call at the bar, no one on the line. Minutes later, he comes out and someone punches him. Badly enough that he passes out. And the guy destroys his camera too. There was hardly anything left on the strap to tell you it *was* a camera.'

Madison drove home with her windows rolled down. Riley had slammed into a wall of bad luck but nothing seemed to connect him to the Sinclairs except for his presence on the crime scene.

Two things: one, the phone call had been made to identify him in the bar. Which meant the attacker had been standing right there to see him get the call. Two, the attacker had looked for his camera and destroyed it. In fact, he had made a point of destroying it.

He had sought out Riley in a crowded bar and, without explanation, without any threats or warnings, he had attacked him and smashed his precious camera out of existence.

Whichever way you slice it, someone had taken offense at Riley's line of work. So had Madison, for sure, and she knew for a fact that if it had been her own loved ones Riley had tried to photograph, her reaction might not have been as contained.

The Sinclairs' next of kin was Nathan Quinn and Madison couldn't see him waiting in the dark for Riley – it wasn't his style. Quinn would never lay a finger on him, they might never even meet, and yet things would happen and Riley would never sell another picture in his life. Quinn would make sure Riley knew why. How far she herself might have gone was something Madison did not dwell on.

The Sinclair house was a dark shape beyond the trees. Madison drove past slowly, catching a glimpse of the patrol car parked out front. In a flash she remembered that she had not returned the keys to the tree trunk. They were still in the inside pocket of her blazer. Madison braked gently. She was about to put it into reverse, her hand already on the clutch.

Not yet.

She slipped the car into first and drove on.

Twenty-four hours earlier, Erroll Sanders drove back to his house. Maybe Cameron was in the car with him, maybe not. Whatever. At that point Sanders had perhaps half an hour to live.

Madison drove past her own driveway and toward Rachel's house. She hadn't done that in a long time, not since the months after her grandfather's death. She pulled up before the turn.

The only light was above the front door; a wreath was pinned to the knocker. Two cars were parked on the side and the curtains were drawn. Madison turned off her engine. It did not worry her that sometimes, after a day of blood and random evil, she would come here and sit in her silent car for a few moments. She could feel Rachel's life inside the house, Rachel's family inhabiting a world that overlapped with her own only in part; theirs was safe and loving and as distant as it could be from the horrors she knew. It was a comfort beyond description.

After a couple of minutes, she left and found her way home.

Nathan Quinn locked the glass door behind him as the office alarm beeped softly. He said goodnight to one of the cleaners who was pushing his cart along the ninth-floor landing and called the elevator. In his right hand he carried his briefcase, in his left a small stack of correspondence he had not yet had a chance to look at. He pressed the button for the underground car park and flipped through the envelopes.

It was the fourth from the top and Nathan Quinn recognized the heavy cream paper before his mind could tell him what it was. He tore it open and took out a card that matched it. On it, five numbers were printed in black ink:

82885

The elevator's doors opened. Quinn looked up as if a voice had spoken.

He got back to the ninth floor, punched in the code for the alarm and went straight for his office without turning any of the lights on. He flicked the switch for his desk lamp and pulled open a drawer in the filing cabinet behind him. It was the first one in the file; he had placed it there himself on Monday. The same paper, the same card, only the message was different. He put the two cards next to each other on his desk.

There was no doubt in Quinn's mind that the same hand that had written the words had taken the lives of James and his family.

He picked up the receiver, punched in a telephone number and replaced it on its cradle. After maybe thirty seconds his cellphone rang and he picked it up.

'Jack,' he said.

Chapter 22

Harry Salinger sits at the workbench in the basement of his house. He looks at a shard of glass through his jeweler's lens, he holds it delicately between his right thumb and forefinger and turns it around until he is pleased with what he sees.

In a corner the fruit of his hard work has taken shape: the base was easy to fix, considering he had to keep it light and portable, but he knows it will be the metal bars that will make or break his masterpiece. He stands up and slips on his welding goggles.

Lynne Salinger was 39 years old when she found out she was expecting a child. She cried for hours: the precarious routine of her life was about to be shattered and within her rigid Catholic background an abortion was out of the question.

Her husband, Richard Salinger, 41, a uniformed officer with the Seattle Police Department, bought a few rounds of drinks in the bar and at the end of the evening was driven home by his partner.

It was widely known within his precinct that his temperament had cost Richard Salinger a promotion many times over. Privately, he was a bully who had never hit his wife because he did not need to: he did his physical work out on the street and kept his darkest moods for the home.

Lynne Salinger gave birth to twin boys, Michael and Harry, and immediately sank into three years of undiagnosed postnatal depression; the week after their third birthday she took her life with an overdose of sleeping pills and died as she had lived, with very little fuss.

Her passing became an adverse reaction to prescribed medication and if anyone at the station wanted to check her death certificate, Richard Salinger would just have to put them straight. It was something Richard did a lot, putting people straight – it was the job and his life and his particular place in the order of things.

Ten years later. Michael and Harry Salinger are riding their bicycles at full speed on the curb, flying toward their house in time for their afternoon curfew. They are tall for their age and blond, their eyes almost colorless. They take after their mother, whom they don't remember at all: soon they will be taller than Richard Salinger, not that it will do them any good anyway.

They hear it as they are locking the gate behind them: the telephone ringing in the kitchen.

It is an acknowledged fact between them that Michael runs faster.

'Go!' Harry yells.

Michael throws the bike on the ground and legs it to the back door. He grabs the key from the pocket of his jeans, shoves it in the lock and turns it. He pushes into the kitchen and gets to the phone in one stride. His hand is slick as he picks up the receiver.

'Hello,' he gasps. 'It's Michael. Okay. Yes, sir. Here he is.'

Harry takes the phone from his brother.

'Hello, sir. Yes. Okay. We will.'

He puts the receiver down and for a moment they stand in the dark room. Then Michael opens the fridge door and starts to make them both peanut butter and jelly sandwiches.

*

Richard Salinger kept his promise to himself: he brought up the boys alone, in the same house they were born in. A local woman in her fifties, Etta Greene, looked after them and did a little housework while he was out; the rest of the time it was just the Salinger men, as he used to call them.

He knew the boys were afraid of him and enjoyed telling them what he had done at work, especially if any violence had come to pass.

One afternoon when the boys were five, during their playtime, Etta Greene asked Harry to name a color with the letter 'b'. Without hesitation Harry said, 'Red.' Etta looked a little disappointed and Harry didn't understand why.

As far back as he could remember, the letter 'b' had always been red – it felt red and it brought a sense of red to any word it was a part of. Even though they sometimes disagreed on what color went with which letter, Michael knew exactly what he meant. It was their mother's gift, undiagnosed and unacknowledged.

She had considered it a kind of madness, but Lynne Salinger was neither crazy nor cursed and the only issue with synesthesia is that it is statistically rare and deeply misunderstood. It frightened her that most sounds carried a sense of color, vibrant and beyond her control. She did not cherish nor begin to understand the experience: she endured it and every day tried to suppress it. Then she would think of her husband, and his name would come to her unbidden, in shades of charcoal and red.

Etta Greene assumed that Harry was confused and left it at that.

By the time the boys started school, they knew enough of the world never to mention the hidden colors, not to anyone, especially their father.

When Richard Salinger was shot in the line of duty by an armed robber he took a bullet in the right knee. Once he left the hospital he had a limp and a disability pension, both guaranteed as long as he lived.

The stream of visitors and well-wishers who had come by in the early days of his injury became a dribble and then stopped altogether. Six months later, they were completely alone.

One morning, while the boys were at school, Richard Salinger went through their room and found a soiled sheet in a bundle in a corner. When they came back, he was waiting for them in the sitting room. He was stone-cold sober and his face was set hard.

'I'm going to ask you one question,' he said. 'Be straight with me and it ends there. Lie to me, and I'll know it.'

From a plastic bag he pulled out the bundled sheet. Harry's insides filled with icy water.

'Who did this?'

Salinger knew and didn't need to ask. He could have washed the sheet and let it go but he was not that kind of man. He waited. Michael stepped forward. Harry's eyes grew wide.

'I did, sir,' Michael said. 'I'm sorry.'

Richard Salinger's eyes did not move from Harry's face. 'What have you got to say, boy?'

At ten years of age, Harry knew exactly who he was: a skinny runt with neither guts nor smarts. He knew that because he had been told enough times. Still, he'd rather get a hiding than let his brother take the rap.

'I did it,' he stammered.

'I know,' Richard Salinger said as he stood up. 'This is how it's going to work from now on: when one of you fucks up, the other will be punished. Michael, you're up.'

Harry Salinger, 37, crouches in his basement. Sparks from the torch flare across the goggles. It's not his best work but he can see the beauty of the idea beyond the faults of his own workmanship, and it pleases him. Salinger peels off his gloves and throws them on the workbench. Time to go.

In the Olympic National Park, a three-hour drive from Seattle, there is a stretch of ground blessed by old-growth trees and ferns, trunks thick with moss and twisting paths that tourists travel days to see and take pictures of with their cellphones.

Harry Salinger does not take pictures and he hardly looks up from the slippery, rocky path. In the depths of winter there are no visitors and in the gloom of the early evening he takes in every detail of the trail. It is in all likelihood the last time he will have the opportunity to do this.

He bends to check that the laces are properly tied on his walking boots and waits, making sure the last little bit of daylight is extinguished, and then off. He runs, trusting his memory of the trail, weaving through the trees because a straight run would get him killed very quickly; his boots cut and rustle through the green, not too fast and not too slow.

In his mind the earth rises to meet his feet and steady his purpose – the forest is on his side. It is the thirty-eighth time he runs the trail, the twenty-first in darkness.

Chapter 23

6.30 a.m. The offices of Quinn Locke were still deserted. Nathan Quinn closed the door behind him. From a filing cabinet he pulled out a clear plastic envelope and passed it to Tod Hollis. The envelope contained the anonymous notes.

Hollis wore a heavy coat with a black roll-neck underneath. He took the envelope and looked at it for a few seconds.

'Coffee?' Quinn asked.

'Thanks.'

Quinn left him in his office and went to the kitchen. From a box he took out a paper filter, shook some fresh coffee into it and turned on the machine.

He knew Hollis would tell him to go to the police with the notes, that they'd have the resources to examine them quickly for prints and run a check on the paper. He would recommend they call the detective in charge and give them to him specifically. It made perfect sense, of course. Except Quinn was not ready to do that yet, not until he knew what the writer wanted.

Hollis would not be happy about it but there was little he could do to change his mind: it all came down to a choice Quinn had made years before, for a time he had hoped would never come. Instead, Judge Martin would be waiting for him in a few hours and everything else was nonsense. The coffee started to drip through.

Quinn's reward had brought in excess of one hundred calls in 24 hours. All the calls had been screened and logged and none had had anything to add to the investigation.

Madison flipped through the typed sheets while Brown was on the phone: a SWAT team was on standby to back them up if they got an address, telephone records could be accessed in minutes and Crime Scene Unit officers had been warned of a possible quick-response situation. Depending on the outcome of the hearing, there might or might not be a press conference where the picture of John Cameron would be made public. The one thing Tully did not have.

'We never did understand why he retied the knot,' she said.

Brown looked up.

'The ligature,' she continued. 'Cameron replaced the ligature around James Sinclair's wrists. We found the hairs but we still don't know why he did it.'

'Do we need to know?'

Do we need to know?

'Quinn is going to blow a hole right through anything we are unsure of,' she said.

Brown stood up, closed the door between them and the squad room and sat back down.

'OK, what do you need to know?' he said.

'What do you mean?'

'Just that. We have four bodies, a motive, a suspect. We have physical evidence. What else do *you* need to know?'

'Everything,' she replied without hesitation. 'If something happened I want to know why. If it didn't, why didn't it?'

'Cameron does exactly what he needs to do. No more, no less.

The murder of Erroll Sanders fits that principle. The murders of the Sinclairs do not.'

'Sometimes people break their own patterns – it depends on circumstance. With James Sinclair, the punishment was Cameron's priority. It is possible that killing him was entirely secondary, and knowing that his family was being slaughtered was more important than Sinclair's own death.'

'Tell me this: why does it matter to you so much to know why the ligature was tied twice? You have seen Cameron's house, you remember his bedroom. Forget about the case in court and tell me why we should ask the question.'

'You know why.'

'You tell me.'

'It's about behavior. The ligature is one tiny part of it. Like the print on the glass.'

'What about the print?'

'When we got the call that Payne had matched the print to Cameron's, you looked like that was bad news. I asked you why and you said—'

'I was surprised.'

'You were disappointed.'

'Maybe you are worrying too much about the small stuff.'

Madison leant forward.

'The glass the print was recovered on was by the sink in the kitchen. I saw it before the CSU officer collected it: it was standing right next to a can of Coke.'

'Okay.'

'They did not recover any prints from the can. Why is that? Cameron, wearing gloves, pours himself a drink. Then he takes off the gloves, picks up the glass and drinks from it. It's sloppy, and he is anything but. There is no small stuff here.'

They regarded each other for a moment. It was the first time she had even half raised her voice with him and God knows why that had happened.

'Why did you join Homicide?' he said.

'Excuse me?'

'It's not for the money and I'm pretty certain it's not for the glory.'

'Why are you asking me now and not five weeks ago?'

'If I'd asked you then, I wouldn't have had any context in which to put your answer. Now I've seen you work. Why Homicide?'

Madison realized she had been waiting for him to ask her since they had first met. She heard herself say: 'It's the only place I wanted to be.'

He nodded slightly. Someday he might ask her again.

The press surrounded the courthouse on all sides. Brown, Madison, Kelly and Rosario had to push through bodies, microphones and cameras. Flashes went off and nobody missed the significance of the primary detective on the Sanders case being present at a hearing for the Blueridge murders. For the occasion Kelly wore his court suit.

It was going to be Sarah Klein's show. Away from the noise of the crowd outside, the courthouse was quiet and people went about their business, their hearing being only one of dozens.

Tony Rosario was still pale from his recent illness; then again, drained pallor might have been his natural state. It didn't help that he was wearing a suit, shirt and tie combination in shades of gray.

'Do me a favor and don't lean against the wall; I'm afraid I'm gonna lose ya,' Kelly said.

'Gray is my signature color,' Rosario replied.

The lift doors opened and they stepped out. Klein turned to them, her voice low.

'If you want to tell me anything during the hearing, write it on a piece of paper and only if it's absolutely necessary.'

'Can you ask him anything about the Sanders situation?' Kelly felt involved but only marginally. They had Cameron's print on the underside of Sanders's car but it wasn't enough in solid terms even for a search warrant of Cameron's residence. Not that a search had done Brown and Madison much good.

'No, it has nothing to do with this. I have to stick to whatever passed between Quinn and Cameron when they first met to discuss the deaths. Anything after that is privileged. You're a tourist, Detective Kelly – just enjoy the ride.' Klein walked into the courtroom and they followed.

Madison had been in court a number of times, both as a witness and as a spectator. She had seen some juries get it right after the prosecutors did their worst and others get it wrong after they had done their best. She believed in the system because it was what they had and it was meant to change and develop as human beings did, in their wisdom and their flaws. She took a seat in the pew behind the prosecutor's table, Brown sat down next to her, Kelly and Rosario behind them.

Brown took his glasses from their case and put them on. He was glad the hearing was closed to the public. Everybody wanted something out of it and though his expectations might not be the same as everyone else's, he knew he wouldn't be disappointed. The night before he had spent an hour on the phone with Fred Kamen. He looked at Madison and hoped that by the end of this long day he'd be able to tell her about it.

Nathan Quinn took his place at the other table. He was representing himself, as Madison had imagined he would. He was alone, and if anything about the proceedings was troubling him it didn't show.

'Sarah,' he said.

'Nathan.' She nodded back to him.

The rest of them did not exist.

Judge Martin took her place on the bench and Nathan Quinn was sworn in.

'Swift and to the point, Miss Klein,' she said. 'There is no jury to impress and we all know why we're here. Mr. Quinn, you're under oath now and you know what that means.'

Quinn sat in the witness box and Sarah Klein stood by her table.

'Mr. Quinn, would you please take us through the events that occurred last Monday from the moment Detective Sergeant Brown and Detective Madison came to your office and told you about the murder of James Sinclair and his family.'

'Detective Sergeant Brown told me that James Sinclair had been found in his house, with his wife and children. They had been murdered by an intruder. They asked me to identify the bodies, which I did.'

'What was the time frame?'

'By then it was early afternoon.'

'What did you do after that?'

'I called John Cameron.'

Klein looked up from the papers she was holding in her hands. It had taken them all of 45 seconds to get there. Quinn held her eyes.

'For the record, who is John Cameron and what is your relationship to him?'

'He is a friend and a client. I represent him in legal matters and we share a business interest in the company we inherited from our fathers. James Sinclair was part of it too.'

'Why did you call him after you left the office of the Medical Examiner?'

'I was told by a colleague at the firm that reporters were already outside James's house and I did not want him to find out that way. I thought I should tell him in person. I called his beeper number to arrange a place for us to meet and after a few seconds he called me back on my cellphone.'

The typist finished tapping his keyboard and there was a beat of silence. Something was wrong: Klein was getting what she wanted and it shouldn't have been that easy.

'Your Honor,' she started. 'The purpose of this hearing is to make sure that Mr. Cameron – who, for the record, has an outstanding arrest warrant for four counts of murder – does not avail himself of the attorney-client privilege in order to escape capture.'

'We are very clear on that, Counselor,' Judge Martin replied.

'Mr. Quinn, how do you contact John Cameron when you need to?'

'As I said, I call his beeper and he calls me back.'

'That's all?'

'That's all.'

'The People request the number, Your Honor.'

'Are you going to object, Mr. Quinn?' Judge Martin asked him.

'No.'

Quinn gave them the number and the typist took it down. So did the detectives. A beeper: Cameron had probably tossed it in the trash five seconds after Quinn told him about the hearing. *Strike one.* Madison drew a circle around the number and two crossed bones behind it.

'When Mr. Cameron called you back, what did you say to him?'

'I told him it was an emergency and that we needed to meet straightaway—'

'Did you mention the nature of the emergency?'

'I did not.'

'Did he seem surprised?'

'He asked me what it was about and I said I couldn't tell him on the phone.'

'Right, the phone. Where did he call you back from?'

'I don't know.'

'Does he have a cellphone?'

'I don't know.'

'This is an old friend and a business partner and you don't know if he has a cellphone?'

Quinn turned to the judge.

'The question was asked and answered, Your Honor.'

'Move on, Miss Klein,' she said.

'So, you called his beeper and he called you back. How long did it take him to find a telephone?'

'A minute maybe.'

'Was he standing right next to one when you called him?'

'Possibly.'

'Miss Klein.'

The attorney half raised her hand in apology and moved on.

'You told him you couldn't tell him on the phone. How did he react to that?'

'He just asked me where I wanted to meet him.'

'Do you often have this kind of conversation where there are subjects you'd rather not deal with on the phone?'

'No.'

'In all your years as Mr. Cameron's attorney—'

'Yes.'

Klein gave him a look.

'Who was it who brought up the location of your meeting?'

'I did.'

'What did you tell him?'

Quinn told them like they were discussing what they had for breakfast.

'I told him to meet me at my house.'

Strike two.

Klein's only reaction was to lean back slightly against her table. Behind Madison, Kelly exhaled through his nose. Quinn's house was a no-go: nothing to search, no witnesses to the meeting. It was the safest place Cameron could be.

'You didn't go to him.'

'No.'

'Where was Mr. Cameron at the time of your call?'

'I don't know.'

'He did not say?'

'I did not ask.'

Klein turned to Judge Martin. 'I would like Mr. Quinn to be reminded that to lie under oath is considered perjury, Your Honor.'

'You just have, Miss Klein. Do you know something we don't?' Judge Martin asked her.

'No, Judge.'

'Then keep it moving. Mr. Quinn knows exactly what will happen to him if he lies in my courtroom.'

Klein nodded.

'Did you go straight home after the identification?'

'Yes.'

'How long did it take you to get there?'

'About twenty-five minutes.'

'How long after your call did Cameron arrive at your house?'

'About an hour and a half later.'

'Where do you live, Mr. Quinn?'

'Seward Park.'

'So, it is reasonable to assume that wherever Mr. Cameron was at the time you called, he was within an hour and a half of Seward Park.'

'Yes. Then again, maybe he stopped for gas, he might have found traffic – I don't know.'

'Sure, that is reasonable,' she said. 'When he arrived at your house, what happened then?'

'Your Honor,' Quinn turned to the judge, 'we are getting out of the communication initiated by me for personal purpose and into privileged information.'

'We're not quite there yet, Mr. Quinn. You may answer the question.'

'I told him,' he replied to the prosecutor.

'What was his reaction?'

'He was very upset.'

'Was he surprised?'

'Yes.'

'What did he say when you told him?'

'Nothing. There was nothing to say.'

'He said nothing at all?'

'He was in shock, and so was I.'

'Looking back on it, knowing what you know now about the evidence found in the house, was there anything off in his reaction?'

'No.'

'It was completely consistent?'

'Your Honor—' Quinn's eyes stayed on Klein.

'Asked and answered, Miss Klein.'

'Mr. Quinn, when John Cameron arrived at your house did you notice what vehicle he was driving?'

'Your Honor—'

'A car is a car, Mr. Quinn.'

Quinn turned to Brown and Madison.

'He was driving a black Ford Explorer.'

Madison returned his look. They both knew cops would be on it the second they left the courtroom and by now the car would be sitting with the beeper in it in a ditch. However, it would have been bought somewhere, driven around, and someone might have seen it.

'Is that the vehicle he usually drives?'

'I don't notice cars.'

'Really?'

'Yes.'

'I doubt that. I doubt there's anything much you don't notice, Mr. Quinn. Would it surprise you if I told you that DMV has a black Ford pick-up registered to John Cameron?'

'No. He used to drive one a while ago.'

'Do you know what happened to it?'

'No idea.'

'Let's go back to the meeting at your house. What happened after you told him about the deaths?'

'We spoke for a while and then he left.'

'What did you speak about?'

'Your Honor—'

'Sorry, Miss Klein. Out of bounds.'

Klein nodded.

'Would you describe Mr. Cameron's appearance at the time you met?'

'His appearance?'

'Yes. Let's start with his clothes—'

'Miss Klein,' Judge Martin interrupted her. 'Is this relevant?'

'Your Honor, I understand that there are boundaries I am not supposed to cross, but in view of the seriousness of the case and the consequences of Mr. Cameron's ongoing freedom, I am trying to gain as much information as possible within my power. I don't need to remind the court that Mr. Cameron is also being sought in conjunction with the murder of Erroll Sanders—'

'I don't believe there is a warrant out for the Sanders case, so you might as well not go there. I'm giving you a little latitude on the question of appearance.'

'That's all I ask.'

'That's all you have.' The judge motioned with her hand to continue.

'What was he wearing?'

'A black jacket with fleece lining and moleskin trousers, dark green.'

From a file Sarah Klein took out the picture Records had altered.

'This picture was created working from Cameron's arrest sheet. How close is it to his appearance now?'

Quinn looked at it for five seconds. 'It is him and it isn't.'

'Would you say this is a reasonable likeness?'

'Yes, it's reasonable.'

'Excuse me?'

'This is probably the best you can do.'

Klein put it away.

'As far as you know, does John Cameron own a weapon?'

Judge Martin was waiting for him to object.

Nathan Quinn thought about one night when they had been playing poker. He had dropped a chip under the table and as he was retrieving it, he had noticed something around Jack's ankle. It was dark; he didn't see it clearly.

'No, not that I know.'

'Counselor,' Judge Martin turned to Sarah Klein. 'I feel you have exhausted the subject dealt with in the subpoena. Do you have any more questions?'

'Many, Your Honor. Unfortunately, not within these terms. We're done for now.'

'Thank you. Mr. Quinn, you are free to go.'

Just like that, it was over.

Judge Martin left the courtroom and everybody else left after her, until only the attorneys and the detectives were standing around.

'You thought fast last Monday, didn't you, Nathan?' Sarah Klein said. 'You might have been in shock, but you clicked real quick that sooner or later somebody would be asking you questions. You do not go to his safe house, because someone might ask and you might have to answer. You make sure you don't have his phone number, because someone might ask and you might have to answer. You have been so careful all these years and still, here you are. This is not a drunk driving charge; you don't *fix* this.'

Nathan Quinn started to leave. 'You know, everybody in this room would get their fifteen minutes if you collar my client – anybody else just wouldn't do. You're looking in the wrong place and asking the wrong questions. Call me when you get your head out of the evidence bag.'

'Let's get out of here,' Sarah Klein said. 'The next case is due in a minute.'

Madison was disappointed. They had Quinn sworn in and they were coming away with very little to show for it. They would work the car angle, sure, and check into the beeper thing, but those were crumbs. Quinn had been prepared for it the second he had left the morgue; everything he did after that was a moat around his number one client. It took a pretty cold heart to get into that mindset right after he had formally identified the bodies of his friends and their children. That's what he does, Madison told herself, and that's why he's good at it.

They left the courthouse from the back entrance. It was time to get the media into the game and John Cameron's face was about to go platinum.

They drove toward the station house. Brown had alerted Lieutenant Fynn of the outcome of the hearing and he was getting the wheels in motion.

'When Quinn identified the bodies, what was he like?' Madison asked Brown as they dove in and out of the lunchtime traffic.

'He was upset.'

'That's what I would have thought. How could he not be?'

Madison had to ask the question.

'Do you think he lied?'

'Now?'

'Yes.'

'Are you asking me if Quinn just perjured himself?'

'Yes.'

'I don't think so. He gave us everything we wanted, only it turns out it's not what we needed.'

'That's what I'm thinking: he gave us everything because there was nothing there that could really hurt him.'

'Something bothering you?'

'Yes and no. I don't think he lied but, why go through all the trouble of being subpoenaed when he could just tell Klein in Judge Martin's chambers? It's a waste of energy and Quinn is not the type. He was all set with the right answers; he should have just given us the car and the beeper and that would be that.'

'You think he held back?' he asked her.

'No. If he was caught in a straight lie it would be a disaster. Klein asked him what he did after the identification and he said he called Cameron, she asked him why and he said to arrange a meeting and tell him to come to his house . . .'

The first time they had met, Madison had seen Quinn deal with tragedy. He had kept his head and asked the right questions; his emotions had been well in check. They had left him to talk to Annie Sinclair's family in Chicago and to his colleagues and then he had met Brown at the Medical Examiner's office.

Between the time they left him and when he had seen the bodies, something had shifted. Madison remembered he had questioned them about the burglary theory: Quinn had not believed for one second that the murders had not been premeditated. He was familiar with Seattle crime statistics and if she had been in his place, she would have drawn the same conclusions: the Sinclair family had been targeted and executed.

'You want to stop for coffee?' Brown's voice interrupted her chain of thought.

'No, I'm good.'

The execution had been flawless except for one thing: evidence had been left at the scene. Evidence Nathan Quinn knew nothing about at the time he made his identification. In spite of that, he saw his friends' dead bodies and made the connection with Cameron – that somehow, somewhere, the whole big mess would come knocking at his door. The rest was just damage control.

Sometime in the past few minutes Brown must have switched on the car radio because it was now droning on with world news.

The point that Madison seemed to get stuck on was that Quinn had wanted to give Cameron the news in person, that he could imagine what it would be like for him to hear about it between jingles and sports chat. At that moment, Quinn was acting as a friend not as an attorney. Madison was sure he had not lied about that.

So, at some point there had been a switch and the legal counsel had taken over. Madison closed her eyes. There are some things you just shouldn't say on the phone. She remembered the time in college when Rachel's mother had called because her father had been in a car accident and was in intensive care.

Madison had called all their common friends. They did not have cellphones then, and after one hour of tracking Rachel's steps, she had found her finally at Neal's place, the guy who years later would become her husband. Madison remembered very clearly what she had said to Rachel: 'I'm coming to pick you up; tell me how to get there.' *Tell me how to get there.*

The twinkle lights were blurred in the rain behind the windshield wipers. Madison sat up. There it was: Quinn's one moment of weakness that could have cost John Cameron his freedom. Quinn had come out of the morgue and called him straightaway. 'I'm coming to see you right now; tell me how to get there,' he had said. And Cameron did. As he was driving to him, Quinn realized he was leaving deniability behind and getting into all sorts of trouble, and he called Cameron back and told him to meet him at his own house.

All he had to do then was to hope that the question would never come up, but if it did – as it had because Klein was not born yesterday – Quinn would fight for attorney–client privilege every step of the way, even get subpoenaed for it.

Once he got them all believing that they were fighting for every answer, he would give them the 'safe' version and they would think they had scored a moral victory, and come away with bupkis.

Klein had not asked how many times they had spoken and Quinn had not lied. The first time, he had called with his heart; the second, with the chilling knowledge he might be talking to a murderer.

The news had turned to the weather: a cold front was going to hit the city in the next 48 hours and a hell of sleet and snow was about to be unleashed over Seattle.

No surprise there, Madison thought. They had just lost Cameron.

They stood in Lieutenant Fynn's office. He was too mad to sit down at his desk and was leaning against the back wall. Brown and Madison had the side next to the door and left the middle to Sarah Klein, who was pacing the small room for all it was worth. Judge Martin's voice crackled through the speakerphone.

'I thought we had an understanding when we spoke in my chambers. The circumstances were *extra* ordinary.'

'Your Honor, he is still under oath.'

'Did he perjure himself?'

'Not exactly.'

'Don't get cute. Yes or no?'

'No, but—'

'Do you have any new evidence not in your possession two hours ago?'

Klein looked at Madison. What they had was best described as a hunch.

'No, Your Honor. If I may, I'd like to explain our concerns regarding Mr. Quinn's testimony.'

'Miss Klein, if you asked the wrong questions that is entirely your problem; you don't get two bites at the apple. Now, let's be done with this and find me someone to indict for real.'

Judge Martin hung up and the line went dead. Klein turned the speakerphone off.

'That went well,' Lieutenant Fynn said after a beat, taking his coat off the rack. 'I'm going to the briefing now: get me a license plate for the Explorer by end of shift or leave town.'

He opened the door and the squad room fell silent. He ignored everyone and left.

'I'm sorry,' Klein said.

'Shit happens,' Brown replied. 'Let's get over it and move on.'

Madison picked up the receiver and dialed Cameron's beeper number. It connected, but there was no message, just an open line and a beep.

John Cameron was now officially a fugitive and as such he had just made the Ten Most Wanted list – before him a man who had shot his parole officer dead, after him a serial rapist who operated in the towns along I-5. The briefing went as predicted: the media lapped it up and the evening papers changed their front page. A hotline was already in place for any tips from the public, as well as Quinn's reward, which had been intended for information that would lead to the arrest of the killer, not specifically Cameron. A subtle difference there, Madison thought, which might escape the general public.

A sandwich still in its wrapper sat on the corner of Madison's desk. She had been online for a while, tapping quietly and making notes.

Once the initial rush of understanding how Quinn had played them was gone, failure was a heavy knot deep in her chest.

'Do you know how many Ford Explorers are registered in the State of Washington?' she asked Brown without taking her eyes off the screen.

He had just put the phone down. In the first 45 minutes after they had posted Cameron's picture, the hotline had received 75 calls. The good ones were starting to trickle through.

He knew the place where Madison was standing very well indeed, had been there himself a number of times. Some of those times had had consequences.

'It wasn't your fault,' he said. 'You made the right connections.'

'Sure, razor-sharp me. If I had been ten minutes earlier on that train, right now we'd be searching his real house.'

'Maybe, and if the Sinclairs had a dog they might be alive today.'

Madison turned to face him. Sometimes she did not like him all that much.

'You don't have time to be sorry. The difference with Quinn is that now we know and that is a good thing,' he said. 'How many?'

'What?'

'Explorers.'

'One hundred and six thousand,' she replied flatly.

'Okay.'

'We can eliminate all those in colors other than black, those registered to women or men other than Caucasian or older than, say, fifty.'

'We'll take it from there. Quinn was told about the hearing yesterday morning, so Cameron might have dumped it in the last twenty-four hours. You have a car you want to get rid of, somewhere it's not going to attract attention and nobody's going to come looking for the owner. Somewhere a car is expected to be sitting unused for a while.'

'Long-term parking.'

'We'll check downtown and the airport first.'

Calls were made and a good number of people whose main job was to sit at a toll booth and watch the world go by had to get up fast and reluctantly join in the general rush.

A couple of hours later, Dunne put his head round the door.

'Hey,' he said.

'Hey,' Madison replied.

They had wheeled a small television with a video player into the room and Madison sat at her desk, flanked by a tall pile of tapes. Something played on the monitor, a black and white shot that didn't seem to change. Madison stared at it.

'What's up?'

'Security tapes from Sea-Tac. I'm going backwards from the most recent to – I don't know – as far as the pile goes.'

Dunne picked up a copy of Cameron's photograph from her desk and looked at the screen. In it, people were coming and going, with and without bags and cases, some with hats, some with hats and scarves.

'You think you can see him in the middle of that?'

'I might. Thing is, I'm actually hoping I don't. If he managed to get a plane out it will be ten times more difficult to get him back.'

'You're looking for someone but you hope not to find him.'

'Pretty much.'

Madison kept her eyes on the screen. When there was no one in the frame she would fast-forward it until there was someone else walking past.

'Sounds like fun,' Dunne said.

'You bet,' she replied.

'What are you doing for Christmas?' he asked her.

'I'll be sitting right here with a turkey sandwich in one hand and the remote in the other. How about you?'

'I'm going to see my folks in Portland.'

Madison pressed the fast-forward button, stopped and pressed it again.

'You're going to miss the big snow,' she said absent-mindedly.

'In any way I can,' he replied. 'Where's the sarge?'

Brown was not at his desk.

'Around.' She looked up. 'He's checking out some calls from the hotline.'

Madison stopped the video, stood up and stretched. 'What are you guys up to?'

'We're going to get roped in the hotline, I think. Did you hear about OPR?'

'No.'

'They managed to get Tully to admit that he had received the information from an anonymous source and that no money had changed hands.'

'They believe him?'

'If you take away the money, what else is there?'

'I know.'

Madison went back to the tapes. Nobody looked even remotely like the man they were after. Somehow that was a good thing.

In the end, inside the fourth hour, she began to see the stories unfolding: the couple arguing, the guy who jumped the check-in queue, the kid who got lost. She also saw a woman who tried to steal another woman's wallet and got caught, and a guy who lifted a briefcase, who didn't.

It was sometime past the end of the shift and before the depths of night when Brown came in and put a pizza box on her desk. They both took a slice – it was olives and anchovies. Anchovies had been something Brown and Madison had always been in agreement about.

Brown's desk phone rang and he picked up. He listened and then took down a number.

'Try this,' he said and passed Madison the piece of paper. 'It's a black Explorer – the sticker says it's been in Sea-Tac long-term parking since yesterday afternoon at about 2.20 p.m.'

He saw her thoughts in her eyes. 'It doesn't mean he's gone; he could have just left it there.'

'I hope so,' she said and went to work on her computer.

It took her two minutes to find that the owner of the car was one Mr. Roger Kay of Bellingham, a Caucasian male.

Brown stood behind her looking at the screen. 'Right age, right colour. Doesn't look anything like him.'

Roger Kay had limp brown hair and a face you instantly forgot. Both Brown and Madison leaned into the screen.

'The eyes are half closed and the mouth looks different,' he said.

'The chin and the jawline are different too. We can call the number we have for him but if his car is in long-term parking, chances are he won't be home.'

'Try anyway.'

Madison dialed. It rang for a while and nobody picked up.

'See if he's got a record.'

It took her a minute.

'Nope,' she said. 'No rap sheet.'

'OK. What's his home address?'

'It's in Bellingham.'

Brown sat at his desk. 'I'm going to keep a man on the Explorer while we get someone to check the residence.'

'I'll get going on the warrant,' Madison said. Judge Martin was off the clock but Judge Kramer, also known as Dial-a-Warrant, was on call. Lucky for them.

Twenty minutes later Brown's phone rang. It was a uniformed officer from the Bellingham Police Department – he was being patched through from his patrol car.

'I'm standing right in front of the address,' he said. 'It's an empty warehouse. Door's been boarded up. Nobody lives here but rats.'

'Okay,' Brown said after he replaced the receiver. 'You want to register your car to someone other than yourself, what do you do?'

'Fake driving license.'

'It's too easy.'

Madison took another slice of pizza from the box. 'It's just twenty dollars, a birth certificate, out-of-state ID, and a couple of letters from the bank for proof of residence. To get a birth certificate just check in the records for a child death, find someone who would be your age now and pay your twelve dollars online. Way too easy.'

She tapped on her keyboard. 'Let me try something,' she said.

'What?'

'There is something called Social Security Death Records. If Roger Kay is an assumed identity and he got it going through records of infant deaths – if, for whatever reason, the original death was registered – then it would turn up in here.'

'Why?'

'Say his parents were receiving benefits or something.'

'Lord, I hope they were.'

Madison waited for the answer to come back on the screen. The pizza was getting cold and she wished she had a Coke to go with it. There was a beep.

'I got him. Roger Kay died when he was eight years old.'

'I'll call the Crime Scene Unit,' Brown said, and within five minutes they were out and driving.

Two men in Airport Police uniforms paced up and down and stomped their feet to keep themselves warm. When Brown and Madison drove up, one of them came to their car and checked their badges while the other stayed with the Explorer.

Brown thanked them both and made sure they were glad they had helped out.

'Either one of you touched it?' he said without making a thing of it.

'I might have when I was looking to see if there was anything in view inside,' one of them replied.

'OK, we're going to have CSU here in a few minutes. Your prints will already be on record. Thanks for heads-up.'

The men left.

Madison wore gloves and had a one-foot heavy-duty torch in her right hand. The car looked spotless on the outside. She got close and shone the beam of light around the seats. Brown did the same on the other side. They moved from the front to the back.

Madison crouched a little, cutting the light sideways on the handle. The beams crossed and parted as they checked the black-carpeted floor.

'Nothing,' she said.

'Nothing.'

Brown turned off his torch.

'We don't know it's him yet,' he said to her quietly. 'Not for absolutely sure.'

'It's him,' Madison replied.

'That a hunch?'

'Yes. I'm on a roll today.' She kneeled by the back and shone her light on the underside.

The Crime Scene Unit van arrived and Madison was pleased to see CSU Officer Amy Sorensen shrug into her jacket and snap her gloves on.

'Sorry I missed the scene on Monday,' Sorensen said as she joined them. 'Got my appendix out at the weekend. They put me on forced bed rest. A waste of time, if you ask me. What have we got?'

Amy Sorensen was a striking five-foot-eleven redhead in her forties. Her father had been a cop, her husband was a cop, one of her two younger sisters was a detective in Vice, the other had just made plainclothes. The family was a legend in the department. She had a mind you could cut glass with and the dirtiest laugh in King County. Madison knew she could use both right now.

They briefed her quickly and she went to work. Her partner was a junior officer Madison had seen around a few times. They set up a couple of strong lights and busied themselves around the Explorer.

'It's been here since yesterday afternoon,' Sorensen said as she examined the concrete around the tires. I tell you what we're going to do. We're going to take a peek at what the inside has to offer, with minimal intrusion: I do not want to disturb any trace evidence we might find. Then we'll take it back and do things properly.'

Her partner called the truck that would move the Explorer off the lot while Sorensen got the driver's door open in less than 20 seconds.

'You're pretty good at that,' Brown said.

'Best in town,' she replied. She picked up one of their portable lights and shone it around and above the seats.

'Smell it?' she asked them. 'Wood polish and that flowery crap they put in dust busters.'

She checked the mirrors and under the steering wheel. She

clicked the glove compartment open and peered in, the bright light reaching into every corner. It was empty.

She shook her head. 'Okay, the longer it stays here, the bigger the chance it might get contaminated.'

'It's a dump job,' Brown ventured.

'Oh yes, and someone had a pretty good go at it.'

'Too clean for trace evidence?' Madison asked.

'We'll see about that.'

Once the truck arrived, they maneuvered the Explorer into it. After they drove off, Brown and Madison stood in the empty space where John Cameron had been only 18 hours before. Without the lights, it had gone back to a chilly gloom.

'I want to check the hotline,' Madison said and flipped open her cellphone.

'Wait,' Brown said. He was only a few feet away, his back to her, looking at the rough uneven ground. 'There's something I want to run by you.'

Madison put her phone away and sank her hands in her pockets. Brown examined the oil-stained concrete.

'What is it?' Madison asked.

'What do you think we'll get from the car?' Brown asked her.

Madison was getting used to his habit of leading her into a new thought by asking her a question about something entirely unrelated.

'Sorensen will find something – if there's anything there to find. How much closer that will get us to Cameron, I don't know, but everything counts. He doesn't know that identity is blown; he might use it again. Something is going to shake loose.'

'And the evidence will lead us to him,' he said.

'Sooner or later. The sooner the better.'

'We have four bodies in the morgue. Sanders makes five. We have a lot of *how* and *what*, we have almost zero *why*. Explain that.'

He said it as if it was a mathematical issue. Brown seemed entirely unaware of the cold, the late hour and the desolate place they were standing in. Madison's eyes felt gritty.

'That's what they told us at the Academy: you get a lot of one, you'll get none of the other. Murphy's Second Law. So, we have motive for the Sinclairs, but not for Sanders. We have proof that Sinclair stole from him but not why. He left the drugs and the money in Sanders's house but no trace evidence. We've got plenty of that at the Sinclairs' but nothing to match it to.' Madison could see that was not what Brown had in mind.

'We need to stand back and see the whole picture.'

'He's been two steps ahead of us all the way,' she retorted. 'How much further back do we need to be?'

'Right now, how far are you prepared to go to find the man who killed those children?'

'As far as necessary. What exactly are you saying?'

'We will find him when we see what he sees.'

'For crying out loud!' Madison heard herself say, suddenly losing the brain–mouth filter. 'Are you holding back on me? Because this Yoda-in-a-raincoat thing is not working.'

A beat of silence between them. Madison did not know what to say – she was as surprised as he was. Then, slowly, like some rare geological event, Brown smiled.

'I don't know any more about this than you do,' he said quietly.

His phone rang: it was Fynn. As Brown briefed him, they got into the car. The people they needed to interview at Sea-Tac would be back with the morning shift.

Madison sat looking straight ahead, not knowing exactly what her next words should be. Brown drove fast toward the lab. After he flipped his phone shut, he was still smiling.

The night shift was going about its business and didn't give Brown and Madison a second glance as they wandered down the quiet corridors, their 'visitor' badges hanging on their coats.

The machine had drinks and snacks. The neon light above was unforgiving and a wave of tiredness hit Madison like a brick wall. She chose a can of Coke and hoped the caffeine would kick in before she fell asleep on her feet. She popped the catch and drank and paced.

Brown drank from a bottle of water. Sorensen's office door was open, on her desk a copy of the *New York Times*. He picked it up and sat on a bench in the corridor, adjusted his glasses and started reading. After a couple of minutes of Madison pacing, Brown looked up.

'Will you sit down already?'

She obliged. He went back to the paper.

'What I said before—' she started.

'The Yoda thing,' he said crisply, still reading.

'Right.'

'Funny,' he said.

After that, they sat in silence for a while, Brown turning the pages from time to time and Madison leaning her head on the cool wall behind them, her eyes closed. It was past eleven when his phone rang and they both knew there was just no way it was going to be good news.

It was a long call and, for most of it, he listened. Then it was done and the only sound around them was the soft hum of the vending machine.

'That was detective Finch, LAPD Homicide. They were called on a crime scene today – the house of a known dealer. Vice had him on their wish list for years but nothing ever stuck. Anyway, they get there and they find three bodies: the dealer and two body-guards. Looked like an assassination. Good news for the civilized world but they still have to work the case, so they look into friends and associates and check out who might want him gone.'

Brown paused.

'The guards died of blood loss from knife wounds to the neck and the dealer was shot with his own gun. Shot through the right eye. The Los Angeles ME puts the time of death sometime on Tuesday. No prints. No witnesses. No trace evidence so far. But it turns out the guy had an associate in Seattle, name of Erroll Sanders.'

He let that sink in.

'And when they checked on him—'

'They are looking at Cameron for it?' Madison said.

'They have nothing that links him to the dead men, except for Sanders and how the guards were killed. They're going to email Kelly the details of the blade for a comparison with the knife that cut Sanders.'

'It happened sometime on Tuesday,' Madison said.

'Yes.'

'That's before Sanders was killed.'

Brown nodded. Madison thought about it for a moment. There must be a chronology to this mess. 'Cameron is here on Saturday night – we have the Sinclairs' time of death to confirm it. He waits for two days. He meets Quinn Monday afternoon. On Tuesday he's in LA, he takes care of business. In the early hours of Wednesday he's back here for Sanders. He speaks with Quinn after the first hearing and yesterday at 2.20 p.m. he drops the Explorer at the airport.'

'Busy week,' Brown said.

Sorensen emerged after a while. 'We have the partial of a thumb from inside the boot; it's smudged as if there was a whole hand there and it got cleaned off. It might not be strong enough for court anyway. The outside and the underside are spotless. No surprise there.' She took a sip from a paper cup. 'We have a couple of hairs from the backseat but – don't get excited – they were shed, not pulled. So, no follicle and no DNA. Also from the backseat, a very small amount of fibers that could be cotton or wool, black. But, best of all, there was a drop of blood under the steering wheel. Could be the palm of his right hand. We're comparing it to the DNA from the Sinclair crime scene. Now, I beg you, go home.'

They walked out into the night. Across the city skyline windows were bright in the deserted offices and Madison longed for that drive home, alone in her car, the music loud enough to go right through her bones.

Billy Rain had spent the rest of Wednesday in the garage, thinking about Tully's article and George Pathune lying dead on the concrete floor of a prison laundry. More than actually thinking about it, he had been in a state of constant recall. It had come between his brain and his hands and he had cut himself twice. Something that had never happened before. His brother-in-law had noticed.

'Don't bleed on the seats,' he told him.

Billy could not have cared less if he tried. The day inched on and at the end of his shift Billy left with the paper tightly folded in his coat pocket. He needed a bar where he knew no one and no one knew him. He found one off Fairview. A dim local enterprise one flick of the broom away from sawdust on the floor.

He finished his first beer, sitting in a corner booth, the paper untouched next to the bowl of peanuts. He ordered a second beer, took a sip and opened the *Star*. He read Tully's piece twice, feeling each time the same cold dread but getting through it nevertheless.

By the time he was starting on his third beer he felt a little more in control. Enough to know that he needed to switch to ginger ale if he wanted to think straight.

He had not been back to that day since he'd been paroled; he had left the memory of it in his cell. No one knew because he had never told. He had never needed to: the body of George Pathune had been added unofficially to the tally of a convict called Edward Morgan Rabineau who was already doing time for two counts of murder, and nobody was particularly surprised at his notching up a third.

Billy Rain, safe in his booth, visited briefly the prison laundry on that day three years ago and, if he had to be perfectly honest, he couldn't say whether the person he had seen was Rabineau. He was familiar with the man, sure, but they had never spoken; they moved in different circles and within the prison hierarchy they were about as far apart as they could be and still belong to the same species. With one major difference now: Rabineau was still in jail. Billy Rain was sure of that.

Tully's piece identified the prime suspect as someone called John Cameron. A name he had not heard in a long time and had seriously hoped not to hear again.

Billy Rain drained his ginger ale. Something else he was pretty sure of was that Cameron had not been in jail at the time Pathune was killed. Which meant Tully might be wrong. It had nothing to do with Billy, of course – none of it had.

He ordered some food and ate watching the sports on cable. He went home to his one-room fold-out – he hadn't sufficiently proven himself to go back and live with his family yet, he just had dinner with them a couple of times a week – and he watched television till he fell asleep in his chair.

By Thursday morning, the news of Nathan Quinn's reward was in all the major papers.

Chapter 24

It had been a hard winter. Michael and Harry Salinger had spent many afternoons at home, prisoners of the rain, the early dark and their father's moods. They endured the seventh grade and prayed for spring and the release of summer.

One Saturday afternoon, as they were coming back from the grocery store, they saw their father waiting for them in the kitchen. Michael noticed him first and took one step back, away from the window. He hadn't seen them. He motioned to his brother to follow him to the back gate.

'He's waiting,' he whispered.

'I didn't do anything,' Harry said quickly.

'Let's go,' Michael said. 'We might as well get it over with.'

They walked into the kitchen and put the bags on the table.

Richard Salinger looked at them. 'Do you guys want to see *Back to the Future* or what?'

They were speechless. The film had just opened and no one was talking about anything else.

They queued for tickets and bought popcorn, the boys still stunned, finding their way in the crowd.

They watched the film and heard their father laugh, an exotic sound. He took them for pizza afterwards, they split a large salami and cheese and drank Cherry Coke. The place was full of parents with kids. The last thing Harry thought that night as he was falling asleep: *that* must be what it's like for everyone else.

Richard Salinger's mood lasted about a week. Then, one day, Michael's 'Yes, sir' wasn't quite as snappy as it should have been and his brother got a quick smack on the back of the head. It would be funny if you didn't have to live here, Michael said afterwards.

They were sitting on the back steps. It was the end of a summer day and above them the sky was turning purple. Their yard was lined by tall trees and once their father had gone to work, nobody could see them.

They shared a cigarette, passing it back and forth between them and knowing how much every drag would cost them if their father knew.

'We could run away,' Michael said. 'It's not impossible.'

They both knew Richard Salinger would use every connection he still had at the Police Department to find them. They would last five minutes on the road.

They buried the cigarette pack and the matches in a small plastic bag under the roots of the farthest tree from the house, the stub next to it.

Two days later, Michael found the gun.

They were tossing a tennis ball as they were going down the stairs. Michael missed and it rolled into their father's room. The boys looked at each other: it wasn't a good idea to go in there without an excellent reason and a tennis ball didn't even come close. But Richard Salinger was out and Michael gently pushed the door open.

'It's under the bed. Get it and get out,' Harry said.

Michael stood just inside the room and looked around. The bed, with the blankets hastily pulled up, was in the corner. A jacket and a shirt had been thrown on a chair at the side. The room had not been aired in a long time and smelled of cough medicine.

'Come on,' Harry called out. The hairs were standing up on the back of his neck just knowing that Michael was in their father's room.

'Okay.' Michael got onto his hands and knees, lifted the bedspread and looked into the half darkness.

Two pairs of old leather shoes lay at funny angles, covered with such a thick film of dust it was impossible to see their color. A shoebox was tied with a piece of string and, wedged between that and the wall, was the tennis ball.

Michael wasn't all that happy about reaching out into the dusty mess but there was not much he could about it.

Suck it up, he thought.

He lay down flat on his stomach, trying to keep his face as much as possible off the floor, and reached for the shoebox. He felt it with the tips of his fingers and grasped it; he pulled it out and went for the ball. His eyes were squeezed shut; he could feel the dust going up his nose with every breath. He closed his fingers around the ball and straightened up. Still sitting on the floor, he wiped the front of his white T-shirt with his hand.

He started to push the shoebox back under with his foot. It was heavy.

'What's taking you so long?'

'Have you seen this before?' Michael pointed at the box.

Harry peeked into the room and shook his head.

Michael picked it up and felt its weight in his hands.

In that house of secrets, none was more closely guarded by Richard Salinger than their mother's death. The boys had no memories of her: he told them nothing and they did not ask. Between themselves however, they sometimes spoke of her and wondered.

Slowly, Michael began to untie the string. He did not know himself what he was hoping to find – maybe a scrap of paper, maybe a photograph.

Harry stood transfixed.

Michael laid the string to one side and lifted the lid. His mouth dropped open. He looked up at Harry.

'What is it?'

'Come here,' Michael said, his voice dead-serious.

'No.'

'Harry.'

Harry stepped into the room and saw it. The revolver was wrapped in a white handkerchief, next to it a small box of cartridges. Even concealed inside the fabric, there was no doubt about what it was.

Michael put the box on the ground between them and they looked at it. Many times, when they were little and their father was still a police officer, he had shown them his duty piece, strapped in the holster and well out of the reach of their small hands.

Michael lifted the corners of fabric one by one, his fingers barely brushing the gun metal.

The weapon was polished to a shine.

After what seemed like forever, Michael picked it up by the butt. Harry was frozen on the spot. They had never thought for a second that their father might still keep a piece in the house. The cigarettes behind the tree were baby stuff. This was beyond trespassing, it was way beyond any rule they had ever broken.

Harry went cold. 'Put it away,' he said.

Michael stood up; he held the weapon toward the window, his arm stretched out and one eye shut, taking aim. 'In a second,' he replied.

Harry didn't know why he was sick with fear. They couldn't get caught; their father would be out for hours. He could see Michael working the loader and looking inside. It was empty. It was his brother's ease with the gun – how he cradled the butt in the palm of his hand.

'Put it away.'

'In a second.' Michael held it out to him, the muzzle pointed at the floor. 'Do you want to hold it?'

Harry Salinger took the .38 from his brother's hand, surprised and delighted by the weight of it. It was the strangest thing. He stretched his arm out and took aim at the falling sun. It felt better than good; it felt right.

They knelt together and put it back in the box, carefully folding the fabric around it. Michael pushed it back where he had found it and they left the room. Without having to explain, they went to the tree and dug out the cigarettes. They took one each and sat on the kitchen steps smoking, as scared and thrilled as they had ever been in their lives.

'It's not impossible,' Michael said quietly.

The rest of the summer was about nothing else but the gun: why their father had it, why he was hiding it and how they could use that precious discovery. Around their father they were as quiet as mice but at every occasion they would resume the same conversation.

'I think we should go before school starts,' Michael said one day, while they were folding laundry. 'I don't think I can stand another winter here.'

Harry nodded. He was used to Michael doing most of the talking anyway. This time though, Michael's ramblings were different – they were *specific*. He had dates and ways of getting out of town; he mentioned big cities where two kids could get lost and no one would find them. Somewhere warm, where they could do small jobs to keep them going. Most of all, they'd be traveling with the gun. They'd be as safe as they could be. Harry nodded.

He started to wake up more often during the night; he would lie in bed listening to the tiny creaks and clicks in the house, feeling squashed between his father and his brother's will to run.

The touch of the gun metal against the palm of his hand had projected cool blues right in front of him and the word itself, 'g' being a rich deep purple. Harry could see it with his eyes closed as it glowed against a black background. It came to him whether he liked it or nor, ready or not.

One Sunday morning, their father was still asleep and the day shone with all the sweetness of summer's end. Michael turned to Harry at the kitchen table.

'Let's go to Mount Baker Beach,' he said.

They took the bus and the farther they got from the house the better they felt. It was Labor Day weekend and the beach was busy with families and kids splashing everywhere. The boys bought two bottles of Cherry Coke and sat at the water's edge. After a while Harry got up.

'I'm going in.'

The sun had been hot on their shoulders and Lake Washington was so cool it made him almost dizzy. He went under head first and came out shaking the water off his hair.

'It's great! You've got to come in.' Harry splashed Michael hard with the cut of his hand.

They got into a water fight and then swam under water until their feet could not touch the bottom anymore. They came out for air and paddled, spitting jets of water at each other. They swam and they lay on their backs letting the water take them where it would.

After a couple of hours, Harry started to swim back to shore.

'I'm staying for a little while,' Michael said and watched his brother's feet disappear like a fish tail, silver under the blue.

Harry found their clothes and lay down in the soft breeze. He fell asleep and when he woke up his hair was dry and Michael was still gone. Harry got to his feet; the sun was lower in the sky and most of the crowd had left. He looked around, all around. The lake was flat and still and he stepped into the water, turning to look at the shore, turning back to the water.

'Are you alright?' The lifeguard put his hand on the boy's shoulder and Harry jumped. The sun had just set when they brought Michael's body out of the water.

Harry couldn't stop shivering. He sat in the back of the patrol car as they drove him home. The two officers spoke to him kindly but their words did not get through. One second the police radio was crackling, a second later it was dead quiet and they were parked by his father's car, the officers knocking on the door. His father appeared. One officer looked at his feet and the other put his hand on his father's arm; Richard Salinger's head moved back and he turned slowly and stared at the car.

A month later Harry watched from the kitchen window as his father picked a fight with their neighbor. When the neighbor's cat was found with his throat cut, no one noticed the scratches on Harry's hands and arms. That day his father smiled briefly. 'Sometimes the world is just, boy. Not often, mind you. Gotta enjoy it when it happens.'

In his basement, Harry Salinger wraps the metal wire twice around the glass fragment. It is a clear piece the shape of a water drop that wouldn't look out of place on a chandelier; when the light is right it throws colors on his hands and on a small wooden box on his table. Michael would have liked it.

The work is soothing. The television monitors are muted and Salinger lifts his eyes from time to time to check if the news has started.

Madison's voice, indigo, is still frozen at the crime scene: it has filled the silence in his house in a way he didn't think possible.

... he came at them and they never even knew it ...

She was describing his work in such detail, with such understanding. It was almost intimate. Plans are made and they can be unmade; it was time to improvise, to go with the flow. What a blessing she was.

Chapter 25

Alice Madison opened her eyes in the darkness. She was suddenly awake and aware; the projected clock on the ceiling showed 05:43 a.m. The telephone by her bedside rang again and she grabbed it.

'Hello.'

'Brown told me to call him *as soon as*. I tried him but I couldn't get through. You're the next best thing.'

'Sorensen.'

'Good morning.'

'Give me a second.' Madison turned on the table lamp and swung her legs out of the side of the bed. She was wearing only a T-shirt and the instant chill woke her up a little – the heating had not clicked on yet. She took a couple of deep breaths, trying to oxygenate her brain into action.

'I'm here,' she said.

Sorensen didn't believe in chit-chat.

'The fibers are cashmere, the blood is human and we have a five-point match for the print, which doesn't hold up in court but, hey, it's the thought that counts.'

Madison was trying to keep up.

'Are you still there?' Sorensen didn't sound like she had just pulled a double shift with a fresh appendectomy scar under her coveralls.

'I think so.'

'Because this is where it gets good. The five-point match is Cameron.'

Madison wanted to take it down. Her notebook was in the coat's pocket, the coat was on a chair in the living room. She walked fast.

'We're still waiting for the DNA results. Five points is way too few to mean squat in court—'

'I know, but it's still something.'

'Gee, you're an upbeat kind of gal, aren't you?'

Madison smiled as she scribbled in her book. 'Cashmere?' she said.

'Black. At least he has good taste. Find me something I can match it to – a sweater or maybe a scarf.'

'I will. Thank you, Sorensen.'

'OK, you pass it on to Brown, I'm off home now for a nap. I'll be back before lunchtime.'

There was no point in trying to go back to sleep. Madison put the coffee on; while she waited she pulled on sweat pants and a heavy top. She took her mug out on the patio, braving the early morning frost and warming her hands around it.

Without even a hint of daylight there was little to see but Madison knew every tree and every bush and she had missed being out there. It was so quiet. She hoped a little of that peace would last her through the day.

The human traffic of the Main Terminal of the Seattle–Tacoma airport flowed undisturbed around them. Madison and Brown were going over payments and ticket purchase dates when Brown's phone started beeping: a young patrol officer, all of six months out of the Academy, had been canvassing cab drivers at King County Airport and had something they might want to hear. Madison felt a drop of adrenaline coming loose.

There is no scheduled passenger traffic at Boeing Field but they still clock on average 833 aircraft operations per day between corporate and private planes and flying clubs.

'His right hand,' George Malden had said. 'I remember the scars.'

Late Tuesday afternoon the cab driver had picked up a single man with one piece of hand luggage. The photograph Officer Jerez had shown him didn't exactly ring a bell but when he had mentioned the scars on the man's right hand, that was something Malden could swear to.

During the fast drive to King County Airport, Brown had called the precinct to get a sketch artist on standby.

Again, they showed him the photograph. Malden looked up. 'If I tell you that the guy I saw is like *this* guy but different, you're going to think I'm a flake, aren't you?'

Brown shook his head with a brief smile. 'We had this picture doctored with a computer; what we had was twenty years old.'

'Well, you got the eyes right. But the guy's leaner, his jaw a little different, he had one of those little beards – a goatee. And the hair was kinda blond, but like peroxide, you know.'

'Let's go inside and sit down for a minute,' Brown said and Madison felt her body tense. They had picked up the scent again.

Malden had dropped Cameron off at the Marriott Residence Inn on Fairview. A hotel.

Two things bothered Madison: why would Cameron need to go to a hotel, given that he had the house in Laurelhurst and probably another somewhere in King County? And the hand – it bothered her that after seven dead in four days, with all his caution and care for details, Cameron would not make sure the driver didn't see his one identifying characteristic.

He was coming back for Erroll Sanders, to finish off the work started with the Sinclairs in the early hours of Sunday morning. He *should* have been wearing gloves. Maybe he didn't pack them, maybe the sun in LA was too warm and sweet and he forgot.

Sure. Madison filed those thoughts with another couple of unanswered questions that needled her from time to time.

The Residence Inn stands on the edge of Lake Union and does well with business travelers and the tourist trade. It has all the amenities one has grown accustomed to in hotel chains with identical rooms in muted pastels, but John Cameron did not avail himself of any of them. It took Brown and Madison just under an hour to establish beyond any reasonable doubt that Cameron had not checked in on Tuesday evening. Not under his own name or Roger Kay's. In fact no one at all of his description had checked in between Tuesday and Wednesday. Madison went through the computer printouts and Brown handled the staff.

Cameron might have had a drink at the bar, the bartender couldn't swear either way, but that was that. Madison couldn't honestly say she was surprised. Disappointed, sure, but not exactly shocked.

They walked out of the hotel, just as Cameron must have done four days earlier. So, he arrives at the airport with his chartered plane, grabs a cab and gets dropped off there. He doesn't register, he walks right back out. What next? Madison sniffed the breeze coming from the water, Lake Union just across the road, dark and still. *Damn.* She turned to Brown. She knew it in her bones.

'He's got a boat.'

Brown held her eyes; he nodded. 'Yeah. That's what Quinn was protecting.'

They stood there, Chandler's Cove stretching out before them, pier after pier, more boats than they could count in the damp salty dusk.

'Let's take a walk,' Brown said.

A boat was bad news, and Madison was suddenly annoyed with

herself for not having considered the possibility before. A boat in Seattle meant he could *go* anywhere and not *be* anywhere. On the water he was practically invisible. The numbers were unforgiving: in the Seattle King County area there are many thousands of licensed boats.

They had no solid proof yet but they knew as if they had seen him with their own eyes, walking out of the hotel, making sure the cab had gone, stepping lightly over to the pier where his boat was moored. It could have been anything – Chandler's Cove fuel dock can take up to 65-footers, it's open 24 hours a day and from Lake Union he could get into Lake Washington or maybe out to Puget Sound and on to wherever. The journey to Vancouver Island, Canada, would have been real pretty.

Madison looked around; hardly anybody else was on the piers and they were going to be short on witnesses. The Ford Explorer had been registered to a different name, Roger Kay – that was very likely standard operating procedure for Cameron, which meant the boat could be registered to a whole different identity. Keep them separate, keep them safe. He hadn't lasted that long without being careful. He probably had several well maintained identities for separate purposes – driving license, boat, properties, airline tickets. Madison was deep in thought when she realized Brown was talking.

'Do you know anything about boats?'

'I have a kayak, if that counts.'

'Well, let's put it this way: you have to moor them, keep them, put in fuel, maintain them in nine months of rain. Just think of taking one of these forty-footers out and you are already burning money.' Brown's eyes moved over the sleek sails and the heavier motor boats with their well-appointed cabins. 'Cameron doesn't mess around; if he has a boat, he's got himself a nice piece of nautical engineering and someone somewhere must have seen him on it. I don't care what he did to his hair.'

Madison put her hands in the pockets of her coat and looked up at the purple sky.

'We have eight square miles of water against eighty-four of land.'

Brown turned to her, about to say something, then changed his mind. The boats bobbed up and down, bumping gently against each other.

Back in the precinct, Madison opened the fridge in the rec room and examined its contents. She had promised herself many times that she would keep something in her desk or in their makeshift kitchenette for occasions such as this.

The fridge was nearly empty and could have done with a quick clean. The same carton of chicken soup had resided at the back of the second shelf since Madison had joined Homicide. Next to it, half a bagel with something green in it that Madison could only pray was salad. Something yellow and sticky had been spilled at the bottom – maybe a soft drink, maybe soup. Never mind OPR, she thought, the World Health Organization would shut them down in a nanosecond.

Andrew Dunne walked over in his shirtsleeves, his tie loosened and the top button undone. He stood next to her and they both stared at the desolation. His red hair stuck out a little at the back and he was pale under the freckles.

'I heard you got boat trouble,' he said.

'Yup.'

'I've got a buddy in the licensing office, if that helps.'

'Thanks, but it's just going to be a papercuts job.'

'Lucky you.'

'Anything from Sea-Tac?'

'No. Except Kelly was ticked off he wasn't with you at Boeing Field. He came right back and kinda yanked the cab driver away from the sketch artist.'

Nothing much Madison could say to that; she raised her eyebrows and thought that was an appropriate reaction. That had been exactly why Brown had phoned in the news about the driver and not taken Kelly with them.

Dunne shut the fridge door with the tip of his index finger.

'It's meatloaf night at Jimmy's.'

Jimmy's was a cop bar three blocks away; if they knew you and they weren't too busy, they delivered. Dunne had their number on speed dial. Twenty minutes later six Friday night specials appeared.

Madison's first instinct was to pick up her carton and go back to her desk where a small mountain of printouts from Sea-Tac airlines and the Washington State Board of Vessel Licensing were waiting. Instead she sat on the edge of Spencer's desk and spent a few minutes not being antisocial. Kelly ignored her, Rosario read his paper, Dunne and Spencer talked about tattoos and Brown sat quietly, picking at his food and going over the fax LAPD had sent them earlier.

Madison took a bite of meatloaf. It was glorious; her grandmother would have approved.

After a while she returned to her desk. The paperwork was arranged in neat piles. She was holding a cup of coffee; to make room for it she picked up a file. It was her notes from the library, her research on the Hoh River kidnapping and the background on Cameron, Sinclair and Quinn. Madison opened the file and quickly scanned her own writing – four more dead since then.

The newspaper articles had the photographs of David Quinn's funeral – the crowd picture and one of John Cameron Madison didn't remember. One arm was in a sling and, with the other hand, he was grabbing the camera off the neck of a photographer. The men and women around him hadn't noticed the intrusion, except for Nathan Quinn. The photographer's face was a flash of surprise,

Cameron's pure hatred. The man, much taller and heavier than the boy, was stumbling back to get away. Cameron looked completely unafraid: something more powerful than his small body had washed over him.

Madison blinked. When she had moved the file, she had glanced at a page under it – another article that she had cut out. Now she reached for it. It was the report on Andrew Riley's attack in the alley behind the bar, so cocky when he had tried to take photos of the Sinclairs' bodies at the crime scene. She remembered how the detective had described him after the attack: the fear, the shock.

Madison blinked. Somewhere far outside her immediate attention, Brown was by the door with Spencer. She looked up at him, hearing nothing. Brown met her eyes, Spencer still talking to him. Madison looked down, in one hand Cameron's picture, in the other Riley's article. And the notion was there, clear and unavoidable and utterly compelling. Because one moment ago she didn't and now she did.

She looked up and Brown held her eyes; he said something to Spencer and he left. Brown closed the door of their office and leant against it.

'Cameron attacked Riley,' she said, still stunned.

'Yes,' Brown replied simply.

' "Yes"?'

He nodded.

'Because he had tried to take pictures of his dead friends.'

Madison paused. Everything she knew was being reshaped and renamed.

She lifted her hand. 'Give me a minute.' Her eyes could not rest on anything. The Sinclair crime-scene report, the pictures, Nathan Quinn's interview notes, Sorensen's preliminary on the Explorer. Everything she had seen, everything she had done.

'DAMMIT!' Madison slapped the wall behind her with the flat of her hand. She felt like she could have punched a hole right through it easily enough, but when she turned to Brown her voice was controlled and her anger in check.

'You *knew*?'

'Yes.'

'And you chose not to share this thought with me?'

'If I told you, it would have been worth nothing to you. I trusted that you would get there. If we have to sell this to Fynn or anybody else, I cannot be worrying that you only half believe it yourself. You had to see it with your own eyes.'

'What if I hadn't?'

'I'd have put in a request for a new partner.'

A look passed between them.

'I need you to think straight now,' Brown said.

'Okay,' she said.

'Okay,' he replied.

They sat down.

Out of all the implications and consequences of what Madison had just found out, the first and most important was the one she was almost reluctant to articulate. After all the hours spent on the hows and whys. She had to say it out loud.

'If Cameron was punishing Riley for his insult to the dignity of his friends, the logical conclusion is that he is not responsible for their deaths.' The words felt strange in her mouth. 'If he were, he would have welcomed the exposure: that would have fit nicely with arranging the crime scene and positioning the bodies. He would have wanted the world to see it.'

'I don't think he did it.'

'When did you start to doubt?'

'When Payne called us about the glass.'

'Last Tuesday morning during the briefing?'

'Yes.'

'*Last Tuesday?*'

'I know.'

'You haven't mentioned this to anybody else?'

'I talked about it with Fred Kamen.'

'The glass was the last straw?'

'Something like that. At that point we had the partial check with the forged signature and the hairs in the ligature knot. It was too much good fortune for us. If you look at Cameron's previous work, the Sinclair crime scene is a completely different pathology.'

'We still have all that evidence that needs to be accounted for.' Madison liked evidence, she relied on it. It stung her pride that someone had taken advantage of her beliefs and she would never have known if not for chance and a cup of coffee.

In her mind things were clicking and finding their place.

'If Cameron didn't kill the Sinclairs, somebody else did. The LA dealer and Sanders were involved and Cameron found out.'

'Do you really think that's their style?'

'Let's go back a second here. You started to think about this on Tuesday. Since then we've had an arrest warrant out on Cameron, we tried to get Quinn to talk, we've been wading through rivers of papers with one single objective – to find Cameron. And the kicker is, he is the *wrong* guy. How, in the name of everything holy, did you not tell anybody?'

'I have *zero* proof; this is a hunch. A guess which I happen to believe we are dead right about. The only possible way to do this is to work both ends at the same time: we follow the trail the killer has left us to get to Cameron and we back up on it to get to the killer himself.

'This thing wasn't thrown together at the last minute: he knew what we would be looking for and he gave it to us. How he has chosen to lay the trap and build the set-up tells us about him and how he thinks and what he wants out of this. Something else: Cameron might not have killed the Sinclairs but three men in LA and one in Seattle are dead because he decided they should be. If the killer is close enough to Cameron he can give him to us on a silver tray, I'm not saying no.'

Madison chewed on that for a moment.

'Let's look at the Sinclairs again,' Brown said. 'We can start with "manner of death".'

'The wife and the children were shot, the husband was tied up and died of a heart attack brought on by inhalation of chloroform. We had concluded that the difference meant that the killer wanted James Sinclair to know his family was being slaughtered. It was his punishment for stealing from him.'

'What happens if we take Cameron out of the crime scene?'

'The killer wanted Sinclair to die after everybody else. He wanted Cameron to know Sinclair's death was slow and painful and he was aware of what was happening to his family.' Somehow it was even worse than their first conclusion.

'Yes. And it doesn't look like something our LA friends would do.'

Madison sat back on her chair. '*Thirteen Days* is a warning to Cameron, and the guy is still out there.'

Brown nodded once. She knew he was right and something cold snaked down her back. Retribution was swift in the circles Erroll Sanders moved in; they were low on detail work and high on ammo. This was something else.

Brown picked up the Crime Scene Unit report and flipped it open.

'From the moment Payne said we had Cameron's print on the glass, it was all about evidence. *Evidence* is how the killer is revealing himself to us. He used DNA and fingerprints to tie his target to the scene and constructed a motive using forgery and embezzlement.'

'Saltzman has finished with the tax records?'

'Yes. He found nothing that indicated Sinclair ever acted inappropriately.'

'We have the check and the money going in and out of the account.'

'How easy do you think it would be for me to open an account tomorrow in a different name? You spent some time at Sinclair's house. What was your gut feeling? Did the guy need extra cash?'

'No.'

'What was your gut feeling?'

Madison shook her head. All that time spent watching their home videos: she had had a gut feeling and pretty much ignored it. Something came to her out of the blue.

'The ligature. You said that the amount of blood and cells on the ligature was not consistent with Sinclair's injuries, that there should have been a lot more given the fight he put up. So we had the question of why did the killer re-tie his hands.'

'Now we know.'

'He did it to place the hairs in the knot. He couldn't have done it when Sinclair was alive and struggling.'

Madison was beginning to get a sense of the madman. To find him, she needed to understand him. To fight him, something else would be called upon: something she was not altogether sure they taught at the Academy.

Her cellphone rang and she jumped. She checked the time on the small screen: it was 10.45 pm. The number was unknown.

'Hello.'

'Hello, is this Detective Madison?'

Adult male, over 20 and under 50 years old, local.

'Yes, who is this?'

'My name is Greg Phillips. You spoke with my father Clyde a few days ago in Laurelhurst. His house is opposite John Cameron's.'

The old guy with the shopping.

'Yes, of course. Is he alright?'

'He's fine, thanks. You left him your card and, well, we just called 911. Someone was trying to break into Cameron's house. My dad said to call you, that you might be interested.'

'Yes, absolutely, thank you. We're on our way.'

Madison shut her phone and stood up reaching for her jacket. 'Somebody's breaking into Cameron's house.'

Brown grabbed his coat.

Chapter 26

They shot through the station, all the other detectives gone out or off shift. The traffic was light and they made good time toward Laurelhurst. The temperature had dropped and anybody with any sense had stayed home.

'What did Kamen say?' Madison asked once they were on 23rd Avenue.

'He picked up on the use of DNA and fingerprints; he said we should look into someone with an affinity for police work. Possibly someone who applied to the Academy and got turned down, who frequents cop bars and strikes up conversations. That kind of thing.'

'What if he applied to the Academy and didn't get turned down?'

'What he did to that family, I'm hoping something might have come up in the Psych. exam. That was not his first piece of work; he's had time to practice his swing.'

'Can we get the records from the Academy?'

'We should have them by tomorrow. I asked Payne to go over the glass again, check if it had been treated chemically in any way. Sorensen is looking at the hairs. It might tell us how he got them and kept them.'

Madison was still getting her bearings. First there was one, now there was *another*. Brown knew exactly what she was feeling. 'Right this minute, Lieutenant Fynn is asking you the question, what do you say?'

She puffed her cheeks and blew out some air. 'You know those pictures that are actually a composite of two images, like a trick of your eyesight? The thing is you can't have both at the same time. You can see one but you lose the other, and vice versa. I just know it was Cameron who beat up Riley, but if I see that, then I lose the bigger picture.'

He nodded.

'We still don't know why,' she continued.

'We've been dealing with why all week and see where it got us. Today I'm just going to be happy with how and who.'

Madison shifted her holster a little and relaxed in the seat. 'We had surveillance on the house.'

'Not enough hot bodies. They put the numbers into canvassing, and a patrol car would look in on the house every hour or so.'

'The chances of this being a casual B&E are pretty slim. Someone wants to have an eBay Christmas.'

'It could be a reporter getting a little too close; breaking and entering ain't what it used to be.'

'You know we're going to have to tell Fynn soon, right?' she said.

'Tomorrow. We'll catch him nice and early.'

'*After* his first cup of coffee.'

'You'd better believe it.'

They found Laurelhurst quiet and still, the residential streets already turned in for the night and a light mist softly rising. Brown hung a right into Cameron's street and slowed down. Left and right, cars were parked in their driveways.

One Seattle PD uniformed officer stood in the middle of the street, opposite Cameron's house. He saw them approaching, a torch in his left hand. Brown parked and identified himself and

Madison as they exited the car. The beam of the torch swept over their feet. The air had a bite to it.

Cameron's house stood deserted just as they had last seen it. Madison noticed a couple of windows still lit in the Phillips home across the road.

'My partner and I responded to the 911 call; the owners are not on the premises.' Officer Mason was tall and wiry, a plain face under the cap.

'We expected as much,' Brown said.

'Front door and windows are secure but my partner has driven around to the other side, in case anybody came out that way.' Cameron's yard backed onto the end of another property on a parallel street.

Crackle came and went from the officer's radio. The sound of glass shattering hit them and they were running, weapons out, up the drive toward the garage.

Behind her, Madison heard Officer Mason calling into his radio.

It had come from the back of the yard. The only way there was following the side of the house, with trees and bushes in your face and getting darker as you went deeper. She had been there before, her heart was racing, but it was only a chemical reaction and it didn't worry her.

'I'll go in first,' Madison said. 'I've walked it in daylight – it's pretty tight.'

'No, I'm on point,' Brown said. 'You watch my back.' He went before she could say a word. She followed him quick, the uniform a few steps behind her. In seconds, they had left the half light from the street.

Madison held her left arm bent in front of her face to protect her eyes from the branches whipping back after Brown's passage. Under her feet the ground was hard and dry. In a minute they would get to the fence and there would be a little more room for movement, just another few steps. Madison heard Brown ahead of her, twigs snapping and a rustle of clothes. Suddenly behind her, loud radio crackle. Madison waited for Mason to appear.

'Turn your radio down.' Quietly but firmly.

'Sorry,' he whispered.

Madison turned to continue. Left arm up and right hand down, weapon pointed at the ground. She smelled the dead cat again – they were almost through. She had been listening carefully but had heard nothing out of place after the glass breaking. They'd see it soon enough – the door probably; there were glass panels there. She could get over the fence and to it in seconds.

She smelled the cat close now and something faint under it. Chloroform. Madison started to turn but it was too late. Her right hand, holding her Glock, was gripped tight behind her. He was trying to get the gun off her. Chloroform, close to her face now. She felt his body almost lifting her off the ground, half spun, her head knocked back against the wall, trying to get the cloth over her face.

No, this is not how it's going to happen. Breathe, try to get some air. Yell. You gotta warn Brown, gotta warn him.

It was seconds and the space between them was the longest of Madison's life.

She kicked back hard. The cloth finding her face, smashed against the wall, something warm spilling over her cheek. Her left elbow thrust sharp and high behind her, all her strength in it. He yelped. Her right arm hurt. He had the strength but she had the anger. Chloroform meant one thing: chloroform was four dead bodies on the bed.

If she got one shot off, Brown would know to take cover. She'd probably just get it into the wall. It would cost her the arm. *Fuck it.* She pulled as far as she could and fired, something snapped, the pain white hot and the cloth over her face. The man swore.

She fired again. The gun dropped to the ground. *Don't breathe, don't breathe it in.*

From far away she heard Brown coming toward them, thrashing through the bushes. His voice calling to her. Madison blind in one eye, her eyebrow cut and blood all over her face, half drugged, on her knees, feeling the ground with her hands, looking for her weapon. 'GET DOWN.' Her voice burned in her lungs.

Three shots in rapid succession cut into the night. She saw the muzzle flashes six feet into the darkness ahead of her.

Brown, find Brown. Madison tried to stand up, her legs gave way. She couldn't hear well, ears still ringing from her own shots, but she sensed no movement around her. The man was gone.

She called out to Brown and heard nothing but silence. She put one hand on the wall, half standing, followed it and kept calling. She found him lying by the fence and even in the dim light she saw the blood, glossy on his chest.

No. She did what she was trained to do. She dropped to Brown's side, saying his name, calling him back. She found his pulse with two fingers, faint as it was, her hand slick with her own blood. She bent to listen and heard him breathe, a thin sound that scared her more than anything else that night. And she kept talking, talking to him all the time, while she put pressure on the wound, and the sirens were already screaming in the distance, and she hoped to God there was an ambulance there and they could find them in the bushes.

Two patrolmen and a medic got to them in minutes. From a window someone had seen Harry Salinger in his uniform meeting the detectives. When she heard the shots, the woman called 911 and said a police officer was under fire; that got a rather snappy response.

'Are you shot?'

'No, I don't think so.'

'Can you walk?'

'He needs oxygen.'

'We know.'

The medic snapped a mask on Brown and tried to get Madison out and into the street but she wouldn't leave until they had strapped Brown to a stretcher and carried him to the ambulance.

By the time they came out there were two more patrol cars, lights blazing, and a crowd was gathering around them. Under the streetlights Madison looked at Brown and he looked dead.

'Is he going to be alright?'

'Get in the car. You'll see your partner in the hospital.'

'Is he breathing?'

'He's breathing. Now, get in the car.' The medics were fast and she knew they wouldn't stop for red lights. Her head was thumping and from the faces of the cops around her she knew she looked pretty bad herself. She turned to one of the two who arrived first – she couldn't remember his name, could hardly remember her own.

'Secure the scene and call for Sorensen from CSU, you understand? Sorensen.'

At that point she leant on the car because standing up was getting difficult, and when she steadied herself with her right hand the pain was so stunning she almost passed out.

Somehow she sat in the backseat of the patrol car and they took off after the ambulance.

'You okay back there?' the uniformed officer asked her, turning fast and leaving rubber on concrete.

'Yeah,' she said, and it was all she could do to prevent herself from throwing up, wrapped in a blanket and sinking into shock. 'Can you do something for me?'

'What do you need?' His eyes were in the rearview mirror.

'Get dispatch to call my boss, Lieutenant Fynn, Homicide. He ought to know what happened.'

'No problem.' For a short while he spoke into the radio. 'You guys got ambushed?'

Madison smelt the chloroform on her clothes.

'Something like that.'

Madison felt her holster and miraculously the Glock was there, automatically replaced, the safety latch on. She closed her eyes for a second and the next thing was the bright lights of Northwest Hospital's ER and someone calling out.

'What's your name?'

'Alice Madison. Where's my partner? He was brought in minutes before me.'

She was sitting sideways on a gurney. A doctor in green scrubs was pointing a tiny flashlight in her good eye, the right one, while a nurse was cleaning the cut on her left eyebrow. It was deep and stung like hell.

'Look up now. They are looking after him – don't worry.'

'All due respect but you don't tell me how he is and I'm gonna go find out myself.'

Big words for someone too dizzy to put her feet on the ground but she meant it and he knew it.

'Adam, please,' the doctor said.

The nurse left to go check. On the table next to them, Madison's X-rays. She had been given clean scrubs. Her clothes, her belt and weapon had been put in a plastic bag. It had been collected a few minutes earlier by a CSU officer who had dropped by to scrape under her nails for trace evidence. Things were moving fast.

The doctor stuck the X-rays on a viewer: Madison's head from both sides and her right arm.

'Your head's okay. It's going to feel bad for a while but that's just the chloroform and the knock you got. No permanent damage there.' He gave her a little smile and pointed. 'You have sprained your wrist and damaged the muscle that extends your elbow joint. Are you right-handed?'

'Yes.'

'Fine. Keep your splint on; no lifting of anything heavier than a cup of coffee. Your shoulder will be sore for a few days. Driving will be difficult and seriously painful and I don't recommend you try it. A couple of stitches on your eyebrow will do it. The scar will go with time.' The doctor always said that because patients always asked. Then again, it didn't look like Madison was the kind who'd ask.

'Bag of frozen peas,' he said. 'It'll help with the swelling.'

She nodded. The nurse came back. Madison turned her head too fast and a jab of pain reminded her to be more careful. 'They got him stable and they are taking him to the OR. Doctor Taylor is taking care of him.'

'Doctor Taylor is our top neurosurgeon; your partner is in good hands.'

'What do you mean *neurosurgeon*? Brown was hit in the chest.'

'There was a second GSW,' the doctor said, and gave her a moment to absorb it. 'One shot went clean through, somehow missed his lungs, and the other, Doctor Taylor is going to deal with now.'

Madison was glad that she was sitting down. She nodded.

'I'm going to give you a breather. A resident is going to be back for the stitches.'

They left her alone. Madison sipped water from a cup. She had been given a painkiller and Fynn was on his way. But all that mattered was that Brown was upstairs.

The room she was in was by the side of the triage area; it was small but private. Madison turned the lamp the doctor had used away from her face; it was still too much and she switched it off altogether. Voices rose and fell somewhere nearby and muted steps hurried past the closed door. Madison was grateful for those few moments alone and the soft glow from the X-ray viewer.

In that drab and functional room, where people had received news that would change their lives, Madison gathered herself and looked for the strength and the clarity to do what she knew she must. She didn't have much time and she only had one chance of getting it right. Lieutenant Fynn would be there soon and he would want to see her.

This was not how it was meant to happen. It should have been tomorrow, catching him early and alone in his office, Brown leading the way and her backing him up. Instead, Brown was fighting for his life in a dreary room with neon lights and she had to convince a sensible man, a good and steady cop, that black was white.

The resident, a young Chinese woman, put in two stitches. The cut fell straight across her left eyebrow.

'One inch south and it could have been much worse,' the doctor said. 'You were lucky.'

Madison took a sip from the cup. The resident got up to leave. 'You should look outside,' she said.

After the door swung shut, Madison put her feet on the ground. She took a few steps and it felt okay, weak but not so dizzy anymore. She got to the door and opened it a couple of inches. In the sudden brightness the waiting area was a sea of blue. Police officers in uniform, more than she could count, and plainclothes and detectives from her precinct and others, all there to make sure that two of their own were going to be alright.

Madison let the door fall back softly, took a couple of deep breaths. They were there for Brown, and in his fight she hoped he knew that.

Five minutes later Lieutenant Fynn knocked and came in. Madison was standing by the viewer and the overhead light was on. She saw him take in her injuries. He wore his dark coat over a roll-neck sweater, looked like he'd dressed in a hurry.

'Madison,' he said.

The splint on her wrist came down to the middle of her hand. He offered his left and they shook once.

'Sir.'

'You okay?'

'I'm fine. You know about Brown.'

'They got their top guy working on him. He has a sister in Vancouver – I called her. Spencer is at the scene; he's going to be the primary.'

'That's good,' she said. Madison knew nothing of Brown's family. Something else to feel ashamed about.

'Would you like to sit down?'

'No, sir. I'd rather stand.'

'Okay. Tell me what happened.'

'We are in the precinct, going over the paperwork from the airport. I get a call on my cellphone. A man says he is the son of Cameron's neighbor, a man I spoke to – I had given him my card. He says they have just called 911 because someone is trying to break into Cameron's house. He thought I might want to know. Anyway, Brown and I drive to Laurelhurst and when we get there there's a uniformed officer in the middle of the street in front of the house.'

'You got a good look at him?'

'Yes, at the beginning. When we were by the side of the house it was too dark.'

'Do you have enough for a sketch artist?'

'Yes. White male, at least six foot to six foot one, no distinguishing marks. He identified himself as Officer Mason from the North Precinct. Said his partner had driven around to the street parallel to Cameron's, in case someone was running out that way. Doors and windows were secured, he said. Then we hear the sound of glass breaking and we start running.'

Madison told him about Brown going first and the radio crackle

that held her back long enough for the man to take them on sep-
arately. About the cloth soaked in chloroform.

Fynn nodded. He'd had little opportunity in the previous weeks
to see what kind of detective Madison would make and this was
not how he had hoped to find out. Still, the scrubs had short
sleeves and there were reddish dark bruises from her shoulder to
her wrist. She must have given as good as she got.

'Sir, it has to be said that if I had managed to warn Sergeant
Brown earlier—'

'Let me put you straight on this, Madison. How did you mess
up your arm?'

'I fired my weapon into the wall; the attacker was holding the
arm behind my back.'

'You did that for Brown.'

Madison didn't reply.

'Right. You said there were three shots. Brown was already taking
cover when he was fired at. The first got him, the second got him,
but the third missed him completely. If you hadn't done what you
did, he'd have been hit three times in the heart and we'd be having
a whole different conversation.'

Madison didn't reply.

'Sir, the attacker used chloroform. That's the same trick he used
to sedate James Sinclair before murdering his family. And I'm willing
to bet Ballistics will match the casings from Laurelhurst to the
ones in Blueridge. It will be a .22, the same that was used on Annie
Sinclair and her children.'

'Cameron.'

Madison looked at Lieutenant Fynn. Black was white.

'No.'

'You don't think he ambushed you?'

Madison held his eyes.

'I'm listening,' he said.

In a few sentences Madison summarized the investigation of the Sinclair murders as they had it. She put it in the context of the LA deaths and the Sanders homicide. Evidence, motives, opportunities.

'Now,' she said, 'I want you to imagine that someone else broke into the Sinclairs' house last Saturday, someone who wanted us to believe that Cameron had slaughtered his friends and their children. And he had been close enough to him to obtain physical evidence, like the glass with prints on it, and the hairs he placed in the ligature knot *after* Sinclair had died. He untied him and tied him back up, which is consistent with the tissue recovered on the leather strip.'

Lieutenant Fynn's head went back an inch or two but he said nothing.

Madison proceeded to destroy their case, picking up every point that had damned Cameron and turning it around. Just knowing that the conversation was taking place would give Nathan Quinn enough to contest the arrest warrant.

When she was done, they stood quietly measuring each other.

'Are you out of your mind?' he asked her.

'That's what I thought at first, but no, I don't think so. I got there today, just by chance really. Brown saw it days ago.'

'You said he was "working both ends".'

'Yes. Fred Kamen at the Bureau can confirm that.'

'Whoa, there. I'm not talking to him or anybody else about this.'

'Sir—'

'Madison, you have just dumped the investigation in the trash. Brown was right not to come to me; you have nothing to support your theory—'

'Except that it is the only thing that makes sense.'

Fynn sat on the side of the gurney. He knew what kind of detective she'd make.

'I can't talk to Kamen and hold up the rightfulness of the warrant at the same time.' He reached for a stick of gum in his pocket.

Madison sat next to him. She was running on fumes, her legs shaking. She wanted to say more, about Brown, about the day they'd had. Instead, they sat for a bit and she let Fynn work things out in his mind.

It occurred to her then, she had no control over how he would decide to pursue the case. The only thing she could control was what she was going to do about it. Brown's Rolodex was on his desk; in it, under K, she would find Fred Kamen's direct number. It was a start.

'Are you in a lot of pain?' Fynn asked her.

'They gave me a couple of Tylenols. It's not too bad.'

'Right-handed?' He looked at her gun hand, half covered by the splint.

'Yes.' Madison didn't know how to say this without boasting so she just said it. 'But I've shot competitively with my left as well.'

Fynn smiled a little smile.

'He could have shot me too if he wanted to. I was right there.'

'But he didn't. Still, you're going to be off the streets for a while.'

'Sir—'

'Let me finish. This is what's going to happen. I'm going to take over the Sinclair investigation from Brown, who's one stubborn piece of work, and I'm gonna tell him in person tomorrow. Spencer is on Laurelhurst – he's probably on his way here now. Kelly stays on Sanders.'

'What about me?'

'You're out. I cannot put you back on rotation until you can at least half pass a fitness test. You cannot handle a weapon, you cannot even type a report.'

Madison opened her mouth to speak.

'You're going to be flying under the radar,' he continued. 'Brown started something and, as much as I wish I could dismiss it, I can't.

You have nothing – you have less than nothing – because you're not going to tell anybody what you're doing.'

Madison nodded.

'You're just going to be clearing up your notes on the case, make a few calls, maybe talk to a few people. Can you do that?'

'Yes, sir.'

'You understand what I'm telling you.'

'Yes, sir.'

'Tell me you understand.'

'I understand.'

'The next time you come to me *on the record*, you are going to give me some honest-to-God proof, 'cause I'm going to keep looking for Cameron and if I find him, I'm going to have to take him. And the son of a bitch won't come easy.'

'I understand.'

'Good.'

'Thank you, sir.'

Lieutenant Fynn shook his head. 'There's people outside who want to show their support. Are you ready for it?'

They came out of the room together and there was an instant murmur from the crowd assembled. Many of the officers Madison knew, many she didn't. They walked through, Fynn first, edging toward the lifts to the second floor. Everybody had something to say or a nod or a pat on the back. Madison just wanted to get the hell out. Whatever anybody else might think, they were cheering the biggest mistake of her career.

Brown was still in surgery. Nobody could tell them anything except to take a seat and wait. They found a sofa and chairs, a small corner made comfortable with a coffee table and magazines. Fynn sank into a chair and Madison perched on the edge, her eyes following every doctor and nurse that walked past.

It was after 2 a.m. when Spencer and Dunne joined them. They had dirt on their shoes, and their ties in their jacket pockets.

'Hey,' Spencer said to Madison, his voice quiet in the wide room. 'You kicked his ass. The lab guys are picking up all sorts of evidence from the scene. Any news yet?'

'Not yet.'

'We need to do it, the sooner the better.'

'Let's do it now.'

'Sure?'

'I'm fine.'

'Okay.'

Madison told them what she could, Fynn watching in silence. Spencer and Dunne left after 3 a.m.; there was still no news. The corridors were pretty much deserted. Madison sat back in her chair, counting the square gray ceiling tiles. She must have dozed off for a moment because she woke up with a start. A doctor was padding toward them and the wall clock said 5.55 a.m. They stood up.

Doctor Taylor turned out to be a woman in her fifties with cropped salt-and-pepper hair and small blue eyes.

'How is he?'

'Your partner is in the recovery room right now.'

'That's good.'

'He is a very resilient man and, technically, the surgery was a success. We repaired most of the damage to the chest and, by some kind of miracle, even with the swelling due to the trauma, the bullet had not penetrated the outer layer of the brain. But his heart stopped beating during the operation. He was down for a little while.' She let them take it in. 'We have revived him and he is on a respirator to help him breathe, but it's too early to say anything except for wait and see.'

'When is he going to wake up?' Madison asked her.

'We don't know. We're going to have to take it an hour at a time.' She looked at Madison, the cut on her brow a vivid red against her ashen face. 'You should go home and get some rest. I'll have a nurse call you if there's any news.' She left.

'I'm going to stay here until Brown's sister arrives,' Fynn said. 'Someone is going to drive you home.' He made a call on his cellphone and a couple of uniformed officers from their precinct appeared.

'I'll call you in the morning.'

Madison didn't move.

'Go,' he said.

Six-thirty a.m., in the beam of the headlights snowflakes swim across the road. Behind them, Three Oaks is still asleep. Madison sat in the passenger seat of the blue-and-white, one of the two officers followed in her car.

She had asked them to go via the precinct so that she could pick up a few things. In the corridors nobody stopped her; hardly anybody was there anyway.

She opened the door to their room. Everything as they had left it seven hours earlier, the takeaway cartons still on their desks.

Her rucksack was hanging on the back of the chair. She grabbed it and quickly unzipped the main section. Her papers were in stacks everywhere: she reached for the library notes and the newspaper cuttings and stuffed them in together with a notepad. Cameron's photograph from the Sinclair boy's birthday party was tacked to the wall – she took that too.

The black Rolodex sat next to the telephone on his desk. Kamen's number. Madison, the rucksack hanging from her good arm, flipped through it, couldn't find the card and bent down. The rucksack fell on the ground, hands shaking now and her sight suddenly blurred.

She grabbed the Rolodex, shoved it hard into the bag and wiped her eyes with the back of her hand.

One last look around and Madison left, turning the light off as she closed the door.

It was the last Saturday before Christmas.

They turned into Madison's drive and a patrol car was parked by the front door. Officer Giordano, who had been the first at the Sinclair crime scene, climbed out.

'The boss said you don't want a car sitting by. I just wanted to let you know we'll be looking in from time to time, should you need anything.' They waited until Madison was inside and then left, turning slowly into the slippery road.

Madison dropped the rucksack by the door. She kicked off her shoes and padded into the kitchen. She poured herself a glass of orange juice and downed two painkillers. She would call Kamen in a couple of hours.

She didn't expect visitors. The man could have shot her there and then but hadn't. The reason, she thought, would probably reveal itself soon enough, like every other dark and twisted thing.

Looking for the comfort of the ordinary, Madison went to the safe under her bed and took out her off-duty piece. With one hand, she cleaned it, oiled it and dry-fired it a few times. The weight felt odd in her left hand, the arm twitching with tiredness. She would need to go to the range.

On the sofa, sitting up with her comforter around her and her eyes wide open, Madison waited to fall asleep.

Chapter 27

Nathan Quinn's house in the Seward Park neighborhood of Seattle has been decorated with much care by its owner, who hardly spends any time in it and, in the last week, has been all but blind to the views of Mercer Island and Lake Washington.

In his study, on the mahogany table, sealed inside clear plastic envelopes, the anonymous notes. Quinn expected a third note within the next 48 hours and his guts told him it wouldn't be a request for money.

This wasn't blackmail: the first note had been delivered on Monday morning *before* the murders were public knowledge, *before* the case had come to rest at John Cameron's feet. For reasons known only to himself the killer had chosen to talk to him, and Quinn believed that once you know what someone wants, the thing they need above all else, anybody can be got to. Anybody can be dealt with.

The news on KIRO said that it was 9 a.m. Quinn checked his watch automatically – he'd been up for two hours, mostly talking on the phone with Tod Hollis. The private investigator had little to report since their last call the previous evening. The morning call was about the ambush on the detectives and what he had managed to gather from his police contacts.

Quinn had listened while Hollis told him about Detectives Brown and Madison. Footage of Northwest Hospital had been on each news cycle and they even had a flash of Madison being driven away in a blue-and-white, her face invisible through the glass. The same brand of evil that had visited his life had quite probably crossed theirs.

He sat at the wide kitchen table and continued reading the *Los Angeles Times*, a well-informed piece on the murder of a local drug dealer and his two bodyguards. Quinn's eyes scanned the story for what he knew he would find and there it was, in the last paragraph – the name of his most reclusive client.

The telephone rang and he picked up the receiver.

'Hello.'

'Is this Nathan Quinn?'

An unknown voice.

'Yes. Who is this?'

'You'll have my name when I give it to you.'

Quinn gently replaced the receiver in its cradle. He waited. Five seconds later the telephone rang again.

'What the hell do you think you're doing?'

'Who is this?'

A long silence, traffic in the distant background. A payphone, Quinn thought; not on a street but nearby – in a shop, maybe.

'My name's not important.' The attitude was gone. 'You have a reward out for information about those murders.' It was a statement.

'This is not the right number to call. I can give you the right number.'

'I'm not going through the police—'

'They are screening the calls and doing the checks.'

'They also have a warrant out for your client's arrest, and what *I* have they wouldn't want, believe me.'

'What do you have?'

'Something that would help the case for the defense.'

'I'm listening.'

'We should meet. It's not something I want to talk about on the phone.'

'You might want to give me something now or we might not meet at all.'

'Okay, what if I can prove to you that the person who killed the family had killed before? What if I could tell you where and when?'

'That would be worth a conversation.'

'I want two things from you: first, your guarantee that my name will never be made known. Second, the minute the cops drop the charges on your guy, that's cash in my hands. Are we clear?'

'Crystal.'

'Pier 52, the ferry to Bainbridge Island, today at 3 p.m. Walk on, don't bring your car. Be on the upper deck. I'll find you.'

Quinn was about to confirm the instructions but the line had gone dead.

Cameron's new beeper number was on the tips of his fingers. His eyes fell on the *LA Times* and Quinn replaced the receiver. He had no idea where Cameron was anymore; he only knew for certain where he'd been.

In downtown Seattle, Billy Rain, standing next to a payphone, shivered in the pale morning.

Nathan Quinn paced around in the house for a few hours, found there was nothing that would hold his attention for more than fifteen seconds and went to the office. He parked his car in the underground garage and took the elevator to the ninth floor. When he came out he gave a brief wave to the security guard on the first floor who had picked up his movements on the video cameras.

The offices were deserted. He deactivated the alarm and let himself in, turned the lights on and headed for his office.

Carl Doyle had been doing a great job of keeping everything running smoothly in the past week. He had left a small stack of files on his desk for Quinn to look at. There was a world where those files mattered, and court dates, and judges' decisions. Quinn sat down and flipped open the first one.

He worked his way through the pile, glad for the distraction but gladder still when it was time to go. He left the car in the garage and walked down Pike Street, then turned on Second Avenue and left on Seneca to the waterfront.

It was too cold to snow, the sky and the water the same shade of pewter.

Nathan Quinn walked onto the ferry, unarmed and alone, knowing full well that he had probably already been clocked and was being followed. Fine with him – he hoped the man he was to meet knew what he was getting himself into.

He looked around: the ferry was vast, one of those that carry a couple of hundred cars and at least a couple of thousand passengers. Today, it was quiet. The journey to Bainbridge Island would take 35 minutes. By the time it started to move off the pier, Quinn had bought himself a tea and found an empty bench on the upper deck, by a window.

The air was warm with the scent of reheated food. There was an old couple a few benches down, a woman alone twenty feet to his left and a family of four, small children running around. Quinn was sitting with his back to the wall; he sipped his tea and missed nothing.

He saw the tall man approach and read him like he would a prospective juror in a trial. Late thirties, maybe early forties, there were fine lines around the eyes. He was wearing a red Gore-Tex jacket over jeans and work boots. Hair short, clean-shaven. The hands were too rough for a white-collar job but there was a kind of grace about the man. He slid onto the bench across from Quinn, a table between them.

'Billy Rain,' he said.

'Nathan Quinn.'

'Yes.'

'Let's get this done.'

'Okay.'

Rain had baby-blue eyes; he looked out of the window. His fingers drummed lightly on the table. His hands, Quinn noted, were scrupulously clean.

'We are clear my name is going to stay out of it.'

'No problem.'

'And the other thing.'

'Mr. Rain, I wish nothing more than for you to be right about this.'

'I know I'm right. Three and a half years ago. Upstate.'

'McCoy.'

'I was doing three to five in the Bones.'

The Bones was what everybody called the McCoy State Prison. It probably started from some *Star Trek* fan enjoying a stretch of hard time but nobody knew for sure.

'I saw something that was very ...' – he hesitated – 'similar to what happened to the family.' Billy Rain's eyes moved quickly beyond Quinn's shoulders.

'A guy got killed in the laundry. The man who did it left him tied up, hands at the front, blindfolded. And he drew ...' – Billy Rain made the sign of a cross on his brow – 'in blood.'

Nathan Quinn nodded. A prison killing.

'You were a witness.'

'I saw it. I was no more than ten feet away.'

Quinn could see where this was going. 'But you didn't tell anybody.'

Rain gave him a look. 'Have you ever done time? Ever spent any time around cons *on the inside*?'

'No.'

'Then we'll get back to your question when you have.'

'What happened after they found the body?'

'It ended up on the tab of a con called Edward Morgan Rabineau. He was doing life for two counts already. They pinned it on him – I don't know what evidence they had. I didn't see anything when I – when I walked past the body. Anyway. Thing is, Ted Rabineau is still inside. And my guess is, always will be.'

Billy Rain wished Quinn would speak; there was something unnerving in the man's silence.

'Let's take a walk,' Quinn said and stood up. The rest of the conversation he'd rather have outside.

They turned up their collars and leant on the railing, Bainbridge Island was approaching fast.

'Tell me as much as you remember about it,' he told Billy Rain, and Billy did.

It had been quick and to the point, no accident there. The man had come ready with a blindfold and a ligature for the man's hands. That in itself was unusual: in prison, if you're going to take someone down you put a shiv between his shoulder blades or in the soft tissue under the sternum. Then you walk away.

'Who was the victim?'

'An arsonist called George Pathune, young guy. Had been inside maybe three months.'

'The man you saw with him was Ted Rabineau?'

Billy Rain looked at the water. Time and time again in his mind he had tried to see the face of the man. It had been seconds, and fear had pretty much wiped out the details.

'I don't know,' he said. 'If my life depended on it, I still wouldn't know. Maybe Rabineau was taller and heavier. Anyway, it's not like he's the kind of guy you would normally look at, you know what I mean? I'm not sure I'd recognize him today.'

'Sure you would.'

'Whatever.'

'Why would Rabineau want the guy dead?'

'I have no idea.'

'The man you saw was *not* Rabineau?'

'I don't know. I know what the body looked like after he was done with it. If your client didn't do it and Rabineau didn't do it, somebody else did.'

John Cameron had never seen the inside of a state prison and Edward Morgan Rabineau had not seen the outside of one for many years. There was a trail there, at the very least a glimpse of one.

'Why didn't you take this to the police?'

'They'd have lost the call. They want your man so bad they can taste it. I'm on parole anyway; I don't see them working hard on something I give them.'

'I see. What were you in for?'

Billy Rain shrugged.

'Which time?'

They were almost docking.

'You should know,' Billy Rain said, 'I've written an affidavit and my attorney will receive it on Monday. Anything happens to me now, or you try to get out of our financial agreement, and he'll deal with it.'

'You should know,' Quinn replied, 'that I believe what you told me is the truth, but if I ever found out you lied to me for money or held back anything that might have helped, I'll rip your life apart.'

Billy Rain nodded. 'As long as we know where we stand.'

'Absolutely.'

Billy Rain was glad to get off the ferry – his hands were shaking. Nathan Quinn watched the waves slapping against the hull. *Now the summer's in its prime with the flowers sweetly bloomin'*.

Nathan Quinn went back inside, bought another tea and sat on the same bench. A prison killing. It made sense: the details would have never made the papers. No one would have made the connections between that and the slaying of a family in a wealthy suburb.

The connections. Blindfolds and leather strips and blood on the pillows. Quinn drank the tea and wished he'd poured a measure of bourbon in it – a double measure.

Tod Hollis would work the prison angle: they needed as much as possible about George Pathune's murder. The report of the investigation must still be in the prison's records.

Quinn dialed Hollis's number and told him about Billy Rain.

'I'm telling you right now they'd rather cut off less useful parts of their own bodies than show us the records.'

'I know, but we need to get there. What chances have we got?'

'There's a guy I can talk to, informally. He owes me one. Billy Rain, I'm going to look up his sheet. You think he was being straight?'

'I think that whatever he saw scared him enough that he wouldn't have picked up the phone if money was not involved.'

'You think someone set up Rabineau.'

'Yes.'

'The same person that set up Cameron.'

For a beat all that Hollis could hear was the open line and a voice on the ferry's PA system.

'Yes,' Quinn said.

'Are you going to tell him about this?'

'Tod—'

'I read the papers, that's all I'm saying.'

'I understand. You'll let me know when you know, right?'

'Yes.'

They hung up.

There was a world of things Nathan Quinn and John Cameron had never talked about and would never talk about. Those were the boundaries that had been set a very long time ago. If in the last few years Quinn had truly believed things had changed and the rules had become redundant, this week three men in LA and one in Seattle could say otherwise. It was time to throw away the book. He dialed a number on his cellphone, punched in a code and hung up. Two minutes later, it rang.

'We need to talk,' he said.

It was after sunset by the time Quinn got home. He picked up his car at the office and drove back. He would forget for hours at a time and then, out of the blue, he'd remember that Jimmy was dead, and Annie and John and David. All dead now. Nothing more would ever happen for them. It was a kick in the stomach and, in those moments, Nathan Quinn understood about rage and the God of the Old Testament. But that was not where he lived his life. His home was in a privileged neighborhood and his work was done amongst rules, bound by law and protected by it, yet still they were gone and no judge's ruling could bring them back.

He put the key in the door and walked in, punched in the alarm code in the near-darkness and stepped into the kitchen. He put the bag of groceries on the table, took from it a bottle of Johnnie Walker Black Label and twisted the cap.

'Want to keep me company?' he said.

'Thank you,' John Cameron replied.

The blinds were drawn and the pool of light on the table was the only brightness in the room. John Cameron sat on the leather sofa in the corner. When Quinn took out two glasses from a cabinet, he stood up and approached his friend. He wore a black roll-neck over dark brown trousers, his hair was back to his natural color and the goatee was gone.

Quinn poured two generous measures. Cameron took one of the glasses and, under the light, the scars on his hand glistened. Quinn didn't usually notice them. Tonight though, he saw them pale against his skin.

Quinn's home had always been one of the few places in the world where Cameron would feel completely at ease. They sat down at the table because that was where they had always come together, and their silence was comfortable.

'How was your day?' Cameron said, taking a sip.

Quinn smiled. Above the rim of the glass, Cameron's eyes were a couple of shades darker than amber.

The last time they had sat at the table, Quinn had told him their friends had been murdered. They raised their glasses and drained them. Cameron poured another round.

'I have a witness to a homicide with very strong similarities,' Quinn said.

Cameron nodded slowly.

'McCoy State Prison. Three and a half years ago. They put it on a lifer who's still inside but the witness has doubts.'

'Ex-con?'

'Yes. He never reported it.'

'What's his name?'

'Billy Rain.'

'Billy Rain.'

'You two ever met?'

'No. I know of him.'

'He read about the reward and came forward. He thought,

correctly, that I might act with more urgency than the police on this matter.'

'He's not lying?'

'I don't think so.'

'Okay.'

'Hollis is going to follow it up.'

'Hollis?'

'We'll do what we have to.'

A beat between them.

'Tell me about the killing.'

Quinn told him everything. Cameron listened. Neither touched their drink.

'He was in jail one hour away from here,' Cameron said when Quinn was done.

'The detectives must have put it through VICAP, and that's why they came up empty. A homicide inside a jail, where they are already holding the culprit, is not going to make it into the database. We are going to narrow the parameters by what kind of crime our man would have been doing time for, the age we think he is, when he was paroled. We will find him.'

'I would like to talk to Hollis.'

'I don't think so.'

'Nathan—'

'We're going to take it to the judge and get them to drop the case against you. That is my priority.'

'I understand. Do you know why he went after Jimmy?'

Quinn didn't reply.

'To get my attention.' Cameron paused. 'Do you know why he went after the detectives?'

Quinn didn't reply.

'To give them a murder weapon. As we speak, I am pretty sure Ballistics is matching the casings to the ones they found in

Jimmy's house. And, just like that, I have shot one cop, maybe even fatally, and assaulted another. You can take *that* to the judge.' Cameron took a sip. 'I think you should get out of town for a while.'

'No.'

'This man I want to meet so badly will come after you. We don't know what's going to happen when the thirteen days run out.'

'He hasn't told me what he wants yet. He will finish what he started with the notes.'

'May I see them?'

Quinn got them, placed them on the table between them.

Cameron did not touch the plastic. He followed the contours of the paper and the typewritten letters, one by one. His eyes held them whole. He spoke quietly, looking at the cards.

'I think you should leave town for a while,' he repeated.

'I'm not in any danger.'

'Jimmy wasn't.'

'No.'

'He wants you *here*, Nathan. He wants you where he can see you.'

'I'll take my chances.'

'That's not good enough.'

'It'll have to do.'

Cameron knew better than to try and change his mind. He stood up. 'You want something to eat?'

When it was hot enough, Cameron put two steaks on a heavy pan, one and a half minutes on each side, a streak of red in the middle.

'Who's taken over the case?' he asked Quinn.

'Mike Fynn, Homicide. He's the shift commander of the two who were hit.'

'You know him?'

'No. I only dealt with the detectives.'

'I saw the woman – you know, at Jimmy's.'

'Detective Madison. When?'

'Tuesday night late. I went by the house.'

Quinn put down his knife and fork. 'You *went by the house*? When every officer in Washington State has got your picture tacked on their dash?'

'Yes, and you would have done the same.'

'You were inside the house?'

'Yes.'

Quinn had seen the crime-scene photographs and the devastation contained within the glossy white borders.

'What was she doing?'

'She was watching their home videos.'

'Why?'

'She was looking for pictures.'

'Pictures of you?'

'Yes.'

'Did she find any?'

'Nothing useful.'

'Tuesday night late,' Quinn said. 'Where were you on Tuesday?'

Cameron wiped his mouth with the white linen napkin.

'I was in LA'

'I know.'

'What do you want to know?'

'Is there anything I need to know?'

'I had some good sushi and the weather was lovely.'

'What did you do in LA?'

'Don't do this to yourself.'

'What did you do?'

'It's not polite to talk about business at the dinner table. My mother was positive about that.'

'What did you do?'

'I killed three men. The bodyguards were in the garden, watching a soap on one of those tiny portables. The dealer was in the house – he didn't have much to say for himself except that he'd shake the hand of the man who put any friend of mine under the ground. I could argue self-defense but, when it comes down to it, they just needed killing.'

Quinn held his gaze. 'What about Erroll Sanders?'

'Erroll. Erroll liked black Formica tables and white shag carpets. Erroll was a pre-emptive strike, in case he'd developed any misguided sense of loyalty to his boss. I'm sure the world is a darker place now they are not in it anymore.'

Cameron folded the napkin and put it on the table. He stood up.

'Check the windows and set the alarm. It was good to see you, as always, and thank you for dinner.'

John Cameron walked out of the front door and the lock clicked shut behind him. After a few minutes, Nathan Quinn heard a distant car start and drive off. It might have been Cameron's, it might not.

The first day of law school they teach you that you never, ever, question your client about guilt and innocence. It would affect your defense and you might find yourself suborning perjury. Quinn hoped his client would still be alive come the end of the month; perjury was the least of his concerns.

He took the plates to the sink and ran cold water on the bloody juices.

'Nathan?'

Some twenty years earlier, Nathan Quinn's office in the King County Prosecuting Attorney's had been tiny: files were stacked on his desk and books crammed on the shelves. He was a deputy prosecutor in the Criminal Division and, in spite of appearances, there was a kind of order in the depth of paperwork covering every surface. He had never lost anything – not a file, not a case.

He looked up. John Cameron, eighteen years old, stood by the door. Quinn checked his watch; he had no idea where the morning had gone.

He stood up and reached for the jacket on the back of his chair. 'I'm starving. Let's go.'

Every couple of weeks they would have lunch together. Jack would come over to the courthouse and they would grab a bite nearby. In the past two months the boy's moods had darkened. Quinn knew that to ask a direct question would have been pointless. If he wanted to talk about something he would do so.

They slipped into the corner booth of a deli on Second Avenue, an old-fashioned establishment that had never heard of the ongoing battle against cholesterol. They ordered salt beef sandwiches.

'How's classes?' Quinn asked.

Jack rolled his eyes. He had started at the University of Washington in the Fall and it had not been an immediate success.

'I've got the tickets,' he said and clinked the ice cubes in his glass.

'You're kidding.'

'Courtside. Dad's guy got them somehow.'

'Jack!'

'I know.' They had been looking forward to the ball game for weeks, unsure if they'd make it.

They devoted themselves for a moment to the plates that had been placed in front of them. Quinn looked like he hadn't slept much and had seen little daylight recently. Cameron saw everything, his eyes sweeping the restaurant.

'Are you still on the homicide?' he asked Quinn.

Quinn looked up.

'Yeah.'

They were about to go to trial against a 21-year-old woman who had shot her boyfriend. She had suffered years of abuse from her parents, left home, fell in with the poorest excuse for a human being and one night, after watching the news together, she had taken his revolver from the drawer and put three bullets in his chest. The neighbors hadn't heard any noises beforehand and she had admitted they had not fought that evening; the bruises on her arms were turning yellow and she said she had just had enough.

The defense attorney hired by a charity for the protection of abused women had tried to plead it down to manslaughter but, given that her alleged attacker was asleep at the time she shot him, that hadn't really made a dent in the prosecution's case.

'Starting in a couple of weeks,' Quinn said.

'Tough case?'

'Yes and no. She shot the guy – nobody questions that. The defense is going to argue that she was provoked by years of abuse; we are going to argue that it wasn't self-defense and she could have walked right out.'

'But she didn't.'

'She shot him while he was asleep.'

'What's going to happen to her?'

Nathan Quinn wiped his hands on the paper napkin. It wasn't the first time he had ever had this kind of conversation with Jack, about fairness and justice and, from time to time, about the absence of either.

'She is going to do some hard time.'

'Are you going to ask for the death sentence?'

'No. There are circumstances.'

Around them, the lunchtime clatter continued. Somebody dropped a tray of glasses and others whooped and clapped. Cameron seemed oblivious to all of it.

'Under which circumstances would you ask for the death sentence?' Cameron took a bite of his sandwich.

'Why the sudden interest?'

The boy shrugged but his level gaze stayed on Quinn.

'Well, if you have a homicide with malice, where there was a clear intent to kill or cause great bodily harm. With premeditation, when the person had thought about it beforehand. Or during a dangerous felony, like robbery or arson.'

Or *kidnap*. The word hung for a moment between them, unsaid.

'What if you didn't have enough to convict?'

'What are we talking about here?'

'What if you didn't even have enough on the woman to charge her, but you knew she'd done it?'

'Then you go back to the drawing board and you find the evidence you need.'

'Still, sometimes you don't.'

'Sometimes you don't.'

'What would you have done then?'

'In this case?'

'Yes.'

Cameron picked up his glass. Quinn wasn't sure what they were talking about exactly.

'I don't know,' he said, and he meant it. 'Sometimes, however hard you work the case, it just doesn't happen.'

'What about eyewitness testimony?'

'In theory?'

'In theory.'

'Without evidence?'

'Yes.'

'It would be very difficult. A good defense attorney would tear the witness apart.'

Cameron nodded.

'But we're the good guys; we have the white hats and we put away the guys with the black hats. That's pretty much my job description. You read up about this in the papers?'

'Yes.'

'If you're interested in seeing how things work you could come in sometime.'

Cameron smiled a little. 'Thank you. It's just that in the papers it looked like there were some reasonable grounds for her to do what she did.'

'*Reasonable grounds?* That is very well put but, here's the thing, she could have walked out. She could have called any of many numbers for the victims of domestic abuse. She didn't have to kill him.'

'Maybe she thought she had to.'

'I think it is a tragedy what happened to her in her life, and it is a tragedy that the man is dead. But no, one doesn't cancel the other.'

'You believe in that, don't you?'

Quinn finished his drink. He had never talked to Jack like he was a kid, even when he was one. 'What are we talking about here?'

'What do you call it? A *justifiable homicide*?'

'That's different.'

'Why?'

'In legal terms, a court-ordered execution is a "justifiable homicide". Everything else is murder.'

'A "court-ordered" execution.'

'Yes.'

Cameron smiled.

'What brought this on?' Quinn asked.

'I don't know.'

'Sure you do.'

'I don't know.' Cameron shrugged.

'Okay.'

As they left the deli Cameron turned up the collar on his sheepskin coat. The rain was thin at sea level but it would be snow higher up, a few inches deep over the hard ground.

Less than 48 hours later, Nathan Quinn would bail him out of a police lock-up.

Chapter 28

Alice Madison woke up on the sofa. Daylight said it was sometime in the middle of the morning. For a couple of seconds everything was fine, then she remembered.

The telephone was on the table. She extended a leg from under the comforter and tried to straighten up. Every muscle in her body hurt. She reached for the phone and pulled it toward her, still sitting down and a little woozy with the movement. She dialed the hospital and was transferred to Dr Taylor. There was no news: they had moved Brown to the Intensive Care Unit as expected but he was still on a respirator. His sister was with him, the doctor said. No one was allowed to visit aside from family, she said finally – no exceptions. *Got the message*, Madison thought.

She walked to the kitchen slowly, and found a bottle of water in the fridge. She twisted off the plastic top and drank half where she was standing. She could still smell the hospital in her hair and clothes. After she put on the coffee, she unhooked the clasps on the splint and spent fifteen minutes under a hot shower, washing her hair and keeping the soap off the stitches.

When she came out, she dried herself with a towel and stood naked in front of the full-length mirror in her bedroom closet. She looked at the bruises on her arms and back. No big deal: she could already feel the benefit of the heat on her skin.

She tested her right arm: the elbow was painful, no way around that one, but at least it wasn't broken. The cut? Well, that had no practical downside, it was just an annoyance.

She pulled on jeans and a navy hooded top and padded barefoot back to the kitchen. She poured herself a mug: it wasn't espresso, but it did the job. From the icebox Madison dug out the remains of a bag of frozen peas, molded it to her wrist and tied a dishcloth around it.

She folded the comforter and put it back in the bedroom. She took her rucksack and put it on the dining table, which was to be her new office.

She arranged all the notes and papers in separate piles. Brown's Rolodex went in the corner.

Madison sat down at the long side of the table and looked over her small domain. She had been in a conversation with Brown ever since they had walked into the Sinclair crime scene and now it was done. She could think about him with tubes sticking out of his chest or she could hunt down the man who'd shot him. She couldn't do both.

She dialed Spencer's cell. He picked up straightaway.

'It's Madison.'

'How are you doing?'

'I'm okay. Any news?'

'Hold on.'

It sounded like he was indoors somewhere: he had put his hand over the mouthpiece and said something to somebody else.

'We're at the lab,' he continued. 'There was a pane of glass rigged at the back of the yard. They haven't put the thing back together yet but he could get the glass to shatter when the time was right.'

'That's what we heard when we got there.'

'Exactly. There were fibers from the uniform on your clothing and the bushes by the fence. But nothing definite yet – they've only had a few hours to work the crime scene.'

'Alright.'

'There's something else. We got the casings checked first.'

Madison knew what his next words would be.

'They match the casings in Blueridge: it was the same gun that shot the Sinclairs.'

There was a beat of silence and Madison realized that she was expected to say something.

'Damn,' she said, and her voice sounded odd even to her. Face to face, Spencer would have known but a bad connection hides many sins.

'You tussled with John Cameron, Detective,' he said.

'Yeah, well, that's definitely something worth thinking about.'

'You okay?'

'Just a little off, you know.' Suddenly she wanted out of the conversation fast. The next word out of her mouth would have to be a lie.

'I'll call you later. Just relax and take care of yourself.'

'Sure thing.'

Madison hung up. This was not going to work. She couldn't not tell Spencer. He was working the shooting, he had the right to know.

Lieutenant Fynn picked up on the second ring.

'Sir, it's Madison. I've just spoken with Spencer. They've already matched the casings. I have to tell him.'

'Madison, how are you?'

'Fine, sir. But Spencer ought to know.'

'You called the hospital yet?'

'Yes. I'll go over later.'

'They only let the family in.'

'I know. Sir—'

'Madison, has anything changed between last night and today?'

'No. But we can't let Spencer investigate without all the facts. He thinks that Cameron shot Brown and I don't believe that's true.'

'Have the facts changed since last night? Can you give me anything else except for a guess inside a hunch wrapped in a leap of faith?'

'No.'

'Then let Spencer work with the facts he does have.'

There was a long silence on the line. The papers on the table and all her notes were puny ammunition and the 3 a.m. strength of her logic had faded.

'Okay, but you will let *me* work this angle, right?'

'You're on medical leave, Detective. What you do with your time is up to you.'

'Alright.'

'Just, whatever it is you're going to do, do it fast.'

'Yessir.'

Well, thanks so very damn much. She wouldn't tell Spencer, not yet. Still, she might have to at some point soon, and if Fynn was going to boot her back to Traffic, she was not in the mood to care, not today.

The telephone rang and her 'hello' was maybe a touch crisper than normal.

'Alice?'

Rachel's voice. Sanity in a world going to hell.

'Hey—'

'Oh, sweetheart, I heard it on the news and I wanted to call but didn't want to wake you. And I thought maybe I should just come over and check on you with the spare set of keys. Except the last thing you want is somebody coming in while you're asleep.'

'It's just a couple of bruises, I swear.'

'How is your partner?'

'Not good.'

'I'm so sorry. Do you want me to come over?'

'I'm kind of in the middle of something and I'm going to the hospital later. You really don't have to worry.'

'You're working?'

'Just looking over some papers.'

Rachel was her friend, but she had also years of experience in dealing with victims of trauma and post-traumatic stress disorder issues at clinical level.

'How was it?'

'Quick – it was very quick. It started and it was over.'

'You'll talk to me if you want to, right?'

'Yes.'

'You should rest. Why don't you come over for a bite later?'

'Thank you, I will.'

'Listen, Tommy overheard us and he understood you were in a traffic accident like his Uncle Robert. I'm going to let him believe that.'

'Fine with me.'

'Babe, take care of yourself today.'

'Don't worry.'

'Take a taxi to the hospital. No driving.'

'Don't worry.'

Her coffee had gone cold and when Madison went in the kitchen for a refill she realized exactly how hungry she was. The fridge looked almost as desolate as the one in the precinct, minus the health hazards. She found three eggs within best-by dates and scrambled them in a pan. She tried to move the pan with her right hand and *that* really did not work, the arm refusing to carry the weight. She managed somehow, poured them on a plate and carried the food to the table with a fresh coffee and a bagel.

It was late enough in Virginia to call Fred Kamen on his home number, if she could find it. Madison looked again under 'K' in Brown's Rolodex – it wasn't there. Not surprisingly, it wasn't under 'F' either.

Let's start at the beginning. She started flipping the cards and realized that, even though the first was an 'A', the second was an 'F' and the third a 'T'. It was Brown's most used numbers. Kamen's was the fifth card.

Madison sat at the table, looking at the number in Brown's neat writing, finishing her eggs. She'd better have something else to say to him aside from 'Good morning', because right now he was the only person she could talk to about the whole damn business.

She had had less than 24 hours to get her bearings – it wasn't much but it would have to do. In her mind, she ran through each day starting from Monday: what they did, what they found out, who they'd talked to.

She dialed Kamen's home number. It rang an impossibly long time, then a soft click and Madison prepared herself to leave a message.

'Hello?' It was a man's voice.

'Hello. My name is Alice Madison. I'm a detective with Seattle Homicide. May I speak with Fred Kamen?'

A beat of silence.

'I know who you are. Stay on the line – I'm going to pick up in my study.'

Another click. Thirty seconds later the voice came back. It was more Boston academic than East Coast FBI and deeper than Madison remembered from the college lectures.

'I saw it on the news. How is he?'

'Not good. They moved him to the ICU after the procedure but he's still on a respirator and they don't say much. We're going to have to wait till he wakes up to see . . . we're just going to have to wait.'

'How are you holding up?'

'I'm okay. Sir, I'm calling because before we were ambushed, Brown and I had a conversation, and the subject of the conversation was the man who set up John Cameron for the Sinclairs' murders.'

'I see.'

'Now, I do believe that the man who shot Brown is also the Sinclairs' killer and I need to know everything that passed between you on this point.'

'You told Lieutenant Fynn?'

'Yes. I can keep looking into it. Technically I'm on medical leave, but he is still pursuing the Cameron angle and he can't dismiss the evidence without solid proof.'

'That's why Brown was reluctant to approach him a few days ago.'

'Brown told me about the trail the killer left. He said that as much as it leads to Cameron we can walk it backwards and it'll lead us to him.'

'Yes. The final objective of his work is the destruction of his target in every possible way. However, the manner in which he achieves that has more to do with his own compulsions and circumstances.'

'We're getting the list of Academy rejects.'

'Good. Something else: it is important that you start seeing Cameron as a victim. You have to consider how he was chosen, how the subject knew where he would be vulnerable, how he used the evidence against him. In any crime you have to work out how the victim was picked from the crowd. This is an unusual situation but the same rule applies.'

'It's going to be a change of perspective.'

'I know.'

'This man, he's thorough – he must have been planning this for months. He didn't hesitate to attack two police officers. I'm thinking he must have done something like this before. You just don't get to this level of – I was about to say "competence" – without honing your skills somehow.'

'I agree. I wouldn't be surprised if he had worked his way up to Cameron.'

'The man who attacked us, he was between thirty-five and forty, maybe early forties. He was very calm, in control; there was nothing out of place when we met him on the street. He was just waiting for us, cool as he could be.'

There was a small pause. 'Did you take his call?'

'Yes.'

'Did he have Brown's number?'

Madison thought about it for a second.

'Yes, the neighbor had both our cards. The killer must have seen us there.'

'He chose to call you.'

'I know, and I walked us right into it.'

'No, he called you and he shot Brown. He could have called him and shot both of you. Am I correct to say he was in a position to shoot you?'

'Yes.'

'He made a choice. This man does not do anything he has not planned and rehearsed in his mind. You are alive because he let you be.'

'I know.'

'Do you have any police surveillance on your home?'

'I don't think I need it. You said it yourself: he could have got me then.'

'What I mean is, with a lot of these types, obsessive rigorous planners, I wouldn't be surprised if he drove past your house, just to see if your car is in the drive, how you are doing with your injuries.'

'Yes, well, I can see that,' Madison said maybe a touch too quickly. 'I'll keep my eyes open.'

'Good. Look, if you need to start somewhere, I'd start with Cameron.'

'Yeah, I'd love to have a chat with him myself.'

'I can believe that.'

'Thank you, Mr Kamen. I really appreciate this.'

'You call me anytime. Do you have my cell number?'

'Yes.'

'Use it.'

In the bedroom, she opened the safe and pulled out her off-duty weapon, a short .45 for concealed carry. She slipped it into a holster that lay flat behind her left hip, put the splint back on and replaced the navy hooded top with a black sweater and a blazer. The lining of the jacket fell away easily from the leather.

She checked the windows, set the alarm and locked the door. The air was crisp and Madison could smell the water behind the trees. She was about to get into her car when she heard the blue-and-white braking softly.

Officer Giordano stepped out. 'You need a ride somewhere, detective?'

'No, thanks.'

'You're going to the hospital, by any chance?'

'Yes.'

'Wouldn't be any trouble to drop you off. Give your arm a little rest.'

She could drive herself, with difficulty, or she could accept the help and be grateful.

She rode in the back of the patrol car and when they got to the Northwest Hospital, she thanked both officers and they knew she meant it.

*

Two officers had been posted downstairs. Madison took the elevator to the ICU. When she got there she was about to ask the nurse at the reception desk but she saw the uniform standing at the end of the corridor.

A woman came out of the room; when she turned to Madison, she recognized her eyes and the pale ginger hair.

'I'm Alice Madison.'

'You're Kevin's partner.'

'Yes.'

'Ellen McCormick.'

'How is he?'

'Stable, but things would look better if he was breathing on his own.'

Ellen McCormick was in her late forties and wore a white T-shirt under a smart navy suit. Her manner was direct and her answer had been plain. 'I'm a doctor,' she continued. 'Which right now is a blessing and a curse.'

'I understand.'

'I was going to get a cup of coffee. Will you join me?'

'Sure.'

Ellen McCormick turned to the uniformed officer. 'I'll be back in five minutes.'

'Nobody's going in, ma'am.'

Which was exactly what Madison wanted to do, and she sensed Brown's sister knew that. She was a couple of inches taller and a good many years younger than Ellen McCormick but there was a grim determination there that Madison was familiar with. They rode in the elevator together and, once they were alone, the woman spoke. 'You were ambushed.'

'Yes. Did Lieutenant Fynn give you the details?'

'Yes.' She quickly scanned Madison's injuries.

'How long have you worked Homicide?'

'Why do you ask?'

'You are younger than I expected. I'm trying to work out whether you have the experience to go after the shooter.'

'I appreciate your honesty.'

There was darkness under Ellen McCormick's eyes and cold anger in her voice.

'Your boss told me that everybody is looking for this man and he will be caught. Once, many years ago, Kevin's partner was shot and killed in an attempted robbery. The shooter escaped but my brother found him three days later. He did not touch him, he did not put a finger on him, the sonofabitch is still upstate, as far as I know. I don't care what you do to him after you find him – what I want to know is that you won't stop until you do. Because that's what my brother would have done for you.'

'I know,' Madison said.

'I want you to see to it yourself that whatever needs to be done will be done. Can you promise me that?'

Madison nodded.

'You hadn't worked with him long, right?'

'Long enough to know what kind of man he is.'

Ellen McCormick smiled. 'Did he give you a hard time?'

Madison smiled, then the smile went away. 'I will find him.'

The woman exhaled slowly. 'Would you like to go see Kevin?'

Madison pushed the door very gently and walked in. Without a sound it swung shut behind her. Ellen McCormick had stayed outside.

There were monitors and IVs and the rhythmic hiss of the machine that was breathing for him, but at the center of it all Brown lay on the bed as if he were asleep.

She approached slowly and kept a respectful distance. He was still Brown and their relationship, with its structure and boundaries, had not changed in the last 24 hours.

The only color on him was the pale ginger hair through the straps of the respirator.

It felt odd to stand there, knowing how private and somewhat formal he was; he would have hated the notion of people coming in and seeing him like this.

Madison dug her hands deep in the pockets of her blazer. She hadn't taken any painkillers; then again, if there was a pill for what she was feeling, she didn't know about it.

She started talking because it justified her being there, her words punctuated by the rush of oxygen through the machine.

'I've spoken with Kamen this morning. He was very helpful – he gave me some ideas, things to look into. The boss is letting me do this quietly and carefully but, as you thought he would, he's not giving up Cameron. I have to give him something and it'd better be good.'

She took one step toward him.

'Spencer is the primary. I'm not supposed to tell him anything and I don't know if I can. He should be given the chance to make up his own mind, you know. Jesus, I wish I understood why all this happened.'

His glasses were on the bedside table next to an upturned cup and a beaker of water. There was a day's growth of beard on his cheeks, darker than his hair, speckled with gray.

'They matched the casings to the Sinclairs',' she continued. 'It was the same weapon. The shooter used the .22 he used on the kids. I'm going to pick up the records you had requested from the Academy and I'll chase Sorensen.'

She was close enough to touch him now. She stood there quietly; she didn't need to make any promises and there was nothing she could say he didn't already know. For a moment, she laid her good hand next to his on the white sheet.

'I'll see you tomorrow,' she said.

Brown's sister was talking to a doctor on the other side of the ICU reception lounge; their eyes met. As the elevator's doors closed, Ellen McCormick's gaze never left her.

There were taxis waiting at the hospital main entrance. Madison got into one and gave the man the precinct's address. They had been on the road for a couple of minutes when her voice startled the driver.

'Stop the car.'

'What—'

'Would you mind stopping the car?'

'What's up?'

'Now, please.'

The driver pulled over. Madison got out and threw up. Cars sped past beside them. She shivered and her guts ached.

'I should take you back to the hospital. It doesn't look like you were ready to leave yet, miss.'

'I'm sorry about this, I'll be alright in a second,' she said with her head still down, waiting for the waves of nausea to stop.

As she straightened up, the driver saw the leather holster and her weapon in it.

'You the cop on TV.' He was leaning on his car door with his arms crossed like they had stopped to look at the view. 'You ought to get some time off – you don't look so good.'

'Yes, well, thank you.'

When they got to her destination she gave him a big tip for almost throwing up in his cab.

Madison spent less than five minutes inside the precinct. She got her mail from the pigeonhole: two letters reminding her of court appearances in the next weeks and one large envelope addressed to Brown, hopefully the Academy records he had requested.

Madison didn't have a bag with her so she folded the larger

envelope around the smaller ones and left. Not a great moment for the sanctity of the postal service but she didn't think twice about it – Brown would have kicked the whole thing off the wall had it been necessary.

She walked a few blocks and felt her stomach settle a little. She found a coffee shop as it was beginning to rain. Tiredness had started to fray her concentration: caffeine would help, at least for a while. She sat on a stool by the window, the pane steamed up, and took a couple of sips. It was busy with downtown shoppers and tourists; nobody paid any attention to her.

Madison tore open the side flap of Brown's envelope. There it was: a list of names going back years. It did not give details; the specifics of the rejections were confidential. Still, if any of those names had even the slightest connection to Cameron it was well worth pursuing.

Madison scanned the list; there must have been over two hundred names. She rolled her eyes – a needle in a haystack would have looked pretty good at that point.

She tried to lift the cup with her right hand and the wrist wouldn't work. Her left would have to get busy, Madison thought, stretching it wide and closing it into a fist. There was something she must do, the sooner the better.

She finished her coffee and walked out, the startling chill finding every ache and pain in her body. Madison's thoughts were already elsewhere and she moved fast through the crowd with her head down.

Under ground, surrounded by darkness, her left hand held out before her, Alice Madison put three quick shots into the target provided by the firing range. She focused on the concentric circles that had taught her to shoot: the innermost was the center of a man's chest, go up a foot and a half and you're aiming for the head.

The air was cool out of the ventilation system, the same temperature all year round, the same low lighting between the cubicles. It was a place where Madison had always found it easy to get out of herself, to let her hands and eyes do the work.

She slowly squeezed the trigger, her front sight clear and her rear sight and the target appropriately blurred. The kick traveled back up her arm like electric crackle. Nobody on her left, nobody on her right. Madison liked to do her shooting alone. She lowered the .45 and took off the goggles. The grouping was good but not good enough. She wriggled the fingers almost covered by the splint, passed the weapon into the right hand and started to extend the arm in front of her. The pain was not unbearable but there was no way she would even hit the target that way.

She breathed deeply, left arm extended, and squeezed on the exhale. And again. And again.

The man had been tall. Madison remembered his voice in the deserted street as she was getting out of the car with Brown. Officer Mason, he had said. Just over six foot. Wiry, with a plain face. Hair, Madison couldn't remember – he had been wearing a cap. Would she recognize him if she saw him again?

Breathe in and exhale and shoot. Lower the weapon and do over.

Madison had reported the ambush in detail but had not spent much time with the memory of it herself. It made her smile out of one side of her mouth that she had chosen to go back to it now, as she emptied her weapon into the target. *I must remember this for the counseling session*, she thought. She would be obliged to attend one before returning to duty – it was a mere formality.

Madison pressed the switch to collect the target and replace it with a new one. It came to her, what was left of it, and she put it to one side. She pressed the switch again and a blank target slid down the line back into position 40 feet away. Then she reloaded, resting the .45 against the palm of her right hand.

The first shot felt as good as the jolt through the arm after the swing, when the bat makes contact with the ball. It tore a neat hole at the center of the target. Madison looked at it. Pretty good by anybody's standards. Still, a day late and a dollar short, her grandfather used to say.

It would be difficult to identify the man in a line-up, that was true, but there was something she knew for sure. They had not been looking at Cameron: the plain face with the small mouth and the straight nose was not Cameron's.

Ballistics might very well say that the .22 used against Brown had shot three members of the Sinclair family, she couldn't argue with that, but eyewitness testimony was a whole different ball game. She couldn't identify Cameron as the shooter – in fact she could positively exonerate him. It was definitely worth a conversation with Spencer.

Lieutenant Fynn would be unhappy, of course. He had asked her to keep her thoughts to herself, try not to give Quinn ammunition to contest the integrity of the warrant, and she had lasted less than 24 hours.

Madison took off the spent target, the center of it now almost non-existent, and put a new one in place.

Her body remembered the fight, sudden and quick. They prepare you for the worst in training; what they cannot do is give you a sense of the fear and the shock of being physically attacked. Had she been afraid? *Goddammit, yes*, Madison thought. Had it stopped her thinking and reacting? Madison lowered the .45. *I can ask Brown the next time I pop in to see him.*

By the time she was done there was a small pile of spent targets at her side and her left hand was shaking with fatigue. Madison took off her earmuffs and goggles and turned to find J.B. Norton, her gunnery instructor, leaning on the wall behind her. He was a welcome sight – a quiet man who looked like a librarian and had taught generation after generation of law enforcement officers.

'J.B.'

'They told me you were down here and I thought I'd bring you a present.' He threw it and she caught it – a squeeze ball to strengthen her left hand. Madison smiled.

'Thank you. I need it.'

He didn't ask her how it had gone – he picked up the target sheets and examined them. He considered the progression from the first to the last.

'We don't see you around here as often anymore,' he said without looking at her.

'I know, I'm sorry. The last few weeks have been full on.'

'Look, Madison, all I wanted to say is that you can shoot if you have to, right-handed or not.' He picked up the last target with two fingers; the inside circle was all but blown out. 'And you've got good judgment, not like some of the cowboys who pass through here. Have you ever aimed your piece at another human being and pulled the trigger?'

'No.'

'A lot of cops never do but you never know.' His glasses glinted in the half light. 'If you have to, aim for the middle of the chest. It will bring a man down before he does the same to you.'

Under her sweater, the tiny hairs at the back of her neck stood up. It was a terrible notion. She nodded and Norton left.

Madison gathered her things and found the exit. Her hands smelled of gunpowder as she dialed the precinct's number.

Lieutenant Fynn always stood during conversations that tested his patience. He was standing now. His office door was shut and Madison, also standing, had come in to make a bad day worse.

'Run that by me again,' he said.

'I'm going to tell Spencer,' she replied. 'The description of our shooter, the man who called himself Officer Mason, exonerates Cameron. Whatever Ballistics says, Spencer ought to know that much.'

'Twenty-four hours you couldn't keep it to yourself?'

'I should have told him last night at the hospital. I was wrong not to.'

'You mean *I* was wrong.'

'I was wrong. My description of the attacker was vague at best but I can tell you for sure who he was not.'

Lieutenant Fynn knew that Madison had told him first out of courtesy and respect. At that moment, though, he'd rather be dealing with an idiot without manners who did what he was told.

'Is this what you want?' he asked her with his hand on the door-knob. There was a grim note to his voice that meant 'consequences'.

'Yes.'

'I cannot physically stop you from talking to them, but I can and will do whatever I can to prevent you from compromising this investigation, you understand that?'

'Yes.'

'Okay.' He opened the door and called out. 'Spencer, Dunne, get in here now.'

Spencer and Dunne had not slept for two days: they had been home for a couple of hours when they were called to the ambush crime scene, and since then they had been on their feet. They came in punchy and tired, but Fynn's bleak expression woke them up fast. Spencer was the primary and Dunne was his partner; if one knew, they both knew.

'Madison's got something to say. You might want to sit down.' Fynn crossed his arms and leant against the closed door.

Spencer and Dunne looked from one to the other. Madison started; she kept it simple and quick. When she was done no one said anything.

Dunne ran his hands over his face. 'What the hell,' he said after a while.

Spencer's reaction was more difficult to gauge. His eyes stayed on Madison. 'You have absolutely no proof of this?'

'No, I'm working on it.'

'You're working on dismantling your own case?'

'I know the man who shot Brown was not Cameron.'

'You barely saw him. Your description said "a plain face", no distinctive characteristics. You don't know for sure it wasn't him; the guy changes his appearance every day of the week – you know that. What about the picture on his driving license?'

'I've been looking at his picture for days. I'm telling you, it was somebody else.'

Fynn didn't say a word.

'And Brown agreed with all this?' Dunne butted in.

'Absolutely.'

Fynn stepped into the middle of the room.

'That's what he was "looking into"; we don't know what he would have said today. He might very well have decided that there wasn't enough evidence to support this angle. Actually, there isn't *any* evidence to support it at all.'

Madison opened her mouth to interrupt.

'Let me finish. We don't know he wouldn't have let this go. You don't know, Madison.'

'No way. He was about to come to you himself.'

'But he didn't.' Fynn sighed. 'I have looked at the file again, I have reread every word of it ten times and I do not see even the beginning of doubt. Madison, you have been through something awful in the last 24 hours. Isn't it possible that you are stuck on this out of loyalty to Brown? He is a great cop, he was checking every angle as he should, but he would have moved on by now.'

'What are you saying exactly?'

'You were attacked and your partner got shot and your judgment is out of whack. You feel guilty because you think you didn't watch his back and are obsessing about something he said that he probably would have taken back today.'

'You think I'm doing this because I'm *stressed*?'

'It wouldn't be the first time it happens.'

'All due respect, sir, but that's a crock.'

'You are on medical leave, Detective. I suggest you go home and rest.'

'And that will make it all better?'

'You might also want to rethink the attitude.'

Spencer and Dunne stood transfixed by the exchange. Fynn turned to them. 'I want to have a few words with Detective Madison, in private.' They left.

Madison lowered her chin and got ready for the fight.

'How long?' he asked her.

'What do you mean?'

'How long do you think it will take for that conversation to filter through to the whole precinct?'

She shook her head.

'Not long,' he continued. 'It means anything you do now is going to be tainted. It means that, as per my recommendation, you will not be allowed back on duty until you have undergone evaluation by a post-traumatic stress disorder expert. And it won't be a formality.'

'That's just—'

Fynn raised his hand. 'It means anything you say or do now cannot be used by Quinn to contest the warrant.'

Madison stopped in mid-sentence.

'It's called "deniability" and it's not a gift,' Fynn continued. 'It's going to be on your record.'

'I don't care.'

'I didn't think you would.'

As she was leaving, she turned to him. 'Brown wouldn't have changed his mind, you know.'

'Go home,' he said, not unkindly.

Spencer was waiting for her to be done. He motioned for her to follow and they went into the rec room.

'What was that about?'

'You heard me. That's as much as I know.'

Spencer was the calm thinker. If Madison had any hope to get through to anybody it would be him.

'You really believe this?' he said.

Madison felt suddenly exhausted. 'He tied the knot twice so he could leave the hairs for us to find.'

'But you don't know why.'

'No.'

There was a moment of quiet between them. Spencer opened the fridge, took out a small carton of juice and pressed the tiny straw through the hole. It was the kind of thing a child might drink. He was making up his mind about telling her something, or holding back.

'We're following a lead from Harbor Patrol,' he said. 'You were right about the boat thing.'

Madison was glad and sorry to hear that. 'I need some time to work through this.'

'I don't know how long you're going to get.'

'What can you tell me about the lead?'

He shook his head. 'I don't think me telling you anything is a good idea right now. You go home and do what you do. We'll see who's going to get there first.'

*

Outside, the sun had decided to call it quits and the sky was white with snow. Madison grabbed a cab. She dialed and lay back with her eyes closed.

'Rachel, I'm sorry, I'm not very good company tonight. I'll come over another time. Thank you anyway.'

'I'll drop something off if you like, so Tommy can see you for just a minute.'

Rachel brought lasagna in an oven dish. They popped open a couple of beers and, while Rachel was busy with the microwave, Tommy examined her injuries. He was a bright six-year-old who knew about running around and getting his knees scraped.

He put his finger lightly on a stitch on Madison's brow. 'Does this hurt?'

'Not really.' Actually, it was just beginning to hum.

Gently, he turned her arm around to see the splint. He touched her fingers to make sure they still worked. He took a step back. 'You don't look too bad,' he said.

'Thank you,' she replied.

'Did you sing "Blackbird"?'

After every cut and graze Rachel had sung the Beatles' 'Blackbird' to him ever since he was a baby. Magical healing.

'Yes, I did,' she said.

'Did it help?'

'It did.'

He was only one year younger than the younger Sinclair boy, David. One week ago at that moment, David was having dinner with his parents and brother. In a few hours, a man would walk into his bedroom and shoot him in the head as he slept.

Rachel and Tommy left. Madison hugged the boy tight before they strapped him in the backseat and was glad she had washed the gunpowder off her hands and changed her clothes. He smelled of cookies.

Madison waited for their car to disappear up the drive and down the road. Back inside, she went into her bedroom and retrieved the holster and the .45 from the safe. She felt stronger after the food, and restless.

The Sinclair house was deserted – the patrol cars that had been posted there earlier in the week had received other assignments. When Madison remembered that she still had the keys, she knew she had to go back.

The neighborhood was quiet and the walk was brief. She put the key in the door and let herself in. In the hall, she stood and looked around. Nothing had moved since the last time she had been there, only her own world had been turned upside down. The Sinclair house was a clock that had stopped a week ago.

Kamen had said that she had to see Cameron as a victim: if Madison could see how he had been chosen it would get her one step closer to the killer. Now, given that Cameron was not available, the Sinclairs were the next-best thing.

Madison breathed in to get used to the smell more quickly; seven days after the fact it felt old and unpleasant, just bad enough to be a distraction.

She would go upstairs, she knew she had to, but not straightaway: the upstairs had everything to do with their deaths and Madison hoped to learn something about their life. If they had been chosen to carry the weight for Cameron, somewhere somehow their paths and the killer's must have crossed.

Madison sat on the sofa. It was comfortable and she sank into it, feeling the last 24 hours in her bones, replaying in her mind the conversation with Kamen, reminding herself that she had to try Sorensen at the Crime Lab for the third time. In the corner, the small table lamp threw a patch of light on the stripped wood floors.

Madison told herself that she was going to close her eyes only for one minute. One minute and she would open her eyes. One minute. She fell asleep, a heavy sleep not unlike death itself, without dreams or movement or sound. For three hours she sat up and when she stirred it was only to stretch lengthways, unaware of where she was. It could have been her own home, her own sofa.

A puff of cold air woke her – that's what she thought at first. Her eyes blinked open as the cool scent of the night outside brushed her cheek. Then she heard the lock of the French doors click shut and the hairs on her arms stood up.

She lay on the sofa, her body frozen in place and her breath caught in her throat. She felt more than heard the presence in the room, a living person behind the high back of the sofa, who could neither see her nor be seen.

There was movement a few feet behind her, maybe someone taking a couple of steps. Madison tried to relax her stiff muscles, but even her stillness had a sound, a humming of blood in her ears that washed over almost everything else. She wanted to gather herself and get her brain to stop racing and just listen.

She was safe where she was. She had the advantage: she was armed and ready to tussle. Never mind that the gun was behind her, pressed against the sofa. Just be quiet and listen. The person wasn't moving, he – Madison decided arbitrarily that it was a man – was standing five to six feet behind her. All her senses were telling her was that the man was standing there *looking around*.

Her eyes blinked, tiny clicks in the middle of the night, in a house where awful things had happened. Only two men in the whole world had any reason to be there. That knowledge bore into her with piercing and sudden clarity: Officer Mason might be standing close enough for her to reach out and touch, or, if she was lucky, John Cameron, alleged murderer of nine.

Then, with a sound no louder than a whisper, the man started to move away. First, he was in the hall and from there he went into the kitchen.

Madison stirred. The adrenaline made her chest ache and she was glad to find the floor under her feet as she slid off the sofa. In one movement her hand found the .45, flicked the safety latch off and cleared leather.

A beam of light danced on the ceiling in the hall, fell on the alarm panel by the door.

Madison, the gun pointed to the floor, leant forward from behind the armrest, her eyes barely clearing the fabric: the man was examining the panel, his back to her, dark clothes, dark hair. He had a small torch in one hand, his left, and the other was on the panel. No weapons – at least none that she could see. If she got to him now, unprepared and unarmed, she could have him on the floor in seconds.

Madison narrowed her eyes; it was difficult to see in the half gloom. What was the man doing? Never mind, she could ask him later, once he was cuffed in the back of a blue-and-white, thank you very much. Now – it had to be now. She had to do it before he turned around.

Madison stood straight up and spoke in a clear, unequivocal voice.

'Seattle PD. Don't move.'

The man didn't so much as flinch. Madison came around from behind the sofa, left arm straight out, front sight at the center of the man's back.

'Do exactly as I say when I say it and we'll be just fine. Do you understand?'

The man did not reply. He stood with his back to Madison, his arms slightly raised as if he had chosen to stop at that moment in time.

With her right hand, Madison found the switch for the overhead light in the hall. She flicked it on.

'Do you understand?' she repeated slowly and clearly.

The man did not reply. There was at least ten feet between them and two thoughts occurred to Madison: the first was that the last time she had been up close and personal with Officer Mason things hadn't gone so well for the home team. The second was that John Cameron had been close enough to slash Erroll Sanders's throat and the guy had probably never even seen the knife before it came for him.

Whoever it was she was speaking to, the wise thing to do was to keep a polite distance.

'Okay, not a big talker. I don't care. This is what I want you to do and it is not optional. I know you can hear me –'

He was a dark-haired man, broad shoulders. Gloves – he was wearing black leather gloves.

Madison edged to one side but still couldn't see his face.

'– and you can understand me. I want you to put your hands over your head and drop to your knees. Do it or you will not get out of this in one piece.'

Her voice was steady, her hand dead still. The man did not move.

Madison flashed back: getting out of the car, the police officer meeting her and Brown, walking together toward the house. The sense of him, his height and body shape, before the attack.

Well, here goes nothing, Madison thought.

'John Cameron, do as I—'

It was the first sign of life, the tiniest flinch when she said his name. Then, in the silence of 2 a.m., the fridge in the kitchen rumbled to life with a shudder and hum and for one split second Madison was startled enough to look away. And he was gone.

'HEY!' Madison had never seen anyone move so fast; he was up the stairs before she knew it and her choice was either to shoot him in the back or to follow. She followed.

She didn't even have time to swear: he was going for the master bedroom and she had to get there before he reached the window and out across the lawn.

Madison was already halfway up the stairs when she realized there was no way on this earth she would catch him up and if she did she couldn't climb with her arm as it was. She spun around and ran back down: if she couldn't catch him, she'd wait for him at the other end.

She made the turn into the living room, sliding on the wooden floor, and bumped into the French doors. She grabbed the handle and turned it. *DAMMIT*. They were locked and the keys were nowhere to be seen.

Without thinking, Madison backed up a few steps, passed the .45 into her right hand and lunged against the doors with her left shoulder, her face covered in the crook of her arm. She crashed through and hit the patio with her side on a bed of glass.

John Cameron touched the ground at the same time and became a fast-moving shadow in the darkness. Madison staggered up and gave chase. The lawn was surrounded by trees on two sides and sloped to the water on the third, the ground frosty and slick under her feet. She ran, following the blur at the end of the lawn. She heard him land with two feet on the pebble beach below – he must have jumped the six foot drop. *If he's got a weapon, he's got it out by now.*

Madison reached the drop and stopped with a sideways slide, lay on her front and looked over the top, left and right. No movement, no sounds. The beach was empty. It was maybe 25 feet to the water with a short pier to her right, and next to the pier, bobbing up and down with the tide, a small rowing boat.

Whose boat is that? Did the Sinclairs own a boat?

Madison leant forward, trying to see a little better. The air stung in her lungs and the ground under her belly was ice-cold. She propped herself up on her left elbow. *What the* . . .

She saw it indistinctly at first: two dark patches that were the pier and the boat slowly moving apart, coming together and then moving a little further away from each other.

He's in the boat. Madison's head came up from behind the grass. Let him take a crack at it if he was so damn keen.

It was moving, it was definitely moving up the length of the pier. Madison couldn't see the rope that had tied the boat to the post. Too dark and too far, and he might very well have a gun.

Madison breathed hard through her mouth. She closed her eyes tight for a second: what would five minutes of Cameron's time be worth to her?

She jumped and landed hard, bent her knees and balanced herself with her right hand on the pebbles. It shot a warning arrow of pain up her arm.

The boat had almost cleared the pier now. Madison straightened up and, just as she was taking the first step, from behind her she heard the clear and unmistakable sound of a branch snapping. She spun around, weapon out, as still as she could be and shivering in the night air in spite of herself. She held her breath and listened.

Out of the corner of her eye she could see the boat bobbing further on, without any apparent haste; it had almost cleared the pier. *It could have been anything.*

If she ran now she could still make it. Madison did not move. It could have been anything, she thought, but it wasn't. Somewhere above her to her right, something brushed against the trees. Madison turned to see the boat floating away.

Nice try, she thought. He must have climbed back up after he released the boat and gone into the dense patch of trees that separated the properties.

Madison looked around. A rickety wooden ladder stood at the other end of the lawn. It would take too long to get there. She holstered the .45. He knew – the sonofabitch knew about her arm.

She backed up a few steps, then took three quick strides and jumped up. Her left hand found a hold above and her boot dug into the rocky ground. She swung her leg high and to the side and grabbed at the earth with her right hand. She hoisted herself up. She knew the pain would come a half second later, and it did, worse than she had imagined, the full Technicolor version. She groaned and crouched, one knee on the ground, the gun back in her hand. To her right, the Sinclair house shone at the top of the lawn, the light spilling out from the French doors Madison had crashed through. A little of it had found the outlines of the trees next to the house; it was too far to reach where she was.

Madison looked straight ahead into the firs and the darkness they held and stepped inside it. The trunks were slightly spaced out and only minimum light filtered through. She proceeded slowly and carefully on the thin layer of frozen snow, twigs and branches crunching under every step. How much time had passed since she had last heard him? Seconds, minutes. She had to think clearly; her gun hand trembled. She stopped and stretched her right hand out, her fingertips brushed the bark of a fir, a low branch bent as she trailed her hand along it. She couldn't hear him. She could barely see one foot in front of her but she should at least be able to hear him: he couldn't have gotten clear to the other side or up to the street yet. If she couldn't hear him, it meant he had stopped too.

Madison, standing stock still, tried to make sense of the shapes around her. A drop of sweat ran between her shoulder blades, chilling on her skin. She closed her eyes. She heard nothing but the lapping of water on the pebble beach. She wiped her brow and was surprised to find it covered in perspiration. Something stirred deep in the gloom to her left, Madison swung her arm, her eyes narrowed. A soft crunch of snow to her right. She held her breath to listen: something, someone circling in the darkness. She started moving toward the sound.

He was there; he had to be. The question was why was he *still* there. Fast as he was he could have found a way out, risked her following him, sure, but he would have made it to the street.

Out of the blue, the photograph of the deck of the *Nostromo* came to her: the wood black and glossy with the blood of the five men Cameron had slaughtered. She pushed it away. She thought of Sanders crumpled on the floor, arterial blood spray all over the walls. *Shit*, she whispered, and a puff of white breath drifted before her.

In the house, she had been the one with the advantage – briefly, she had to admit, but she had caught him unawares. Now she was blind as a bat, waiting for the tiniest click and snap. For the first time Madison realized that she didn't know what she would have done with him if she had got him in the first place. A sobering thought, it quickened the thumping in her chest: she could not take him in. If she arrested him, it would be all over. If they got cuffs on him, not even Nathan Quinn would be able to get them off. Cameron was the only living connection to the killer. If she took him in – if she managed to take him in – they would never know.

She remembered Brown's words in the airport parking lot after they found the Explorer, her own snappy reply. She had known nothing then, understood nothing. *What are you prepared to do?*

She saw a small clearing ahead and the canopy opened above her, enough for shapes to become distinct. She stepped in that direction, careless of the rustle of clothes and branches caught in her movements. Her steps loud as she left the tangle of roots and shrubs behind her and walked out under a clear patch of sky, a perfect target. *Remember Sanders*, a thin voice told her. Standing in the middle of the clearing, Madison counted in her head to 60.

I hope you're watching, you sonofabitch.

A bird flapped its wings on a nearby tree. When she felt she had given him enough time to follow, she lifted her .45 high above her head and the muzzle caught a glint of light, the weight of the weapon so familiar and welcome in her hand. *First day in Homicide, a lot of hand-shaking, a lot of do-you-know-so-and-sos, Fynn taking her around to meet everybody, keeping Brown for last. They hadn't shaken hands.* The thin voice spoke to her again: *If you have to, aim for the middle of the chest. It will bring a man down before he does the same to you.*

Madison placed the .45 back in the holster and hooked the leather strip on. Then, arms stretched out to the side, she turned around, all the way round, weapon holstered and secured.

There were flakes of frozen condensation in her lashes and particles of glass in her hair and on her shoulders. John Cameron saw them catch the light as she stood unarmed under the open sky. That was not what he had expected, not at all. He took one step toward her.

'We need to talk,' she said, her voice steadier than she felt.

Madison did not like the empty silence after her words, as if hers was the only heartbeat in the woods. Nothing stirred. Maybe he had made it to the other side, long gone and far away. Still, she waited.

Cameron had known her instantly when she had spoken in the house. She was the one who had been looking through the videos and the pictures the last time. The one who had been attacked only the night before.

He had read the papers: he knew that she must think he had shot her partner and he was not going to let her get any closer to him. He had checked the front before going in. No cars – the woman must have walked to the house. And she had fallen *asleep*, Jesus Christ. More than anything Cameron had been annoyed at himself.

He stood feet away from her and looked her over. Under the black leather gloves, he felt the blade of his knife resting flat against his leg.

Madison waited. If he wasn't moving, neither was she. If he was taking measure of her, wondering how long her patience would run, how cold she could stand to be, they were in for a long one. She stared into the darkness, he stared right back.

Cameron had enjoyed her crash through the French doors and the chase. The boat had been merely a distraction: he wanted her in the trees, he wanted to take a good look at her. Twenty-four hours ago she had been close enough to touch the one person he was dying to meet. They certainly had a few things to talk about.

There was activity in the top of the trees above them; something flapped and dislodged a handful of snow. It fell in the clearing between them.

It had been a long time since John Cameron had stood that close to a cop. Madison kept her hand well away from the holster.

'Do you have any idea how easy it would have been to shoot you in the back?' she said. 'What are the chances that you are carrying a weapon right now? Everybody thinks you shot my partner; how hard do you think they would have looked into a self-defense homicide? They'd just give me a medal.'

She let her words drift between them.

'And the man who murdered your friends would get away.'

Madison wiped her brow, the perspiration on her skin ice-cold. She didn't know whether she would be able to convince him to talk; she didn't know whether she'd still be standing in five minutes.

'No more poker nights, no more birthday parties. I saw them in the morgue, Cameron – the children. And Quinn will be next; you must know that.'

If the murdering piece of shit doesn't take a step forward right now—

Loud voices broke onto the lawn from the house. Madison was startled and she turned. Someone was on the grass. Voices calling to each other – three, maybe four men. It must be cops, patrol cops. Some helpful neighbor must have called them when they heard glass breaking.

Thank you very much. She couldn't think of worse timing for the Neighborhood Watch to swing into action. Cops on the lawn. No way he would show now. No way.

Madison hesitated; the voices were getting closer. She stared into the pitch black around her.

Cameron had heard the cops too; he hadn't moved an inch. Even if five of them combed the wooded patch, he knew he'd get away. If it came to it, he might just have to *make* his way out. No problem there. The detective hadn't made a sound yet.

Madison felt like she was hitting the dregs of her adrenaline. What would happen if she called out to them? Just then it started to snow. Madison looked up; flakes floated to the ground. *I must be out of my mind.*

'We need to talk,' she said quietly and started to make her way toward the lawn. Her eyes unaccustomed to the sudden gloom, she brushed past John Cameron, who stood no more than an arm's length away, watching her.

She came out on the grass to find four uniforms, three men and a woman, with their pieces out, walking toward her.

She had already taken out her badge and held it in front of her. 'Police officer,' she said out loud. They crowded around her.

She turned back once toward the spot she had come from and only seconds later she thought she heard a car engine coming to life in the street. Good job, she thought. Brown would have got him to show.

*

Thirty minutes later, Detectives Kelly and Rosario arrived with snow on their shoes. Sure, Madison thought, it could have been Spencer and Dunne, but no, that would have been a whole different day. Kelly looked grim: the Sanders investigation hadn't thrown up anything solid as yet and patience was not a notion he lived his life by.

She had already told the story once, to the responding officer, and went through it again with them. She showed them exactly what had happened where and walked them out to the pier.

Back in the hall a solitary Crime Scene Unit investigator was dusting the alarm panel.

'You fell asleep?' Kelly snorted.

'Yes.' There was no way around that one and Madison wouldn't lie about it.

'You still had the keys,' Kelly said. 'Even though you're on leave.'

'Yes, I realized I had them in the pocket of a jacket at home.'

'You would have brought them back first thing tomorrow,' Rosario said, without any apparent trace of sarcasm.

'You bet,' Madison replied.

'There you go,' he said to his partner. Kelly ignored him.

'What did you hope to find? We've been through this place with a nits comb.'

'I don't know. Maybe something I missed the first time.'

'Will you give her a break? Her partner is in ICU and she had to do something.' Rosario smiled at Kelly. 'I'm sure you'd do the same for me.'

'Not necessarily. You didn't see his face at all?'

'No.'

'You have no idea who it was?'

'No.'

'But you had to chase him through glass doors?'

'Yes.'

She gave them a description. Accurate, as it happens, but one that would fit about a quarter of the population. Kelly took it all down, Madison saw that he was itching to start an argument and she didn't exactly feel shy herself. Sooner or later she would have to confront him. It had little to do with Kelly and everything to do with her place within the precinct.

Kelly didn't like her. It had been an immediate thing with him and Madison didn't really think gender or anything else had played a part. He just didn't like her. He smiled tightly and was about to say something when Rosario stepped in.

'You said the guy was wearing gloves?'

'Yes.'

Madison and Kelly didn't break eye contact.

'No prints then,' Rosario continued.

'I guess not.'

'Alrighty.'

'How's Sanders going?' Madison asked Kelly.

'We're working it,' Rosario replied.

It meant they had zero leads aside from Cameron's print on the axle and no way to link him to the crime scene.

Kelly lit up. 'There's a rumor going round that you got cold feet about hunting down Cameron.'

'Meaning?'

'That you lost your nerve after last night and are coming up with all sorts of screwed-up theories. You've been with Homicide what, a month? A rookie mistake: pressure got to you and you couldn't protect your partner.'

Madison took a step forward and in one totally unexpected moment of clarity she knew that she was about to lose it.

'What?' Kelly said in her face.

It would have been so sweet to let him have it, to wipe the board clean after four weeks of his yard-dog manners and the stench of cheap cigars that hung on his clothes. Kelly straightened up and shut his mouth, the cigar clamped between his lips.

Everybody had stopped what they were doing. It had to be now, and Madison spoke quietly because she knew she didn't need to shout.

'You know, of all the awful things that have happened this week, you don't even make the top ten: you are somewhere between *I forgot to pick up the dry cleaning* and *I should gas up the car*. You are less than an inconvenience and I don't care what you think because you are nothing but a bad smell. You are the lint in the toilet bowl I wouldn't bother to flush. Now, are we done here?'

Kelly blinked. Rosario came to his rescue.

'My feeling is maybe we can call it quits,' he muttered.

'Sure.'

'Kelly?'

Kelly nodded.

'Okay then, boys and girls, we're done.' He clapped his partner on the shoulder. 'Let's go.' Kelly didn't move. Rosario took his arm. 'Let's go.'

Madison wanted everybody out so that she could have one last walk-about. The uniformed officers had boarded up the broken door.

'We'll wait and drop you off,' Rosario said.

'No, thanks. I feel like walking.'

'It's 4 a.m.'

'I'm okay.'

'You'll drop off the keys tomorrow?'

'Sure thing.'

He lowered his voice. 'Get some rest. We don't know each other real well but I'm betting your natural color is not green.'

Everybody left and then it was just Madison in the empty house, and she didn't know whether she'd rather have a shot of bourbon to end the day or a coffee to start it. She walked from room to room, too tired for inspiration, just letting her brain record what her eyes were seeing.

Given the state she was in, walking was better than getting into a car with Kelly, even if by the time she got home Madison had to peel off her clothes with shaking hands and put herself under a hot shower. The anger coursing through her had nothing to do with Kelly – he was just noise. She had to remember that.

Madison stayed under the water, as hot as she could take it, until it started to turn cold. In her white robe and bunny slippers she padded into the kitchen. With the possible exception of her hair, everything ached. She poured herself a glass of milk, shook a couple of painkillers into the palm of her hand and downed them in one go. She had no trouble falling asleep.

Chapter 29

John Cameron drove his deep green Cherokee Jeep at exactly the speed limit as he left Three Oaks. At 4 on a Sunday morning, it would have been nice to slam his foot down on the pedal but there was snow on the ground and patrol cars with his face taped to the dash. It had already been a good night in some unexpected ways; he wasn't about to force his luck.

He had gone to Blueridge looking for a connection that would put Jimmy and his family together with the man who had taken their lives, the man who apparently had started his trade in prison. Instead, he had found something entirely different and, possibly, equally useful. He checked the clock; the digits glowed pale green. It was too early and too late to call Nathan; he owed him at least another three hours' sleep.

Cameron understood Quinn's reluctance to let him talk to Hollis. They both knew that once the investigator came up with a name, the lifespan expectancy of that person would be dramatically reduced. Quinn had his way of doing things, and so had Cameron.

There is a house in the Admiral neighborhood above Alki, almost on top of Duwamish Head – an unassuming three-bedroom set in its own grounds, surrounded by the same trees as every other house in the street, protected by the same wrought-iron gate. No living being has crossed its threshold in seven years except for its owner: the day the workmen finished laying the new wooden floors was the last time anyone other than John Cameron walked between those rooms.

Cameron opened the gate with a remote and drove the car into a garage on the side of the house. There was enough distance from the street to allow for a sense of privacy without it being the obvious reason for someone to choose that house over any other. It wasn't its structure in brick and wood that had attracted Cameron in the first place. He stepped into the living room and paused: one side was entirely glass, the water black and still and beyond it a handful of flickering lights, downtown Seattle across Elliott Bay.

He owned a bungalow in Westwood, Los Angeles, and an apartment in New York, yet this was what he always came back to: a simply furnished house bought in another man's name. No one, not even Nathan Quinn, knew about it and nothing inside it had any connection to any part of his life – not a scrap of paper with his name on it, not a family photograph.

For many years he had lived in a fine balance, the fragments that made the whole close enough but not quite touching. Cameron poured himself a shot of bourbon and sat in a deep leather chair that faced the glass wall; he took a sip and felt the warm rush in his chest. The system had worked until seven days ago.

Cameron was calm and could think clearly: that privilege had been bought at a price. He knew it in Los Angeles, he knew it as he slashed Erroll Sanders's throat and put a swift end to his life. There was a point in LA when he had realized that the dealer was not responsible for Jimmy's death and he had gone ahead anyway.

He sipped the bourbon and hoped that there would never come a time when he'd lie to himself about it: Sanders had died because he needed killing and because Cameron knew he would enjoy killing him. It was that simple.

Earlier that night, as he had walked into Jimmy's house, one moment of unguarded grief had almost cost him his freedom, possibly even his life. One razor-sharp memory: James and Annie showing him the home they had just bought, their children not yet born and their lives extending into the bright forever. Cameron drained the glass. He had been distracted and now he couldn't even be sure that it wasn't a composite of other memories, if it had happened at all.

He stood up to refresh his drink and instead found himself making coffee. He could look at the situation straight on or he could recriminate and rationalize and damn well put a bow on it but it wouldn't change a thing: for all his care and caution, *he* had drawn the killer to them, *he* had invited him into their lives. Seven days ago something had followed him home.

Cameron poured the coffee and took it back to his seat by the window. Detective Madison had surprised him and that didn't happen very often. She had known to keep her distance even though she'd followed him like a terrier and wouldn't have budged if the patrol cops hadn't turned up. She had put her weapon away, a nice touch – he had enjoyed that moment. Nevertheless, she was a homicide detective and that was where her priorities lay. Did she want a collar that would make her name in the ranks? Quite possibly. Did she want to find the killer? Very probably. Did she want to nail the piece of shit who had put her partner in a coma? Absolutely. That's what he could count on. Strangely enough, he had believed her when she said she knew he hadn't done it. So the question was really quite simple: what would he have done if the uniforms hadn't broken up their party? What indeed? Cameron thought. Detective Madison didn't know about the firebug who had been murdered in jail – however, she must know something.

It was worth a conversation and, the next time they met, he hoped for her sake that she would keep that .45 snug and well secured in the holster.

He checked his watch: barely gone 5 a.m. He wanted to speak to Nathan, he wanted to get him the hell out of town. Something about Detective Madison, how determined she had looked in the small clearing: she had been standing there with nothing between them except her words and cold night air. He was not the one she was afraid of; what she was after was altogether different and they both knew it now.

Cameron waited for dawn. Without exception, anybody he had ever met in his travels had been moved by a desire for power or money and, again without exception, he had never done anything in his life in pursuit of either. Still, the man who had murdered James and his family was not driven by those hungers: his rewards, Cameron suspected, were measured by darker scales.

Then we have something in common. Cameron looked down at the scars on the back of his right hand.

Chapter 30

John Cameron, eighteen years old, sat across Nathan Quinn in the corner booth of a deli on Second Avenue. It was stuffy and busy with the lunchtime crowd, the waitresses yelling the orders to the cook above the general din. They ate their salt beef sandwiches, Quinn talking and Cameron listening. He talked about justice and the legal system and the homicide case he was on, and Cameron was a good audience. Truth be told, that day John Cameron was not in the mood to talk; he sat back in the red leather seat and looked his friend over.

Nathan Quinn's brother, David, had been dead just over five years; the family had been hit hard and everybody had gotten on with their lives in the best way they could, but it's not like it was ever going to go away. Quinn had been there for him and James; maybe it had helped him a little too. Before, they were only his kid brother's friends; after, they were a living reminder of what he might have done, what he might have become, had he lived.

Cameron nodded at the right points and Quinn talked on. Nathan Quinn was a prosecuting attorney who had come to terms with the fact that his brother's body would never be found and the men responsible for his death would never be brought to justice.

It wasn't peace of mind; it was a fight every God-given day to keep his life straight and good and not let the rage take over. Until recently Cameron had never quite understood how hard that fight could be, but things had changed.

Six weeks earlier to the day, John Cameron was nursing a beer in a bar in Eastlake, between Yale and Pontius, when a man from a table at the back approached the bar and started giving the bartender a hard time about something Cameron couldn't quite hear above the music. The bar itself was a low-rent, dank-smelling excuse for a neighborhood joint with a rather relaxed attitude to fake IDs.

It was a quiet night and the bartender was going about his business washing and drying glasses; the customer, late forties with a lot of muscle turning soft on a six-foot frame, was following him along the bar, getting closer and closer to the stool where Cameron was perched. The bartender was nodding and obviously trying to get away from the conversation yet the man kept at him. Cameron realized he must have met him somewhere: he didn't look familiar, his voice did – the way he just hammered on at the guy.

Maybe he knew him from the restaurant, although there was something unpleasant about him and he didn't seem like the type his father would be friends with. Still, he had definitely heard that ranting before.

Don't make me do this.

The hairs on the back of his neck were already standing when his brain caught up.

Don't make me do this, you little shit.

He covered the back of his right hand with his left before he knew what he was doing, and for the first time in years he felt the cold blade resting against his skin. The man got closer and Cameron looked down into his glass, feeling a mouthful of beer coming back up. He swallowed it and tried to stand and his legs wouldn't move. The man was maybe five feet away from him and Cameron could do nothing but sit there and force himself to breathe in and out. At some point he looked up because it would have seemed odd if he didn't. The man was leaning on the bar, propping himself on one elbow, the bartender was refreshing his drink and filling up a bowl of peanuts. The man turned to Cameron as if he'd been part of the conversation.

'Do you believe this shit?' he said pleasantly. Then he shook his head, picked up his drink, bourbon straight, and the peanuts, and went back to his table. Cameron waited until he could safely get up and walk to the door; he put a bill on the bar, leaving a large tip for the bartender, and found his way out, his legs just about carrying him.

Out of the door he turned left and walked a dozen yards where he knew there was a deserted alley. Bent double with his hands on his knees, he threw up between two dumpsters; then he went back to his car and sat with his head back and his hands shaking on the wheel. There was no doubt in his mind, absolutely none. Sometimes he went a few weeks without thinking about it in detail and then it would come to him every day for a month. No more than a few seconds, but it was enough.

August 28, 1985. He was twelve going on thirteen. They were fishing at Jackson Pond, David had nicked three cigarettes from his father and they were smoking with their feet in the cool water and their bikes in a heap on the ground. They were discussing whether to take off their T-shirts and get bitten by a million mosquitoes or keep them on and suffer the heat. Jimmy had put his head under water and then shaken it like a dog, David had told him that his ugly face would scare the fish away. He had trailed a thin gold chain with a tiny St Nicholas medal on the surface of the water; it was better than bait, he said. The chain was a gift of his father's

Scottish relatives who thought his mother's Jewishness was not a good reason to deny the boy the protection of the patron saint of Holy Souls. The chain glittered in the water, the fish stayed away.

So far, so good: the day was glorious and school was in the distant future. Then the blue van appeared on the path and things got fuzzy.

John Cameron came to in the back of the van, blindfolded, hands and feet tied and pinching. He thought he was asleep and dreaming, a hell of a dream really, then he bumped against someone lying next to him on the floor and lost consciousness again.

The next time, men's voices were whispering nearby and he lasted a while. It was so hot under the blindfold he could barely breathe and it smelled of something awful like they'd used it to wipe grease off an engine. The shirt was stuck to him and when his head started to pound he knew they were in trouble and it was for real. He wanted to call out for the others but he lay still, disoriented and rigid with fear until the van came to a rocky stop.

The blindfold was tight around his face and he couldn't see anything above or under it. He felt someone large and strong lifting him clear off the grimy mat on the van floor and out; the fresh air was wonderful and it was so quiet, they must be somewhere out of the city. The men, three maybe four, worked quickly and spoke little.

He was pinned against a tree and a coil of rope was tied around his shoulders and thighs. The grass was cool under his feet and he remembered they had taken their shoes off at the pond – they must still be there. He heard a rustle of clothes and movement to his left – David and Jimmy. What was happening? They had been kidnapped; he had read about that kind of thing in the newspapers. Last year someone took a kid in Spokane, returned him after a couple of days. Was that it? Thick silence hung over them; he could smell cigarette smoke and heard the suspensions in the van creak a little when the men sat down. The clearer his head became, the heavier the sense of dread, like somebody kneeling on his chest.

For the longest time no one said a word, then a man spoke. 'Boys, I want you to listen to me and listen good. Say yes.'

Nobody spoke.

'Say yes.'

'Yes.' John heard two faint voices like his own.

'This is a message for your daddies, I want you to remember it. The message is: it's not personal, it's business. You got it? Repeat it.'

John was blacking out; the rope was tight and he couldn't get his voice to work. He wanted to run, he wanted to be home, he wanted his mother.

'Repeat it.'

'It's not personal, it's business.'

He heard David and Jimmy and he opened his mouth and nothing came out.

'Again.'

'It's not personal, it's business.'

'Hey, little guy. You heard me, right? You want to go home?'

John nodded. The man was standing close by, tobacco and August sweat beyond the filthy rag on his face. There was something so ugly and nasty about his voice that John was almost glad he couldn't see him. What kind of face would go with that voice?

'C'mon, sweetheart, say it.'

With the smallest voice, John said the words.

'Louder.'

John yelled the words out.

'Ooh, this one got a set of lungs on him,' somebody sniggered.

John took great gulps of air and tried not to sob; he wouldn't give them the satisfaction.

'C'mon, boy. Let's hear it.'

John yelled the words out again.

'Good job. Now, we are going to let you go home in a while but I want to be clear about something: you ever, ever tell the cops about this and I'm going to come back and take you. You ever tell anybody at all about this and I'm going to come back and take you, and I will hurt your mom and dad too. You understand? You saw nothing and you heard nothing. You just pass on the message to your daddies and everybody stays alive. You understand?'

'Yes.'

Now they knew, it was about the restaurant. The grown-ups didn't talk business around them but that had to be it.

'See if you can get louder than that, you little girl.' John felt something sharp slashing at his arm.

'The hell are you doing, man?' One man's voice yards away.

'Shut up. Don't make me do this, boy. Let's hear it.'

John yelped as the blade cut his arm again.

'Hey!'

'Get into the van and shut the fuck up,' the man said calmly.

'C'mon, man, let's get out of here.'

'What are you doing?' It was David's voice.

'Leave the kid alone. Let's go.'

'Don't make me do this, you little shit. Let's hear it.'

John yelled out the words. He thought of the frogs they gave them to dissect in school: some kids couldn't wait to start. *I bet he's like that and I'm going to die*, and for a second he felt as if that terror was going to squeeze him right out of his body and into death.

'Stop it!' David's voice.

'What did you say?' The man moved away.

'He's just a little kid. We'll do what you want – just stop hurting him.' David's voice sounded out of breath, scared into a higher pitch than normal.

'If you want to go home in one piece, boy, you're going to have to shut up right now.'

And it happened, quicker than he would have ever thought possible: David was breathing fast, he wasn't speaking. John had seen a kid once having an asthma attack; David sounded like that but worse.

'What's wrong?' Another man's voice.

'He's not breathing. Cut him loose.' Another man.

'Don't touch him. He's going to be fine.'

'He can't breathe. Do something.'

They were speaking on top of each other and under it that awful choking and gasping.

'Shit! We have to do something.'

'Touch him and I'll cut your hand off.'

'There's something wrong with him.'

'We can see that, you moron. Cut him loose.'

'No.'

The other men wouldn't go against him; they were standing around and the breathing was getting faint and shallow. John was straining to hear.

'Dave?'

'Dave?' Jimmy's voice.

Cameron was pulling at the ropes, leaning as far as he could, but suddenly he couldn't hear David anymore. He couldn't hear anything anymore.

'Dave?'

The longest silence. Somewhere above him the ticks and rustles of the tree he was tied to.

'We're done here,' the man said finally.

'What happened?' Jimmy's voice.

They heard someone starting to cut through ropes. 'This shit we hadn't signed up for.'

'Just do it.'

'What are we going to do with him?'

'He's coming with us.'

'What are we going to do?'

'Shut up and start the van.'

'This is not—'

'Shut the fuck up and start the van.'

John Cameron couldn't speak, couldn't move, couldn't think. The blackness in front of him spun and closed in. He smelled the acrid cigarette smoke and felt the man near him.

'You remember what we talked about.'

'How's David? What happened?'

'You and your friend don't say anything to anyone. Not to the cops, not to your father, no one.'

'What did you do to him?'

'Not to the cops, not to your father, no one.'

'What did you do to him?' John's voice cracked.

'Maybe I should make sure you do remember.'

John felt the blade on his skin and the searing pain and he passed out. The voices followed him into the black. 'What now?'

When he woke up a while later, his arms stung, his hands burned and he was soaked with sweat.

'Jimmy?'

'I'm here.'

'Where are they?'

'They're gone.'

'Are you okay?'

'I think so. And you?'

'My arms hurt.'

'I think they took David.'

Neither of them could bring themselves to say it.

After a while Jimmy whispered: 'Do you think they're going to come back?'

'I don't know. Maybe.'

It was a terrible notion, the men coming back, but if they didn't, who would find them and was anybody looking for them?

'I'm going to try to get free, Jimmy. You try too. We must get away before they come back.'

By rubbing his head up and down against the bark John managed to undo the blindfold a little; after an hour it slid off his face and rested around his neck like a cowboy handkerchief. He opened his eyes wide, blinking the grittiness away: they were in the woods and night was falling. They could have been anywhere and no one knew they were there.

John looked around: there was no road, no path, nothing. How did they get there? He didn't know. He looked up: the tree he was tied to seemed absolutely huge, the kind they make you count the inside rings of when they saw it off. The rest was just tall grass, ferns and more ferns, as far as the eye could see, which wasn't very far because the woods were thick and the gloom was already coming in. Then he looked down and what was left of his courage disappeared: he was covered in blood, encrusted on the slashed fabric of his T-shirt and on his skin; he could barely see the color of the sleeves. He gasped and Jimmy turned to him, his voice panicky again. 'What is it?'

John looked at his hands dark and slick, and felt the tears come. He could cry, Jimmy wouldn't see. It wasn't the pain – he was completely numb; it was everything inside him suddenly letting go. He moved his fingers a little and they still worked. The burning pain came in waves.

'It's okay, it's nothing,' he said and started on the rope around his shoulders, twisting and turning to make it looser, his face wet and his lips pressed tight.

Darkness found them still struggling. Jimmy was making slow progress and hadn't even gotten his blindfold off yet. By the time it was pitch black they reckoned maybe the men wouldn't come back; they had left them there to get free or stay lost forever. And the boys talked, non-stop, about anything but where they were and what had happened to them. They talked through the night because they thought the noise would scare any wild animal away and, most of all, because the other's voice was the only real proof they were still alive.

It was a warm August night, they were cold but they could stand it, even joke about it when Jimmy had to pee and he said he didn't understand how it could come out so hot when his thing was frozen. Neither admitted they had wet themselves when the men were still there. The night drew on slowly, small clouds of bugs visiting around their faces and the odd stretch of silence when one fell asleep and the other sort of kept guard for a few minutes, before hollering his friend awake.

At some point John wriggled under and out of the rope around his shoulders. It was a small victory but it felt damn good. Still, he was so weak that he was almost glad his legs were tied to the tree or he'd have fallen right on his face. He was hungry and thirsty and the 3 a.m. chill was something neither of them felt like joking about anymore. Jimmy was asleep for longer stretches and John would keep talking to him until he stirred.

It was dawn when he got free, biting at the rope around his wrists, so cold that he wasn't feeling anything in his arms and hands. His bare feet slid out easily and he found himself on his knees, hands flat on the ground, trembling as if he would need to learn how to walk again. He grabbed a handful of dewy grass and rubbed it on his forehead and cheeks. He staggered to Jimmy, who was asleep, and put his hand on his shoulder.

'Hey.'

'Hold on. I'm going to take the blindfold off first.'

His fingers were so chilled he couldn't undo the knot; instead he carefully pulled it over his head and threw it in the bushes. The first light was glowing through the mist and the boys looked at each other. Jimmy's eyes went to the dark streaks on John's shirt and he opened his mouth.

'It's okay,' John said quickly, but in fact he was so light-headed it was difficult to keep things straight in his mind. First, he had to free Jimmy. Alright – he could do that. Except that he couldn't; his ropes were still tight and they wouldn't budge. John worked on them for an hour with no result aside from a slight fraying in a couple of places.

'You have to go get help,' Jimmy said.

'I'm not going to leave you here.'

'You are not leaving me, you are going to get help. Somebody must be looking for us. I mean, your mom goes bananas if you are five minutes late for dinner, right?'

'Right.' John smiled weakly.

'You'd better go.'

Neither of them wanted to say how pitifully feeble they felt; it would be like saying they were a girl or something.

'Okay.'

John looked up where the sunlight seemed to be coming from. It was as good a place as any to start. He walked off into the bushes and turned around once before going down into a dip. Jimmy's head was resting back against the tree and his eyes were already closed. John started running.

Just over five years later, John Cameron sat in his car. Now he knew exactly what the man who had given him his scars looked like. The man had seen him. He had spoken to him, for Chrissake, and not recognized him – not even a second look while the very air around him hummed with his fear.

The door of the bar opened and closed. John slouched in the

seat. In the rearview mirror, the man was slowly walking away. The key was already in the ignition; all he had to do was turn it and go. The man was getting to the corner; a few more seconds and he would disappear from his life. John could not let that happen, not this time.

He pocketed the key quickly, slid out of the car and closed the door gently. He could still see him; maybe he was walking home. There was nothing else to do. Cameron crossed the road and followed.

He kept well back. The streets were deserted; between them there was little aside from a block of dingy two-stories, with shops on the ground and one-room apartments above them. Ten minutes later, the man stopped and let himself into a door with peeling red paint next to a launderette. Seconds later, two windows lit up and curtains were pulled close.

John Cameron walked past the red door slowly, close enough to see that there were two doorbells and neither had a name on it. He got to the corner, crossed the road and came back, his eyes never leaving the windows. There was no further movement: the man was in for the night. John Cameron stood by the end of the block, pretending to look at a pawn-shop window through a metal grid. He could go now, but he was reluctant to leave. In the end, he walked back to his car and drove home; his parents were asleep and his mother had left some cake for him in the fridge.

He was still stunned and shaken and, if he had to be honest, somewhat exhilarated by the whole night. He ate the slice of cold chocolate cake standing over the kitchen sink; he wasn't hungry but the food tasted like everything that was good and steady in his life.

His mind raced and his common sense tried to keep up. He had to call Nathan; he had to tell him. In his nightmares, in the terrifying dreams he'd had after they had been rescued, there was only ever one man: the others had disappeared, their roles were minor and unimportant. He was the one responsible for the others. He had forbidden them to help David and David had died because of him.

In the chaos of the investigation, with the two main witnesses saying little of any use, there had been only one certainty: David Quinn suffered from a mild form of arrhythmia, a heart condition that affected his heartbeat. He had taken medication from time to time and had been expected to live a normal life but when his parents were told what the boys had heard, they knew instantly what that meant: their son was gone.

John Cameron went into the living room and poured himself a small measure of his father's Johnnie Walker. It was something he had never done before; then again it was that kind of night. He sat at the kitchen table and went back to the place where nightmares came from.

They had talked about it, Jimmy and himself, before they had given statements, but only once. For months after, they had been terrified the men would come back for them and their parents. It hadn't been hard to lie, to tell the officers that they had never seen the men's faces and couldn't recognize their voices. They had been taken from Jackson Pond, drugged, taken someplace in a van. When they woke up blindfolded in the woods they were tied up, and after that, David had been sick. No one had told them why they were there; no one had said one damn thing about anything.

As the years had passed theories had come and gone. John Cameron knew now with the wisdom of his late teens that it had been a shake-down gone wrong.

He looked at the wall-mounted phone next to the door. It would take him exactly ten seconds to call Nathan and tell him – and then what? He'd get the man picked up, get a formal identification, charge him, put him in a cell and throw away the key. John had kept his ears open all the time Quinn had worked in the County Prosecutor's Office. He knew what was what and that knowledge fell on him suddenly: they didn't stand a chance. He was the only witness that could identify him – he doubted Jimmy could – and what kind of case was that? The defense attorney, even those public defenders with a hundred cases in one day, would blow his testimony right out of the water. They would never indict; the man would walk away.

John Cameron washed the glass and put it on the draining board. He knew where the man lived, he knew where he drank his beer. That was more than he had three hours ago.

He went to bed and somehow, in the morning, he managed to sit through two hours of English Lit. and one hour of Introduction to Philosophy.

When the time came he drove to Eastlake, parked in the same spot and turned off the engine. He was scared again. So what? The guy didn't know who he was: all he had to do was sit on the stool and drink his Coke. He had decided earlier that he needed to be stone-cold sober, even if alcohol would kick-start his courage. Fear was only a normal animal reaction, he said to himself. He walked in, saw the man sitting at the usual back table and was about to turn and leave. Instead he found his seat and ordered.

A short while later, the man came to the bar for a chat with the bartender. John's insides were frozen solid but he didn't blink. The man recognized him from the night before and nodded to him, Cameron nodded back. His eyes followed the man as he returned to his table and something in John Cameron's world began to shift.

Over the next month he would drop by maybe three times a week, and more often than not the man would be there and each time the spike of fear would be a little smaller. The bartender was a friendly guy who'd get bored behind the bar and chat to whoever was around – sometimes that was Cameron. One night, John asked him the man's name because he thought he reminded him of someone his father used to know. The man's name was Timothy Gilman, he worked in the docks and had spent time upstate on some kind of embezzlement beef.

'Really?' Cameron said but privately he thought that if the man had been away it must have been on a violent felony charge: nothing about him said *fraud*, everything said *I'm going to hurt you and hurt you badly*.

One Saturday evening they were all at the restaurant for Jimmy's father's birthday. The group of friends and family had taken over the private room. There was loud cheering when the cake was brought out from the kitchen, the candles lit and trembling.

Cameron's skin tingled, he couldn't focus on anything. He knew that Quinn would have believed him but Quinn and his family had barely survived David's death the first time round. This time it would kill them too.

They had walked into that same room years before, the walls still only half painted and the restaurant a week from the grand opening. The grown-ups hadn't noticed Cameron, who was sitting behind a cardboard box and playing with a brush.

'I understand that kind of thing has happened before but no one approached us yet, and we don't know they ever will,' his father said.

'It's just something we have to be aware of,' Quinn's father replied. 'Someone might come knocking. This is a new business and there are people who might see us as easy targets.'

'Are you saying we should just pay protection money to whoever comes calling?'

'No. I'm saying we don't know if there are feathers to be ruffled here. Hopefully, we'll be left alone.'

'And if we're not?'

'We'll cross that bridge when we have to. *If* we have to,' Quinn's father replied.

They had come for the boys one August afternoon, and the bridge was unequivocally crossed.

Just as his father was standing up to make a toast, John Cameron wondered how good it would feel to get Gilman back in the woods and what he would say to him if he managed to get him there. Often, in the quiet nights at the bar, he had played around with that notion. They certainly would have a lot to talk about. The fear wasn't completely gone – some of it was still there as well as something else he couldn't define.

His eyes met Jimmy's across the table. Cameron picked up his glass. Of all the things he was ever going to do in his life, what he was about to do would be the one thing he would never regret and whatever came of it, he would be able to live with the end result. If that made him a little less of a human being than they were, Cameron thought as he looked around the room, well, that was just the price of doing business.

It was six weeks to the day John Cameron had first laid eyes on Timothy Gilman. He had had lunch with Quinn in their usual diner on Second Avenue and had spent the afternoon taking care of the last details of his special project.

When he walked into the bar, his eyes went automatically to the table Gilman and a couple of his friends would sit at. He was there. Cameron perched on a stool and ordered a coffee with a shot of bourbon. Two men sat with Gilman – one skinny guy with a tattoo on the back of his hand and a tall Scandinavian-looking fella. Cameron didn't want to get to know either.

He put a coin in the public telephone in the corner and called Quinn at home. There was something about hearing his friend's voice while looking at Gilman a few feet away – it steadied his hand and his heart. You find courage wherever you can, if you can.

Minutes later he couldn't have remembered what they'd spoken about – maybe the ball game, maybe something else.

He exchanged a few instantly forgettable remarks with the bartender, just to prove it was a night like any other, finished his drink and left, maybe a little earlier than usual but not so that anybody would notice.

The snow had just started to fall as he came out. The coffee and the bourbon had somewhat counteracted each other and he was grateful for the sharp, clean air. John Cameron had bought new clothes especially for that evening – nothing special, just something warm he wouldn't mind burning in a fire at the end of the day.

The streets were predictably deserted. He checked his watch: it was 10.20 p.m. His car was already in place, in the alley opposite Gilman's house. There was no light in the alley; it started dark and went to pitch black in a matter of steps. Cameron leant on his car with his arms crossed; someone on the pavement ten yards away wouldn't have seen him and that suited him fine. Gilman was a creature of habit but he was also six foot tall and built to match his temperament. Cameron waited. His heart was pounding but his head was clear. He didn't have to do this, he could walk away without shame or regrets, and if his hands were shaking inside the gloves, it was as much the cold as his nerves.

He didn't think about his family or his friends, he didn't think about David. He focused on the street ahead, the thin snow which wouldn't last the night, the cars in the distance on Eastlake Avenue, something small scurrying across the alley behind him.

Cameron heard Gilman before he saw him. The man appeared around the corner and Cameron pulled down his black ski mask. He let him reach the door with the peeling red paint, he saw him pull out the key from his pocket. He covered the distance between them in seconds, the sand-filled sap already in his right hand. He hit him once hard on the back of the head and Gilman fell heavily without a sound. Cameron stood over him breathing fast inside the wool and looked around. Nobody and no one. He had to be quick. *Be quick or be dead.*

He rolled Gilman onto his front and tied his wrists firmly with a length of plastic rope, the kind used to hang out laundry – three colored strands, blue, red and white. He tied his feet in the same way, fast and careful, his hands working in the thin leather gloves. From his pocket he took out the end of a black plastic bag, fitted it over his head and tied it loosely around his neck. The last thing he wanted was for the guy to choke right there.

Cameron looked up. Nobody and no one. He backed the car out of the alley and close to Gilman, popped the boot open and grabbed the man under the arms. He lifted him like a firefighter across his back and slid him in, made sure hands and feet were well inside the boot and then shut it gently. He scanned the street, pavements, windows. It was all clear. John Cameron got in the car and drove off, at the legal speed limit, out of the city and toward Mount Rainier National Park.

Chapter 31

'Wake up.'

Timothy Gilman opened his eyes. He was sitting with his legs straight out in front of him and his back resting against a tree. His hands had been re-tied and rested on his belly. He was disoriented and his head was killing him. He tried clumsily to get his legs under him and get up.

'Don't do that.'

Around his neck, something tightened slightly, then released. He couldn't have stood anyway; he flopped back down.

'What is this?' he mumbled.

'Are you thirsty?'

'What?'

'There's a bottle of water by your side.'

His mouth was dry and he was thirsty enough to risk it. He found it, unscrewed the top and drank deeply. Maybe that would buy him a little time to understand just what the hell was going on. He took another small sip and another after that. He looked around, his eyes narrowing in the effort to get everything into focus.

The only light came from the beams of a car parked some few yards away. They cut through the clearing and disappeared into the firs. About ten feet in front of him, a man sat on his heels, slim build, a black ski mask covering his face. A mask was good, Gilman thought. It meant the guy didn't want to be recognized, which meant he was planning to let him go at some point, which was going to be a big mistake.

A length of the same rope he had been bound with was coiled around the man's left hand. Gilman followed it. It went straight up into the tree he was leaning against, wrapped itself once around a heavy branch and came down to end with a noose around his own neck. Enough slack to let him turn his head but tight enough not to let him slip out.

His eyes went back to the man crouching. He looked much slighter than he was; still, with all his weight behind it, the bastard might just be able to hang him sitting down.

His throat was scratchy and his voice came out in a low rasp.

'You're dead,' Gilman said.

John Cameron stood up, took the slack in the rope and wrapped it slowly around his forearm. His heart was punching its way out of his chest and his breathing inside the mask was faster than he would have liked but there they were now, the two of them, and the voice that came from him was hardly his own.

'I don't think so, not tonight,' he said.

'Is this a joke?'

'No, it's not.'

''Cause I'm freezing my butt.' Gilman shifted on the ground. 'And I'm just about ready to break your neck, you don't tell me what's going on.'

John Cameron had rehearsed this moment so many times in his mind, he knew the words by heart – what he would say, what he would do. Yet as he stood in front of Gilman, holding his life at the end of a rope, everything felt wrong and pointless. He opened his mouth and nothing came out. He was suffocating inside that mask.

'What do you want?'

His left hand holding the rope firmly, John Cameron took the ski mask off with his right and put it in the pocket of the jacket.

Gilman leant forward to get a better look. 'What the—'

Feeding the slack as he moved, Cameron crouched again so their eyes would be level and waited for Gilman's thoughts to come together.

'You're the kid from the bar.' Gilman was incredulous. He was being held hostage by a boy. He got his legs under him and started to get up.

'Sit.' Cameron gave the rope a sharp yank and Gilman fell back down. He stared at the slight figure almost within reach. 'Are you insane?' he rasped.

'My name is John Cameron.'

'John, I don't give a shit what your name is, are you out of your mind?'

'Possibly. But not in any way that matters right now.' Maybe he had been crazy to take the mask off but it felt so much better. 'My name is John Cameron,' he said. 'I have been looking for you for a very long time.'

Gilman was more stunned than scared: the boy's name sounded familiar but it still meant nothing to him. His voice cut the air like a blade. 'What do you want?'

'I want to know who paid you to take us. I want to know what happened to David.'

Gilman blinked. 'What?'

Cameron took off his glove, stuffed it in his pocket, looked at his right hand casually and flexed his fingers. There was enough light for Gilman to see.

'I want to know who paid you to take us. I want to know what happened to David.'

The change came slowly over Gilman's face. He sat back against the tree, his eyes hard and his breath coming out white and heavy.

The rope around his wrists was pulled tight and his hands closed into fists. He remembered.

'I'm going to take you apart,' he whispered.

'You tried once,' Cameron said quietly. The old fear was nipping at his heels but there was such an unexpected relief in finally meeting the man face to face, each knowing the other. 'Tell me about David.'

'And then what?'

'And then I'll let you go.'

The man smiled. 'I don't think so. You didn't bring me out here for conversation.'

'If I had wanted to hurt you I could have done it a hundred times, those nights you came home from the bar alone. Like tonight. If I wanted you dead, you would be dead.' The words felt odd in his mouth. Cameron realized he wasn't lying.

'How did you find me?'

'By chance. I'd been in the bar a few times and one night I heard your voice.'

'Brought back memories, I guess. By the way, how's the hand?'

'Pretty good. What happened to David?'

The man shook his head. 'The kid was dead by the time we cut him loose.'

Cameron went cold. He didn't know whether it was the man's words or the night pressing in. 'His name was David Quinn.'

'Whatever,' Gilman said. 'You're going to have to untie me if you want to know where we buried him. Wouldn't you want to know?' He held out his wrists.

'Sure,' Cameron said and he did not move.

'It was an accident – you must realize that. He was sick. It wasn't our fault.'

'You could have helped him.'

'How did you know we didn't try? You were blindfolded.'

Cameron wound the rope around his arm once more and tightened the grip in his hand.

'Do you want to know who paid us? I can tell you. I can take you right to them.' Gilman turned his head left and right. 'But you have to take this thing off my neck first.'

A beat of silence. Nothing stirs around them.

'Sure,' Cameron said softly.

'Sure,' Gilman replied. He started to get up. Cameron let him get halfway up and then suddenly yanked on the rope with two hands and almost all his weight. Gilman gasped, tried to grab at it. 'Stay,' Cameron hissed at him.

Gilman slumped back, the noose still taut, his head bent a little sideways, his feet fighting to find the ground.

'Where's David?'

'Nowhere you can find him.'

Cameron pulled the rope tighter. 'Where is he?'

Gilman stood on tiptoe. He had only so much breath left in his lungs.

'In the water. We put him in the water.'

'Where?'

'Does it matter?'

Cameron dug his heels in the ground and pulled.

'In the Hoh. We dropped him in the river.'

'Who paid you?'

'I don't know.'

'Don't lie to me.'

'It was a cash order. We never met the client.'

There was a rush through Cameron's blood. He could have hung on to the man till they were both dead but anything out of the man's mouth was going to be a lie. He had to force his aching arms to move; he gave Gilman some slack and they both tried to catch their breath.

Gilman looked at Cameron. The boy had more nerve than he'd thought but he was still just that, a kid. Five years older maybe, but still a kid. Gilman bent double and started coughing hard, holding the noose away from his neck as if he couldn't breathe. The irony of it, Cameron thought, and gave him some slack; Gilman bent even lower, measuring the distance between them out of the corner of his eye. Twelve feet.

The boy wasn't armed – there was nothing in his hands. If he had a gun or a knife in his pocket he would have to reach for it. In his coughing fit Gilman stumbled forward and felt the kid feeding him a little rope. The boy wasn't a killer – maybe he wished he was but he wasn't, and, even with his hands tied, by the time he was done with him he'd wish he was dead anyway. Ten feet.

John Cameron stood his ground. The rope was slowly coming unwound from his arm. He knew Gilman was getting close but he wasn't going to pull it while the man was choking all by himself.

'Get back,' he said.

Gilman knew that the further he got from the tree the harder it would be for Cameron to yank him back to it. He kept his head down, coughing and inching forward, and raised his hand as if to excuse himself. Cameron took one step back and still fed him the slack. Jesus, the kid was dumb.

Gilman looked up and saw Cameron take another step. Now he was holding the end of the rope in his hand; he would need more than that to stop him.

Now.

Gilman straightened up, grabbed the noose with his hands and went forward. John Cameron opened his hand and the rope flew away. Their eyes met and locked; the boy didn't flinch. Suddenly released, Gilman surged on with a growl. 'You're dead.' His voice thick with every ugly memory in Cameron's heart.

The boy went back as the man lunged forward and the earth

gave way: Gilman's foot landed on the thin snow and a layer of leaves and branches and he felt the void opening under him but he could not stop himself – he was falling into it, crashing through the slight cover, his feet kicking out for support and his hands scrabbling for a grip. He howled and fell six feet into the hole and screamed when the spikes went clear through his chest and legs. After that, a heavy silence – the kind Cameron had heard only once before in his life.

His legs shaking, John Cameron went back to the car. From the backseat he took a torch. He stood over the edge of the hole and flicked it on. Gilman was face down, completely still. There was very little blood. He ran the beam across the body. He must have died instantly.

John Cameron braced himself but nothing came. As the punch of adrenaline went away, he was calm and his hand barely shook. He didn't know what he should feel as he stood by the pit that had taken him seven days to dig, almost clawing it out of the hard earth. Yes, he would have been glad to see him fall all the way down into hell. In his heart, if he dared look deep enough, Cameron hoped he would find a sense of peace, but maybe that would come later. For now it was done, it was over, Gilman was dead.

As he started to collect branches and greenery to fill as much of the hole as possible, Cameron wondered whether it was a good thing he had enjoyed that moment, as Gilman was about to fall, quite so much. He covered the body and worked hard with a shovel to put the earth back where it came from. Timothy Gilman's body had a grave – it was more than David ever had. The work kept him warm while all around him the snow fell light.

Driving back to the city, he stopped by a liquor store and used his fake ID, and by the next dawn Nathan Quinn would bail him out of a police lock-up.

Chapter 32

Harry Salinger trails a finger on his ribcage, following the dark line of the bruise that marks his meeting with Madison on Friday night. He stands bare-chested, mesmerized by the red and purple, in front of a full-size mirror in his bedroom, a spartan room almost devoid of color.

There it is, the point of contact – he can almost feel her anger radiating out from it. It is fierce, which makes sense to him because the letter 'f' is purple, just like his bruise. The thing is, he is counting on her anger and, as he presses lightly on a rib, he flinches at the sharpness of the pain. A little of her spirit has passed into him during the fight; he can feel their connection and he welcomes it. In her house in Three Oaks, she might be looking at the marks he has left on her, she would see them clearly, and yet she would miss their meaning.

Harry Salinger stretches his arms out to his sides and the light catches the long, thin scars etched all over his chest and back. Prison scars – dozens of jagged lines made with whatever was at hand as someone held him down. The scars remind him of where he came from and where he's going like his own personal map of Hell. He remembers each cut and who gave it to him. His sallow skin will not let him forget even one day of those 48 months.

Salinger puts on a clean white shirt and returns to the basement. On the wall, he has taped enlargements of the photographs he had given to Fred Tully at the *Star*. They had got the ball rolling on Cameron in the media, yet more than that, he thought they were really good shots and he was quite proud of them. Especially the black and white where James Sinclair was still alive and struggling. They might not win any prizes but he enjoyed looking at them. On the worktop, he has placed the .22 that he has used to shoot Annie Sinclair, her children and Detective Kevin Brown. An Anglepoise lamp is pointed at it and the metal sings in the light. Salinger has spent a long time polishing it today, delighted by the memories of the muzzle flash.

He shifts his chair so that he can see the object in the corner of the basement. It has traveled out of his mind and into the sketches on the wall and now, unbelievable as it is, it sits there. The glass shards on the metal bars catch the light but it is the steel knife blades that give the cage its very reason for being. Salinger is grateful: he expected it to fulfill his purpose but never in a million years would he have imagined it would be so beautiful.

He turns on one of the monitors and presses the 'play' button on the video remote: out of the evening darkness Alice Madison's windows are bright, the front door opens and the zoom kicks in, framing three people in the doorway. Madison's cut above the eye and the splint on her arm are clearly visible and unconsciously Salinger rubs the side where she hit him. Madison says goodbye to the woman and hugs the child tight. He pauses the video. Madison is hugging the boy: it tells Salinger all he needs to know.

Chapter 33

Sunday morning, early enough to order food and call it breakfast. Amy Sorensen stepped into the diner and looked around for Madison, who sat at the bar with a cup of coffee and a notebook spread open in front of her. Madison wore black jeans and a black roll-neck; the outfit made her look pale but her eyes were bright and she smiled when she saw her. Sorensen noticed the leather holster under her blazer, the butt of her weapon on her left side now.

They moved to a booth and ordered: Sorensen was just coming off her shift when she had called Madison, waking her from a brief sleep, because for what they had to discuss they needed a face-to-face. Madison had welcomed the chance to get out of the house and the drive had been tricky but not impossible. Halfway through she had taken the splint off her arm and thrown it behind her on the backseat.

Sorensen looked her over. 'Nice stitches,' she said. 'An inch lower and you could have a pirate thing going.'

Madison smiled – she felt about ten years older since the last time they had seen each other. Then the smile went away. 'Brown's still on the ventilator.'

'I know. I called the hospital earlier.'

They didn't need to say any more about it; they both cared about the man and he was fighting for his life. The waitress brought them their order: French toast and bacon for Madison and a fruit salad for Sorensen.

I met Cameron last night. Nice fella, good runner. Madison took a bite of toast – everything tasted like cardboard. She liked Sorensen and her opinion mattered a great deal to her, but what she was about to say might drive a wedge between them that their friendship would never completely recover from. A crime-scene unit investigator worships at the altar of forensic evidence and Madison was about to pick up a hammer and smash the thing to bits.

'I heard about your meeting with Fynn.' Sorensen had never been big on chit-chat. 'It was all over the department, and there was a lot of bull about you saying the evidence was *tainted*.' The word itself was distasteful. 'I'm here to hear your side and make sure you haven't lost your fucking mind. And, by the way, the blood in the Explorer matches the hairs in Sinclair's ligature.'

Madison had never heard Sorensen swear; in her crisp tones it was the equivalent of somebody else putting their fist through a window. It was simple: if the case against Cameron went to trial Sorensen would be right there batting for Homicide.

'I don't want the complete history of the universe from the big bang; just give me the bullet points.'

'Fair enough,' Madison replied. 'The hairs in the ligature – Brown asked you to run a check a couple of days ago. I'm going to tell you what you found, and we'll take it from there.'

'Shoot.'

Madison sat back in her seat. 'Glue.'

Sorensen looked up from her food and Madison knew she had her, and she went on, 'You've found trace residue of an adhesive, possibly the kind used in your everyday scotch tape. Also a cleaning agent in a minute quantity, sodium hypochlorite, bleach – you can find it under any kitchen sink. A tiny amount and concentrated at the tip of the hair, nowhere near the end holding the DNA.' She paused. 'How am I doing so far?'

Sorensen had finished the tests herself two hours ago and nobody else had had access to the results. She took a sip and her eyes stayed on Madison's.

'So far so good. The hairs were washed in a very mild solution of water and bleach after they came in contact with the adhesive.'

Madison blew air out of her cheeks. 'Excellent. It's what I was hoping for.'

'I'd say it was a pretty damn good guess. How did you get to glue and bleach? Neither was present in the immediate vicinity of the crime scene or the victims' bodies.'

'What you heard about me saying that the evidence was tainted – I never said that. What I said, what I think, is that someone manipulated the evidence.'

'Stop right there: you know that if I'm questioned by Quinn under oath this conversation is going to make his day.'

'If I had a dollar for every time I heard that in the last thirty-six hours—'

'You think this is funny?'

'Not yet but it's getting there. You check it out yourself: every item recovered from the crime scene that carries Cameron's finger-prints or DNA could have been brought *into* the house. We didn't find any prints on the bodies, on the furniture, on the kitchen surfaces. Nothing on objects that could not be dropped in, like a bedside table; everything we have could fit into a bag. Still, suppos-edly, he took off his gloves to pick up a glass and left it there for us to find.'

'Sometimes a cigar is just a cigar.'

'Not this week it isn't.'

Sorensen wasn't going to be turned quite so easily. 'How did you get to glue and bleach?'

'Pull up your sleeve.'

'Why?'

'Indulge me.'

Sorensen rolled her eyes and pulled up the sleeve of her flannel shirt. Madison put her hand on Sorensen's bare forearm, leant forward as if to say something, and her other hand bumped the tall plastic tumbler. A little water spilled over the counter and they both dabbed it with paper napkins.

Madison picked up her fork and speared a piece of bacon. 'All done.'

'All done what?'

Madison raised her hand. Around her two middle fingers, like a child's pretend rings, two small clear circles of tape, on them a couple of fine blond hairs from Sorensen's arm. 'The glue comes from the adhesive; the bleach is how he tried to wash off the glue without damaging the follicle and the DNA.'

Sorensen pulled her sleeve down.

'Did you feel the tape?' Madison asked her.

'I felt something but if that's the only problem, it can be fixed with a big enough diversion.'

'That's what I'm thinking.'

Sorensen shook her head. 'Neat trick. Do you think it'll work in court?'

'Did I give you something to think about?'

'You haven't given me a motive.'

There was no way around that one. 'I don't have one yet. I've been having the same conversation over and over for the last forty-eight hours. Sometimes I do think I have lost my mind.'

'Do you feel strongly enough about it you're going to pin your career on it?'

'I'm looking for Brown's shooter and it's not Cameron.'

'That's not what Ballistics says.'

'Ballistics says it's the same .22 that shot the Sinclairs. We don't have the weapon, we don't have Cameron's prints on the weapon, and we don't have a positive gunshot residue test that says he shot the weapon.'

'Cameron is a killer,' Sorensen said quietly.

'I never said he wasn't,' Madison replied.

For a minute or two neither spoke. They finished their food and drank their coffees.

'We had a call this morning,' Sorensen said. 'I don't know why I'm telling you this because it has no connection whatsoever with the case. A private investigator called very early today – he calls us on a Sunday – to ask whether we're holding the paperwork for a homicide that happened a few years ago upstate, in the Bones. The name of the victim was George Pathune, and as it happens it wasn't our jurisdiction at the time, so he wasted his dime. However, the name of the PI is Tod Hollis; we crossed paths before and his main client is Quinn, Locke & Associates, specifically Nathan Quinn. I thought you might like to know that.'

'No connection whatsoever with this case?'

'You're the one with the bright ideas.'

'Quinn has a PI looking into a prison death?'

'So it seems.'

'Why?'

'You tell me.'

Around them, the place had filled up and some customers had looked at Madison over their shoulders.

'Thank you. I mean that,' Madison said.

'I haven't decided whether I should wish you good luck or not,' Sorensen admitted.

Madison shrugged on her jacket. 'Take another crack at it, that's all I'm asking.'

They stood outside Brown's room. 'I've seen people come back who looked much worse,' Fynn said to Madison and possibly to himself. 'There's media outside; they'll be on you faster than you can spit.'

'I have nothing to say to them.'

'It's never stopped them before. By the way, I'll have the Sinclair keys in my hand by end of shift today, right?'

'No problem.'

'I didn't think it would be. Do you need someone to get your car for you?'

'No, thank you. I'll go now.' She turned as she was leaving. 'How are Spencer and Dunne doing?'

Fynn didn't know Spencer had told her about the lead on Cameron's boat.

'They're working it,' he replied, revealing nothing except for the hollow place between them.

'Good,' Madison said and felt a sudden biting sadness. Neither was going to say any more about anything.

Madison took the elevator to the ground floor. As she walked down the corridor, a door opened to her left and a nurse came out closing it behind her. The pungent hit of chloroform found Madison and stopped her where she was. Her body recognized it for what it was: the smell of the man who had tried to kill them. She looked around: nobody was paying attention. A cold sweat broke out and her heart was drumming fast. *What the hell.* It was hard to breathe. There was a small sofa a few steps ahead and she found it and sat on it and put her head between her knees, dark spots before her eyes.

The blue fabric had a checkered pattern, the texture rough under the damp palm of her hands. Madison closed her eyes. *It's only*

*chemistry, I'm fine, it's nothing but an automatic reaction to stress, breathe
slowly. One Mississippi, two Mississippi, three . . .*

'Are you feeling alright?'

Madison looked up: the nurse was standing by her side. She was
in her twenties, Japanese–American and pretty, an electric-blue
streak in her jet-black hair held back in a ponytail.

'I need a minute.'

'Would you like a glass of water?'

'I can get it.'

'Stay where you are.'

She came back with a paper cup. 'What happened to you?'

'It was nothing. I just got a little dizzy.'

The nurse eyed her cut and bruises. 'Do you want to see a doctor?'

'No, it's not necessary. Thank you.'

Ten minutes later, a half dozen camera lights came on as she
walked out of the glass front doors. She made for her car with her
head down and managed to reach it without having to physically
remove anybody from her path. As she eyed the pack in her rearview
mirror, she almost wished she'd had to.

Madison bought as many Sunday newspapers as she could find
at a stand on 6th Avenue and drove home. She thought of George
Pathune and how his murder fit into the case, and before she knew
it she was turning into her drive.

She dropped the bundle of newspapers on the table in the living
room and drew the curtains wide open. Alice Madison had never
had a panic attack in her life: what happened in the hospital was
a kind of post-traumatic stress reaction, that's all. No need to get
worked up about it; anybody who's ever been assaulted goes through
it on some level. It was to be expected.

Madison had a degree in Psychology and could rationalize the
hell out of it but what bothered her the most, what made her mad
enough to wish she could have picked a fight with a reporter, was

the shot of fear that had coursed through her when she had smelled the chloroform.

Madison needed clarity and if she wasn't quite there yet, she wanted light. She turned on every switch. She put on a pot of coffee and waited for it in the kitchen with *The Times*. Front page, an unbelievably young photograph of Brown from his days in uniform next to a snapshot of the Sinclairs, all victims shot by the same gun and by the same man, John Cameron. His arrest photograph was also on the front page, together with a couple of the sketches they had shown around Sea Tac airport.

Till now he had been very careful and very lucky, but with this kind of exposure, Madison didn't know how long he would last out there. Fynn was right about one thing: if they were going to take Cameron down, it wouldn't be dainty.

The doorbell went as she was going back to the table, a mug in one hand and the paper under her bad arm. She wasn't expecting anyone and Rachel would call before dropping by. Madison did not rush: she placed the cup on a side table and the paper next to it. She let the doorbell go once more and looked through the peephole. One guy, forties, glasses, shirt and tie under a windbreaker. *I can take him*, Madison said to herself because she needed the small joke. She opened the door and the man smiled warmly.

'Detective Madison, so good to meet you. I am Fred Tully from the *Star*. Do you have a couple of minutes?' He was still smiling.

This was the worm who had splashed the details of the case all over his paper; OPR were still itching to find a leak in the department. She looked him over, her temper rising.

He continued: 'I've been to the hospital. The doctors say—'

Madison lifted one finger and his voice sort of petered out. She stared a hole through him.

'You've got to be fucking kidding,' she whispered and slammed the door shut.

Given that Madison's weapon was still in her holster and her mood seemed less than cooperative, Tully thought it was probably best not to force the issue. She heard him drive off as a patrol car slowly cruised past – Officer Giordano was still keeping an eye on her. Madison went back to work.

The dining table was covered with all the notes and paperwork and sketches she had managed to take with her from the precinct. Hidden somewhere in all that information were the details that could triangulate the identity of the killer. *George Pathune*. Madison checked her watch. About now her contact in the Bones would be having lunch with her kids.

'Arnelle? It's Alice Madison. Sorry to call you on a Sunday.'

'Detective, I saw you on the news. Are you alright?'

'I'm okay.'

'Your partner?'

'He's still in ICU.'

'I couldn't believe it when I heard what happened.'

'Arnelle, let me get straight to it. I need a favor. I need to look at the file on the murder of an inmate called George Pathune; it happened about two to three years ago.'

There was silence on the line.

'The late George Pathune is getting kinda popular all of a sudden.'

'Someone already called you?'

'Three hours ago, a PI asked me about him.'

'What did you say to him?'

'I said, "I don't know how you got my private home number but you can sure call me in the office. I'll be there between and nine and five, Monday to Friday."'

Hollis would have offered to compensate her for her time and she had turned him down.

'Good one.'

'Does the Pathune file have anything to do with you and your partner getting beat?'

'Most probably,' Madison replied. Today, Quinn had only one client.

'Look, give me a couple of hours; I'll leave your name with security.'

'Arnelle—'

'Yeah, yeah. See ya later.'

Madison stood up. She had a good drive ahead of her and ought to get going. If Quinn was after the file it was definitely worth her time to find out why. She put some of the leftover coffee in a chrome travel mug and checked her cellphone was charged. She was almost out of the door when she remembered that Fynn wanted the Sinclair keys back and she hadn't had a chance to copy them yet. Well, she could always crash through the French doors if need be.

Outside, the early afternoon darkness had dulled the colors and a thin veil of snow softened the lines of her car. The engine started easily. Madison dug a couple of painkillers out of her jacket pocket and downed them with a sip of coffee. It was time to find out how George Pathune had left his wicked life.

Madison gave the keys to the desk sergeant and got back to the car, engine still running. Sorensen had asked her if she was going to pin her career on something that was little more than conjecture. Funny thing is, she had never thought of being a cop as a career. One week ago all she had wanted to do was to learn from her partner and do well in her new post. Just as well. It made her think of the old Chinese curse 'May you live in interesting times'.

She drove north on I-5. The roads were nearly empty but the weather held her back and her right arm hurt in regular waves of pain. In her thoughts she tried to organize a timeline of events that ended with the Sinclairs and went back to a point where the killer had crossed paths with Cameron. Somewhere along that line George Pathune might turn up.

Madison was convinced that the killer had spent some time working it all out: he needed to get the fingerprints and the physical evidence that would lead them to Cameron. He needed to set up the bank account and pay funds in and out of it, transactions that would throw the shadow of embezzlement over James Sinclair.

All of it took patience and a passion for detail. A bitter taste in her mouth reminded Madison that they had only about five days left. The Thing that had drawn crosses in the blood of the Sinclair children wasn't done.

Sorensen's results seemed to confirm how thorough he had been in his preparation and how familiar he was with police forensics. Madison had scanned the list of Police Academy rejects – it went back years and if she didn't have something to run it against, it might as well have been the Seattle phone book.

Hollis had called Sorensen even though it wasn't their jurisdiction at the time; there was a small chance that he should have known that. He wasn't interested in the man's life or what crime had led him there, just in the manner of his death.

Madison pulled into the McCoy State Prison, also known as the Bones. It rose from the concrete parking lot into a combination of high chain-link fences, towers and walls within walls. There were different levels of units, graded in degrees of security: some of the two thousand-odd inmates would get to work outdoors, grow something maybe or build something and go to classes. Others would have no meaningful contact with anybody but prison wardens for the length of their stay.

Madison was used to jails – through the years she had certainly done her bit to increase their population. She stretched and breathed deeply and her arm ached like a sonofabitch.

Twenty-five minutes later, sitting in her car with the engine idling and the windows fogged up, she read the pages that Arnelle had copied for her. She scanned them, running her fingers along the lines, cursing the dim light above her and the faint ink. Her mouth was dry when she was done and she laid ten inches of rubber as she sped out of the parking lot.

Poulsbo, Kitsap County. On Sunday afternoon the shops close early: the weekend tourists had come and gone and the pretty main street with its Norwegian–American bakeries and grocery stores was deserted. Strands of twinkle lights carefully wound around the shop fronts and the naked branches of the trees by the marina shivered on and off. The seven piers were three-quarters full and the boats, sails tightly secured, rose and fell.

A Kitsap County Electricity Board van drove into the waterfront park and stopped by the Harbormaster's office, and two men in regulation gray and red jumpsuits got off. One of them took a key from his pocket and opened a black metal box that hung on the back of the small brick building. Ten seconds later the whole marina and the front street plunged into darkness. They locked the box and went back to the van, where a cellphone was ringing. After a brief conversation, one of the men swore loudly and slammed his side door shut, the other turned on the engine and they drove off.

Two streets away and around the corner the van pulled up to the curb and the men got out. The taller one said: 'A little over-done maybe.' His companion rolled his eyes, opened the back of the van, unzipped his jumpsuit and stepped out of it. Under it, he wore a black uniform and a ballistic vest; on the back, in large yellow letters, it read SWAT.

'Let's go,' he said. From the carpeted floor he picked up two assault rifles and passed one to his colleague, also in SWAT uniform. The tall one adjusted his earpiece and a steady stream of voices crackled into life. He clicked on his night vision goggles and the world glowed bright and green. Snowflakes, like black specks, found their way to the ground.

Madison flew south on I–5, her mind vaguely aware of a speed limit being broken. No wonder Quinn was interested in how Pathune had died: when a guard found his body he had been blindfolded, hands tied at the front and the sign of the cross drawn in blood above the blindfold, smudged on the skin but still perfectly visible. The Medical Examiner's report said his neck had been broken and a piece of ripped denim had been found in his right hand. The cloth was then matched to the shirt of an inmate called Edward Morgan Rabineau; he had been working in the laundry up until a few minutes earlier and there was a window of time when he could have committed the murder.

There had not been a trial but the warden would have a quiet word with the board every time his parole came up, and Rabineau wasn't going to come out any time soon. He was still inside, within the walls of the aptly called Intensive Management Unit. On the other hand, the Sinclairs had been found blindfolded, hands tied at the front with a cross neatly drawn in their own blood.

It would have been an impossible coincidence if the similar circumstances were the work of two different men. Of the two suspects, Rabineau was still in jail and Cameron had never been in it, which meant neither of them could have committed both murders.

Whoever investigated Pathune's death had no reason to doubt the evidence, even if it was no more than a scrap of cloth and no motive had ever been proved. Madison, though, had every reason to doubt. The murder gave her a time frame: the killer had been in prison at the time Pathune died and she was willing to bet he had been released shortly after that; he would have wanted to get the hell away from Rabineau and his pals. Rabineau must have been going nuts knowing someone had set him up and jail retribution comes swift and sharp.

If he had ever applied to the Police Academy it would have had to be before he went to jail. Nobody is stupid enough to apply with a record and this guy might have been crazy but he wasn't stupid. No, he wasn't crazy, he just liked playing with cops.

Madison remembered suddenly the night of the ambush – the man who called himself Officer Mason, dressed like a cop, using the right language. She was sure he had applied to the Academy, he wanted to be one so badly. Madison saw him looking at himself in the mirror as he buttoned up the uniform, thinking of her and Brown and how he was going to draw them into those trees and do what he did to please his long-dead heart.

She rolled down the window and let the air brush her face. She suspected that it had pleased him to shoot Brown while he was himself a police officer; it had made things right, almost legal.

George Pathune. The killer must have left some physical trace of himself on the body of his victim but the investigators had followed the ripped cloth all the way back to Rabineau. She wondered if Sorensen would have looked further than that and remembered her skepticism in the diner.

There was little Madison could do that would have shaken her confidence in the evidence. Madison might as well have picked up Sorensen's spoon, with her prints and DNA on it, and shown her how easy it would have been to – and in that instant Madison was lucky that the road was empty and lay straight in front of her because for a moment she saw nothing but the killer picking up the glass that held Cameron's prints, the glass the police had found in the Sinclairs' kitchen, picking it up from the table where Cameron had put it down *because the sonofabitch worked at the restaurant.*

One hand on the wheel, the other dug into her inside jacket pocket for her cellphone, Madison made a conscious effort to keep her eyes on the road. She dialed the precinct number by touch and got through to Jenner, the desk sergeant.

'It's Madison. Could you put me through to the lieutenant?'

'He's not in his office.'

'Okay, I'll try his cell.'

'He's out with the detectives. They're all out.'

'What do you mean?'

'I better patch you through.'

'Jenner?' Madison held the phone close against her ear but the static silence on the line lasted a lifetime. *Brown.* Something had happened to Brown and they had all gone to the hospital. Brown was dead.

Madison, driving like an arrow through the night, waited for the voice that would tell her he was gone. As long as she wasn't told, Brown was still alive. As long as she wasn't told . . .

She waited alone in that awful silence and seconds later Andrew Dunne's voice came on the line. 'Madison?' Voices all around him.

'Andy? What's going on?'

'We got him.' His voice came and went in the static.

'What?'

'We found Cameron. The boat's in Poulsbo marina. I'm looking at it.'

Madison had to find her bearings, had to come back to herself quick and think. Relief flooded warm through her.

'Is he on the boat?' She wasn't sure she was going to like any answer he was going to give her.

'Yes. He was seen about an hour ago.'

Talk fast.

'Andy, is Fynn with you? I need to speak with him.'

'He's kind of busy.'

'I need to talk to him right now.'

'He's with the Assistant Chief, the SWAT commander, the Kitsap

County Sheriff and the Poulsbo Chief. He's got his hands full and we're about to go in. You tell me and I'll pass it on.'

'You've got SWAT there?' she said.

'We got *everybody* here. We locked down the marina and two blocks around it.'

'Put me through to Fynn.'

Something in her voice reached Dunne.

'What happened?'

'Two years ago in the Bones someone was killed and the body left just like the Sinclairs'. Put me through to Fynn now.'

'That's impossible.'

Madison didn't know if he meant the murder or Fynn. 'Andy?'

Silence.

'Andy?'

Radio crackle.

'Madison, I'm going to call you back.'

'No—'

He was gone.

They were about to go in. They were seconds away. Madison was gripping the wheel so tight even her good hand hurt. She knew every single one of the officers on the SWAT team. Good people all of them, they were well trained and did their job carefully so that at the end of the day everybody on either side would go back home alive. And then there was Cameron, and as far as they knew he had shot one of their own. Madison rolled the window all the way down. In minutes someone was going to die – from either side, it didn't matter, a life would be taken. They thought they were about to grab Brown's shooter and he would never let them take him alive.

One day soon, Madison thought, they would get Cameron for Sanders and for the LA dealers, but not like this. Because like this, the killer would win.

Madison picked up her cell. She remembered the number from all the times she had dialed it days before.

'Hello.'

His voice was soft and close and Madison asked herself what in the name of everything holy she was doing.

'Mr. Quinn, it's Detective Madison.'

'Detective.'

'Quinn, Tod Hollis works for you. You told him to call Sorensen, knowing it would get back to me somehow. Cameron called you, he told you we met last night, he told you what I said and Hollis must have known it wasn't Sorensen's jurisdiction.' She took a breath. 'You *gave* me Pathune, didn't you?'

'Maybe.'

'You were right: I think it was the same man and we are going to find him. But we need time and that we do not have. Does Cameron trust you?'

'What do you mean?'

'If he does this right he'll live. If he harms even one of them, nothing you or I can do will save him.'

Madison imagined the boat, the SWAT team ready to storm the pier, unmarked cars with officers crouched behind them and snipers on the roofs of the pretty houses.

'Detective—'

'You can get him out of there alive but you must tell Cameron to give himself up.'

'What?'

'If he harms any one of them I'll take him down myself, I swear to you.' Madison hoped that what she was about to say would save lives. 'The killer worked in the restaurant. Now, tell Cameron to give himself up and get off the boat.'

The line went dead and Madison dropped the phone on the passenger seat. She drove past Everett and the Snohomish, a ribbon of black water barely visible through the snow. It must be snowing in Poulsbo too. She could drive there, catch a ferry to Winslow and make it in under two hours. It would all be done by then; whatever was going to happen would have happened. What are you prepared to do? Brown had asked her once. Madison felt the tear spilling onto her cheek and wiped it off with the edge of her sleeve.

'What are we waiting for?' Detective Tony Rosario asked no one in particular. He stood behind a Kitsap County Electricity van parked in the Poulsbo marina parking lot and rubbed his gloved hands against each other. Rosario wore a navy windbreaker with SPD on the back on top of his coat; underneath it the Kevlar dug into his armpits.

'Marine Control is not in place yet; they had an emergency they needed to deal with first,' Dunne said. He was next to him, his night vision binoculars trained on the E Pier, the second one in from the right, opposite the Harbormaster's office. Kelly was edging close to Dunne, trying to see through the windshield, ticked off that SWAT was going in first. He looked up: on the roof of the Scandinavian Grocery Store a sniper would be keeping his sight on the third boat from the water, the one with the cabin lights on. Kelly couldn't see him but he knew he was there.

Everybody was in place: a dozen SWAT officers were covering the ground between the pier and solid land, ready to go on the signal. The chief had decided against a negotiator – it was better to get in fast and grab him before he managed to shoot another cop. Lieutenant Fynn stood with the other chiefs at the end of Pier D, behind a small brick building that matched the Harbormaster's office. It was his operation, but technically speaking the Poulsbo Chief of Police ran things: they had all got into position when the agents had cut the power to the block and had said little since then, four somber middle-aged men stomping their feet to keep warm.

The seventeen commissioned officers of the Poulsbo police force had looked on as the Special Weapons and Tactics Unit had taken charge. A couple of them had grumbled half-heartedly about territory and jurisdiction, but everybody remembered the bodies on the *Nostromo* that had set sail from their very own harbor, and they quickly shut up.

The SWAT commander, Marty Karlsson, had briefed his team before going in.

'Cameron's boat is the third from the end of the pier. We have something like twenty-four vessels, left and right, to pass before we get to his. I know we got him eyeballed in the cabin but if I see you cross a boat you haven't checked first, I'm going to dunk your ass in the freezing water myself.' There were nods and yes-sirs all around. 'This guy's a heel, slippery and fast; you give him half a chance and you'll get yourself shot. No special privileges here – if he doesn't want to end the day in one piece, he doesn't have to.'

A few times the curtains in the cabin of the sleek thirty-footer fluttered as if someone was brushing past them, and every time it happened thirty-five men and women with heavy artillery held their breath.

'How long?' Fynn asked Chief Rogers.

Rogers raised three fingers. Voices came through his headset – the patrol boat was almost in place.

Yards away, Dunne turned to Spencer, radio in hand. 'That was Madison just now,' he said. 'She wanted to talk to Fynn.'

'Why?'

'She's found something.'

'Did you tell her it's happening?'

Dunne nodded.

'Where the hell's my partner?' Kelly turned around.

'He had to go,' Dunne said.

'Go where?'

'He had to go.'

Shadows moved fast on E Pier. There was a burst of crackle and voices in Spencer's earpiece. 'They're going in,' he said.

Tony Rosario was annoyed that the public lavatories had been locked for the duration of the operation. It was too damn cold to stand around with three large coffees kicking around in his system, and Kelly was getting on his nerves.

They had parked their car out of sight by a dumpster in a back alley behind the front street. It was still within the block that had been plunged into darkness and he figured he could take care of business without going too far. He smiled to himself. It was so dark, he ought to be careful not to pee on their own car by mistake.

He found his way more easily than he thought he would and after a couple of minutes he was standing between their unmarked Ford and the dumpster, taking his gloves off and unzipping his pants – and, Lord Almighty, was it cold out there.

When he heard the bumblebee, at first it didn't register, and he was zipping himself up when it buzzed again: with sudden clarity, Rosario knew that you don't get bumblebees in December and it was a beeper that had just gone off three feet behind him.

He half turned and someone grabbed him by the hair, smashing his head against the brick wall in front of him. His nose broke on impact, a pain so sharp he almost lost consciousness. Things moved awfully slowly: the ground came up to meet him and he tried to reach for his weapon but his brain couldn't quite get the hand to move fast enough. *Not like this, sweet Jesus, not like a fool.* He felt the butt under his fingers.

The voice spoke low, close to his ear: 'Stay down.'

Someone patted his pockets. Rosario tried to breathe through the warm flood, his eyes filled with tears.

'Stay down now.' A man's soft whisper and an open hand pushing lightly against his back.

Then the pressure was gone and Rosario found enough balance to stand up with the help of the wall. He leant his back against it and looked around – he was alone. He felt for his gun and the police radio that was in the pocket of his overcoat and then the ground around his feet.

At a road block three streets away, Kitsap County troopers flag down the deep green Cherokee Jeep. The passenger flashes his Seattle Police Department badge.

'How's it going back there?' Officer Carey asks the man, nodding toward the marina; he wishes he was close enough to the action to have a story to tell – any story.

'We got him locked down,' John Cameron replies. 'He's not going anywhere tonight.' He waves at the officers as he drives on. The heating in the car is turned up full blast and he's glad his clothes are dark over the rubber diving suit, glad that Officer Carey didn't notice they were soaked, and glad for that first instant when the SWAT officers cut the power and he had lowered himself in the black water, the chill taking his breath away. Cameron's hand shakes as he adjusts the air vent and picks up the beeper from his belt: it's Quinn's number. Cameron drives with one hand; with the other he undoes the straps on the waterproof backpack on the passenger seat. He dials the number with difficulty, his fingers aching and stiff as the blood comes back.

'Nathan?'

'Jack. Where are you?' Quinn's voice is controlled but Cameron hears the steel in it.

'Driving.'

'The police have the boat under surveillance. You can't go back there.'

'I'm coming *from* the boat.'

A long pause as Quinn considers the implications of what Cameron has just said.

'Are you alright?'

'I'm fine. How did you know they found the boat?'

'Does it matter?'

'Well,' Cameron smiled. 'Your timing was impeccable.'

'Jack, Detective Madison told me that—' Quinn paused for a second. 'She confirmed that the inmate who was murdered in prison was very probably killed by the same man. She is getting close to a name.'

'How did she know about the prison murder?'

'Someone in CSU told her Hollis was digging around. And Jack—'

'What?'

'How did you get off the boat?'

'I took a swim in the dark. I don't recommend it.'

'That's not what I'm asking you.'

'I know what you're asking me and the answer is no.'

'Okay, where are you now?'

'Are you sure you want to know?'

Quinn's voice is colder than the black sea. 'Go to hell, Jack.'

But Cameron had regretted the words as soon as they had left his lips.

'Home. I'm going home.'

Quinn stands in the kitchen, the cellphone in his hand. He hasn't told Cameron that the killer worked at the restaurant and he doesn't know where Cameron's home is anymore. In the other hand he holds the tape recorder that he has used since Billy Rain called him, on it Madison's voice telling him his client is about to be taken down. He takes out the tape and turns it around in his fingers. It was entirely accidental but there it was, her career and her future contained in a small piece of plastic.

*

Rosario made his way back to the marina, his coat front soaked in red. By the time he got back the spotlights had come on, flooding every corner of the waterfront park. SWAT officers criss-crossed, jumping from boat to boat, searching every inch with the flashlights clamped on their rifles. Rosario, breathless and shaky, got through a group of local patrol officers who were sweeping the parking lot and headed for Lieutenant Fynn.

Fynn was being briefed by the SWAT team sergeant and they both turned as he approached them.

'Medic!' Fynn shouted as Rosario crumpled on the ground.

'I'm sorry,' he rasped.

Within seconds Fynn and the County Sheriff were on the radio organizing road blocks all over the peninsula. It was as if a great gust of wind had suddenly come upon the marina and dispersed the crowd: the Crime Scene Unit was on its way to work Cameron's boat but for everybody else the fun was now elsewhere. Small SWAT teams went through downtown Poulsbo, each accompanied by a local officer familiar with the streets. In their hearts they all knew their prey was long gone.

Kelly stood at a distance, watching, as a paramedic packed Rosario's nose and tried to stem the bleeding. His partner got his gun taken and couldn't identify his assailant for sure. A voice ident in court was like pissing in the wind. Kelly was angry and hurt as if Rosario had slighted him personally. What business did he have going out there on his own anyway? Their eyes met and Rosario looked away. Kelly walked over and sat down heavily next to him.

'Could be worse,' he said.

'How?' Rosario replied.

'I could be talking to a body bag.'

Lieutenant Fynn questioned Officer Carey personally, the young trooper flustered and upset. This was not the story he would have wanted to tell.

*

The cellphone rang and Madison snatched it from the passenger seat.

'It's Andy,' he said.

'What's happening?'

'He's gone.'

'How?'

'By the time SWAT hit the boat it was too late; he must have taken a dive. Don't know when – we had people watching the boat for hours. Anyway, he must have made them at some point because when they got in they found the lights on and one of those little fans with a revolving head flapping the curtains about. We went through the boat but we got nothing; now we're just waiting for CSU.' He paused. 'And Rosario was attacked from behind while he was taking a leak.'

'What?'

'SWAT was about to go in. Tony goes back to the alley where they had parked their car because Poulsbo officers have locked up all the toilets in the marina, and just as he is finishing his business, he gets smashed against a brick wall. He's got a broken nose and his eye doesn't look too good. Worse than that, his weapon and his badge were taken.'

'Cameron.'

'He couldn't say. Thing is, they have like next to zero violent crime here. What are the chances of somebody else walking around who doesn't mind attacking cops?'

'Is he okay?'

'He was taking a leak, Madison. My guess is he feels pretty raw. And the next time Cameron takes a shot at somebody with his gun, his mood is not likely to improve.'

'No, it's not.' It was small consolation that Cameron had left the boat before she had called Quinn; Rosario's nose was still broken and his piece still gone. 'Can I talk to Fynn?' Madison asked Dunne.

'He's not here. He's questioning the troopers who let Cameron through the roadblock and he's feeling real pissy, so unless you have something good to say to him, and I mean *gold*, I'd just leave him alone for a couple of hours.'

Madison could sure use the time to make her point sharper and fill in the details; they hung up. She was sorry that Rosario had been hurt, no question there, but her heart knew things could have turned out much, much worse and for that, if nothing else, she was grateful. She stopped for coffee on Mercer Street and dialed her next call.

Nathan Quinn answered after the first ring.

'Your client attacked a police officer,' she said.

'Is the officer still alive?'

'Yes.'

'Then it's a good day for both of us.'

She paused. 'I want The Rock's employment records. Do I need to get a warrant?'

Madison hoped that the urgency of the situation would temporarily blur Quinn's appreciation of the law.

'With what you have, you wouldn't even get in to see the judge.'

Madison rolled her eyes.

'I'll meet you at the restaurant,' Quinn said. 'How soon can you be there?'

Thirteen minutes later they pulled into the empty parking lot at the same time.

It felt strange to stand on the steps of the dark restaurant as he unlocked the door. Neither had said hello.

Quinn disabled the alarm and flicked a switch. Madison came into the light and he saw her face for the first time – the deep cut held together by the stitches, the bruises, and in her eyes something that hadn't been there four days ago. He didn't look away.

Madison had disliked Quinn from the instant he had decided

to protect Cameron; he had believed in his innocence against everything they had and was proven right. It didn't make Madison like him any better; in his way he was just as dangerous as Cameron and anything he offered was a gift to be treated with extreme caution. She was glad he regarded her with neither warmth nor sympathy. She returned his gaze; they were in uncharted territory.

'Say we do get a name here tonight,' he said. 'All due respect, but is anybody listening to you?'

'If I can back it up they will.'

'What if they don't?'

He didn't give her time to answer and walked off. Madison knew he was trying not to think of every single time he had shot the breeze with one of the waiters or a busboy or the kitchen help. If the killer had worked at The Rock, Quinn had met him, known him, talked to him.

Their steps echoed in the gloom of the main room, the tables set and ready with their china and white linen napkins, eerie in the half light coming through the vast windows.

He was already unlocking the manager's office door. 'Why is he doing this?' He had kept his tone neutral, as if this was nothing more than one of the cases on his desk.

'I don't know yet. We find *who*, we find *why*.'

Days ago, hours ago, she had been in that office with Brown, talking about poker nights and knives. The air smelled stale and cold, the air conditioning turned off since the early afternoon. Quinn pulled metal file cabinets open and his fingers ran through index markers.

'The last thirty months?' he asked her.

'Yes.'

Madison didn't have the list of parolees in the weeks immediately after Pathune's death but she could get that tomorrow. The date of his murder was a good starting point.

Quinn sighed. 'They're in alphabetical order. We have to check every single one.'

'Thanks, but I'm going to make copies and get on with it by myself. I don't need your help.'

'No, you certainly look like you're doing just fine. Let's go into the kitchen.'

Madison hesitated. 'If I find what I'm looking for, what guarantee do I have you are not going to share that particular piece of information with your client?'

'You have the word of an officer of the court,' Quinn replied without sarcasm. 'Or you can come back whenever you can find a judge willing to sign a warrant.'

They grabbed a bunch of files each, moved into the kitchen and spread them on the immaculate steel work surface in the middle of the room.

They started by eliminating all the women; that cut the number down by about a third. He picked up a file and flipped it open; she did the same.

'Have you told him about this?'

'What do you mean?'

Quinn knew exactly what she had meant.

'Cameron.'

'Are you asking me about my communications with my client?'

'I'm asking whether before or after you told him to get his ass off the boat you happened to mention the killer worked here.'

'The subject didn't come up.'

'It didn't?'

'No.'

Thirty months is a long time in the life of a busy restaurant with full-time and part-time staff; each file held résumés and references and contact details, not necessarily in the most useful order.

They scanned the pages, found what they needed to know and put them on the no-good pile; there wasn't a second stack so far.

'How did you know he didn't do it?' Quinn kept his eyes on the paperwork.

'I read about a photographer being beaten up and I remembered a picture I saw of Cameron when he was a boy.' Too late Madison realized it was Quinn's brother's funeral she had just casually mentioned; she looked up. 'I'm sorry,' she added quickly.

Quinn ignored it. 'Go on.'

'I think that last Monday, sometime after he met with you, Cameron assaulted Andrew Riley because he had tried to photograph the bodies of James Sinclair and his family. It just reminded me of what had happened before.'

'That's all?'

'Yes.'

'That's what turned you around?'

'Yes.'

'I'm not surprised you couldn't sell it to your boss.'

'Were you hoping I had some secret piece of evidence?'

'I was hoping you would have had more than a hunch by now.'

'You and me both.'

'What was he like?'

'Who?'

'The man who shot your partner.'

'He is strong and fast and determined to do his thing. He was comfortable impersonating a cop and had no problem shooting one.'

Madison pushed a file toward Quinn. 'Dicky Boyd,' she said. 'In prison at the time of Pathune's death, he started working in the kitchen here eight months later and resigned last June. Do you remember him?'

'Boyd? Yes. I don't think we ever talked.'

'What does he look like?'

Madison's memory flashed back to the man dressed as a police officer who had met them at Cameron's house.

'About six foot, dark hair, built like a heavyweight. What did he do time for?'

'Fraud. And the man who shot Brown was much lighter.'

'It's a big step from fraud to murder.'

'Do you remember any details about him?'

'Nothing.'

Madison put Boyd's records on one side and they went back to the pile on the table. An hour later they had two more names, Owen Burke and Paul Telling.

'Is that it?' Madison asked him as she pushed her last file on the no-good side.

'That's it.'

'Burke is Chinese–American and Telling is five foot five. Both of them with drug-dealing offenses. Neither of them looks anything like the guy I met.'

Madison had been so convinced she would find the name in that kitchen that it hadn't even occurred to her that she might be wrong. Nathan Quinn went to one of the fridges, took out two bottles of water and handed one to her.

'Thanks. I'm going to go through them again; we must have missed someone,' she said.

'Maybe we didn't.'

He picked up the receiver on the wall phone and pressed one of the speed-dial keys.

'Donny, it's Quinn.'

Donny O'Keefe, Madison thought. The chef of The Rock was one of the regulars at the poker nights. He had offered them clam chowder. Madison stood up and stretched and took a few steps in the long narrow galley to get herself ready for the second pass.

'Donny, I have some names in front of me. I'm looking for a guy who worked in your kitchen fresh out of jail. He would have started here about three and half years ago.' Quinn looked at Madison. 'Six foot, slim build. I have Boyd, Burke and Telling, but they don't fit.'

Quinn listened for a beat. 'No, I can't tell you why. Thank you. I'll call you tomorrow.' He replaced the receiver.

'What did he say?'

Quinn stood there with one hand still on the phone.

'What did he say?'

'He said, "What about Salinger?"'

Madison blinked. 'Who's Salinger? I haven't seen a Salinger file.'

'No,' Quinn replied. 'Harry Salinger worked here until a few months ago, and when he left he must have taken his employment records with him.'

'Harry Salinger.'

It felt good to be able to call the man by his name. Madison took a deep breath and flipped open her cellphone. 'This is Detective Madison, Homicide. I need to run a check on a name. Salinger, Harry. I'll hold.' Madison opened her notebook, clicked her pen and silently prayed that she would have something to write down.

Thirty seconds ticked on. Madison couldn't sit or stand still. Quinn waited with his eyes closed.

'I'm here,' Madison said into her phone. She straightened up and jotted something down.

'Yes, dates please.' She looked up at Quinn and nodded once. 'And the address. Great, thank you.' She hung up. 'Salinger was released three days after Pathune was murdered; he was doing time for an assault charge.'

She slapped her notebook shut.

'There is a series of things that need to happen,' she said. 'One, I need to put Salinger on the crime scene. Two, I need to convince

Klein and the Prosecutor's Office. Three, most important, you must get your client to sit tight for a few hours. You can tie him to a chair, right?'

Madison started to gather her things. 'And you cannot, must not, give him the name.'

'How are you going to put Salinger on the crime scene?'

'Cameron attacked a police officer and that's not going away – I'm just putting it to one side for the moment. It's the difference between being investigated for four counts of murder instead of eight. I wouldn't want you to break open the champagne.'

'Salinger,' Quinn said crisply.

'I don't know. Klein is not going to want to listen. He's left us a breadcrumb trail and he's been very meticulous: all prints recovered and checked for match were the victims' aside from the glass, and *that* came from right here in this kitchen. The more I think about it, the more I feel he must have visited the Sinclairs' house before – he's not the type to go in blind. Can you remember any occasion he might have been there?'

'A few months ago there was a party at the house. I know James borrowed glasses from the restaurant. Maybe someone from the staff took the cases over; someone must have gone to pick them up. It's a possibility.'

Madison wrote down some telephone numbers from the employees list. People who worked together day in and day out had to know something.

'Do you remember him?'

He thought about it for a moment. 'No,' he said, and Madison believed he was glad he didn't; the memory of the killer standing close, talking to the children, would have been almost too much to bear.

'Thank you for this,' Madison said, awkward and already halfway out of the door. 'It made a difference.'

'I have your voice on tape,' Quinn interrupted her.

'What?'

'I have your voice on tape warning me to get Cameron off the boat.'

Madison turned to face him and hoped she would look and sound suitably unconcerned.

'How?'

'By chance. I've been recording calls as a matter of course. I wasn't expecting you to call; I wasn't expecting you to give me the perfect reason to go to Judge Martin and bury the case.'

'Is that what you're going to do?'

'Isn't that what any reasonable attorney would do?'

'Probably.' Madison thought about it for a second. 'But the tape changes nothing; they got ready to discredit me the second I told my boss. They will put it down to post-traumatic stress behavior: I couldn't handle my partner being shot and I hadn't stepped up for him. They can dress it how they want it, what it means to you is that my words or my actions are not going to damage their case. They knew you'd try to use me to contest the warrant.'

'They didn't know you were going to call me and throw the arrest. Would they put that down to post-traumatic stress behavior too? You've been with Homicide less than five weeks; you have a promising future. How do you think they'd like you now?'

'What do you want from me, Quinn?'

'Tell me why I shouldn't go to the judge tonight.'

'I'm not in the mood to ask you for special favors, Counselor.'

'Not even to save your career?'

'Not in a thousand years. I will lose my badge and you will lose the one person who believes your client is innocent. You can take that to the judge.'

'I have Salinger's name.'

'It's not enough.'

Quinn smiled and there was no joy in it, only the embers of a thought Madison couldn't begin to fathom.

'Nothing is ever enough, Detective, but we do what we can with what we have.'

'I agree. Use the tape, don't use it – I don't care.'

'Yes, you do,' Quinn said. 'Not about the job, but about being able to do the job. You care very much indeed.'

At that moment Madison knew just how dangerous Quinn could be. She'd rather call Fynn and tell him herself.

'This name has bought you a little time, Detective. Use it well, because one way or the other I'm going to get that warrant scrapped tomorrow. And one more thing.' Quinn's voice was barely a whisper. 'Don't be a fool and call your boss and tell him all about your phone call. I can see you're tempted. Don't. Consider what it is that you hate the most, me holding that tape or Harry Salinger getting ready to finish the job on your partner.'

Madison wished the anger away from her voice. 'I will do what I need to do. If I don't have a badge it might slow me down some but it won't stop me.'

'I've never thought it would,' Quinn replied quietly as her steps were already receding through the main dining room.

Alice Madison sat in her car, engine turned on and windows fogging up. She could deal with her anger but she couldn't afford to worry about the future. *If I don't have a badge.* Quinn had let her look at the employment records to find a name to take to the judge; that was the only reason he had agreed to meet her. Well, good for him; he had what he wanted. Then again so did she, and the only thing she regretted was that she could not tell Brown.

First things first. If she was going to hunt him down, she wanted to look into his eyes – the eyes of the man who had almost killed her partner. She had felt the same about Cameron less than a week earlier. *See how well that turned out*, she thought. Salinger's mugshot would have been good but she'd rather not go back to the station house as yet; his driver's license picture would have to do and she knew how to get that.

She put the car in gear and got to the edge of the parking lot: turn right and she'd be on her way home, turn left and she could pay a quick visit to Harry Salinger.

Nathan Quinn locked the restaurant door behind him. He turned into the chilly night and saw Madison's car at the lot's entrance. The road was empty but the car wasn't moving, the indicator flashing a right turn. Quinn sank his hands into his pockets; he knew where Madison lived and he knew where else she might be thinking of going. The road was deserted in both directions and the car wasn't moving. Quinn stood and watched the red pinpoint of light until the indicator suddenly flashed left and Madison's car took off at speed.

He knew she was going to the *last known address* and was glad it was Salinger's and not Jack's, this time at least. He wouldn't always be so lucky. She knew how to handle herself – her injuries said as much – and she might even find Salinger before Jack did. After that, she would be coming after his friend, and that, he reflected, was going to make things lively for everybody involved.

It was only going to be a quick look at the house to get a sense of him, nothing more than that: the address he had had before the halfway house the parole board had put him in. The sky had cleared and the Sunday evening traffic was light, Madison streaked through it, heart pounding.

It was Salinger, she knew it, and there was no way to prepare for this. She thought of the crime scene, the bodies on the bed and the weight of his body fighting against her. She slowed her breathing; she wasn't going to knock on his door yet. When the day came she wouldn't knock, she'd kick the damn door down with an arrest warrant in one hand and her piece in the other. And yet, if she could positively identify him as the man who had shot Brown, there was no way she'd sit on her heels. She needed just one good long look.

They had Salinger's address at the time of his arrest; the chances he would still be there were roughly the same as finding his file in the restaurant employment records.

The drive was short enough for Madison to settle into quiet anxiety. It was a Ballard address near Sunset Hill and the street was mostly single-family detached houses. Madison could have parked and walked but Salinger knew what she looked like and luck hadn't played a big part in her recent past. She didn't want to be seen before she was ready to let him see her.

She shouldn't have worried: it was the worst-looking property on the block and it was clearly boarded up and empty. A realtor sign said it was for sale and Madison memorized the phone number. She drove slowly past. A pane of glass in one of the downstairs windows was missing, there was a minimal front yard covered in weeds and an ugly padlock ran from the post through a hole in the wooden gate. Leaflets were crammed in the mail box and a large sticker from Seattle City Light on the front door announced to the world that the electricity had been cut off.

Harry doesn't live here anymore, Madison thought. The realtor had been employed by a development company that had gone belly-up two months earlier. He had no idea who Harry Salinger was and to be quite honest he didn't care.

In no particular order, she was tired, hungry and ticked off. She would work, eat, and maybe sleep a little if she could manage it. Other than that, life was swell.

One hour later Madison was in front of her laptop with a cup of coffee and the fire crackling in the fireplace. There's not much that you can't find with the right software and a positive attitude and it took only minutes for the data on Salinger's driving license to come up.

His picture appeared in pixels in the top left-hand corner of her screen and Madison sat back in her chair and looked at the thin face. Sure he was much younger, but there was no mistaking the pale eyes of the man who had met them wearing a police officer's uniform. She could pick him out of a line-up without hesitation. So much for eyewitness testimony, Madison thought. Salinger would never see the inside of a police station unless they could put him on the crime scene; somehow she was less concerned about finding him than about building the case. He was bound to the city, he was contained within Seattle grounds by his own rage and the pathology of the plan he had designed; he wasn't done yet and he wasn't going anywhere.

When she realized that she had been staring for minutes at the same line on the Academy papers, she got up and took a couple of painkillers with the leftovers of Rachel's lasagna.

Harry Salinger had been arrested on an assault charge and Madison knew that often that is the first felony for offenders who graduate to much more serious business. The assault is the appetizer and something stopped them before they could get to the main course.

She found his name in the list a little after midnight: Harry Salinger had been officially rejected by the Police Academy two days before committing the crime that would send him to jail and into the life of George Pathune. Madison allowed herself a very small smile. At least she had been right about that; to know that the horror brought upon the Sinclairs had been committed by someone who had aspired *to protect and to serve* gave her a cold feeling in her gut.

The file didn't specify the reasons why Salinger had been turned down; maybe he had failed the psych. evaluation, maybe he had failed the physical. Madison hoped that it was the former.

Chapter 34

Harry Salinger wipes his hands on a cloth. He is not a patient man but, God knows, he has done his best with what he was given and now it's almost all gone. He can see the finishing line; it is within the reach of his hand and the extent of his accomplishment nearly takes his breath away. He could never have foreseen this seven years ago, sitting on a bar stool, the rejection letter from the Police Academy burning a hole in his pocket.

He had applied because it was all he had ever wanted to do and because it would have pleased his father, had he been alive. Sometimes the reasons blended into one dull ache. The letter had come that morning and with it the end of everything.

Seven years ago he sat at that bar and drank as people and time flowed around him. When someone grabbed his shoulder he turned and saw it was night and the bar had emptied except for the bartender and this man. His voice was charcoal and he couldn't hear the words. He wasn't sure who threw the first punch but he let anger take over.

The fight was brief and by the time the police arrived the bartender was lying face down on the wooden floor on a bed of shattered glass; the other man put up a struggle as they cuffed him, Salinger went quietly. He hadn't even touched the bartender.

They had sat them down with their lawyers in a room that smelled of bleach and for the first time Salinger had understood that he was in serious trouble. The evidence was inconclusive, the prosecutor said; either of them could have hit the bartender with the broken bottle.

He was wearing the scrubs he had been given; his public defender hadn't had the time to pick up any clothes for him. The other man had shaved and wore the suit his attorney had brought him: it looked expensive, though not as expensive as the one he himself was wearing. He had introduced himself as Peter Hansen from Quinn Locke. He looked like he was on his way to his first million dollars; his public defender looked like he had graduated last week and once called Salinger 'Henry'. He knew he was in trouble but how deep and how black the water was he couldn't have fathomed.

Today Salinger folded the cloth and put it to one side. *Patience.* He had fought hard the temptation to go to Poulsbo on Sunday afternoon and witness with his own eyes the result of his anonymous tip on the Cameron hotline. He had known about the boat since October and had waited for the appropriate moment to drop it in the lap of the Seattle Police Department. He had checked first thing in the morning, mixing with the tourists along the Scandinavian shops: beyond the twinkle lights and the bare trees, the boat was there.

Sitting in his basement Harry Salinger waited for longer than he thought he could bear, his monitors all showing local television stations. At some point the news would come on and he would know that John Cameron had killed again in the process of being apprehended by a SWAT team. He had not had a moment's doubt that Cameron would get away; he just wanted him to leave a trail of law enforcement bodies behind him in his escape, like so many more nails in his coffin.

The news came on and the reporter stood by the cordoned area so that the police cruisers with flashing lights would be in frame. Salinger sat forward in his chair. Disappointment washed over him and he covered his face with his hands. He didn't want to weep over it, but who wouldn't? The frustration was immeasurable.

He forces his breathing to slow down and closes his eyes; by touch he finds the remote and mutes the offending report. It is a setback but he has to stay positive. He has already packed what he will need for the next few days, and a few days are all he wants. He places his hand on the small wooden box that has sat on his table for the last six months; the simple touch gives him all the comfort he needs.

The van is gassed up and ready, his major piece of work dismantled and wedged safely behind the boxes, under a tartan blanket. He has timed himself: it will take him 42 minutes to set it in place.

In his kitchen Harry Salinger fixes himself two sandwiches, hard-boiled eggs and mayonnaise on white bread. His plans are fluid and he can go with the flow, if that's what's required. He wears headphones and Madison's taped voice keeps him company; he even finds the strength to smile.

Chapter 35

Monday morning, 6.30 a.m. Billy Rain woke up with a start. He hadn't slept well – sleeping was one of the things that everybody else in the world seemed able to do, but not him. He hadn't slept properly since he was a kid and last night wasn't any different: Nathan Quinn and the continuous coverage of the Blueridge murders had not done much to improve his sleeping patterns.

After coming back from the bar he had knocked himself out with some sleeping pills, seeking at least for a few hours the comfort of that blessed darkness. He came to, drowsy and thirsty. The dim light in the gloom of his one-room apartment came from a neon sign on the outside of the building that flashed yellow on the floor above him.

He had a carton of milk in the fridge. His six-foot-four frame could cover the length of the room in three steps. He slid one leg out from under the covers and his foot touched the tiled floor.

'Stay down,' the voice said, and Billy Rain felt a thump as if he'd been hit in the chest. He stayed down.

'I have thirty dollars on me, no plastic, my wallet is on the dresser. Take it and leave.'

He could hear him but not see him. Someone stood up from his armchair. Billy heard the springs creak, and footsteps crossing to the chest of drawers in the corner. The table lamp was switched on.

'Oh, fuck,' Billy Rain whispered as John Cameron sat back in the armchair.

'Billy Rain,' Cameron said.

Billy nodded and sat up, grabbing the covers around him while his heart pounded away. He shouldn't have called Quinn. Fuck the reward, he shouldn't have got involved.

'Do you know who I am?'

Billy nodded.

'I would like you to tell me what you told Quinn. Everything you remember, everything you know. Can you do that?'

Billy nodded.

'Do you want a glass of water?' Cameron asked him, and for a moment he flashed back to another time, to a night somewhere in his distant past and a man about to die.

'Okay.'

'Stay down, I'll get it. You're doing fine, just relax and don't be a fool.'

Cameron took a clean glass from the sink and poured some water from the tap. He put the glass on the night stand and went back to the chair. Billy picked up the glass and drained it.

'Do I need to tell you what will happen if you lie to me?'

'No.'

'Good. Start at the beginning and tell me everything.'

'You want to know what I saw?'

'Everything.'

'Okay.' Billy took a deep breath and went into it. John Cameron listened without taking his eyes away from him, the words being not so much heard as absorbed.

Billy Rain had calmed down a little. For years every detail of that day had been a tiny hook caught on his skin. It all came out like poison.

'You're doing well,' Cameron said. 'You mentioned it happened in the laundry. Is that where you normally worked?'

'Yes, it was my second month there. It's part of the rehabilitation program – it was a rotation. You learn a skill and then you get a job when you get out.'

'Everybody was on the same rotation? I mean, Rabineau and the man who was killed?'

'Yes, it was a group of ten inmates from my block. Before the laundry we were in the kitchen.'

'The kitchen,' John Cameron said.

'Four months of washing trays.'

Cameron looked like he'd gone away for a second there and Billy Rain found the silence unbearable. He continued. 'It works for some; they get jobs in restaurants or whatever. It didn't work for me.'

'No,' Cameron said as he suddenly stood up. 'You work in your brother-in-law's garage.'

That was more than Billy would have liked him to know. Cameron headed for the door.

'Is that all?' Billy said. 'Are we done?'

'You can keep your wallet,' John Cameron replied and he was gone, the door closing softly behind him. Billy Rain, quick out of bed, locked it gently and leant with his back against it, eyes closed.

John Cameron looked left and right: the narrow corridor was empty and all four other doors shut. He left the building and took a left into the alley behind it. It was no more than a 20-foot-wide gash between the brick walls; the frost had sealed the litter on the ground and it crunched under his boots. He dialed a number from memory.

'Donny? It's Jack.'

Donny O'Keefe took a sip of his coffee. 'I thought you might call,' he said. 'You spoke to Nathan?'

Cameron thought of their last conversation and he realized that Quinn had known since last night. 'Tell me exactly what you told him; I need to hear it from you.' It was less than the truth and both men knew it.

O'Keefe did as he was asked because Harry Salinger had worked in *his* kitchen and he had not seen it, not until last night, and now in spite of himself he was glad that Cameron had called.

Cameron drove home. He had ditched the Jeep after Poulsbo, thinking, quite correctly, that the entire Seattle Police Department would be after the guy who had smashed Detective Rosario into a wall and driven away through the police block. The red GMC pick-up had been on standby. It was a little battered and worn; in the back a few crates of building equipment were covered by a tarpaulin in case anybody wanted a peek. On the side it read 'Scott Carpentry Seattle' in white letters.

Cameron had liked the Jeep and he had been sorry to get rid of it. It was the second car he had had to lose that week but he hadn't liked the Explorer quite as much.

He had decided that he would not think about Salinger until he got home, until he could devote all of his attention to how to find him and kill him. He could not afford to be distracted with a police cruiser stopped at the traffic lights next to him, the driver seeing an unshaven, tanned face under a faded Seahawks baseball cap.

The lights changed and the cruiser took a right. Cameron made it home without a glitch. He poured himself some orange juice and dialed Quinn.

'I spoke to Billy Rain,' he said, and knew that Quinn was bracing himself for bad news.

'You did?'

'Yes. He told me about the rehab program where they learn new skills for life on the outside, like kitchen work.'

'Yes.' Quinn had hesitated but there was no point now.

'I just spoke with Donny,' Cameron continued.

'I wish you hadn't done that.'

'Harry Salinger. We must have seen him dozens of times.'

'I know.' He had been thinking about little else since last night.

'Maybe we could have dinner tonight and talk things through.'

'Here?'

'Yes.'

'Okay. Today I need you to stay put. Detective Madison is working on reversing your warrant and getting a lock on this guy.' *This guy.* 'It's almost over. Don't go out, don't talk to anyone, don't do anything.'

'Sure.'

'Jack?'

'What?'

'Do you even know him?'

'No. I have no idea who he is.'

'I'll call if I have any news.'

'You mean like last night when you found out his name?'

'I'm sorry, that's just the way it has to be.'

'No, you're not sorry. You're my attorney, you were protecting me. And you're very, very good at it. I'll see you later.'

They rang off and both knew they had just exchanged lies, Quinn would never tell him how to find Salinger and he would never stop until he did.

Cameron ran himself a hot bath and took a couple of Tylenols; he had felt cold since his unscheduled swim last night. He took off his clothes and untied the holster on his ankle, took out the weapon and placed it over a folded towel on the floor by the tub. The hot water felt wonderful.

He slid into it and let his head go under for as long as he could bear it. He didn't know Harry Salinger, never met him before he had come to the restaurant, never heard his name mentioned by anybody before this morning. The first time he had ever laid eyes on the guy he was wearing a waiter's uniform, or maybe it was kitchen whites. He honestly could not remember. Harry Salinger was the black hole into which everything was disappearing, and Cameron came up for air.

He would find him. After all, he had found Billy Rain pretty quickly. Salinger would just take a little longer, and when the two of them met face to face, he would get his answers and Salinger's reward would be swift and final.

It was all the compassion Cameron was willing to show him and even so he was going to enjoy that moment a great deal. The dead stay dead but we are allowed our small pleasures.

Chapter 36

Monday morning. Madison, startled out of a deep sleep, turned to switch off the alarm clock and found herself not in bed but still on the sofa, her phone ringing on the coffee table. She reached for it.

'Madison.'

'It's Quinn.'

It was enough to wake her up.

'What happened?'

'I just spoke with Jack. He knows. You don't have much time.'

Shit. It was bad news, it was horrible news. Cameron would move fast: unlike her he didn't have to deal with legal technicalities.

'What did you do?'

'I didn't tell him if that's what you're asking. When are you going to talk to Klein?'

'I'm going to see if Salinger's DNA from his records can be matched to anything found in the Sinclair home. Then, and only then, I will call Klein. Sit on your client if you have to, because today any cop will shoot him on sight.'

'Fine, but get to it fast.'

After the last week, there was very little left of Madison's natural goodwill; she felt the anger rise.

'Does he know him?'

'No.'

'How did Cameron find out?'

'He figured it out like you did. Just do your job and we can all go home.'

It was too early in the day and Madison hadn't even had her first cup of coffee. She stood up and the words flew out of her mouth.

'When you wake up in the morning, Quinn, your only thought is "How can I make it possible for my client to get away with it today?" That's your job. And then you cross your fingers that he won't kill somebody else. Don't tell me how to do my job; you can kid yourself that you are serving the law, that you're *an officer of the court*. All you really do is hide behind the small print and hope for the best, like a cheap used-car salesman with a good suit.'

The harshness of her own words shocked her into silence. Quinn didn't reply for a few seconds. Madison closed her eyes.

'Eloquent and to the point. I'll bear that in mind, Detective,' he said, his voice unexpectedly soft.

Madison started to speak but the line had gone dead and she suddenly felt awful. She ran a hot shower and stood under it till all her cuts and bruises had stung for long enough. All things considered, it might very well be her last day as a cop.

She was drying herself when the telephone in her bedroom rang.

'Detective Madison? This is Ellen McCormick.' *Brown's sister.* Madison didn't have time to think the worst. 'I'm calling to say they took him off the ventilator and he's breathing on his own.'

Madison smiled. She couldn't remember the last time anything had meant so much.

'That's great news,' she said, even though it didn't begin to describe how she was feeling.

'I know, one hour at a time, one day at a time. How are you doing?'

It struck Madison that, with everything going on at the hospital, it was a little strange that Brown's sister would choose to call her herself instead of letting one of the detectives do it.

'I'm okay, given the circumstances. If I may ask, how are you dealing with it?'

'I'm wondering what's going on. I saw the news last night: they almost had him and he got away and I'm concerned this . . .' – she searched for the right word but nothing seemed appropriate. 'This man might come after him again.'

Madison wished she could be entirely honest with her; maybe in a few more hours she would be able to.

'I don't think that Brown has anything to worry about from the man they went after yesterday. He's on the run; he's not looking to get jammed in a hospital surrounded by cops.' Madison was reasonably sure that applied to both Cameron and Salinger.

Ellen McCormick had seemed a rather good judge of character, much like her brother in fact. Madison was glad they were not face to face and very glad there was still an armed guard on Brown's room. She would want it there until they had Salinger in leg irons.

She took her coffee out on the deck and dialed Sorensen.

'Amy, it's Madison. Do you have a minute?'

'I'm reconstructing a pane of glass that has shattered in roughly a billion pieces on the off-chance I might get a print off it. One minute is all I have.'

'I'll be quick. The heads-up you gave me yesterday, the name of the convict who died, it was a solid lead. The man's body was posed in the same way as the Sinclairs', down to the cross drawn in their own blood. At the time John Cameron was not in prison but someone else was – a man who was paroled days after the murder and went to work in the restaurant that Cameron owns with Quinn and Sinclair. Are you with me so far?'

'Yes.'

'Okay. Was there any trace evidence from the Sinclair crime scene that wasn't matched to the victims or Cameron? I mean anything: hair, skin cells, fibers, anything that was put to one side because we didn't need it at the time.'

A print was out of the question: he was an ex-con. If Salinger had left a latent anywhere near the bodies, it would have been picked up and identified straightaway.

'There was a massive amount of specimens collected and not all of them were processed.'

'He must have left something behind.'

Sorensen was quiet for a second.

'There was a small amount of talcum powder on the bathroom floor,' she said. 'It was the same brand as the one in the Sinclairs' cabinet so it didn't raise any flags.'

Talcum powder.

'Amy, talcum powder is used under latex gloves and he had to take off his bloodied gloves and put on a pair of clean ones when he planted the hairs in the ligature knots.'

'We also found something else with it – a very small amount of coagulated blood.'

'A scab?'

'That's what it looks like.'

'Test it. Run it as a priority.'

'We have a billion—'

'It's *his* blood. He's been in jail — we have his DNA. Test it as soon as you can.'

'Okay. I'll let you know.'

It was a crisp, clear morning; one hundred feet out a couple of kayaks broke the surface of the water. What Madison would have liked to do was to get her own kayak from the garage, wipe the dust of weeks off it and spend a couple of hours with nothing more on her mind than the sound of the paddle slicing the waves. She picked up a couple of flat pebbles and threw them in one after the other with her good hand. They skipped across the glassy surface and sank with a satisfying *plop*. It was easier to breathe outdoors.

Harry Salinger, born with a twin brother who died when he was a boy; his father was a cop, his mother died of an accidental prescription drug overdose.

As she threw more pebbles harder and harder in the water Madison felt a stab of nausea. She was as much a part of his fantasy as Cameron and Quinn, otherwise she'd be lying next to Brown.

If everything so far had gone to plan, he had never meant to harm her more than he had managed to during their fight. It was only his way of testing her, getting a little closer, a little more personal, and Brown was the uninvited guest. *Thirteen Days*. Madison shivered. Salinger wanted more. The horror in the Sinclair home had pleased him, sure, but the real reason must lie elsewhere. He needed more from them and Alice Madison suddenly stepped back from the edge of the pier: four days to go till the thirteenth day from the murder of the Sinclair family, the worst was still to come.

She had wrapped herself up against the cold but the weather was turning and in some patches of the lawn she could see the dirt under the thin layer of snow. The sky was deep and blue and Madison wished she could feel that beauty again: the colors of earth and water that had pulled her back to Seattle after college, when the world had been wide open before her.

She picked at her food and thought of Harry Salinger and she wasn't sure anything would ever feel right or beautiful again. Salinger had done his time for an assault charge; how did it progress to the murder of George Pathune in jail and the Sinclairs after that? By all accounts the first one had not been self-defense: Pathune was a firebug who was just trying to get by in prison. The Sinclairs were part of a much bigger plan to destroy Cameron, and Brown and herself were somewhere on the same drawing board – right next to Cameron, if she thought about it.

Madison flipped through her notebook and the pages she had written while talking with Salinger's prosecutor and his public defender. She remembered that Salinger's father had been a cop and she wondered what he thought of his son's accomplishments. Maybe someone in the precinct would remember Salinger Sr. As she got up to go back inside, the doorbell went and she jumped.

Madison wasn't expecting any visitors; she put down the plate and the coffee and unhooked the leather strip on her holster. She realized how tense she was by how long it felt to walk to the front door. She collected herself and her left hand rested on the butt of her piece as she looked through the peephole.

The man stood ten feet back and there was ex-cop, maybe even ex-army, written all over him; he held a brown envelope in his right hand and Madison guessed the heavy coat could easily accommodate a shoulder holster on the left. *Private dick.*

She unlocked the door.

'Detective Madison, Tod Hollis,' he said, showing her his private investigator's badge. 'I have something for you from Nathan Quinn.'

They stood in the living room and Madison knew Hollis was taking in every detail: the table covered in her notes and sketches of the crime scene, the paperwork she had managed to get out of the precinct and, on top of it all, the printed photo from Salinger's driving license.

It wasn't a social visit and he got right to it. 'I've been looking into the black pick-up truck that was spotted on the Sinclairs' driveway on the night of the murders.'

Madison had to think for a second. 'Yes, a neighbor saw it and it was the basis for the arrest warrant issued against Cameron last week.'

'You might want to take a look at this,' he said and handed her the envelope.

Madison undid the flap and took out a sheaf of papers. The letterhead said Alamo. It was the rental agreement for a black pick-up truck from three days before the Sinclair murders to the Monday after, the day the bodies had been discovered. The name on the agreement was Peter Welsh; the photograph in the photocopy of the driving license was Harry Salinger's. Madison looked up.

'It took me a while to go through all rental agencies this side of Washington State and frankly, until we had a name, there was nothing I could match it to. He just got himself fake papers and rented the truck for the week, put a bit of mud on the car registration plate should your witness have really good eyesight, and that was that. He was hoping that someone somewhere would see him.'

'How long have you been working on this?'

'I started looking the second the warrant was out.'

'It's the Alamo at Sea-Tac.'

'He's local. He figures enough people coming and going and no one will pay much attention.'

'If the truck hasn't been rented to anybody else we could get the Crime Scene Unit to go through it, even though he's probably cleaned up after himself.'

'The truck hasn't been rented.'

'How do you know?'

'Because I have paid a nice chunk of change to the guys there to call me if anybody wants it and so far nobody has.'

'They can't hang on to it forever. I need to go to my boss now.'

Hollis made to leave.

'I know that you're looking for him and I am very grateful for this.' She held up the papers. 'But do not forget what he is: do not attempt to make contact, do not let him see you.' She gave him a card with her cell number.

His hand was already on the doorknob when she remembered. 'Were you on the force in Seattle?'

Hollis turned. 'Some of the time.'

Madison had seen a flash of the holster under the coat, Hollis carried himself like he had put his regular twenty on the job and then some.

'His father was a cop – uniformed officer, I think. Ever run into him?'

Hollis thought about it for a moment. 'Not that I know. He must be real proud of his boy, though.'

Madison left the house ten minutes after Hollis. She paged Sorensen and left a message on her machine, then called the precinct to make sure Lieutenant Fynn was in his office. Sarah Klein's voicemail told her that the prosecutor would be in court until 4 p.m. Madison checked her watch; she wanted her there when she talked to the others. She tried her cellphone.

'It's Madison,' she said when Klein picked up. It sounded like she was still in the courthouse, loud voices around her.

'I was glad to hear you gave as good as you got.'

'Thank you. Brown is off the ventilator.'

'I know, news travel fast around here. For once it's good news.'

'I'm on my way to the precinct, I'm going to see Fynn and you ought to be there too.'

'Madison, I've already drawn a line across your name in my Christmas list.'

'I'll give you the short version: the pick-up truck that Cameron's arrest warrant was based on has been rented with a fake ID by the man who shot Brown. He has killed before and posed the victim like the Sinclairs; his job put him in contact with them and with Cameron. His name is Harry Salinger.'

Madison could hear Klein walking away from the noise and finding a quieter spot.

'Can you put him at the scene?'

'The Crime Scene Unit is working on it; they have his DNA. He left it at the scene when he took his gloves off.'

'Do you have a motive?'

'Not yet.'

'What about Cameron?'

'He's innocent.'

'Relatively speaking.'

'That's all I have for you today, I'm afraid.'

'I'll see you there.'

Madison flew north on 509. She was driving on automatic pilot, barely aware of the commuter traffic. Since the last time she had spoken to Fynn, she had deliberately warned their prime suspect that a couple of dozen armed officers were about to pour onto his boat. As it happened, Cameron had already left by then and Rosario could swear to it, but the betrayal remained.

In the light of day, it was difficult to understand how she had ever thought she was doing the right thing, and yet not even 24 hours later they might be withdrawing Cameron's arrest warrant and issuing one for Salinger. How would she be feeling if police officers had lost their lives trying to catch a snake only to set him free in the morning?

She wished she could talk about it with Brown. When it came down to it, it was pretty simple: no officer would ever serve next to her again if they knew, her boss would gladly hand her over to the Office of Professional Responsibility, and her future in the department would be measured in nanoseconds. Well, Madison thought, that's the cost of doing business, and she almost missed her turn off the highway.

The door of Lieutenant Fynn's office was ajar and Madison had managed to get to it without stopping to chat with anybody on the floor. She had heard Spencer's and Dunne's voices from the rec room and, a small blessing, Kelly was nowhere to be seen. She knocked and waited.

'Come in.'

Fynn was seated at his desk – he looked like three hours on the corner sofa and yesterday's suit. He had been watching a monitor on a steel trolley that had been wheeled into the corner. It was black and white and he had paused it.

'I was about to call you,' he said without small talk. 'Take a look at this.' He pressed 'play'.

'What is it?'

'Just watch.'

As far as Madison could make out it was CCTV: some kind of reception desk, a woman sitting behind it answering the phone, talking briefly. She put down the receiver and took a sip from a mug on the desk.

'What am I looking at?'

'Wait.'

Two men came in from outside at the same time. The first signed a visitors' book and exited the frame, the other handed the woman an envelope and turned to leave, giving the camera one good shot at his face. Fynn paused the video.

'Do you know him?'

The definition was poor but Madison nodded. 'Where was this taken?' she said.

'Who is he?'

'His name is Harry Salinger,' she said.

Fynn sat back in his chair.

'It's CCTV from the reception of the *Washington Star*. OPR has been after the leak to the reporter from the beginning. First they thought it was a cop, then they managed to squeeze out of Tully how he got the details of the crime scene. The little turd was sent a picture –

turns out it was hand-delivered. OPR thought we might like to know who delivered it.' Fynn threw across his desk a photograph in a transparent plastic folder. 'We had this enhanced. Check the time on the bedside clock.'

Madison's eyes swept over the slain bodies. The digital clock read 2:15: the picture must have been taken minutes after James Sinclair had died. Madison found a chair and sat down.

'Start from the beginning,' Fynn said, and she did.

Twenty minutes later he beckoned Spencer and Dunne into the office. Madison felt their eyes on her as they came in. Fynn closed the door behind them.

The timeline had started with Salinger's rejection from the Police Academy; two days after that he was arrested and convicted. While in prison an inmate was murdered and posed exactly as the Sinclairs had been. On his release on parole he had started work at The Rock, where he had come into contact with John Cameron, the Sinclair family and Nathan Quinn. He stayed there long enough to finish his probation, then resigned. Days before the Sinclairs' murder he rented a Ford pick-up identical to Cameron's, using the alias Peter Welsh.

Once the murders had been discovered he made sure that the *Washington Star* had a picture of the crime scene and enough on Cameron to guarantee a guilty verdict. Those were undisputed facts.

'What about crime-scene evidence?' Spencer asked.

'He got what he needed when he was working in the restaurant: a glass with Cameron's prints and the hairs he put in the ligature knot around Sinclair's wrists.'

'This is the man who shot Brown?' Dunne said.

'Yes.'

'You're positive?'

'I don't know why or what he wants, but I know it was him.'

'The weapon that shot Brown is the same that shot the Sinclairs. That's enough to pick him up.'

'Klein is on her way.'

'What about *Thirteen Days*?'

'We still have as little time as we had before. Today's Monday, thirteen days still take us to Friday.' Fynn turned to Madison. 'Find out if the date means something special to Salinger – an anniversary, a funeral, anything that might help us to anticipate what he's got planned.'

Spencer and Dunne were quiet; it was a massive change of perspective to adjust to and there were questions that only time would answer.

'First, I want a picture of Salinger distributed around the hospital and I want the officers guarding Brown to tape it to the inside of their eyes,' Fynn said.

'What about Erroll Sanders?' Spencer asked Madison.

'Cameron killed Sanders.'

'Revenge for the Sinclairs?'

'No, he just wanted to. Anything good from Rosario?'

'Nothing useful. He didn't see anything and the Crime Scene Unit drew a blank.'

'Something else,' Fynn said. 'Cameron knows, and we can expect he is *actively* looking for Salinger.'

Dunne rolled his eyes. 'How do you know he knows?' he asked Madison.

'Quinn told me.'

'You've been in contact with Quinn?'

'Yes. It was his investigator who came up with the truck lead and Quinn gave me the restaurant records that got us Salinger's name.'

Fynn watched Madison closely. 'That would have been last night?' he said.

'Yes.'

'How did Cameron find out?'

'He worked it out the same way I had.'

'Quinn didn't tell him?'

'No, I don't think he did.'

Fynn stood up. 'Alright, I want that car turned inside out. Our man is still in the city: he's got to be living, sleeping, shopping, putting gas in his car. He doesn't know we're looking for him and I'm not planning to tell him: we're still after Cameron and his plan is ticking on beautifully. Klein can talk to Quinn but nobody is going to talk to the press.'

Spencer and Dunne left to get the ball rolling.

'I feel like I've been using somebody else's toothbrush,' Dunne muttered to himself.

Salinger was still frozen on the screen.

'Madison,' Fynn said.

'Sir.'

'Officially, you are still on medical leave; I can't have you on the street with that hand. You got it this far with forensics, you can follow up anything Sorensen finds out. That's as far as it goes. And you're going to have to talk to a counselor.'

'About what?'

'The ambush, Brown's shooting.'

'Can that wait a few days?'

'The sooner, the better.'

Madison nodded.

'You got Quinn to help you without contesting the warrant,' he said. 'That was good work.'

Madison didn't say anything; she knew that there was more to come.

'He did what was best for his client and he would have dropped you in the glue without a second thought,' he continued.

'I'm sure he would have.'

'You don't need to explain. I put you in a corner and you did what you had to. By the way—' Fynn took a printed sheet out of a folder, crumpled it up and threw in his waste-basket.

'That was the report on your behavioral *difficulties* after the ambush.'

It meant there would be nothing on her record about endangering the investigation; even better, there would be no compulsory psych. evaluation.

'Now I need to call the Chief and spread the joy,' Fynn said.

Madison left him to his work. In the two hours that followed, she saw the news spread through the precinct, making the horror of the crime worse than anybody thought possible and the reality of the investigation a nightmare. The notion that there was a man out there who had baited John Cameron, ambushed two of their own and was conceivably biding his time before taking somebody else's life apart was almost unbearable. She was at her desk when Sarah Klein found her.

'Judge Martin wants everyone in her chambers when she signs Salinger's arrest warrant,' she said.

Madison looked up. 'Everyone?'

'Everyone.'

'Why?'

'Because she can.'

Chapter 37

The silence in Judge Martin's chambers filled the room and pushed against the small group gathered there. Spencer and Dunne were next to each other at the back, Lieutenant Fynn and Sarah Klein in front and by the desk. Madison stood to one side; in her pocket her hand was tight around her cellphone, willing Sorensen to call back with the result of the DNA test. They all waited on the judge as she read through the warrant's application, her fountain pen already in hand.

Somewhere to Madison's left, away from the others, Nathan Quinn had watched them file in together, his face betraying no emotions as the judge prepared to lift the warrant for John Cameron's arrest. Madison had felt a single sting of guilt remembering their exchange earlier that day; she had swiftly suppressed it and reminded herself that the man had, maybe even there in his Italian leather briefcase, the means to yank her out of the only place she had ever wanted to be, should he wish to, now that she was no longer the only other person on the face of the planet believing in his client's innocence. Quinn seemed entirely unaware of her presence or anybody else's.

'A lesser man might indulge in a small amount of gloating, Nathan,' Judge Martin said as she signed the warrant, 'considering that last Thursday we were all ready to throw attorney–client privilege to the dogs.'

Sarah Klein had the decency not to look down at her smart designer pumps at that point.

'With what I had, I'd do the same today, Your Honor,' she said.

'With what you had, you'd have the same results, Miss Klein,' the judge replied. 'Lieutenant, what are the chances of locating Mr. Salinger with more success than you had with Mr. Cameron?'

'We have just started looking, Your Honor. His last known address has been vacant since he went to jail; after his probation was done he went to ground. He has no family and no ties to the city. We don't even know for sure that he is still in Washington State.'

'He's still here,' Nathan Quinn said. 'Someone tipped you off about the boat. It wasn't the Kitsap County Tourist Board.'

'It was an anonymous tip on the hotline from a public phone in Poulsbo Harbor,' Fynn continued. 'The area is not covered by any CCTV. We have local officers canvassing the shops but I'm not holding my breath. He has had a lot of time to set this up; he's not going to get sloppy now.'

'What's our best chance?' Judge Martin replaced the cap on the fountain pen.

'Blanket coverage. We put Salinger's face everywhere from Seattle to the Florida Keys. We build a profile, we keep looking until we find him. This thing is hours old – we still barely know the man.'

'That should make you happy, Nathan. Your client is now only the second most wanted.'

Quinn did not reply.

'Are we done here?' Judge Martin extended the warrant for Salinger's arrest to Fynn.

Madison's cell started vibrating and she took the call.

'Yes. Thank you. We are there right now.' Madison flipped her phone shut. 'The small amount of coagulated blood found on the Sinclair crime scene matches the basic markers of DNA we have for Salinger. He was there. He shot them and he shot Brown with the same .22.'

It was a start. The group moved to leave.

'Detective Madison, Nathan, a word if you please.' The judge waited until they were alone. 'I am not entirely sure that I understand the sequence of events that brought Harry Salinger's name to our attention, but my gut is telling me that there were a number of conversations and actions that your superiors were not in any way aware of, Detective. And you, Nathan, have done everything in your power to aid that line of enquiry. Now, I'm all for this – shall we call it – strained and unwanted cooperation if it leads to the arrest of a wanted felon. However, if anything you do on my watch forces me to throw out the prosecution's case because *you* have a partner in ICU and *you* have a client with blood on his hands, were I in your place I'd just pack up and move to another state – better still, make it the other side of the country.'

Judge Martin slipped on her navy coat and tied a silk Jersey scarf around her neck, the light blue Hermès pattern doing nothing to soften the steel in her voice. 'That's all. Have a lovely evening.'

Alice Madison and Nathan Quinn left the chambers. They managed the ride down in the elevator without exchanging a word and it was only as they reached the main entrance that Madison turned to Quinn.

'Am I right in assuming that Cameron has already asked you to leave the city for a while?'

'He might have done.'

'It's good advice. Salinger's face will be everywhere in a matter of hours. He still wants to get to Cameron and you are close enough to him to be in as much danger as the Sinclairs were. The *Thirteen Days* thing might get shortened to thirteen hours if he feels hounded and under pressure. And, believe me, he will feel hounded and under pressure.'

'You don't know what he wants.'

'He wants to destroy Cameron and he almost succeeded.'

Nathan Quinn thought of the notes on the heavy cream paper. *82885*.

'I wish it were that simple,' he replied. 'I wasn't the one he went after last week. You are as much of a target as I am.'

'I am alive because he let me. I don't say this lightly – he could have had us both if that was what he wanted. He's not going to come after me again, whatever his reasons and his plans. You are the only person on the planet who is seemingly able to contact John Cameron and he is the only one who might have any idea why any of this is happening. I need to talk to him and I need you to tell him that.'

There were shadows under Quinn's eyes and under the harsh public building lighting Madison could see just how pale he was.

'You are very frank, Detective. Your thoughts seem to just flow out without much consideration for circumstance or propriety. If I put you in a room with John Cameron, both of you curiously unencumbered by the slightest regard for consequence, what are the chances that you will say something, he will say something, and fifteen other open cases from here to LA will suddenly come into play? How many people will read every word of your report, pore over the details, look for admissions and confessions and every scrap of information they can scavenge? And you, won't you be looking for a little of that currency yourself?'

'There will be no report. I'll take notes and they will be for me alone. It will be in a place of your choice and you can check that I will not be wearing a wire. This is what I'm interested in – Salinger

and the Sinclairs' murder and my partner's shooting. The rest is
for another day. I'm not saying I will not investigate other cases
to the best of my abilities and hunt him down with everything I
have, should it come to that. But, right now, this is what I have –
Salinger and the Sinclairs and my partner. The rest is not my business, not today.'

'Do you know what you're asking me?'

'I'm asking you to trust me, while we are doing this in the name
of people you cared for and in the name of a man I would gladly
trade places with.'

Quinn's eyes glittered with something akin to humor – Madison
didn't know him well enough to be sure.

'How much is it costing you to ask me for this, this tiny little
thing, given the recent history of our acquaintance?'

'More than you'll ever know,' Madison admitted, the time to be
coy come and gone.

'I can believe that.'

'We are on the clock and this has to happen as soon as possible.'

'And here you are, asking me to barter the future of my client
and put my trust in someone whose career I could put a final stop
to with one phone call – someone who despises what I do and how
I do it.'

Madison had no answer to that; she held his burning gaze for
as long as he held hers. The things she had said would not be
taken back, and an apology would be tacky and insincere. On the
other hand, what he'd do with the tape was not something she
could let herself think about too much.

'I would still make the call, Quinn, even knowing what I know
now. Do with it what you like.'

Madison had no doubt she was being measured by parameters
she couldn't possibly fathom, and that might prove to be a good
thing in the long run. She was aware of others walking around

them, footsteps on the marble floors and voices and snatches of conversations. Still Quinn held her eyes.

'You gave me George Pathune. You knew I would do what I had to do. Let me finish this,' she said.

'I will think about it.'

'No report, no wire, and you can chaperone the hell out of the meeting.'

'I'd expect nothing less.'

'Thirteen days. Definitively not more, probably much less.'

He looked away then and the icy draft from the open doors suddenly found her.

'I will think about it,' he said.

Quinn walked out into the early evening, his coat whipping around him. Madison felt winded, like after a particularly hard run. She hoped she had done enough, said enough, tried hard enough. There was no way to predict what Quinn would do and she had to prepare herself to go forward without the benefit of an audience with his precious client. She felt coarse, like a tool too blunt to do a piece of work that required a subtle edge and a nimble hand.

Fuck it, she thought. The shortest prayer in the world indeed. Madison screwed up her eyes as she walked outside and into the bitter wind.

Lieutenant Fynn beckoned Madison into his office as she walked into the detectives' room. He closed the door and shrugged on his jacket.

'I'm on my way to the press conference. Joy. What did the judge want with you and Quinn?'

'She was wondering why Quinn hadn't contested the warrant straightaway. She thought there might have been some quid pro quo between us and wanted to make sure we knew that if she had to throw out the prosecution's case against Salinger – because of something I did for Brown or Cameron for the Sinclairs – she'd have our skin. The message was direct and to the point.'

'You might want to have it tattooed on the palm of your hand and read it every hour on the hour.'

'I think I got it, sir.'

'Good. The ME called but I just don't have time to get back to him. Check in with Dr. Fellman, will you?'

Fynn was already halfway out of the door.

'Lieutenant, I asked Quinn to arrange a meeting with Cameron. He might know something, anything, that could help.'

'What did he say?'

'He said he'd think about it.'

'What do *you* say?'

'I honestly don't know. Quinn is . . .' – Madison struggled to find the thread of that image – 'unpredictable. He hates the idea of the meeting but he might see the point of it if it gets Salinger off the street before he gets to his client, or vice versa.'

'Why would Cameron have any interest in talking to you about anything?'

'I went a few rounds with Salinger. Cameron will want to know about that.'

Fynn considered it for a moment. 'You don't really think it's going to happen, do you?'

'No way. Hell freezing over and all that,' Madison replied. 'I'll let you know about Fellman.'

At her desk, Madison looked at Brown's empty chair and neat work surface for a few minutes as she gathered herself. She had no ego about this: if the meeting was going to happen it should have been Brown who would meet John Cameron. He had years in Homicide, she had five weeks. She'd check in with Fellman and then call Fred

Kamen in Quantico: in the extremely unlikely event that Quinn agreed to it and if, even more unlikely, Cameron agreed to meet someone who had chased him through French doors, she should be as ready as possible. *A good point: how do you prepare to meet an alleged murderer of ten?* She dialed the ME's number by heart. *Speak softly and carry a big instrument designed to measure unobserved constructs.* Psych./Criminology student humor.

'I need to show you something. What's your email address?' Dr. Fellman sounded like he'd had a very long day. Madison gave him the address.

'I need to ask you,' he continued, 'are you at your desk and is it private? No members of the public coming and going behind you?'

'It's very private, Doctor. We set up here for that reason.' Something cold started to coil itself around Madison's insides. 'Why do you ask?'

'The trooper who found the second body lost his breakfast at the scene. I have seen you at autopsies before but this is not for anybody to walk in on unprepared.'

'Alright.'

'I'm sending you two sets of pictures. I'll take you through as you open the files.'

'Got them.' Madison's hand hovered for less than a second over the key, a fresh new hell about to unfold. She pressed the key and opened the file.

She sat back in her chair and blinked once, slowly.

'What—' Her voice caught. 'What am I looking at, Doctor?' *Please don't say it's a human being.*

'Unidentified set of human remains. The first of two. Both found in Pierce County in the last three weeks.'

Madison gulped down a sip from a bottle of water in her bag. It was lukewarm.

'Is it an animal attack?'

'We wish. What do you see?'

'Massive tissue damage, deep cuts all over the body, especially the chest. The cuts are lengthways and deep. Blood loss would have been fatal and internal organs would have been affected too.'

'That's the least damaged of the bodies. Open the other file.'

Madison did. When she hadn't spoken for a while Fellman's voice came back as if from a great distance.

'Detective.'

'I'm here.'

'You are looking at the second set of unidentified human remains. Actually, this John Doe was found first but he died after the other. Both men were killed in the last five weeks, give or take a few days; they were left outdoors and if it had been summer the injuries would have been almost impossible to read due to post-mortem insect activity. The cold weather worked in our favor for once.'

'What did this?'

'The Pierce County ME thought *animal attack* until the second body turned up and he realized the pattern of injuries was identical on both remains. In the case of the first man to die, the victim had a very specific pattern of cuts but he actually died of a gunshot wound to the head. In the case of the second man, the victim has the same pattern of cuts except his are much more extensive in length and there are new ones that don't appear in the first body. He died of shock and blood loss. Detective—'

'I'm here.'

'A person could not have easily duplicated the injuries from one victim to the other. Someone has constructed something that does that, some kind of mechanical thing, and the person who is locked in has no choice but to go forward, and that's what creates the injuries. Steel blades, most likely.'

'What do you mean, *go forward*?'

'From the depth and the slant of the injuries, we think the men were forced to physically go through this thing. They had to crawl through it with a gun to their heads; no one in their right mind would do it voluntarily. And that's why the cuts are lengthways on the body. The first man to die couldn't do it and was rewarded with a gunshot wound to the temple, the second man went further but the damage was too much and he died of his injuries.'

Madison's eyes over the photographs, trying to understand and visualize, then abruptly trying not to.

'It's a box, some kind of cage?'

'Maybe. It's still very much guesswork.'

The slimy cold feeling inside her coiled itself tighter.

'Doctor, why did the Pierce County ME call you?'

The pause was only a moment but Madison knew it before he said it.

'There was a piece of glass placed inside each man in one of the chest injuries, close to the heart. It couldn't have ended in there by chance and not in the same place for both men. The glass matches the kind of glass we found Cameron's print on in the Sinclairs' kitchen; it comes from an identical tumbler. The first John Doe was shot with a .22, no casings to match, but it could be the same weapon that shot James Sinclair and Brown.'

Salinger.

'The men are not on the local missing persons lists?' Madison found herself speaking while her brain was trying to absorb what she was seeing, her voice steady while her mind stuttered.

'No, homeless probably, picked them up somewhere discreet, wouldn't have been reported missing by anybody who knew them.'

'Thank you, Doctor.'

Madison clicked on the files and the pictures were gone. Spencer's knock on the door startled her.

'The press conference went well. Fynn is on his way back, Salinger is all over the news—'

'Get Dunne, please,' Madison interrupted him. 'I need to tell you something. Both of you. I need to tell you right now.'

The drive home had been awkward: her arm was not cooperating and Madison had decided not to take any painkillers until after she had spoken with Kamen.

Earlier she had sat Dunne and Spencer down and explained what Dr. Fellman had told her. She had done her level best to describe what they were about to see and they had listened without interruption. Maybe her description would be enough to lessen the impact of the actual pictures. Probably not.

Madison had clicked on the icon and opened the files. Neither man had made a sound. After the longest time Dunne stood up. 'Okay.'

Nobody had said it but everyone was thinking it: *Thirteen Days.* What they were looking at were pictures of the rehearsals.

Back in her house, Madison lit the fire and gave herself a moment of that healing warmth. She hoped Kamen was in the mood for grim because she was fresh out of everything else.

'Mr. Kamen, I'm sorry it's so late.'

'I did say day or night and I meant it.' Kamen sounded like he was still in his office. It must have been near-midnight in Virginia. 'I saw the news: you had a good day.'

'Yes and no, actually.'

She told him about their brief victory with the Salinger warrant and the horror of the John Does from Pierce County.

'I'd like to see the pictures, if possible.'

'Thank you. Anything you might get from them would be welcome.'

'You think what happened to the John Does is connected to the *Thirteen Days* message?'

'Yes,' she replied.

'It could be.'

'The victims were not part of the narrative Salinger gave to the reporter, Tully. He wanted to identify them as his own work, hence the glass placed near the heart. But they were incidental, merely tools to aid his main objective. There might have been more we haven't found yet.'

'Makes sense so far.'

'Sir, I have asked Nathan Quinn to pass on a message to Cameron. I need to speak with him, and even though there's barely the shadow of a chance they might agree to it, I need to be prepared.'

'Quinn didn't say no straight out?'

'No, he said he'd think about it. Which is a partial victory, I suppose, except that we don't really have time for partial victories here, as the discoveries of the day have pointed out. Cameron is – well, honestly I don't know what or who he is or how he will deal with a direct conversation on any subject. What I know about him personally I could put on the back of a very small stamp. But for all these years he has followed patterns and has been incredibly careful, private and spectacularly successful at keeping his life in watertight compartments. If he will talk to me, it will only be because he's curious about Salinger and my meeting with him last week.'

'What do you need from him?'

'He is the reason Salinger started all this. Salinger created the illusion of embezzlement perpetrated by Sinclair to taint an innocent man. He created the perception of guilt for the murders of people who were in fact Cameron's only family, forcing Quinn to defend him for an atrocious act that he, for once, had not committed. If I met Cameron I would know so much more about the man who is trying to destroy him.'

'Are you afraid of him?'

The question surprised her but her own answer did not.

'No. It would not be the first time we run into each other, strictly speaking: we were both on the Sinclair crime scene at the same time one night last week, I followed him and we ended up in a patch of wood near the house. I tried to speak with him then. I knew he was innocent, and I put my weapon away. If he had meant me any harm he had his chance then.'

Kamen was quiet.

'If you're asking me whether I can handle being in a room with him, the answer is yes.'

'I asked about fear because I expect you might have had some PTSD episodes after you were attacked and it might affect your judgment.'

It was Madison's turn to be quiet.

'I did, and they won't,' she said, wary of sounding weak and even warier of a levity she did not feel. 'I seem to react badly to the smell of chloroform. For the rest, I'm fine.'

Kamen's voice was kind; he would be a deadly interrogator.

'Just be aware of yourself. He will be watching you and he will try to get as much as he can out of you. I imagine he believes he will get to Salinger before you do and before Salinger gets to him. But he hasn't survived all these years by being overconfident; be honest with him about what it was like to go up against his enemy, and you have nothing to lose. If he thinks you are lying to him, he will have no reason to talk to you. Would Quinn be there?'

'Most definitely. He's the gatekeeper. He will make sure Cameron does not incriminate himself on other cases.'

'What about your relationship with Quinn?'

'He wants Salinger dead as much as his client does; he just goes about it in a different way. And his main objective is to protect his friend.'

'Does Quinn trust you?'

'No. He thinks I despise what he does and how he does it.'

'Do you?'

'Sometimes.'

'Again, nothing but the truth with Quinn. He already knows how you feel about them both. Madison, do not ask Cameron anything to do with anything else; none of the other deaths matter at this point. You will be tempted; the conversation might very well go in other directions. He will pick up on your interest and you might lose the rest of the conversation. If you don't want to answer a question, say so and why, don't be glib. Cameron will probably bait you a little, just to test you. Quinn will not be pleased.'

'That's not my problem.'

'Detective, whatever it is you haven't told me about your dealings with Quinn, I hope it won't get in the way.'

'What—'

'You answered all my questions very directly, including the one on fear. Except for one. *What about your relationship with Quinn?* You admit he doesn't trust you and he knows you despise him. Always a great starting point for any exchange of information. What else?'

Madison closed her eyes. If she lied to Kamen he would know; if she told him the truth it could be a disaster. The question was whether his counsel was worth her confidence, whether his experience and support were potentially worth her badge. Quinn was right – she did not care about advancement but she cared very much about being where she was and doing what she was doing.

'Detective.'

'I'm thinking about it,' she snapped.

Kamen let out a short bark of a laugh. 'At least you're not trying to lie to me.'

'I might be economical with the truth, if I thought I'd get away with it.'

'With all due respect, Detective, it's past midnight in Virginia. Talk to me or put the phone down. Neither one of us has the time for the cosmetic version. Brown trusts me completely, if that means anything to you.'

'It does.'

Madison told him about the tape. 'Quinn said he'd use it to contest the warrant against Cameron if I didn't get it scrapped in twenty-four hours. I told him to do whatever took his fancy with the tape. Hours later the evidence was in place and the warrant was scrapped. That's all.'

Kamen sighed. 'Quinn holds this over your head and you tell him to go hang.'

'He will do whatever he needs to do. That much I know of him. The rest I'll find out soon enough.'

'Were he to say "Do this thing or I will take your job away from you", what would you do?'

'Look, now that Salinger is the prime suspect he has no hold over me; the investigation will go on with or without me and—'

'This is not about today, it's about Nathan Quinn two years from now and you about to charge Cameron with some God-awful felony he will undoubtedly commit.'

'Frankly, Mr. Kamen, if we were all alive and able to get into that kind of trouble two years from now I would consider it a personal victory.'

'No wonder he's thrilled at the idea of you meeting his client.'

'We both know he'll never let that happen. The more I think about it – never mind, we'll just do what we do and find Salinger some other way.'

'Let me know what happens, Detective.'

'I will. Thank you for the advice.'

'They won't thank you for it but your call saved a few lives,' he said.

'I'll probably get a medal.' She was too tired for funny but she could do wry.

'Madison, don't allow your lack of professional self-preservation to put a dent in your career. Brown will need a partner when he wakes up.'

'I'll try to remember that.'

Madison sank into the sofa, leaned back and closed her eyes. The house was quiet except for the soft noises from the fireplace, a few clicks and pops as the wood shifted and settled in the heat. She could still find comfort in the crackle of a fire even though her Psych. degree had explained to her the mechanics of her reactions; she was grateful for that small pleasure.

The sound of the car pulling into the driveway had her on her feet in an instant. Too late for Rachel – she'd call first anyway. Her left thumb unhooked the safety strip on her piece. The car door slammed shut, a polite gesture from someone not afraid of announcing himself but considerate of the neighbors. Madison ran through a list of possibilities and the worst came first: Brown had died and the news was being delivered in person. She was at the door in an instant, her eyes at the spyhole.

Shit.

She yanked the door open. Nathan Quinn stood a few feet away; he made no move toward her.

'Good evening, Detective.'

'Mr. Quinn.'

'You said it should happen as soon as possible.'

'Yes, I did. Are we doing it now?' Madison's heart pounded; nothing but adrenaline – it would slow down in a minute.

'Yes.'

'Where is he?' Madison looked beyond him, at the car and into the night around the house.

Quinn hesitated. 'He's already here,' he said.

His face was blank and he still made no move toward her. Madison's hairs rose against the sleeves of her sweater and she felt more than heard the presence moving through the room behind her. She turned and looked into the amber eyes of John Cameron, standing easily in the middle of her living room. *Tall, dark clothes, no visible weapons, gloved hands in sight, looking straight into her eyes, still now, barely breathing.* The fire behind him crackled and hissed.

He was there. He had been there all the time.

With the clarity that comes from being on a very fine edge, Madison realized that how she handled this moment would reflect on the rest of their acquaintance, however long or short that might be, given their situation. What she wanted to do was cold-cock him for breaking into her home; then again a threat of blood and gun metal meant little to this man.

What she said was this, her voice calm, her hand away from her piece. 'Mr. Cameron, I understand that tonight circumstances are what they are, but this is unacceptable. We need to operate with a level of trust for this to work and this is one sure way to blow it to hell.' She didn't grace him with the time to reply and she turned to Quinn. 'Counselor.' She stood aside and let him in.

Madison locked her front door, ironic as that seemed to her at that precise point, and knew without a doubt that for sheer surreal value, whatever twists her life might have, this moment would always take the gold.

Chapter 38

Alice Madison turned and faced the two men standing in her living room. It was her job to make this work, it was her one chance to do this and she had to do it well. She could not – would not – let herself be wrong-footed. *Fuck it*, she already knew Cameron could get into other people's houses. *Let's just get on with it.*

Her eyes went to Nathan Quinn; he looked like he'd rather be somewhere else, anywhere else.

'Mr. Cameron, am I right in assuming that you had ample time to look at my notes on the table there and anything else that took your interest before I came back tonight?'

'Yes.' Cameron's voice was soft. 'I had all the time I needed.'

'Fine, then I won't need to move things out of the way. Please sit.' She motioned to the table. 'I'm going to make some coffee.'

If either man was surprised by the old-fashioned gesture, they didn't show it; then again Quinn could probably beat an Easter Island head in a staring contest.

Madison made coffee, her hands working on their own, her mind busy down the dark alleys of the past ten days. She thought of the little girl who had watched poker players for hours, who had read their faces and divined their hands. If any of those skills were still rattling around inside her, now might be a good time to call them forward.

She found them standing in silence by the table, as guests would do.

'Okay, we ask questions, we reply to questions, as far as it is feasible or until Mr. Quinn stops us,' she began. 'There will not be an official report, just some notes for my own use. And I'm not wearing a wire. All agreed?'

'Yes.' Quinn answered for both of them.

Madison relaxed in her chair; she wouldn't let herself be rushed into anything. To understand the dynamic between these two men was almost as important as finding a way to Salinger. Kamen had been right: chances were two years from this day she might be chasing down Cameron for any of a number of charges; what she could learn by watching them tonight would be invaluable.

Madison gave herself a chance to study Cameron's features and made a note to revise the photo identikit Records had produced. He was exactly the older version of the 18-year-old boy who had been arrested, but something had been taken away: the years had shaped the cheekbones and the jaw and something else that wasn't tangible – something that had settled around him like a moat.

'Go ahead,' she said.

'The ambush, Detective. Tell me about the man who attacked you and your partner.'

His focus on her was the unblinking gaze of a predator; somehow the timid concerns of polite society had been left behind. *Good, no time for small talk tonight.*

Madison felt Quinn lean back in his chair. She was expecting the question. The kind of detail Cameron would be interested in would tell her as much about him as if it were her question he was answering.

She took a sip. 'Last Friday night, in the precinct, I got a call on my cell.'

Cameron listened with his arms crossed and his head slightly tilted to one side. She gave them the tale in simple words because it didn't need any elaboration; what details he wanted he would ask for. She described the physical attack as she might have written it on a victim's testimony sheet. As if on cue her arm started aching again.

Cameron let her finish, amber eyes narrowed and absorbing every word. He looked at the cut with the stitches on her left eyebrow and her injured arm. He was thinking, and clearly he was not someone bothered by pauses in the conversation.

Madison memorized everything about him that she could see, from the way his short dark hair was cut around the ears to the midnight blue cashmere roll-neck he wore. He looked so familiar, a childhood friend lost to time and growing up. In her mind, Madison made lists of details to keep in a file that one day she knew, ready or not, she would use against him.

She felt Quinn's eyes and the weight of his understanding. This was what the night was about: he had given her a little of something he could ill afford to waste and hoped the potential gain would be worth it. He was perfectly aware that everything Madison was learning about his friend would one day be used against him, from how he drank his coffee to which hand he favored. *Right-handed*, Madison thought. The fact that Quinn was so wary of her was a backhanded compliment, that he had agreed to the meet in the first place was the grim sign of just how close to the bone they all were.

'How badly was he trying to restrain you?'

'Badly enough that he wanted me unconscious.'

'But not enough to do you a serious injury.'

'I'll never know for sure.'

'Do you think he held back?'

'I couldn't swear on the nuances of his body check. I was busy trying not to breathe.'

'When you smelled the chloroform, did you make the connection with the Sinclairs?'

'Yes. I knew who had me in a headlock and I knew it wasn't you.'

'Were you afraid?'

'Yes.'

'But you didn't freeze.'

'I reacted without too much thought.'

'You have had time to think now, though. All those notes on the table, the hours spent watching a machine doing the breathing for your partner, shooting targets with your left hand.'

Madison blinked.

'Don't worry, I wasn't tailing you. You shoot with both hands; I'm sure you put in some time at the range. Your piece is on the other side and you've cleaned it recently.'

Madison waited for a question.

'He wanted a connection with you,' Cameron said finally. 'He wanted your partner out of the way; with the added bonus of ballistics on the .22 that would be linked to me.'

'I see it the other way round,' she replied. 'His main objective was to draw a line between you and the .22 that had shot a police officer.'

'No. His main objective was a physical connection with you, Detective. The fact that he could get rid of your much more experienced partner was just gravy; he wanted you by yourself. And, frankly, he probably enjoyed the fight much more than you did.' The embers of an unpleasant thought came and went. 'You were good against him but mostly you were very, very lucky. It was a date, Detective. You just didn't know it.'

Madison felt the chill crawling down her spine. Cameron had taken no pleasure from the comment; he was merely dissecting the event, making his own mental lists and footnotes. *What was he learning about her and how would he use it?*

'Was he at the crime scene in Blueridge?'

The Sinclair crime scene. Brown had wanted footage of the crowd and Dunne had checked it only hours earlier.

Madison leant forward. 'Yes.'

'That's where he first saw you.'

'Why would he have noticed?'

Cameron smiled, so quickly it might never have happened at all. It was not a kind smile.

'The photographer,' he said.

'Andrew Riley.'

'Yes.'

'He had a bit of bad luck that night.'

'Did he?'

Quinn had not moved or uttered a single word but his focus on their exchange was like a hum in the air around them.

'Go ahead,' Cameron said.

Madison had thought about this since the night she had crashed through French doors and followed him into a dark wood.

'Tell me about your relationship with James Sinclair.'

The question had surprised him; she had seen it in the fleeting tension around the eyes. It was gone in a heartbeat.

'Why?' he asked.

'Because it's my question.'

'It's a very broad question.'

'It's a very broad issue.'

Cameron did not reply.

'I'm trying to determine why he chose James Sinclair and his family. Why not Mr. Quinn here? Why not wait for you after one of the poker nights at the restaurant? Why not lie in wait when you went to visit your old house? He knows enough about you that he could have picked any of these options,' Madison said. 'Tell me about James Sinclair.'

'Andrew Riley knows exactly—'

'Jack,' Quinn interrupted him quietly.

Cameron stopped and sat back. Madison realized she would not get him to talk about his dead friend and that was that.

'Is it fair to say that he chose the most vulnerable target?' she asked.

The fire let out a loud hiss.

'Yes.'

'What would you say you value most in your life?'

'Excuse me?'

'What would you say you value most in your life?'

'I can tell you what I value and then we can move on to my favorite color if you like.'

'You don't think Salinger has been thinking about it? You don't think he has looked at you, frankly not someone easily upset, and has asked himself, How do I get to this man? You don't think he has been working out how to take away from you what you value most?'

'And what would that be?'

'I don't know you well enough to guess.'

'I think you have your own theories, detective.'

'I'd rather hear yours.'

'I'm sure you would.'

'Whatever it is, I suggest you build a wall around it because Salinger is going for it.'

'Let him come to me.'

'Believe me, you do not want that. You had never met him or had any dealings with him of any kind before he started working at the restaurant?'

'No.'

'As far as you know is he connected with anyone you have had dealings with in the past?'

'No. If he was I would have found out—'

'Jack.' Quinn's voice stopping his train of thought.

Sanders and the dead men in LA.

'The cooks in the restaurant,' Madison said, thinking aloud. 'Someone there must have told him who you were. He watched you, over months, and then he made his move.'

'Nothing you have said adds up to a motive,' Quinn said.

'He attacked two police officers while dressed as a police officer; before he went to jail he had applied to join the Seattle Police Department and was turned down.'

Madison saw Salinger clearing tables and watching Cameron, Quinn and Sinclair having dinner.

'He didn't need a personal motive,' she said. 'Pick any of the felonies you have never been charged with. He was just redressing the balance.'

Rage in John Cameron was barely a shadow across his face but it was there alright. Madison saw it clearly as she had slapped him with the truth. Cold rage for sure. *Not the type to throw breakables around and definitely not someone to play poker with.* She glanced at Quinn: the man was staring hard into the fire and all she could read was crushing guilt. He stood up and paced to the French doors, nothing but pitch black beyond the glass.

Madison could keep her own silence too and there it was: one man was moved by rage, the other by guilt. It begged the question, if Quinn felt so guilty about the deaths of his friends, how much did he know about the deeds that had drawn Salinger to Cameron in the first place? Guilt is not about vague unease and suspicions, it's about specifics: blood and dates and murder weapons. Quinn *knew*.

'How will you measure your success in this case, Detective?' Cameron asked. 'Four dead and your partner in ICU. What will it take for you to draw a line under it and go home happy?'

'I think the going-home-happy time has come and gone but I will draw a line under it, one day soon, when Salinger is in custody and my partner is awake.'

'In custody,' Cameron repeated.

Quinn's protective instincts slammed back into place. 'Jack.'

Cameron paused; his thought didn't need to be articulated for Madison to know what he had meant. 'To each his own,' he whispered.

'How will you measure your success?' Madison baited him.

Quinn simmered, Cameron sighed. 'One day, Detective, it would be very nice to have a conversation without legal significance. This much I can tell you today: there will be no success at the end of this, however many times your judicial system puts him to death, or however many times mine does.'

'Enough.' Quinn's voice was so soft Madison would have missed it altogether but Cameron had heard and stopped. One had to wonder at the balance of power between them.

'I need more coffee.' Madison stood up and took their empty mugs as well as her own. She was struggling with a decision and needed to clear her mind. Bizarre as that might seem, she was beyond worrying about John Cameron in her home like some slightly unpleasant relative she had to have over. He was a target for the horror that had visited the John Does in Pierce County and he didn't know. They were exchanging legally cautious pleasantries and he had no idea. And neither did Quinn.

She stood by the stove, gripping the edge of the oak worktop, eyes shut against the memory of the pictures. She didn't hear Quinn arrive.

'What is it?' He was leaning against the doorframe, arms crossed and looking as drained as she felt.

'You look—' Quinn wasn't happy with whatever words had come to him and he let the sentence hang between them.

'You don't spook easily, Detective,' he said in the end. 'And tonight you definitely look spooked. I doubt it's our impromptu little get-together.'

The fresh coffee percolated in the stove-top machine, the roasted scent a blessing in that moment when everything else in her mind was brittle and ugly. She leant back against the kitchen worktop.

'I have seen you tonight,' she said. 'You and Cameron have some kind of understanding and he listens to you. I spoke with our Medical Examiner today and something's come up. I guarantee you, neither one of you has ever dealt with anything like this.' *And neither have I.*

A few minutes later, they found Cameron reading the titles on her bookshelves. Madison told him plainly about the John Does and what they could reasonably expect was the work of Harry Salinger. At the end of it Cameron's first words were to Quinn. 'Tell her about the notes.'

'What notes?' Madison asked.

'The day you came to my office with your partner and told me about James and Annie and the boys, that morning I had received a card, a simple cream card and envelope. It read *Thirteen Days.* Last Wednesday I received an identical card. It read *82885.*'

'Eight-two-eight-eight-five.'

'No. Eight, twenty-eight, eighty-five,' Quinn said. He didn't expect the numbers to mean anything to her.

Madison's anger bubbled up and she just grabbed the thing with both hands because anger felt better than fear. 'You mean to tell me that Salinger contacted you personally, and you must have had no doubt it was him when you read in the papers that he had carved *Thirteen Days* on the Sinclairs' bedroom door. And you said nothing. And he writes again, this time with the date of the Hoh River kidnapping. Something so personal to you and Cameron and Sinclair. And you still say nothing? What in the sweet name of everything holy were you thinking?'

Quinn was surprised that she had made the connection with the date but nothing showed in his voice. 'Twenty-four hours ago, Jack was the prime suspect in the investigation and the notes were the only link to the man I knew was the real murderer. If I knew what he wanted he could be manipulated. I wasn't going to give up that chance.'

'You are now. You're giving the notes to Forensics and they'll take them apart. Prints, paper, ink, spit under the stamp, forensic botany, what-have-you. He contacted you, he chose direct communication with you, the person most likely to be standing on the right of Cameron when he was sentenced for four murders he had not committed.' Madison ran her hand over her face and gathered herself. 'Could you drop the notes tomorrow early at the precinct? Or, better still, can I pick them up now?'

She calculated that Sorensen would be back in the morning and she would deliver them like gold into her hands and nobody else's.

Quinn nodded. 'Tomorrow morning. Seven-thirty at your precinct.'

'Fine.'

'Thank you for your hospitality,' Cameron said, and before she knew it the front door was unlocked and he was gone.

She stared at the door for a long moment.

'This was . . . interesting,' she said.

'It always is,' Quinn replied.

Chapter 39

Twenty years ago. Nathan Quinn sits in his cramped office in the King County Prosecuting Attorney building. He has been checking telephone records for hours and the boredom is slowly but surely killing him. Six months previously there had been some phone threats to the attorneys involved in the Reilly–Murtough case and he had been one of those who had received calls at home. In their wisdom, his superiors had decreed that all calls should be recorded and kept track of. Hence Quinn sat at his desk, going over the numbers, ticking them off and waiting for his eyes to fall out of his head.

He found an unidentified number from a call received a few months earlier at home and checked his own log. The log said, *Jack called from bar, brief conversation.* Nathan Quinn blinked slowly. He looked at the date of the call. It was a date he wouldn't easily forget – it was the night he had bailed Jack out of a police cell, the boy reeking of alcohol. He ticked off the call.

A few days later a major spring thaw hit Washington State and the body of Timothy Gilman, or what the winter had left of it, was found by hikers very much as John Cameron had last seen it weeks before, dead and impaled on the spikes he had carved. It took them a week to identify him, two days to track down the bar where he did his drinking and twenty minutes to accept that in all probability the file would remain unsolved.

Apparently he had had an appointment with one of his pals which he hadn't turned up for and the friend remembered very clearly the last night they had met at the bar – the last time anyone had seen Gilman alive. Everyone at the bar had been interviewed but nothing had come of it.

Nathan Quinn read the report because Gilman was well known to the King County courts and their paths had crossed before. Gilman was an enforcer who did low-level cash work: intimidation, extortion – nothing that required more than muscle and two brain cells. There, in the middle of the report, was the address and telephone number of the bar. A number he had read only a few days ago on his own phone records: *Jack called from bar, brief conversation.*

Nathan Quinn looked at the number as if it were some kind of alien code. He took out the file with the phone records and checked. It was the same number. Jack had called him from that bar that night, the last time Gilman had been seen alive, the night he had bailed him out of the police lock-up.

Nathan Quinn did not know why he drove to the bar and what moved him to talk with the bartender. He didn't know why he asked him about Gilman, his friends and all the people who had already been interviewed by the detectives. And when the bartender told him that of all the people there that night, only the kid who always sat at the bar had not been interviewed because he had never been back there again, Nathan Quinn didn't know how he drove himself home. Work had been relentless and he had hardly spoken to Jack in the last eight weeks, and the last meaningful conversation he remembered was at lunch in the diner, when Jack had been so interested in his work as a prosecutor and the case he had been working on.

Quinn sat in his parked car, his thoughts running away from him, unable to simply get out and get into his house. Two months ago, in the diner.

'What are we talking about here?'

'What if you didn't even have enough on the woman to charge her, but you knew she'd done it?'

'Then you go back to the drawing board and you find the evidence you need.'

'Still, sometimes you don't.'

'Sometimes you don't.'

'What would you have done then?'

'In this case?'

'Yes.'

'I don't know. Sometimes, however hard you work the case, it just doesn't happen.'

'What about eyewitness testimony?'

'In theory?'

'In theory.'

'Without evidence?'

'Yes.'

'It would be very difficult. A good defense attorney would tear the witness apart.'

Quinn saw Cameron in the lock-up, the boy's eyes dead and glazed and his voice saying over and over 'It's done, Nathan. It's over. It's done now.' He hadn't understood then. The spring air was sweet as Quinn left his car. He lay on his bed in his suit and tie, only kicking off his shoes as he turned and wrapped himself in the bedspread.

The understanding of what Cameron had done and why he had done it had reached into his chest like fire smoke; it burned and choked him. When dawn came the decision had been taken. He showered, put on a fresh suit and went to the office. His letter of resignation was a surprise to all his colleagues; then again it wasn't the first time someone as good as Quinn left to make some proper money in the private sector. Two days later, Quinn and Cameron met for lunch in the diner.

'Hikers found a dead body in the woods – guy fell in a hole and was killed by wooden spikes.'

Cameron didn't so much as blink. 'It's called a trapping pit – they are used for bears. Maybe he was a hunter.'

'No, he was a cheap, boorish enforcer. A bad guy. I knew of him.'

The waitress came and Cameron ordered pie. He took out a schedule of the Sonics games and pushed it toward Quinn. 'Get busy and decide which ones you want to see. Pie's great today.' Cameron's eyes are bright and hold Quinn whole. 'Try some.'

A quiet kid. A beer or maybe coffee with a shot. Trying to look older than he was, you know, but looking like he was passing razor blades half the time. Oh yeah, I remember thinking there was something odd with one of his hands, always in his pocket. I notice things like that – it passes the time.

Quinn circled a few dates with his black pen. Jack would never say, he would never tell him, so he would never have to know that the legal system he believed in – the life he had carved out of his grief – would have failed him again in the only way that mattered. Gilman had been one of the kidnappers, one of the men who had taken David away and lost him in the woods forever, and Jack would carry Gilman alone.

Quinn opened his private practice a few weeks later. His colleagues were right: it would be hugely successful.

Chapter 40

The call came in from an early commuter into Seattle, driving past and noticing the eerie light behind the trees. A neighbor would later say she thought she'd heard an explosion around 1 a.m. The Everett Fire Marshall's Office engines raced to the isolated property; the flames were still high beyond the firs in the distance. A circle of bare ground had spread out and around the house, the snow withdrawing to the treeline.

A row of firefighters in full gear stood and watched the burning hell. No one had made it out of the house: they had checked the perimeter, sweeping the gritty snow with their torches where the light of the flames didn't reach.

The second floor had collapsed into the first, which had folded into itself and crashed into the basement. A wooden house built at the beginning of the last century like so much tinder waiting for a spark. The fire had burned hot and fast. The criss-crossing jets of water did what little they could, but by the dawn's first light Harry Salinger's house was no more than blackened stumps and a pile of ashes.

Madison grabbed the phone on the second ring and automatically swung her bare feet onto the cold wooden floor.

'Hello.'

'Madison.'

Spencer.

'I'm here.'

'Listen. The hotline got a call from San Diego last night: a woman says she's Salinger's aunt, saw him on the news, gave us a lead. His grandparents left him a house in Everett while he was in jail; he just never bothered to register the property in his own name.'

Madison was already walking to the bathroom to shower. She froze mid-step.

'Tell me you have an address.' She flashed to a sudden memory of green, Everett's Forest Park in spring.

'Slow down, Madison. We're all about five hours too late.'

'What—'

'There was a fire. The house has burned down to nothing; there might have been accelerants involved. Right now we know diddly-squat. The FMO investigators are already all over it.'

'Spencer, we can't let ourselves believe he was inside the house. Life is just not that kind.'

'I know. But apparently there was an explosion. We can at least hope.'

'Hope – I can go for a little of that.'

Madison held the cell in her hand for a minute after the call ended, still slightly dazed by broken sleep and new information. This was unexpected; this was a turn in the road.

She checked the time. Six-ten a.m. She was due to meet Quinn in a little less than an hour and a half to pick up the notes. Spencer had mentioned accelerants: that meant either Salinger had quite literally burned his bridges behind him and moved on to the next thing on his to-do list, or he had accelerants around the house and they had blown up on him.

She turned on the cold water and stepped into the shower. In her experience, life was definitely not that kind.

*

It was after her second cup of coffee that Madison realized that she hadn't told Spencer about Quinn and Cameron dropping by. Then again, only the mugs in the sink confirmed beyond doubt what, even a few days ago, she would have filed away under *surreal dream*.

There was no way around it, the fire had deprived them of a wealth of details about Harry Salinger: how he lived his days and how those days sometimes had measured hours filled with death and horror. Madison adjusted her holster and tightened the strap. If the house had held evidence that could connect him to the John Does, that evidence was gone too. Forever.

Spencer's call came just as she was getting into her car.

'They found a body inside the house. Everett FMO is making sure the site is safe but they have definitely seen human remains.'

Madison leant her head against the steering wheel. For one brief sickening moment a dead body in a burnt-down house had felt like a good thing. Was that where she was now? Because the only thing worse than that would have been to pretend it hadn't happened. Madison wound down the car window and breathed deeply. She wasn't going to turn away from it; she had been glad a body had been found in what could only be described as a pit of hell, and she had hoped it was the man whose work she had witnessed in the photographs from Pierce County.

It occurred to her that if she had been at the house when the fire had started, in the twisted way our hearts turn, she would have tried to get him out.

She turned on the ignition and the familiar purr broke the silence, a bird flapped away from the branch above her and a handful of snow drifted onto the windshield.

If the fire had got to him before the King County Prosecutor's Office, before John Cameron and his judgment, then maybe fire was a more appropriate resolution.

*

Madison was on 509 when the cell started vibrating on the seat next to her.

'Make that three sets of unidentified human remains,' Spencer said, his voice rough from lack of sleep.

She didn't quite know how to respond: if he had blown himself to hell then he had taken company.

'Spencer, wait. I have to drop something off at the lab first and then I'm going to brief Fynn. You really want to be there.'

'Brief him about what?' He yawned.

'I met Cameron last night. We had a chat. Anyway, I guess that's one way to describe what happened.'

'You do keep things interesting, don't you? Yeah, I'll be there.'

Madison stepped on the gas. What she really wanted was to drive straight to Salinger's house and go through the smoking ruins on her hands and knees and find something, anything, that would confirm he'd been there. Instead there were more victims to identify, more relatives to inform, and all she could do was wait for DNA testing and the will of a Fate which, quite frankly, had been pissing in their shoes lately.

Just as she recognized that schoolyard swearing was oddly comforting, she also knew that at some point that day she would be standing on the edge of the snow looking into the wreckage for an answer she wouldn't get, and, without a doubt, Quinn and Cameron would do the same.

Nathan Quinn came out of his Jeep as Madison pulled into the precinct parking lot. A large padded envelope changed hands and she took it without looking inside.

'Thank you,' she said.

He nodded.

'You know what to do if you receive another one.'

'There might not be another one.'

'You heard.'

'Yes, an hour ago.'

Madison didn't ask how he knew. 'Three dead in the house so far,' she said.

'Three?'

That he hadn't known. Good news and bad. Madison watched her very own reaction play on his face.

'How long will it take for the tests?'

'I don't know. It depends on so many variables.'

Quinn sank his hands in his coat pockets, snowflakes touched and melted on his shoulders.

'When you want to kill a search in court, you send your opponent a blizzard. Every document they ever requested in triplicate and everything even vaguely mentioned in discovery. Before they can find what they are looking for, they are drowning in paper.'

'He sent us a blizzard.'

'Do you believe our luck would have him blow himself up?'

'Not this week.'

'Exactly.' He started to move away.

'You know what to do if you receive another one.'

Quinn's eyes found hers for the briefest moment.

'Absolutely.'

Madison groaned inwardly. It wasn't so much that Quinn couldn't even bother to lie effectively – there had been a flash of something there and, way down the line, it would be trouble.

'I thought we were working on the presumption of transparency,' she said to his back.

'I've never lied to you, Detective, and I'm not about to start now.'

'Why is that no comfort to me whatsoever?'

'Because you're wise beyond your years.'

'If he is still alive, he will write again.'

Quinn didn't reply.

'You get another one of these, you get on the phone to me like your life depended on it. Which it does.'

Quinn didn't reply.

'Last night it was Cameron who mentioned the notes, not you. Since when is he the one with common sense in the partnership?'

'Don't you have a briefing to go to? Sit with the photo-kit artist, make changes to Jack's computer picture for posterity?'

'I expect there will be a certain interest, yes.'

Quinn turned on the ignition and the engine came to life. 'Have fun.'

Considering all they had gone through in the last week, Quinn should have been at least moderately relieved that now they were getting close to the real killer. Madison had seen no trace of that.

In the small pool of light Sorensen's tweezers gave a flash of steel as the first envelope revealed the card inside. Their heads bent above the table, Sorensen's red hair held back in a ponytail and Madison's under the collar of her blazer; the rest of the room was in darkness.

To know in her mind what the notes contained was one thing, but to see *Thirteen Days* on the handsome cream paper was to see it carved on the doorframe of the Sinclairs' bedroom, the letters pretty against the white gloss, and to see that brought back the heavy scent of flesh decay and wood polish. Madison held her breath.

The room was quiet, the unnatural silence of a number of bodies in a small space; no one dared shift their weight from one foot to the other for fear of missing a single word.

'He was wary but confident,' Madison said an hour into her briefing with Fynn, with Spencer, Dunne, Kelly and Rosario sitting and standing around them.

Kelly looked ready to burst, the unfairness of the youngest and most inexperienced of the unit briefing *them* about anything was beyond him; the fact that she'd had coffee with the man who'd broken his partner's nose two days earlier was beyond belief itself.

Madison had spoken carefully: this was not the place for conjecture and she was aware that a false sense of familiarity with John Cameron might give any of them something much more serious than a broken nose.

'Sorensen will call when she has any results on the cards,' she concluded.

'Good job,' Fynn said.

I need to tell Brown, Madison thought. *Then the briefing will be complete.*

Madison sat at her keyboard. Originally her email to Kamen would have only contained the Pierce County pictures, then Quinn had turned up on her doorstep and twelve hours later she was staring at the blank email box trying to put some order in last night's revelations, this morning's fire, and the bone-deep knowledge that Salinger's letter-writing days were not done yet.

After she had been typing for a while, she stood up and paced the tiny length of the office her desk and Brown's still occupied. It felt pretty much like her mind did at the time, crammed but missing something vitally important.

We don't know why he singled out Quinn, and these cards, this unfinished message, carry the weight of his promises, his hopes for what he wanted to achieve. And unless we understand what that is, if he is still alive, we will not be able to stop him.

Madison signed off the mail, attached the pictures and pressed 'send'.

Fynn had been pleased with her unofficial report and had given her the task to walk backwards, so to speak, in Salinger's shoes and build up his background and anything from his past she could dredge up in order to make sense of the present. Every available warm body was out interviewing anybody Salinger had ever met.

Madison set out to build a timeline that started with twin boys learning to walk and ended with one of them shooting children at point-blank range. Her note-taking was interrupted by the appointment with a young man from Records.

On the screen, Cameron's already altered picture from his twenty-year-old arrest glowed bland and unremarkable.

'You met him, right? How did we do?' the technician asked her, his voice too full of hope for Madison to answer directly.

'Well, he's a difficult customer, this one. We need to adjust some details.'

'That bad?'

'The aging of the original picture was effective but the lines here and here are different and the hairline—'

'Wait. I'll work in the changes as we go.'

He cracked his knuckles and tightened the blond ponytail. 'Let's start with the hairline.'

Madison closed her eyes and went back to the previous evening, turning around and seeing him for the first time, sitting at the table and studying him, Salinger's own Rosetta Stone.

A while later, there he was, on the screen.

'Done. Did I get the slant of the eyes right?'

Madison leant forward.

'Yup,' she replied. 'Now, can you take away *conscience* and *morality*?'

She left with a few freshly printed copies, put one under a stapler on Spencer's desk and grabbed her car keys.

Madison took 99 northbound and hoped that the Everett Fire Marshall's office would let her get close enough to Salinger's house or whatever was left of it. She had to remind herself every mile that there would be no immediate answers, no sudden epiphanies just because she would be physically closer than she had ever been to the man's life and its mysteries.

The sky was heavy and low and she drove as fast as legally allowed to get there before daylight began its slow fade.

She found it easily, emergency vehicles backed up all the way down the drive, the trees hiding the object of their interest. News helicopters circled overhead and at least a dozen camera crews were trying to frame anything worthy of note in their lenses.

She parked, hooked her badge on her coat breast pocket and left her car with her head down. She pointed at her ID when she reached the police barrier and was waved through. It was the smell that found her first: in the chill it was a sharp blade of acrid and bitter air every breath she took, underneath it an oily residue that clung to the inside of her mouth.

Her eyes watered and she wiped them with a sleeve. In a couple of minutes she reached the clearing and the crime-scene tape; beyond that point all the snow had melted, dirt showing through like a ragged gray carpet. A deep flush of anger surprised her: his home, but he was not there; his work, but nothing she could reach through and grab with both hands. Madison walked the perimeter of the tape. A few men in full protective gear were sifting through the ground, slowly and carefully. Every so often one would pick something up with his gloved hand and place it in an evidence bag.

In the distance, on the other side of the house, Madison saw Dunne in conversation with a fireman. He noticed her and lifted his right hand, the thumb folded in and four fingers straight up. *Four sets of human remains.* Madison nodded, message understood. The count had gone up to four.

In her limited experience of house fires and arson, Madison did not know whether her body's reaction to the physicality of the place was due to her own filter of the situation or if it was exactly what was to be expected. There was something toxic and foul hanging over the ruin. Her eyes swept the trees around the back of the house: darkness had already pooled under the heavy branches. Somewhere in there Cameron had stood and watched them work; maybe he was there still – she couldn't tell.

'They found traces of heavy-duty accelerants,' said Dunne next to her. 'And some gas canisters exploded. Seems like he was doing metalwork in the basement. There's a whole mess that can't be easily identified but is definitely not furniture.'

'What about the bodies?'

'Some of the remains were still intact, others were in severed parts. Four human skulls have been found in total. Whatever it was, the fire burnt hot and fast. I'm saying, if the engines were already at full speed up the drive when the first explosion kicked in, they wouldn't have been in time to stop it.'

Chapter 41

Deep under ground, in the concrete bowels of the range, Madison's left hand shot a tight grouping into the middle of the target. The ear-protectors took away the worst of the explosions but the pain in her right arm rang out with every recoil.

She paid no attention to the other shooters: she reloaded, changed target and efficiently shot the center out of the new one, glad for the rhythm of the action and the respite from her own thoughts.

Her key was in the front door when the cell went.

'Madison,' she said.

'There was a new card in my mail today. I have just found it.' Quinn.

Madison stood in the hallway and didn't turn on the light.

'This morning's post?'

'Yes. I got to it only about an hour ago.'

'It would have been sent—'

'Before the fire.'

'The last thing he ever did or just one more step in his plan.' Madison blew out the air in her cheeks. 'Okay, what does it say?'

'I could show it to you in about five minutes.'

'That's fine.' She turned around in the dark hallway, the house quiet and still.

'Just out of curiosity, is Cameron already here?' Her voice dry, her hand on her holster.

'He's with me,' Quinn replied.

In all her years as a police officer, Madison had always taken off her weapon as soon as she was home, washed her face and hands of crime-scene and gunpowder residue. Tonight her left hand rested on the butt of her piece as she leant against the back of the sofa, her eyes on the front door. They were coming to her home, bringing a small piece of horror crafted out of cream paper. She should be glad she'd get another shot at Cameron, never mind that it would be around her grandmother's dining table.

She lit the fire. *Be dead*, she thought, her hands scrambling with tinder and matches. *Be dead and be gone. Let this be your cold dead fingers trailing behind you while you're on your way to hell.* Then the warmth of the fire was on her face and Quinn's car was pulling into her driveway, doors opening and closing. Madison stood aside as they walked in.

It was Cameron who heard them first, soft steps on the wet ground; he turned and put his body between Quinn and the door. Rachel came out of the darkness with Tommy on her hip and a brown paper bag in her hand.

'She's my friend,' Madison said quickly – too late to stop Rachel, already smiling hello, from coming in.

'Hi.' Rachel stepped inside the door. 'My mom dropped by and you know what she's like.' She paused as she saw the tall dark men standing by Madison, her best friend since she was 13. She paused because their photographs had been in the newspapers for days and though one only vaguely looked like the computer picture on the front pages, Rachel knew exactly who she was looking at and knew that the other man was the attorney who defended him, who had stood between justice and the alleged killer of children. The news might have been full of reports on Salinger but John Cameron and his past were still fodder for the goriest appetites. Rachel hugged Tommy tight.

'It's okay,' Madison said gently, standing close. 'We're working on this thing. They're here to talk. I can't ask you in right now.'

Rachel nodded. She held her boy and passed Madison the bag.

'You smell funny,' Tommy said.

'I've been near a fire, sweetheart.'

'I like bonfires,' Tommy said, and just in that moment he wriggled in his mother's arms and dropped the baseball he was holding. It rolled on the wooden floor and stopped at Quinn's feet. Quinn picked it up with his left hand, in his right a clear plastic folder, a cream envelope inside it.

'Here,' he said and extended his hand toward the boy. A look passed between Quinn and Rachel; his hand paused for a heartbeat then shifted only inches to let the ball fall into her hand.

'Thank you,' Madison said and ushered them out into the cold.

'Are you sure you're alright?' Rachel had paled.

'Funnily enough, yes. I'm perfectly safe with them.'

'I don't understand.'

'Neither do I, but I have to work with them to finish this.'

'Be careful.'

'I will.'

She found them in the living room, at ease in her home, and for a moment Madison wondered about Nathan Quinn, who had given Rachel the baseball because he had seen the flash of contempt in her eyes, that nothing from his hand should touch her son. He had not looked away. The slight rested uneasily against Madison's skin until she saw the envelope and all other thoughts went away.

'Let's see it,' she said.

She found the tweezers in the small kit tucked in her bag. 'Did you touch it with your bare hands?'

'Gloves and a letter opener,' Quinn replied.

John Cameron had sat in a chair by the fire, eyes closed, as if what lay on the table had nothing to do with him.

Madison slid the card out slowly and placed it next to the envelope. Same black ink. Same small font. *3 a.m.* She checked the other side. That's all there was.

She reached for her notebook and ripped out two pages. With her pen she wrote in capital letters THIRTEEN DAYS on one page and *82885* on the other. She placed them on the left side of the cream card and stood back. For maybe two minutes the only sound was the crackling of the fire. Quinn had had some time to think about it and, if she was reading him right, he had already reached a conclusion.

'You know what the cards mean, don't you?'

Quinn nodded. He pointed at the first one. 'On the thirteenth day after the murder of James and his family,' he pointed at the second card, 'in the place where my brother died on the 28th of August 1985,' he pointed at the third, 'at 3 a.m. Day, place, time. It's an invitation to meet him.'

He was right. Everything in Madison's bones told her that Quinn was right on the money. Salinger had taken his time to make sure he had his attention but those were definitely instructions to meet. *82885* was keyed to Quinn's brother's death; no one would have understood the meaning of that sequence of numbers except for Nathan Quinn and John Cameron, and that date would be forever tied to the clearing where the Hoh River boys had met their destiny.

'That means this Friday,' she said. 'And he would have sent it at least twenty-four hours before the fire, before his face was on every news bulletin on every channel. They are working on DNA identification as fast as they can but it will take some time. At least four bodies at the last count, not all of them intact. We might not know before Friday. When he sent this last card he thought you would be alone in this, trying to protect your client from us and failing, and Cameron racking up the body count.'

'You overestimate me,' Cameron said into the fire.

'Not for a second. Salinger knew what you would do, just as he knew that, things being as they were, Quinn here would have gone to meet him on Friday to save your life, whether you liked it or not.'

'Do you think I need saving, Detective?'

'I think it's not over, not until I see Salinger's DNA-certified skull on the coroner's table.'

'You are more gothic than I would have given you credit for.'

'It was a figure of speech.'

Cameron turned and held her with eyes the color of warm honey. 'I don't think so.'

Madison returned his gaze, then she picked up the card and placed it carefully back in the plastic sheet. 'I'm going to drop this at the lab tonight. They're pulling triple shifts and the sooner we get this looked at the better.' She looked from one to the other. 'We have two days between now and Friday; whatever he meant to happen on that day it's blown to hell. His cover is ruined and his plan is shattered. If there has not been positive DNA identification of one of the remains as Harry Salinger, we will be there, on Friday, at the appointed time. On the off-chance that he is crazy enough to be where he pretty much told you he would be, the area will be covered by SPD detectives, State Troopers, Park police and SWAT. You will not be there, neither one of you.'

'Two days is a very long time,' Cameron said. 'Who knows where any of us will be come Friday?'

There was much to discuss but nothing more to say for the night. As she drove north toward Seattle, it occurred to Madison that, between them, they had finally and definitively dispensed with the niceties of polite interaction. There had been no greetings or goodbyes and the headlights of Quinn's Jeep had simply disappeared from her Honda's rear window as he took the South Michigan Street exit off 509.

Madison dialed Lieutenant Fynn's cell and let him know that she was on her way to the lab and why; he didn't like the meaning of the cards any more than she did but had to agree that Quinn was probably right, Salinger had given him directions to meet him. One in his study surrounded by family pictures and encyclopedias, the other streaking through the evening with her piece digging into her side, they both thought the same thing: there was a chance that this world around them contained Harry Salinger only as remains in a morgue vault.

'Sir, one last thing,' she said.

'I'm only surprised you haven't brought it up before.'

'We have to do it. We have to check.'

'I know. Judge Hugo will sign the warrant first thing tomorrow morning. I want to get an early start.'

'Do you already know if any vandalism has been reported in the last few weeks?'

'Not that we know. We'll speak with the caretakers on site. The ground is going to be frozen; it's not going to be a breeze to get down there.'

'Makes me think if he's done it, he's done it a while ago, when it was softer and easier.'

'Maybe. It's not like he threw this thing together at the last minute. Anything to report on Quinn and his client?'

'Cameron was very quiet tonight. He's waiting for something to shake loose, whatever that might be. Quinn? I don't know. But I can say without a doubt that he would have gone to the meet. If we were still after Cameron, Quinn would have kept his mouth shut about the cards and gone to the meet armed with a sharp wit and a Law degree. Maybe that private detective of his would have been in the bushes with a sniper rifle. I couldn't swear one way or the other.'

The traffic was light and so was the rain; it turned to wet snowflakes every so often, then it forgot itself and reverted to rain. Madison found Sorensen in the lab, on a sofa in her office with her arm over her eyes.

A while later Madison lay in her bed, after showering and soaping until she was sure the acrid scent of the fire was gone. Her last thought, one breath away from sleep, stilled then popped like a bubble. *Be dead and be gone.*

Chapter 42

Madison woke up before her alarm, feeling not quite inside herself. She was waiting: waiting to hear, to breathe properly, to gather her guns and go into battle again. Just waiting. Waiting for Brown to wake up. Nothing much to do about any of that except roll up her sleeves and tick items off her list, while a sound like a kettle whistle blew right through her and scattered her thoughts.

There was much of the same going around the station, Lieutenant Fynn had gone to get the warrant signed that would authorize them to dig up Michael Salinger's coffin. They would open it with the appropriate tools and reluctance, and check carefully whether any of the remains had been removed to be placed at the house before the fire. No one had forgotten that Michael and Harry Salinger had shared the same DNA.

The other detectives were also out, probably glad to have found avenues to pursue that would keep them driving, walking, talking and not looking at the clock.

At her desk, Madison organized her notes in small piles. Her arm felt better, good enough to lift a cup of coffee if not yet to shoot a gun.

She sent off a quick email to Kamen letting him know about the latest card and their meaning, and added every detail she could about Quinn and Cameron's second visit. She wasn't sure what she expected him to do with that information; it was sort of like talking to Brown – less acerbic, equally sharp and extremely useful in unexpected ways.

The Salinger file had grown a couple of inches overnight with all the interviews from the previous day; Madison read through it quickly, hoping for a thread she could pull at and finding none. His co-workers at the restaurant had barely any memories of him, and if not for Donny O'Keefe they would still be days behind.

His prison file had also been checked. No visitors and no mail, but regular stays in the jail's medical center. His time there had been as hard as they come. Harry Salinger had existed in an utter void of human relations. Madison's index finger ran down the SPD Training Academy letter, looking for and finding the date she wanted: three weeks after his father had died of post-op complications, Harry Salinger had applied to the Academy; two days after his rejection from the Academy, he had been arrested for assault.

A knock on the doorframe startled her. Kelly stepped in and leant on the wall, a mottled green tie and his usual light gray Barneys suit. Not a court day.

'I have to ask,' he said. 'With all that's been going on it's easy to lose sight of what's what.'

'Go right ahead.' Madison settled back into her chair and felt, literally *felt*, her hackles rising. *What do you know? Humans do have hackles after all.*

'Am I right in thinking that Quinn gave you the last card yesterday evening at your place, that he came calling like the gentleman he is, and that Cameron was with him?' Kelly paused. 'Like he came the night before, and Cameron had come too.'

'That's right.'

'Let me get this straight. This guy, this guy we have wanted in our crosshairs for longer than you've been polishing your shield, comes and goes from your own home and you don't think it would be a good idea to give us a heads-up, stick a tail on him and try to find out where he lays his head at night? You met him twice and all you can say is that he favors roll-necks?'

Madison thought of all the information she had just sent off to Kamen and her own private notes. What would Kelly make of those?

'You're right,' she said, and enjoyed the nanosecond of surprise on his face. 'If it had been anybody else and any other situation I would have done. But not on this, and not Cameron. The man is – I don't know what he is. But he would have known, and all I got going for me right now is a little bit of trust on their side. I lose that and I lose both of them. I can't risk that.'

'I hope it's worth it,' Kelly said, clearly thinking it wasn't, and turned to leave.

'Cashmere,' Madison said, already back to her notes.

'What?'

'Cashmere roll-necks, actually. Blue.'

If Kelly answered he did so in the privacy of his own mind.

It was frustrating. Madison felt like they were grabbing at smoke. They had all of Harry Salinger's life statistics and no living human they could interview who would give them more than the vaguest sense of the person. The aunt in San Diego had spoken for hours to local detectives who had relayed Fynn's questions. All well and good, but she had not seen him for decades. All she had said of any importance was that the father had been a source of terror for his young wife and in all likelihood she had taken her own life. What the life of the boys had been like since then, she could barely guess. *The Waltons* it was not, that's for sure.

Madison saw Fynn slice through the middle of the detectives' room. He shouldn't have been there. She approached cautiously and found him already on his phone. When he saw her he put a large hand on the receiver. 'Judge Hugo said no. He said to get back to him if there is a positive identification; he doesn't want to put the cart in front of whatever. Anything at your end?'

'Not yet.'

She left him to his call and went back to her desk. Somewhere in her notebook she had made a note of the realtor who was dealing with Salinger's childhood home. That one had definitely not burnt down. One hour later, with Fynn's blessing and a key from the agent who had come to meet her, she was standing at the front door.

The agent had given her the key before getting back into her silver Camry. 'I'll be honest with you, I don't think we were going to move this unit before this. I mean, look at it. Thirty years of neglect and it wasn't much to start with. After this, it will be the weirdos and the crazies breaking in to steal the wallpaper to sell on eBay. Keep the key – we have a bundle.'

The house had already been checked by patrol officers as soon as Salinger had been identified. They had made sure that there were no signs of forced entry – the house had been repossessed while Salinger was in jail and the locks changed – and no illegal dwelling.

The agency that had repossessed the house had itself gone under and thus the realtors found on their hands a property they didn't want and couldn't sell; in a few years' time, she said, they might as well blow on it and it would sure collapse on itself like the ruin that it was.

A front door, a side gate on the right side, the color faded to a pale green. Madison felt the sun edging out of the cloud cover: not even heavenly blue skies could have ever made this house pretty. She fit the key in the lock and stepped inside.

Her eyes adjusted to the gloom – 'No electricity,' the realtor had reminded her – Madison held a heavy-duty torch in her left hand.

The sunshine was fighting its way in through the dirty windows and she stood the torch upright by the door.

The smell was chemical lavender over dust; someone had left plastic air fresheners in every room that she could see. They had swept the floors and removed all the furniture, all of Salinger's possessions, all curtains and carpets. Madison paused and listened; the outside sounds barely registered.

She walked from room to room, looking for something that would give her a sense of the family who had lived there first, then a father and two boys, a father and his surviving son, and ultimately Harry Salinger alone. All Madison saw was a bare house that told her much about low-income lives and little about murder and obsession.

She climbed the stairs and found the bedrooms. The largest would have been the parents', the bed gone as everything else. The wallpaper was blue, small flowers that looked like monkshood in orderly rows. Madison looked out of the window into the yard and the tall firs that lined it on all sides. The grass was overgrown; there was a time when it would have been Salinger's job to cut it.

Madison was painfully aware that she was looking for significance where there was none by now. She had not felt any connection between this place and the horrors visited on the Sinclair family and the John Does in Pierce County. It was a sad wreck of a house with large patches of damp where the windowsills met the walls, but all the traces of the lives inside it had been washed out with economy-size bottles of Clorox.

She looked around. Had Salinger continued sleeping in his childhood room after his father had died? Had he locked the man's old room and thrown away the key?

She turned and instantly felt the floorboard creak and shift under foot. The wood was a darker color; a rug must have rested there for years, protecting it from the sun. With the tip of her boot Madison tested the floorboard again. There was definite movement there, more than its neighbor was allowed.

Madison dug into the back pocket of her black jeans; she flicked open her grandfather's switchblade knife and eased the tip into the narrow gap at the short end of the floorboard. It was partly stuck. She knelt on the floor, careless of the dust and splinters, and tried to get a look through the gap at the space under the floorboard, too dark to see. She ran downstairs and retrieved the torch. With the full blast of the beam on it she could see it – a shoebox. Her heart thumped once. She put more pressure on the knife but it did little except dent the wood.

This could be nothing. This could be nothing at all. But whatever it is, it's coming out.

She straightened up, went back to her car and took out a crowbar she kept next to the jack. She threw her leather jacket in, slammed the trunk shut and looked around. The road was deserted.

Back in the bedroom she carefully pushed the crowbar in the gap, making sure she had given enough length to lever and the wood wouldn't just break off. She started pushing slowly and quietly as if the floor wasn't really supposed to notice, and one short thrust later the board came off, falling sideways on the floor.

Madison took out a crumpled pair of gloves from a pocket and put them on. She snapped open her cellphone and took a couple of pictures, the flash harsh against the muted light through the panes.

She placed her fingers around the shoebox and tested its weight. It came up easily, a dirty gray that would once have been white, a string tied around it.

This was it – all that remained of Salinger's life that had not been thrown out, sold off or incinerated. The string had been tied in a bow, twisting around the box as if it was a gift. She took each end between her thumb and index finger and pulled delicately, and the bow came apart. For two full breaths Madison waited and then in one movement she lifted the lid. The handkerchief was deeply stained with dark brown that Madison knew to be blood, wrapped around a large irregular shape. She lifted the corners of the fabric, avoiding the blood, and laid them over the sides of the box like petals. There were dozens: different sizes, textures, colors, small pretty ones and cheap worn-out ones. Pet collars, both cats' and dogs', encrusted with blood and grime and fur. Red velvet and thin shiny leather, little tags with names and telephone numbers. Dozens of them. The sudden scent was copper and offal. Madison half slipped and half sat down on the floor. *How long? How long did it take him to kill them all?*

In the fading light Madison spent a couple of hours testing floorboards and looking for hiding places, but the house had already given her everything she would find there. From the kitchen door, opened with a key found on a nail and a shoulder push, she measured the garden and wondered how many small shallow graves the boy Salinger had dug in the soft earth.

Madison locked the front door and walked back to her car, the shoebox and its contents inside an evidence bag in her trunk. She drove back to the station with all her windows down.

The young associate at Quinn Locke had been speaking for a few minutes, briefing Nathan Quinn on the latest developments in Headley vs. ClearGen Ltd. Quinn had stopped listening pretty much immediately and his eyes had found the digital clock on the mantelpiece of the conference room: 6.07 p.m. Less than forty-eight hours. Less than two days to a moment that might never even happen.

He realized that the young man had stopped talking. 'Thank you, Mark. I'll look over the file later.'

Mark Rosen gathered his papers and left. Carl Doyle came in –

he had obviously been waiting outside the room. Quinn didn't need to ask the reason for the thunder in his face.

'Given what happened, it's a necessary formality,' he said.

Doyle was neither naïve nor in the mood for letting things go.

'What do I need to know?' he said, politely but with an edge that Quinn had come to recognize over the years.

'It's a straightforward change. Nothing to worry about.'

Carl Doyle sat on a chair and ran his freckled hand through his hair. This was anything but straightforward. If he was kept in the dark he wouldn't be able to protect Quinn and the practice in the only way he could, by doing his job right and may the rest go to hell.

'What do I need to know?' he repeated.

Quinn let the sun disappear entirely into Puget Sound, then walked to the door and closed it.

'Let me tell you a little about this,' he said.

Doyle left the conference room ten minutes later. He went to the restroom and kept his wrists under the cold water tap until the chill had spread to his whole body.

After a short run through the neighborhood and a hot shower, Madison heated up the stew from the previous evening. She had resisted the impulse to call Sorensen and Dr. Fellman to check on their progress. Everyone had her cell number in triplicate.

She started watching *The Apartment* and fell asleep on the sofa before Shirley MacLaine got her heart broken.

In his house above Alki Beach, John Cameron sits in darkness and studies the lights of downtown Seattle framed in the floor-to-ceiling glass, pinpoints sliding on the Alaskan Way Viaduct across the Sound. He knows there will be no peace to be gained from the view; he has been reading a copy of Salinger's original arrest sheet and all the information Tod Hollis had gathered about Salinger's case. The understanding has come late in the game but it has come, and he swears under his breath.

There are weapons in the house: some he will carry on his person and some he will leave behind. Whether he will get to be in this room ever again, watching strangers driving in the distance, he really could not care less. In the end, it will be speed more than strength or ammunition that will get the job done. Speed and the will to do it. The hunter's instinct was rarely far from the surface, and right now he feels that what little human decency he has carried around in the last few years is fast unraveling into nothing. He hopes Detective Madison will not get in the way and even then he knows she probably will.

He crumples the arrest sheet, lights a match and watches it curl up and burn to ash in the empty fireplace.

Chapter 43

Thursday morning. Madison sat at her desk, cradling the receiver on her shoulder and making notes. A fleeting thought pulled at her sleeve just as Dunne burst through the door.

'They're going through the test again for confirmation. One set of remains matches Salinger's DNA.'

Madison managed a polite if extremely quick 'thank you and goodbye' and hung up.

'Salinger's DNA?'

'Fynn has gone to get the warrant signed. The first round of tests confirms that a complete set of human remains from Salinger's house matches his DNA and the coagulated blood found at the Sinclair crime scene.'

Madison's hand was still on the receiver. 'We need to see with our own eyes that the brother's body is still in its grave. We need to know for sure.'

'Grab your coat. I've never been happier to go to a cemetery.'

Madison stood to follow, her hopes and her fears a single weight pressing against her chest. She hoped to be wrong; more than anything she hoped to be wrong.

*

Farmer Joe's in Burien was Tommy's favorite shop because they had Strawberry Freezer Pops. He loved squeezing the chilled fruit on the tip of his tongue and the way his fingers would go a little numb from the cold. Heaven.

He looked up at his mum; they were in the canned fruit and vegetable aisle and it held absolutely no interest for him at all.

'Just a couple more things, sweetheart,' Rachel said and let go of his hand to pick up a tin of peaches to put in her basket. She checked the ingredients for the sugar content.

Tommy knew where the Strawberry Freezer Pops lived – they were in a freezer a couple of aisles back. He was under strict instructions not to go wandering off by himself but that was not wandering, that was shopping, like his mum did. He took two steps toward the end of their aisle.

'Tommy, stay where I can see you, baby.'

'Yes, Mommy,' he replied. Tommy looked around: few things in his life were more boring than shopping for groceries. A police officer in uniform stood a few feet away by the end of the cereal aisle, holding an empty basket, a long coat folded on his arm. Auntie Alice was a police officer too. The man turned and looked at the boy.

The rain found them under umbrellas on Queen Anne Hill. It was a gentle slope and the water ran downhill through the patches of thin snow – Madison was glad she was wearing boots. Fynn, Spencer, Dunne, Kelly and Rosario, their shoulders and trouser hems already soaked, spread out wide and went from stone to stone looking for Michael Salinger's grave. Within those forty acres they had a rough idea of where it would be: it could have been a lovely walk, evergreens and a neat lawn, the universal markers of eternal rest. Still, when it came down to it they were there to dig up a casket, and Madison looked around for visiting mourners, hoping to find none.

A cemetery official in a long gray parka did his best to keep up with them and reply to Lieutenant Fynn's questions. No, there had been no vandalism in the last three years, no disturbance of any kind; the maintenance crews checked the grounds regularly. Madison half listened as she crouched and ran her fingers over worn-out marble. The wrong name. She straightened up and walked on.

'Here,' Kelly hollered and raised his arm.

The official spoke quietly in his walkie-talkie to give the digger directions. They clustered around it: a granite headstone, identical to the two stones next to it. No angels, no ornaments. Only the dates told them it was a child's grave. It was stark and yet twenty-five years of Pacific Northwest climate had bought it something that money had not.

Two Crime Scene Unit officers in full all-weather gear joined them; Sorensen had stayed back at the lab, fighting her own private war against the pile of evidence.

Madison crouched down and a few raindrops found their way into the back of her collar. The ground around the headstones was intact; there was no visible mark that told them anyone had touched, disturbed or even visited the three Salinger graves. One CSU took pictures, the other held a small video-camera.

The digger arrived, an efficient machine that could do the work faster than men would.

'Here we go then,' the driver said, and the engine came to life. It was a miniature version of the JCB type Madison knew well, built for precise work and neat edges. She stood back and sank her hands in her pockets.

She couldn't say how long it took; at some point the driver stopped and used a shovel to clear off the last of the dirt, the metal scraping against the wood. Nobody spoke.

The CSU officers had already set up their lights; they blazed a circle around the hole. One of the men dropped into it and disappeared. There was little room to move and the other stayed above ground, the video-camera held at eye level.

Fynn's cellphone rang; he flipped it open and stepped away from the light.

Madison closed her eyes and raised her face; the rain had almost stopped and she let the veil of moisture settle on her brows. *Be dead and be gone.*

Fynn's voice brought her back. 'It was the ME. The tests are confirmed. It's Salinger, the body they recovered – the DNA matches.'

'The seals are intact!' The officer inside the pit had to yell above the voices all talking at once.

'Are you sure?' Madison yelled back.

'I'm looking right at them. They would have had to twist and break them in four places. The original seals have not been messed with since this thing went into the ground.'

Madison dropped to her knees on the edge of the hole; around her she could hear the others move and talk and speak on their own cells.

'Open it up already,' somebody said.

Madison could not look away. The CSU man made short work of it, tools releasing the seals on all sides. When they shifted the lid, everybody crowded on the edge of the pit. The human remains inside the casket wore the threadbare rags of what had once been clothes. The body, such as it was now, was there, every bone in its place.

The cemetery official looked them over. 'Happy now?' Nobody replied. 'Lieutenant, I'd like to put everything back just as it was as soon as possible. I'm sure you understand.'

Madison stopped listening. Harry Salinger was dead. She had to tell Quinn, she had to tell Brown. Harry Salinger was gone, blown to hell by his own hand. She felt Dunne's light slap on her shoulder; he was smiling. Even Rosario, his nose still under a bandage and nearly as pale as the dead, was smiling. A group of people standing around an open grave like it was the best thing that had ever happened to them. It was over.

Madison said her goodbyes and started walking down the hill; her world had just shifted and she needed to adjust. *Quinn*, she thought. She reached for her cellphone inside her coat just as it started ringing.

'Tommy's missing.' Many voices around Rachel's and she was speaking and trying to keep her sobs down and breathe. 'Tommy's missing.'

Madison froze. She turned and saw the CSU lights at the top of the hill.

'When did this happen? Where are you?'

She hoped to God that her training would slam into place or she would be no good to them at all.

'Farmer Joe's. I was taking something from the shelf and he was there, and I turned and he was gone. I told him so many times – Alice, I looked everywhere in the store and outside. I don't understand—'

'You called the police?'

'Yes, they came and we've all been looking. Everybody has been looking. Everybody. Where did he go? How could he—'

'How long ago did you notice he wasn't with you?'

'About thirty minutes.'

'Rachel, sweetheart, put the police officer on, please.'

'Alice—'

'I know,' she whispered, hoping that it would convey what Rachel needed to hear. 'Officer? This is Detective Madison, SPD Homicide. Who am I speaking to?'

'This is Officer Clarke, Burien PD.'

'Officer Clarke, the missing boy is my godson. Have you been given a complete description? His mother usually carries a picture in her wallet. It's a recent one. Has she given it to you?'

'She has.'

'Good. Have the store's cameras been checked?'

'Yes – no good. We went through the footage. You see them coming into Farmer Joe's and that's it. Next thing the mother comes tearing out of the door and calling for the boy. Nobody left with a child in the time between, and the staff door was locked and monitored. You need a swipe card to get to the back and the staff exit.'

'I see what you're saying, officer, but a six-year-old boy doesn't just walk off and disappear.'

'I know. Nobody saw him leave alone or with anybody else but he is not here. There are officers checking every store.' Officer Clarke dropped his voice. 'And every trunk of every car in the parking lot. Do you understand what I'm saying?'

'I understand.'

'We're working through the criteria for an amber alert. I have to go now.'

Madison gave him her cell number.

'Alice?' The expectation in Rachel's voice was heartbreaking.

'I'm on my way, I'll be with you as soon as I can.'

'Okay.'

'They're doing all the right things.'

'Okay.'

'We are going to find him.'

'Okay.'

Madison rang off. Her eyes had never left the CSU lights on the top of the hill, still blazing in the falling dusk. *Salinger is dead.*

She hit the trail at a dead run and her tires peeled off a layer of rubber as she skidded out of the cemetery parking lot and streaked south.

'Spencer, it's Madison. I have a family emergency.' She had gone straight to voicemail. 'My godson is missing. Six-year-old boy. It's a possible abduction. It's just happened and we don't know anything yet. You can reach me on my cell.'

Madison had worked cases of missing children before and she knew the statistics: almost seventy-five percent of children who were abducted and murdered were dead within the first three hours from the moment of the abduction. Tommy was not a statistic. Tommy was a six-year-old boy who liked to wander off. *He is safe and we will find him.*

She was torn between reason and a howling wind in her chest screaming the worst possible scenario. Logic and reason told her over and over again that the original seals were intact and the DNA was a match, and yet the memory of the scent of chloroform filled her nostrils. Nothing, not even the icy air rushing through the open windows, could wash her clean of it.

She picked up her cell from the passenger seat and speed-dialed a number.

'Detective Madison calling for Dr. Fellman. I know he's busy. I appreciate it. I wouldn't ask if it wasn't an emergency.'

A long silence as her call was put through. Minutes rolled by.

'Detective, I'm in the middle of—'

'Dr. Fellman, I'm sorry to interrupt but I have a possible abduction on my hands and I just need to ask you something.'

'What abduction?'

'A six-year-old boy connected to the Salinger investigation.'

Fellman took that on board. 'Ask me.'

'You harvested the DNA from one of the bodies found at the Salinger house. Was it a complete set of human remains?'

'It was.'

'And you tested it yourself. Twice. And twice it came back a match to Harry Salinger?'

'Yes, we used mitochondrial DNA because it was all we could recover and it was a match. It survived the high temperature and the destruction of soft tissue.'

'Mitochondrial – that's DNA only from the mother's line?'

'Exactly. We could harvest enough for a match. Tested twice, confirmed twice. What is this about, Madison? I thought you guys would be popping corks tonight.'

'Salinger has a pattern of manipulating evidence and going after family members. The missing boy is my godson.'

'I'm sorry to hear that. But not even that murdering piece of— not even he could alter DNA at will.'

'I'll let you get back to work.'

Madison almost missed his last words as she rang off.

'Good luck.'

Chapter 44

Madison sliced through the rush-hour traffic. There were questions to be answered and she saw the police officer going through the list, following procedure, not knowing whether he was dealing with a wandering child, an abduction, or a parent who had intentionally harmed her six-year-old boy. *Has this happened before? How often? How long before you noticed? Was the boy upset? Show me again where it happened ...* They didn't know Rachel Abramowitz but Madison did. She ran through the options: Tommy was lost, he had gone off and got distracted and was still walking around alone. Possible but unlikely. Tommy was smart and he would not have left the store. Second option, he had wandered off and, without someone to hold his hand, had tried to cross the busy road. From that point on, all the possibilities led into darkness.

Madison had felt before the random cruelty of the world flutter against the edge of her life; you can't work law enforcement and not feel it brush past you every so often. Today, it had found her and woven its way inside.

Brown had asked her why she wanted to be in Homicide, the OPR detectives had asked her the same thing: in the end, it all came down to a dog barking twenty years ago.

She tried and failed to forget the long lines of shrubs and trees close to the store, the dense patches of green where it would be so easy to hide the body of a little boy. She tried and failed to forget the map of Burien marked with the addresses of registered sex offenders. There are very good reasons why justice is not left in the hands of the victim's relatives. The cell kept its silence and Madison drove on, mile after mile.

She rounded the corner and there they were: a motley crowd and the sweeping beams of flashlights. Tommy was still lost and even the thin comfort of daylight was gone.

Madison pulled into the parking lot of the Five Corner Shopping Center and quickly scanned the groups for Rachel and Neal. She spotted them talking to a police officer by Rachel's car; their boy had been missing for over an hour now and they looked as if they had not drawn breath since; around them Christmas carols played softly from invisible speakers.

Rachel's voice on the phone had broken her heart but their faces, gray with shock and fear, were a fresh new hell. Neal had his arm around his wife, both listening to the officer as if he was the path to salvation. Others streamed around them like a river, searching and calling out, under cars and over hedges; some local workers were checking inside the dumpsters. No family member would ever do that.

Madison strode up to them and took Rachel's hand; her friend grasped it in both of hers. She hoped her eyes would tell her what words could not.

'Officer Clarke.' Madison read the name on the Burien PD tag. 'We spoke on the phone.'

'Detective.'

Clarke was thickset and short, an army haircut and cheeks that would need to be shaved in another couple of hours. He registered who Madison was – there had been enough news reports in the last week – but he made no comment.

'Has the amber alert been broadcast yet?' she asked.

'We don't know enough to be sure it was an abduction. If it doesn't fit the criteria we can't send it out.'

'What about regular television and radio news?'

'We are taking care of that. As well as the rest.'

'What's *the rest*?' Neal's voice cracked.

Madison and Clarke exchanged a look and he left it to her to fill in the details. She tried to offer a possible scenario. Nothing she could say would sound reassuring. 'Say that someone here saw Tommy and he had tripped and fallen when he left the store; however minor the injury they might have taken him to a hospital. The police will check the hospitals for a boy who looks like Tommy and has just been brought in.'

'But I don't understand. He didn't leave the store – we looked at the film and he never came out. He should be there.' There was anger and pleading. Rachel was trying to keep calm in a world that made no sense.

'I'm going to watch the CCTV,' Madison said.

'Go ahead, but there's nothing of value on it. Shame though. An SPD uniformed officer was in the store at that time and he might have seen something. We've called around but haven't been able to raise him yet.'

'A Seattle Police Department officer?' Madison repeated.

'Yes.'

'Okay, I'll be right back,' she said and squeezed Rachel's hand. She didn't want her friend to see her face and remember that it had been a man wearing an SPD uniform who had put her partner in the ICU. She didn't want her friends to see her face at all.

The guy would probably turn out to be five foot six, heavy and balding; he could have stopped to buy groceries for dinner and that was that. A uniform meant nothing.

*

Personal courtesy and a badge got Madison sitting in front of the monitor in seconds.

The teenager who had shown her in smoothed her pink Old Navy sweatshirt, the same color as her nails. 'Is it true you know the boy?'

'Yes,' Madison replied without turning.

The girl hovered as Madison ran the footage back to find the moment Rachel and Tommy had arrived. The teenager had finished her shift and changed out of the store Hawaiian shirt; in the backroom Madison could smell her freshly applied perfume, something flowery named after someone famous, and wished the girl would leave.

'I have a little brother the same age.'

Madison didn't reply: there they were, walking into the store, Rachel holding Tommy's hand. Her heart thumped. Tommy. The man came in a few seconds afterwards; he wore the uniform cap and looked down, away from the camera. He was tall and wiry, striding into the store with purpose and grabbing a basket almost as an afterthought. Madison froze the image; her world became that one single frame. She couldn't bring herself to say it even in the privacy of her mind, not when she had stood by the open grave only hours earlier.

The man carried a bulky parka on his arm and he never looked up; his gaze was glued to the floor tiling. A few minutes later he came into frame again – no shopping basket, the coat thrown on his shoulder now – and he just walked out. He hadn't bought a thing.

Madison played the same few seconds over and over again.

'What are you looking at?' The girl was still there.

Madison did not reply.

'You're looking at the police officer.'

'Yes.'

'I saw him.'

Madison turned. 'You remember him?'

'Yes.' The girl looked embarrassed.

'What is it?'

The girl looked away and back at Madison. She hesitated for a moment and then stepped closer. When her voice came it was whisper-low. 'He smelled. It was really bad, like an animal smell. I saw a goat once and that's what he smelled like. He walked right past me and he smelled something awful and also chemical.'

'What kind of chemical? Cleaning fluids? Soap? Bleach?'

'No, he smelled of goats and hospital. You know what I mean?'

Madison knew what she meant and ran the footage again. 'Are you sure? Are you absolutely sure?'

The girl nodded. 'Yes. I broke my arm last year and I went to Harborview.'

Madison watched the man leave, the bulky parka thrown on his shoulder, and Rachel running to the checkout counters seconds later, calling out for her son.

'It's Hayley, right? Hayley, tell me everything you remember. Where were you when you first saw him?'

Madison pulled out the other chair from under the monitor table and the girl sat down, their knees touched. Her eyes were baby-blue and made up with much more care than Madison had ever been capable of when she was seventeen, or now.

'I was standing by the coffees and checking on the stock because it was getting low on some ranges. I guess people buy more coffee at Christmas, I had been back and forth all day.'

'Go on.'

'I looked up because he was walking fast, I mean faster than most customers walk around the store, you know. And he just walked right past me. That's when I smelled him.' The memory was enough to make her scrunch up her nose.

'And then?'

'Nothing. He got to the exit and left. I thought he forgot something and was in a hurry, that's all. He hadn't bought anything.'

'Did you see him on his way in? As he came into the shop, maybe walked about?'

'No, I didn't. I only saw him on his way out.'

'How clearly did you see his face? Could you recognize him if you saw him again?'

Hayley bit her lip; she wanted so badly to say 'yes'. Madison saw that and it was obvious that the answer was 'no'.

'Maybe.' The girl drew out the word. 'He walked real fast. I don't know.'

Madison looked at the image on the screen: the checkout counters, Rachel in frozen panic.

'Hayley, think back for me if you can. After the police officer left, what did you do?'

When Hayley thought with any degree of intensity a little crease appeared in her perfectly smooth brow. It appeared now.

'I finished with the coffees?'

'After that?'

'Well, there was the lady looking for her boy and we all went to listen to the front of the shop and then back into the aisles to see if he was there, but he wasn't.'

'Did you call out to him?'

'Sure. We all did.'

'Did you go where his mom had seen him last?'

'Yes. It's like he was there and then he was gone. I went all around that aisle like four times.'

'Give me as many details as you can remember.' Madison was dreading what the girl would say next.

'Someone had left a basket in the next aisle. I picked it up and carried on.'

'An empty basket?'

'Yup. Someone just dropped it on the floor in the middle of the aisle. People, you know.' Hayley shrugged.

Goats and hospital. The air had gone out of the room and the world made no sense.

Madison sat back in the plastic chair. After a minute or so of her silence, the girl started to squirm on her seat.

'Was that the wrong thing to do?' she asked.

'No, you did great,' Madison replied, her mouth full of ash, and checked her wristwatch.

The girl smiled wide.

Madison splashed water on her face in the staff restroom. She had taken Hayley to Officer Clarke and he had taken her statement even though he did not fully understand why that would be of any use in finding the SPD officer.

Madison found out there were no working CCTV cameras that covered the outside of Farmer Joe's and the parking spaces closest to the entrance. The moment the man in uniform had left the store he had turned to smoke. The footage from local traffic cameras on 509 and 160 Street could be pulled, but if you don't know what car you are looking for you are pretty much wearing a blindfold and spinning in circles.

Madison ran cold water over her wrists. The officers had gone through the storeroom inch by inch. Madison knew they would find nothing, just as she knew the hospital checks and television and radio alerts would not help. There had been no witnesses; in fact apparently there had been no crime at all.

Back outside the sky was clear and stars lurked beyond the orange glow of the city. It had been hours – long past the time for harmless misunderstandings, long past Tommy's bedtime. Rachel and Neal were searching on foot beyond First Avenue South; it seemed more likely that Tommy could have walked in that direction than crossing 509.

Madison checked her watch. She was glad they were not there, glad they would not see her leave. If she went too early it would upset the plan and the consequences would be unthinkable, too late, and what brittle hope she held would simply crumble away.

Logic had no place here; she had nothing more to go on than the fleeting impression of a girl who couldn't even identify the man. It was less than nothing, and yet it was everything. It was the trail that would lead to Tommy. Madison had held the ransom note in her very hands and not known; it had been sent and received days ago when Tommy slept safe in his bed. It did not look like a ransom note; then again the world had tilted and nothing was quite right anymore.

The memory of Tommy in Rachel's arms was a blade drawing out. Quinn had returned the baseball with one hand; in the other he was holding the last card from Salinger, the promise of a hell none of them had foreseen. The last piece of the ransom note.

Madison left the girl with Burien PD; it would have taken too long to explain to them something that was more instinct than reason. Instead, she looked around for the best potential place to park if she wanted to hit 509 as fast as possible after the snatch. The spaces were empty now and the ground had kept nothing for her; her breath puffed out white close to the concrete as she searched for evidence.

It was almost time to go. She looked in the direction where she knew Rachel and Neal had gone and hoped to God that they were right and she was wrong. She hoped that it would be someone else who would find Tommy, safe and unharmed, and that she would not find him where she was going. She hoped.

Madison turned back towards her car just as the black Ford Explorer pulled in next to it. She stopped suddenly where she was, and a volunteer with thermoses in her arms bumped into her, apologized and kept going.

Nathan Quinn stepped out of the Explorer and looked around the lot. Their eyes met and Madison let out the breath she was holding: she would not need to explain, they already knew. John Cameron leant against the side of the car with his arms crossed, watching her.

Quinn wasn't wearing a tie. The pale smooth skin in the open collar made him look oddly vulnerable. He came halfway and Madison closed the distance.

'What are you doing here?' she asked.

'I knew you'd be on your way soon. We have to make the ferry at Edmonds.'

'You shouldn't be involved in this. Neither one of you.'

'It's the other way round, Detective. You shouldn't have been involved in this, neither you nor the boy. But it's time, and our ride is faster.'

Police all around and her ride was a murderer and his best friend. Madison held his eyes for a moment and then started walking toward her Civic. She gathered a few things quickly from the back seat and the trunk and shoved them into a gym bag. Cameron climbed into the back of the Explorer – Quinn would drive. Madison got into the front passenger seat without looking back: her car would remain in the parking lot of the Five Corner Shopping Center, together with all of her life up to that point, and if she was lucky she might be able to get back to pick up one or both.

The Explorer had been on 509 for a few miles when Quinn broke the silence.

'How did he do it?'

Madison stared straight ahead. 'He wore the SPD uniform he has, walked into the store, wrapped him up in his coat in the nanosecond his mother wasn't looking, and walked right out.'

'Did you tell anyone?'

Madison shook her head. 'Couldn't tell them. The CCTV was not conclusive but a witness smelled chloroform. That's all I have. If I'm wrong – I couldn't let the parents think he has him. How did *you* know?'

'SPD released the news that Harry Salinger had been confirmed dead in a fire at his house. The item after that was the missing boy in Burien – they showed a picture.' Quinn turned to Madison. 'He's fooled them before.'

The landscape was a streak of orange lights and concrete, Madison counted the miles on the street signs that blurred past. She made an inventory of what was in the gym bag at her feet, how much ammunition she had, the last time she had cleaned and dry-fired her piece. As if any of that mattered. Something actually relevant struck her out of the blue.

'We need to stop at a drugstore. I need to get – I need to have things in case Tommy's hurt. First aid, bandages, hypothermia blanket.'

The words were almost too much.

'Everything is in the back,' Quinn replied.

'You carry hypothermia blankets and splints in your trunk?'

Quinn didn't reply and, after a moment, Madison understood.

'You would have gone anyway. You would have gone to meet him even after SPD said he was dead.'

'He's fooled them before,' Quinn repeated.

'Why go to him?'

'To finish this, once and for all.'

Behind them, John Cameron was stretched out on the backseat. He had not said a word since they had come for her, a piece of the same darkness that had crafted Harry Salinger, lying behind her with his eyes closed.

Madison knew without asking that he carried a piece, probably more than one, maybe the knife that had killed Erroll Sanders. And she wondered in what world she lived now, where that was both a threat and a comfort.

'Tod Hollis has been looking into Salinger's assault case,' Quinn said. 'Into his trial.'

Something in his voice made Madison turn.

The MV *Puyallup* left its dock at Edmonds as per schedule: the journey to Kingston would take thirty minutes. The late hour meant an almost empty ferry. Once the other passengers had left the car deck, they each took a row of parked cars and went slowly and silently from one to the next, looking inside as they walked past, listening out for any sounds above the thrum of the ferry engine. As they expected, none of the vehicles seemed suspicious. Salinger would have traveled hours earlier, his cargo bundled in the parka in the back; he would have stood among the commuters and day-trippers, the SPD uniform already in a bag on the floor of his car.

The white interior of the passenger deck was almost too bright for Madison; she narrowed her eyes and went to the small food stand. She was not hungry, she could not imagine ever being hungry in her life again, but she had to keep her mind busy and her body functioning. She piled something on a plate – she didn't even see what – paid, and sat down in one of the booths. She forced in a mouthful which tasted like cloth and swallowed it with a gulp of water.

Quinn sat down on the other side of the table. He had bought a black coffee that he was not drinking, and didn't speak. Madison was grateful he hadn't offered platitudes. She wasn't going to get a *He will be alright* from him and she was fine with that. Salinger had killed children before; they both held that knowledge on their skin.

Small groups of people and lone travelers were dispersed in the wide space; five teenagers, crammed in a booth a few steps away, suddenly exploded into laughter. Madison flinched and stood up. 'I'm going outside.'

Quinn nodded and let her be. Madison pushed open the doors and was hit by the cold. She took out her cell and dialed. She had to make the call but hoped it would go to message.

When it did, she thought of the words she had prepared and found them pitifully inadequate.

Truth be told, there were no words for what she had to say. 'Lieutenant Fynn, this is Madison. I'm on the Edmonds–Kingston ferry . . .'

She spoke for a minute and then rang off. The outside deck was deserted and in the clear night Kingston was a few lights scattered somewhere ahead. Beyond it lay the bridge to the Olympic Peninsula and Highway 101, a ribbon that looped around the Olympic National Park. Its heart was mountains and glaciers, and somewhere deep in those woods Harry Salinger was holding Tommy.

So much had already been lost in those woods: tonight some of what had been stolen away in David Quinn might be returned in Tommy.

There were stars in the west, right above the Hoh River Valley. Maybe he could see the same stars. *We're coming to get you, Tommy. Be strong, we're coming.*

The Explorer came off the ferry ramp with a thud and speeded off on 104 toward Port Gamble and past it. They hit 101 and raced along the side of Discovery Bay. Quinn had been right – he drove faster than Madison would ever have been able. She wondered briefly how many times he had visited the place where his brother had died.

After Port Angeles, the woods closed in on both sides and the canopy of firs in the headlights was a tunnel they were shooting through. The road rushed up to them in winding turns; at times it would open unexpectedly onto an expanse of moonlit water only to dive back into the pitch black a moment later.

Quinn took the exit into the Upper Hoh Road. They shot past the Hard Rain Café in the direction of Willoughby Creek and after a few minutes he pulled up to the side of the road.

The air was damp and had a bite to it. Cameron settled a small backpack on his shoulders.

'Jack's going to approach on foot,' Quinn said to Madison. 'He'll get to the clearing from the north side.'

Cameron wore black from head to toe. Madison was sure he could be standing next to her and she wouldn't know.

He turned to Quinn. 'I have your word,' he said.

Quinn nodded.

'Your word,' Cameron repeated.

If there ever was a moment when John Cameron seemed human it was in the instant he took his leave, too fast for Madison to be sure, and yet something had passed between them. There was barely a whisper through the green as he disappeared into the forest.

'It's not far now,' Quinn said.

'Wait.' Madison reached inside her gym bag and dug around for something. When she found it she walked around to Quinn's side.

'Put this on,' she said, and pushed a ballistic vest in his hands.

Quinn looked down at the stiff navy-blue garment with SPD printed in yellow lettering.

'No,' he replied simply.

'I wasn't asking.'

'Do you really think this thing will be sorted with bullets?'

'I don't know. What I do know is that I will handcuff you to this car if you do not wear it, and I'll continue on foot. Put this on.'

Quinn snorted. All he heard was a small clink as the metal closed around the car door handle; and the feeling of cold around his wrist. For the first time in their acquaintance, Nathan Quinn was speechless. Madison took three steps back.

'I have to go now, so either you do as I say, or I'll leave you here. I have no idea what we'll be facing and it would make my life a good deal better to know that you, unarmed as I think you are, have this small and in all likelihood inadequate protection. If he wanted me dead he could have shot me a thousand times.'

After a beat he nodded. Madison released the handcuffs.

'It goes under your jacket,' she said.

Quinn slipped on the vest, heavier than it had felt, and adjusted the lateral straps.

'They need to be tighter,' Madison said, and found the buckles on his side. Her hands shook slightly as she secured them. Quinn saw them tremble and she didn't care: it could have been the chill, the adrenaline coursing through her body, her rage or her terror that it was already too late. She only cared whether the tremor would affect her aim.

'Thank you,' Quinn said.

They got back into the car and drove on. Madison checked the digital clock on the dash.

It was time.

Chapter 45

The mouth of the thin trail was almost completely hidden. Quinn pulled in a few yards before it as if he had done it a hundred times. Madison zipped up an extra layer of fleece under her jacket, checked her piece, shoved a few items in a light backpack and shrugged it on.

Once they were ready, Quinn turned off the car lights and complete darkness swallowed the world around them. They kept the beams of their flashlights low and close; Quinn went ahead, Madison followed.

After a few minutes he stopped and turned to her, his voice a whisper. 'We're going off the trail. Mind your feet and don't fall behind.' He started moving before she could reply. Quinn's progress was quiet and confident; Madison had no doubt it had been bought by years of visiting the place where his brother had last drawn breath.

Around the edge of her light Madison could see the twisted roots of firs and spruces covered in moss and the ferns in between. They were walking under trees they could not see but Madison perceived their height and breadth above them, just as much as Salinger's proximity. He was there, he was waiting.

Abruptly they stepped into moonlight and froze: the overgrown path had opened into a meadow. They both instinctively took a step back into the gloom and clicked off their flashlights. A breath of wind brought the sweet scent of resin and a rustle high up in the trees.

Across the meadow and into the thicket, the light of the first torch flickered in the distance, then a second, then a third. The glow of the flames quivered in the breeze and Madison's heart thumped.

'Stay behind me,' she whispered. She unhooked the leather strip on her holster and drew her piece.

They kept to the treeline as they closed in, away from the open and in the shadows.

The first torch was fixed with a metal grip six feet from the ground into the trunk of a spruce; even without looking up Madison knew it was massive.

As they came closer they realized that the torches marked a path: the points of light were spaced evenly every twenty feet.

Quinn touched her shoulder. He pointed slightly to the left of the path. 'The clearing where my brother died is two minutes further on *that* way.'

Madison nodded. Salinger had got something wrong, finally.

He had laid out the invitation: all they had to do was follow the light. They passed the first, then the second torch; the warmth of the flames came and went on her cheeks. She felt Quinn by her side when they passed the third, and they stopped dead shoulder to shoulder when the voice rang out in front of them.

'You're here,' it said, and there was delight buried deep in the words.

All the hours spent watching men playing out their lives at a card table and she sensed it straightaway, tinny and shrill, the thread that had connected them from the beginning: hope.

'Let me see you,' Madison said to the darkness.

'Where is Cameron?' the voice asked.

'Where is the boy?' she replied, more gently than she would ever have thought possible.

Harry Salinger stepped out of the gloom and faced them. Tall, wiry, a shirt and no jacket – the man in the CCTV, the man who had shot Brown and slaughtered the Sinclairs. Pointing at the ground and close to the body, he gripped a .45; the muzzle caught a flicker from the flames. His pale eyes slid over the cut above her left eye. 'Where is John Cameron?'

A puff of breeze brought Madison a fetid animal smell.

John Cameron came into the light. He had gone all the way round and now stood twenty feet to the right of Salinger, who had to turn his head to see him. Cameron's piece pointed straight at the man's head. Madison had not heard him at all.

'You brought me what I needed,' Salinger said, and Madison noticed the fresh, shiny stains and spatters on his clothes, over his chest and arms, a small tear in his shirt by the shoulder. It looked like blood and dirt.

'Where is Tommy?'

'He's near.'

Keep your head, engage, connect, get him to tell you where he is. 'What do you want, Salinger?'

'I heard you in the Sinclairs' house. You spoke about what I did with such clarity, such understanding.'

Quinn's arm shivered against her shoulder; she prayed he would keep his mouth shut. Cameron was a statue barely visible except for his face, his .22 in line with his dead eyes.

'Cameron for the boy. John Cameron dead by your hand and I will take you to the body. It's more than Quinn's brother ever had. It's safe – I've put it under ground for you.'

It took them all a moment to absorb what Salinger had just said. *Shiny blood and dirt on his shirt.*

'No.' It wasn't a human sound. Madison lunged forward as Salinger lifted his piece and pressed the trigger three times in rapid succession. It jammed. Cameron was already moving, almost there.

Salinger, eyes wide, spun and disappeared out of the circle of light.

Madison scrambled behind him, yelling to Cameron over her shoulder.

'You can't shoot him! You can't kill him!'

Cameron was beside her. 'Better catch him before I do.'

Out of the torches' reach, they plunged into the murky undergrowth. Madison's eyes adjusted to it, and she was running.

Harry Salinger sprinted across a small patch of moonlit dirt. The pine needles barely had time to settle back onto the ground when John Cameron and Alice Madison flew one after the other in close pursuit.

He was fast – God, he was fast. Madison had holstered and secured her piece in her first steps and switched to running mode in the space between heartbeats. She was chasing hard the rustling sounds ahead, Cameron slightly to her left. Even with eyes adjusted to the gloom, they were all running through near-complete darkness.

Her foot caught on a root and she went sprawling, found her balance and sprang forward again. Her breath came out in bursts and her heart thundered. A couple of times she slammed into low-hanging branches and her cheeks stung with tiny cuts.

Salinger was working on his advantage; she heard him crash through with great speed and little desire to cover his tracks. She dashed between the huge trunks, slipped on the moss, straightened up and became aware they were going down an increasingly steep decline.

Cameron was close, sometimes in front, sometimes to her side; she couldn't see him. They were both running as fast as they could and making hardly any progress. The ground dropped abruptly from under her feet and Madison was sliding and striding downward on a bed of wet leaves; she found purchase on the trunks of fallen trees and kept her balance. Cameron swore as dry branches splintered and snapped.

*

Salinger's feet hit the soft ground and he let his body's memory guide him and stir him in the direction he needed. It was a relief. He had shed his jacket as he heard them approach and had already warmed up as he knew he would. Seven years ago, wearing scrubs and sitting in the room that smelled of bleach with his public defender, the door had opened and the tall, dark man had come in. Salinger's lawyer had sworn under his breath.

'Mr. Quinn, good of you to join us,' the prosecutor said.

'It's not my case, Mark, it's Peter's. I'm only keeping an eye on things. I'm not even in the room.'

Nathan Quinn never looked at Salinger and never said another word, and yet he was very much in the room.

In the end they had gone to trial, both men pleading innocent and the bartender still in hospital. It all came down to *reasonable doubt*.

The morning of the last day his attorney had turned to the other lawyer. 'Nathan Quinn wrote your closing argument, didn't he?'

The jury provided the answer: 48 months for Harry Salinger. The other man paid a fine for the broken glass and walked free. It might have been someone else who had delivered the closing statement but Salinger knew who had written it, who had planned the other man's defense, who had given the jury the reasonable doubt they needed and the sinner they wanted. The bartender was still in hospital and someone had to pay that bill.

The forest was a blur, his pain was a blur. Forty-eight months. He remembered each scar and who had given it to him, he remembered each day in jail and who had given it to him. Rabineau would never leave the Bones: killing Pathune had seen to that and the cross on his brow had sealed it. And then, Quinn.

It had been easy to be hired at the restaurant but that first night, in a waiter's uniform, Salinger had looked at the two men sitting next to Quinn and he had understood in a moment of dazzling clarity that this was bigger than his own pain, bigger than anything he had ever contemplated. This had *meaning*. And he was standing there, blinded by that complete awareness, with his most recent injury still under a bandage, because that was where he was always meant to arrive. Everything in his life had led to this moment and he was merely an instrument as the universe corrected his axis and everything Quinn had ever touched and tainted would turn to ash.

Madison's voice, indigo, had expanded and filled up every bit of his consciousness that wasn't taken up by running. He could have done this blindfolded, but that would have been showing off. How long would be long enough?

The terrain leveled out under her feet and Madison splashed through water inches deep, pale stones on a bank only just visible. Salinger had changed direction and she followed through the shallows, up on the other side and back into the undergrowth.

She ran, stumbled and smashed through anything in her path as she tracked him. At times she smelled the putrid, decaying smell and almost retched. Blood and dirt. A searing pain burned in her chest and she almost lost her breath but they were suddenly on a trail, thin light in patches and clear ground, and Madison picked up speed.

Salinger was in sight. Cameron tore onto the trail and started gaining on him. Madison dug for everything she had and pushed forward; they were side by side and their target only seconds ahead.

It was a long stretch. Twice Salinger pounded on almost within reach of her outstretched hand. A sudden rushing of water and, one after the other, they burst onto the Hoh river bank. The moonlight was shockingly bright. Salinger staggered and lost his footing on the rocks; they fell on him and pinned him to the ground. It took Madison a couple of seconds to notice that he wasn't struggling, he was breathing almost normally while Cameron held his left arm and leg and she held his right, both heavily out of breath. Her brain fought for oxygen, it faltered on the memory of his last words.

'Tommy. Where is he? What did you do?' She spat out the words, aware that the muzzle of her gun was jammed against the tender flesh under his jaw, but not sure how it got there. The point of Cameron's knife rested lightly against Salinger's cheekbone.

He was limp under them, his eyes looking to the sky above, his face so devoid of fear, of that most basic human reaction to imminent death, that Madison paused, too shaken for clear thinking but wary that something was wrong. Definitely and irreversibly wrong. Cold sweat trickled between her shoulder blades.

'You brought me what I wanted,' Salinger rasped, and his eyes flicked toward the forest.

'What *did* you want, you sick fuck?' Madison's voice cracked.

'Quinn,' he whispered.

Madison and Cameron looked at each other, both realizing at the same time that Quinn was not with them, that he had stayed behind alone.

'Quinn,' she said.

'Yes.' Salinger turned to Cameron. 'He won't be able to get you out of this one, will he?'

Pieces of understanding clunked into place and the horror uncoiled itself.

'Where's Tommy? What did you do to him?' Madison stood up and Cameron reached over to keep Salinger down. The man was utterly still.

Salinger had not made a single mistake in the last 12 months, he had not misjudged where Quinn's brother had died. He only wanted for Quinn to be alone when he got there. Madison bent over, her hands on her knees, dizzy with the notion.

'Tommy is alive, isn't he?'

Salinger allowed himself a small smile.

Madison turned to Cameron. 'Pierce County,' she said. It was all she could manage. She started back toward the woods and ran – she ran as if the Devil's wail was behind her.

'No!' Madison howled, springing toward Salinger, and in an instant the three of them were out of sight. Nathan Quinn heard the sounds of the pursuit fading in the distance and then it was only the sputtering of the torches around him and the forest's deeper silence.

He walked back the way they had come and when he reached the final torch, on the edge of the meadow, he lifted it easily from the metal bracket – something almost medieval, his brain registered.

Quinn stepped out. No need to stay hidden in the shadows; the trees around the field created a circle of stars in the open sky. He looked up and the breeze chilled the perspiration on his face. He had read Hollis's report and he knew why Salinger had sent the notes to him. He barely remembered the case and his own part in it. In his mind he had gone back to it, and to the restaurant, a hundred times in the last day to try to see Salinger. There had been no recognition when he had come out to meet them. He hadn't known seven years ago whether Salinger or the Quinn Locke client was guilty, and he didn't know today. The only thing he knew was that James and his family were dead and Tommy had been taken because *his words* had been better than another lawyer's on a given day. And because once, twenty years ago, his life had turned left instead of right.

The notes had specified the clearing and, so far, Salinger had not made a single mistake.

The path that would lead him to the place that he had visited at least once every couple of months in the last two decades was before him. He had never been there at night but if he closed his eyes he could see it clearly. He let his memory take over and followed it out of the meadow and into the undergrowth, holding the torch away from low-hanging branches.

Quinn had been right: it took him two minutes and he was there, the ground leveled and the thicket opened into a clearing. It was harder being there at night: the boys, James and Jack, had spent a night here alone and terrified, David already gone by then.

The flame threw shivering light over the first of the trees he knew so well; it was the one Jack had been bound to and that held him up while they had tortured him. *Timothy Gilman like a bear in a trapping pit.*

James had been tied to the second tree. The flame wavered on the rough bark and past it and lit the third, David's tree. Quinn stopped: the hole had been dug in the hollow between the massive roots. It opened like a black wet mouth into the earth and for a moment he could not bring himself to go any closer. He had to look. He must look.

He stood over the hole and held the torch above it. The cage was metal bars and fit tightly against the pit's walls, the boy curled up inside it, wrapped in a blanket. Quinn wasn't even aware of the cry that passed his lips; he wedged the torch between two rocks and threw himself flat on the ground, his right arm stretched inside the hole. He reached through the bars, tight but not impossible, and the tips of his fingers brushed the face of the child. The boy was on his side and Quinn's hand trailed around the edge of his collar until he found it: a slow but steady pulse and the mere suggestion of body warmth.

Something shifted under his body and water started to trickle out of an opening in the wall – a hole the size of his fist, below his reach in the cage and level with the boy's feet.

He grabbed one of the bars on the top; he could see the damn spring lock now and a red wire from the mechanism that disappeared into the earth. He yanked the bar with all his strength. It barely moved.

The water was starting to pool on the surface where the boy was resting. How long did he have?

Quinn didn't need a toxicology report to know the child had been drugged: he wasn't moving, he wasn't responding, his breathing was shallow, and if the water rose high enough he would stop breathing altogether.

He had to think. He had to stop and think because that's what Salinger had meant to happen – and there *had* to be a reason.

Quinn stood up and something came loose under foot. He ran his fingers through the damp leaves and the pine needles. The flat tile was barely concealed – a pressure switch. He had caused it to happen, he had started it, his weight on that piece of ground, lying down to check if Tommy was alive.

A wire was connected to the tile, a thin brown wire that popped out of the dirt as Quinn lifted the switch. The cable snaked his way for a few feet and disappeared behind a shrub.

Nathan Quinn had known madness in his years in the courts, he had known grief and the cloud of violence that takes over from people's humanity in their worst days, but this was beyond it all.

He checked on the boy, the water rising slowly – soon his clothes would be soaked. The choice was drowning or hypothermia. Quinn followed the wire to the shrub and pushed the branches out of the way. It was a bad piece of camouflage that anyone would have spotted in daylight from ten feet away, greenery hastily thrown that he flung to the side until the object was clear.

Nathan Quinn took an involuntary step back and stared at it. He stared at it until awareness came back and slapped away any silly notion of rescues and resuscitations. *Pierce County*. The hard plastic tank which held the water leaking into the pit was kept within a metal cage with bars secured with stakes hammered into the earth. It was all Quinn's mind could contain: steel blades and glass shards welded and pointing inwards in a birdcage that curved like the spiral of a seashell. Low on the ground but wide and long enough that the tank could not be reached unless one was *inside* the cage. A pipe must be running under ground. The tap and the red wire from the spring-lock mechanism were obvious, and if the valve was turned it would empty out the tank, stop the pit from filling up and unlock the device.

Quinn looked to the forest in the direction they had disappeared. How long before any of them would come back? And who would come back? He tried to use logic: either Jack or Madison. It must be one or both. Salinger could not get away from both of them, not without a weapon and he had not heard any shots.

He checked on the boy again – there wasn't much time. Looking at the thing that Salinger had created, he understood the photographs of the ravaged men that Madison had shown them and how they had been slowly and inexorably killed by it.

The water was rising. Quinn shrugged off his coat and was surprised by the hard texture of the ballistic vest over his shirt – he had forgotten all about it. He took out his cell and dialed and spoke to someone. He was trying to make sense so that they would understand, but he wasn't sure they did and his mind was already onto something else: the pattern of wounds on the dead men as they had been forced to creep through the cage. He would need to follow its curling shape around the tank in order to reach the tap.

He laid the cell gently by his feet, the call still connected – no more time now – and looked back behind him to the forest. One of them would come back; one of them would find the boy.

Quinn, his belly flat on the damp ground, steadied himself to crawl inside the cage and pushed in. The first cut was a long stinging slash on the underside of his forearm, a blade grated against the ballistic vest and something pierced his side between the straps. He groaned.

What would happen if his body gave out before his mind? Quinn's focus batted against the searing pain. He closed his eyes briefly: only one way to find out.

Chapter 46

John Cameron saw Alice Madison disappear back into the woods. The last glimpse of her face had been a mask of dread and disbelief. He was pinning Salinger down and the point of his knife was still resting against his cheekbone.

Cameron exhaled. He had tried to keep Quinn safe by hunting this man down and he had failed. Whatever had already happened . . . Cameron stopped that train of thought. Everything was different from even two minutes ago, and spilling the blood of this fraction of a person would bring neither satisfaction nor balance in his books.

He cocked his head to one side. 'Are you sane?' he asked Salinger.

The man seemed to give the question some thought. 'I don't know,' he replied.

'I wonder how the courts will deal with what you've done. So much preparation, so much thinking ahead.'

His grip tightened around the man's throat and Harry Salinger understood that his careful plan had gone to the dogs, and he was in the hands of a man who wanted him to suffer and if he had to let him live to do so, then so be it.

'I've dug the pit at the foot of the tree where David died. Do you remember where that is?' Salinger whispered. 'How long will it take for *your attorney* to make up his mind? Do you know that he still visits every month? How far will he manage to crawl before blood loss and shock will take over?'

Cameron said nothing; his eyes held the man whole.

'Do you have any idea how hard your friend fought for his family? How long before his body grew still lying next to theirs? One of the children tried to hide under the bed—'

Cameron hit him hard on the temple with the handle of his knife and Salinger fell back, sprawled on the rocks of the Hoh riverbank.

'I don't have much time. You need to be restrained, you need to be punished, and you must be alive for the law to find you and drag you through the long life of pain and misery that you so much wish to leave.' John Cameron knelt down. He had never worked within those parameters but he could certainly learn.

The patches of moonlight disappeared behind her as Alice Madison raced along the open stretch, her flashlight giving her streaks of forest and rocky ground. Soon she would get to the steep incline and would need both hands – if she was going to do it she had to do it now. She dug for her cell and prayed for a signal. The bars were barely there but it would have to do.

When the call connected her voice burst through. The operator made her repeat everything three times – Madison gave her badge number and quite calmly, given the situation and the fact that she was running full tilt, assured the young woman that if she asked her to repeat her details a fourth time she would find her way back to civilization without her assistance, haul her into the darkest woods and dump her there. Could *she* repeat that?

She rang off and called Fynn, hoping that this time it would not go to message; when it did – at the bottom of the hill – Madison skidded to a stop. She knew she had spoken and yet, just seconds later, trying to climb back up the slope and sinking in the wet leaves, she couldn't remember what she'd said.

None of this had been about Cameron; all of this had been about Quinn. She saw Salinger, new at the restaurant, one of the busboys looking over his shoulder with a sneer. *Do you know who that is?'* *'Yes, I do.'*

Enough. Nathan Quinn's body could go no further. He tried to slither forward, the vest now slack and twisted, and he could not. Something had jabbed into his leg and he could not move it; the other leg he couldn't feel at all. Agony had given way to numbing cold. He couldn't see the tap anymore because he couldn't see anything.

The fingers of his right hand, slick with blood, stretched along the side of the tank; he could feel something under the tips, something that he couldn't quite grasp.

Time had lost any meaning and his body was turning into stone. Maybe if he just rested for a moment he could gather his strength and continue. Just one moment.

Alice Madison tore out of the undergrowth and into the clearing. She saw it all at once – the pit, the cage, the blood. She called out their names even if she could not hear her own voice over her thundering heart, and she didn't stop calling when no one answered back. Lying at the mouth of the hole, her voice cracking, she pulled on the bar of the cage and the lock mechanism sprang open. She pushed the damp blanket out of the way and managed to slide her hand under the boy's arm. Gently, nearly losing him once, she pulled him out, laid him down, wiped her grimy hand on her trousers and looked for a pulse. *There*, there it was.

All the breath whooshed out of her. 'Quinn!' she yelled. 'He's alive, he's breathing.' She scrambled to the cage, holding Tommy against her, but Quinn's body was curled facing the inside and she could not see his face, his eyes; all she could see was ripped clothing and red. His left arm was bent behind his back. Madison stretched through the bars and her hand closed over his.

'Quinn—' She could not find a pulse; her fingers kept slipping. 'Quinn—'

Madison rested Tommy on her lap and shrugged off her backpack, pulling out a handful of small heat pads and two hypothermia blankets. Tommy had to be warmed up slowly: she inserted the pads on the inside of her own coat, swaddled Tommy in the blankets and wrapped one arm around him so that he was held against her and under her coat. The other hand found Quinn's – it was ice-cold.

'Quinn—'

Tommy sighed. 'I have you, Tommy. It's going to be okay. I have you.' Tommy whimpered in his sleep. Madison held him close, her voice a whisper in his soft hair as she sang 'Blackbird'.

Quinn's hand, clasped tightly in hers, twitched.

Alice Madison didn't know how long had passed but she raised her eyes and Cameron was there; he dropped to his knees. His face was smeared with something she could hardly look at – it was all over his hands and clothes. His eyes were dead. He reached inside the cage and touched Quinn's arm.

'Where have you left him?' she asked.

'On the riverbank,' he replied without looking away from Quinn. 'Alive.'

Their eyes met. The sound of helicopter blades was thin but getting closer.

'If you want to leave, leave now. If you stay, do not say anything to me or to anybody at all. Do you understand?'

Cameron settled on the ground. His hand never left Quinn's arm.

*

They came in waves: the Hostage Rescue Team was first, swarming the clearing with their long-range rifles and their lights; Madison held up her SPD detective badge and Cameron laced his hands behind his head. Medics pried Tommy from her arms and put him on a warm-air inhaler as officers patted Cameron down for concealed weapons and found none.

The cage drew their silence and more focused work than Madison had ever witnessed; within seconds Quinn had an IV in the arm they could reach and his stats were constantly monitored out loud while it was being generally agreed that trying to get him out of it in the middle of the forest was an impossible risk. The low temperature and the metal structure had in fact kept him alive, barely, and if they freed him he would bleed out. Simple as that. He would have to be airlifted as he was and dealt with in a hospital if he survived the journey, which was unlikely.

A man was found on the Hoh riverbank. He was stabilized and stretchered, and no one asked him any questions as he was not in any condition to speak.

Chapter 47

Billy Rain handed the bank teller the check for $100,000 to deposit into his account, which at present held $147.27. He wore a suit – his one suit – because Carl Doyle had issued the reward check in the offices of Quinn Locke and invited him to pick it up there, where Tod Hollis would meet him and drive him to a bank of his choosing if he so wished.

The bank teller didn't so much as blink. Billy Rain, dazed and in shock, accepted the confirmation slip he had asked for. He had just that morning resigned from his job in his brother-in-law's garage and was on his way to the family home, a house he did not have keys for anymore, for a conversation with his wife. Today there were things to talk about she couldn't possibly imagine.

Carl Doyle sat on the thin bench that had been his office, his home and his watchtower for the last three days. He was the gatekeeper to Nathan Quinn's hospital room, as of three days earlier also his next of kin, and no one had been allowed in except for doctors and nurses. Even Alice Madison had been kept on that side of the door in spite of her numerous visits; Quinn would decide who, if anyone, he wanted to see when he woke up. That had been Doyle's mantra.

The thread that was keeping Quinn tethered to his life had been dangerously thin in the last 72 hours but it had not snapped. The doctors had been surprised by his resilience as much as by the scale of his injuries: a few of them had dealt with survivors of bear attacks and some of those had looked a darn sight better than the man who had been delivered to them inside a metal cage.

The residents had stopped keeping count of the stitches once they had reached 400, the spleen had gone almost completely and the ophthalmic surgeon was offering positive if as yet unproven updates. It wasn't much, in fact it was pitifully little, but it was what there was.

So Carl Doyle ran Quinn Locke from a bench in a hospital corridor and would do so for as long as necessary.

The woman who was approaching hesitantly looked as exhausted and drawn as he was. When she stopped in front of the door Doyle looked up from his papers.

'No visitors and no comment,' he said, politely but without room for misunderstanding.

'I'm Rachel Abramowitz. Tommy is my little boy,' Rachel said.

Doyle took her hands and she sat next to him, trying to hold it together.

'How is he?'

Rachel smiled weakly. 'He doesn't remember anything. He woke up, he seems fine, he eats and sleeps. But one of us is always with him. Always.'

Doyle nodded.

'How is he?' Rachel asked and looked at the closed door.

Doyle explained. She had earned the right to know the truth.

'Would you do something for me?' Rachel said.

'Sure.'

'Would you give him this from my boy?'

Rachel Abramowitz left and Doyle went into Quinn's room. The blinds were drawn and the man on the bed was deeply asleep in the comfort of a medically induced coma.

Doyle didn't know what the object meant. It didn't matter anyway, Quinn would know. He slipped the baseball under his good hand and closed his fingers around it.

Mary Sue Linden hurried down the long corridor, a lunch tray held tight in her hands. For the past three days she had been the youngest member of the nursing team treating Patient X: he had come in without a name and under police protection. The rumor was that he was a witness to some hideous crime and a drug cartel was on his tail.

Mary Sue walked past empty rooms on either side and nodded hello to the two police officers standing guard. She pushed the door open with her hip. Patient X was awake, he could not speak but he was breathing on his own. The doctors could not fathom his injuries. Maybe a shark with a knife, someone had suggested.

Mary Sue approached the bed and he followed her with eyes as pale as rainwater. She placed the tray carefully on the bedside table and her eyes flicked to the door. She leant forward, her voice as quiet as she could make it.

'I have a special message for you,' she said. 'From your detective friend with the Irish red hair.'

His eyes narrowed.

'Can you hear me okay?'

Harry Salinger blinked once.

'He said to tell you this and make sure you understand.' A whisper. 'The boy lives, he is fine, and the man is alive too. They are both going to be just fine.'

When the patient turned his face away she patted his arm gently. Men could be funny about showing emotion – no news there.

*

John Cameron stood in his cell and let the light from the thin window slide over his face. He wore the orange overalls of a man charged with a very serious felony who has been denied bail. It didn't surprise him or worry him in the least. Detective Madison had visited regularly with news of Quinn's progress and so far that was all he was interested in.

They had sat on either side of a pane of glass, different clothing but identical cuts and grazes on their faces and hands.

'They found a wooden box in his van, a small bone in it. Could be the brother's,' Madison said.

'Have you found out where they're keeping him?'

'Yes. He's in protective custody.'

'Good. The man needs protecting.'

'We made sure he knew that he had failed, that they both lived.' She passed a sheet of paper through the slit in the glass, the court record from Salinger's trial and the closing argument Quinn had written.

Cameron read: '. . . *It is something at the heart of every human being that makes us seek justice for those who have been wronged, those who have been harmed . . .*'

Madison stood to leave. 'Before you went into the forest you said to Quinn—'

'He had given me his word that he wouldn't do anything foolish, put himself in harm's way.' He sat back in the chair. 'Ask me the question, Detective. I know you've been wondering.'

They could have been talking at her dining table, the fire lit and coffee scenting the room.

'How long are you planning to stay?' Madison asked him.

'For as long as it suits my purpose,' Cameron replied.

For a moment there is no glass at all between them.

John Cameron was kept in isolation for his own safety, which everyone knew was a rather pathetic lie. Nevertheless he had managed to get hold of a newspaper. It seemed Harry Salinger had switched gravestones and the body that had been found in the ground was actually his father, while his dead twin had been removed to die again in the fire.

When tested, the body in the coffin had no mitochondrial DNA in common with Salinger. On suicide watch and charged with four counts of murder and one of kidnap, Salinger, wherever they were holding him and treating him, probably wished he was his brother. Cameron closed his eyes: the cell meant little to him. Above him the sky was so blue it hurt to look at it.

Sgt. Kevin Brown woke up and let awareness come back slowly as he got his bearings. He was in a hospital, that much was reasonably obvious, and yet the last thing he remembered was a conversation with Madison in the precinct. Winter light filtered through the slats in the blinds and the clock on the wall said it was 3.07 p.m. on December 28. He couldn't work out how long he had been there because he had no idea what day the thing had happened that had landed him there in the first place.

He tried to move and nothing much happened. He turned his head a little and saw Madison, fast asleep on a chair by his bed with a heavy book open in her lap; she looked like she'd run through a rosebush. She sighed in her sleep and Kevin Brown remembered something just then, out of a dream – her voice speaking and reading to him. Speaking and reading for hours and hours. *Call me Ishmael.* At least for today then, their day's work was done. He watched her sleep for a while, until the nurse came in and she stirred.

Acknowledgements

Some of the names of the locations in the story are fictitious because I'd rather not set murder and mayhem in a specific house on a real street. Similarly, the various precincts and jurisdictions of the Seattle Police Department have been slightly adjusted.

This story would not have seen the light without the enthusiasm and reckless faith of friends and family: Sue and Bruce Berglund in Seattle, who opened their home and their hearts to us, and gave my tale the view from their deck; Kezia Martin, the first reader, for her encouragement and the fortitude to read the manuscript as it was being written; my mother, who taught me that the world is indeed full of possibilities, and, finally, Gerald, who made everything possible.

This book would not exist without my agent Teresa Chris, whose support, trust and vital humour has been invaluable, and Jo Dickinson at Quercus, who has been incredibly kind and tactful while making sense of a 142,966-word monster. They have made this a better story in more ways than I can count. My deepest thanks also to Kathryn Taussig and the wonderful team at Quercus for all their energy and the magic that turned loose pages into a book.

the dark

*Read on for an exclusive extract from
the chilling sequel featuring
Detective Alice Madison*

Ancient trees rise a hundred feet, red and yellow cedars next to black cottonwood and vine maples, their roots twisting out of deep green slippery moss and rotting wood.

Four men walk in single file. Young enough that the difficult terrain doesn't slow their progress too much, old enough to know this is the day their lives have twisted and turned; they don't speak to each other because there is nothing to say.

Their leader wipes the perspiration off the back of his neck with a ragged square of gray cloth; he points at a dead branch that curves out of the dirt, ready to catch their feet; the others step carefully around it. He's not a considerate man; he's a nasty piece of work in a hurry to get his business done and get out of the forest.

The others follow him, wary of his moods and of the uneven ground; they look ahead and never turn around. If they did, they would see the boy held in the arms of the last man in the file, the boy who hasn't drawn breath for what seems like hours. Eleven, maybe twelve years old, fair wavy hair and pale lips. They grip their shovels and walk on.

The man carries the boy and keeps his eyes on the back of the guy in front. The child's thin arms dangle low and his hands brush the tall ferns. Then, as loud as a gunshot, a sharp intake of breath and the boy's eyes open wide. The man recoils *and the child slips from his arms onto the soft moss.*

The boy doesn't see the others turn as he lies on the cool ground; he's breathing deeply and above him, beyond the highest branches, the sky is so blue it hurts to look at it.

Last night

Homicide Detective Alice Madison tried to find in herself the last shreds of stillness. The woods creaked around her and a puff of breeze soothed the cut on her cheek.

All the time she would ever have was right now. She was frayed with exhaustion and dread, and sanity seemed a lifetime away. It always came down to the same question, over and over: *How far are you prepared to go?*

She pointed her Glock at the man in front of her and wondered if the soft evening wind would affect the bullet's trajectory, whether the small chunk of metal would do what she was asking it to do or the twilight would affect her aim. Precision was all she had, carved out of intent and determination.

Alice Madison had never aimed and shot at a human being before walking onto this field, and this was not what the Police Academy had taught her. Her target was not a threat to her, himself or others. Her target could barely stand on his feet.

Madison squeezed the trigger and in her heart she knew she had a hit like the pitcher knows how the ball is going to curve as soon as it leaves the hand.

Chapter 1

Three weeks and five days earlier

Alice Madison shifted in the comfortable upholstered armchair and adjusted the holster that dug a little into her right side. She stole a glance out of the wide window. Puget Sound shone in the pallid January light, the silver creased white in spots, and Mount Rainier rose from blue shadows in the far distance. She turned when she realized the silence had stretched for longer than was polite. Dr Robinson was watching her.

'Don't worry. I know people come here for the sharp psychological insights but it's the view they stay for,' he said.

He had made that joke the first time they had met a few weeks earlier. She smiled a little today as she had then, not entirely sure he was unaware he was repeating himself.

The sign in the lobby said Stanley F. Robinson PhD. The office on the fifteenth floor was smart, the colors muted.

He was early fifties, salt-and-pepper hair in a short cut and big brown eyes. A useful look for a psychologist who worked with cops: fairly unthreatening with bouts of inquisitiveness, she mused.

'How was your week?' he asked her. Dr. Robinson's desk

was mercifully free of pads and pens. If he took notes he did so after their sessions.

'Good,' Madison replied. 'Paperwork from a few old cases to tidy up. A domestic incident which turned out to be nothing. Pretty standard stuff.'

'Did you think about the forest incident? I mean, longer than for a few seconds during your day.'

'No.'

'Did you experience any unusual thoughts or have unusual reactions as you went about your business? I'll let you tell me what's unusual for you.'

'No, nothing unusual.'

'Any reaction to chloroform or other PTSD events?'

'No.'

'Anything at all about the last week or in general that you'd like to talk about?'

Madison had the good grace to at least pretend she was pondering the question. 'Not really,' she said finally.

Dr. Robinson mulled over her reply for a few moments. He sat back in his chair. 'Detective, how many sessions have we had to date?'

'This is the third.'

'That's right, and this is what I've learnt: you are a Homicide Detective; you joined your squad last November – that's, what, about two and a half months ago, give or take. You have a Degree in Psychology and Criminology from the University of Chicago – good school, great football team. Your record at the Seattle Police Department is impeccable. You play well in the sandbox and there are no red flags in your private life. Not so much as a traffic violation. With me so far?'

'Yes.'

'Good. Last December all hell breaks loose and once the smoke clears the Department sends you here to make sure you're fit for work and ready to protect and to serve. You are very frank: you admit to a reaction to chloroform as a consequence of Harry Salinger's attack on you and your partner, but that stopped weeks ago. No panic attacks, no incidents of post-traumatic stress disorder. Nothing, after what happened in the forest. The boy, the rescue, the blood.'

He paused there and Madison held his eyes.

'Do you know how long it took me to gain all this perceptive knowledge?' He didn't wait for her to reply. 'Seven minutes. The rest of the time what I got was "good" and "pretty standard stuff" and "nothing unusual".'

'What do you want from me, Dr. Robinson?'

'Me? Nothing. I'm quite happy for you to come up and just look at the view. You can do with the break and I get paid either way. But here's the thing: even though I will certify that you are indeed fit to work and ready to protect and to serve – because you are – it is simply unthinkable that those thirteen days in December left no trace on you somehow. So, these goodies I'm giving you for free: you have occasional nightmares, possibly an exact memory of the event but more likely your own perception of the event and whatever troubles you about the nature of your own actions in it. And, most of all, I'm willing to bet you are careful never to be alone with your godson since you got him out of that forest. How am I doing?'

Madison didn't reply.

'Good meeting you, Detective. Have a nice life.'

Dusk. Alice Madison parked her Honda Civic in her usual spot by Alki Beach. Her running gear was stashed in a gym bag in the trunk but she leant against the bonnet and let the clean salty air into her lungs. The Seattle-Bremerton ferry was going past, seagulls trailing in its wake. Bainbridge Island was a blue-green strip across the water and downtown Seattle shimmered in the distance.

As far as she could remember, even as a newbie officer with her crisply ironed uniform, Madison had come to Alki Beach and run after her shifts. The comfort of the sand under her feet and the rhythm of the tide after a hard day; the sheer physical release after a good day. It had been a constant in her life and Madison knew very well that there were precious few of those, and she was grateful for it.

Then, the last day of the year just gone, after the end of those thirteen days, Madison had come back to the beach, changed into her sweats, started running and promptly slipped into a recall so vivid, so physical, that she had to stop: the sweet smell of pine resin still in her nostrils. Hands on her knees and water up to her ankles, her trainers soaked. *Any dreams you want to tell me about?*

Her arm had healed; the rest of her would take whatever time it would take. Madison changed in the back of her car. Her first strides were hesitant but she ignored the forest floor shifting under her feet, and the sudden scent of blood. And she kept running.

The rush-hour traffic carried Madison into California Avenue SW without any apparent effort on her part; she followed the flow south with the windows rolled down and her faded maroon University of Chicago hooded sweatshirt stuck to her back. She wiped the perspiration off her brow with a sleeve and drove, listening to the local news on the radio and not thinking about Stanley F. Robinson PhD.

We find our blessings where we can and Madison pulled into a parking space opposite Husky Deli and stretched her sore limbs as she locked her car.

Her grandfather had brought her here for an ice-cream cone her first weekend in Seattle. Her grandmother was busying herself in the market nearby. They sat at the counter; he looked at the 12-year-old girl he barely knew and spoke to her like no one had spoken to her before.

'I hope you will like it here – I really hope you will. All I'm asking is that should there be anything troubling you, anything at all, you talk to me, to us. I don't know what happened with your father and I'm not asking that you tell us. I'm just asking that you don't run away, that you don't just leave in the middle of the night. And we'll do our best to help you in any way we can.'

Then he put out his hand. Alice looked at it; no one had ever asked her word about anything. She passed her Maple Walnut cone into her left hand and shook with her right, sticky with sugar. They kept their word, and so did she.

Madison rubbed the sole of her trainer against the edge of the pavement to get rid of a significant amount of Alki Beach that had insinuated itself into the grooves. She mingled with the shoppers and filled a basket with food for home as well as a Chicken Cashew sandwich – no parsley – and broccoli cheese soup that would probably not make it home.

Standing at the counter she was no different from anybody else.

'Whole or half?' the man asked.

'Whole.'

'Cup or bowl?'

'Bowl.'

'Roll?'

'No, thank you.'

The man's gaze lingered for a fraction of a second over the two-inch fine red line across her left brow; it would fade in time, the doctor had said. Madison hadn't cared then and didn't care today. All that mattered was that it made her a little bit more recognizable after the flurry of articles and media reports in early January.

The man nodded; he must have been working there since bread was invented.

'Cone? Caramel Swirl's freshly made.'

Madison smiled. 'Not today.'

She started on the soup in the car, engine already running, and by the time she turned into Maplewood and her driveway, the carton was empty.

Three Oaks is a green neighborhood on the south-western edge of Seattle, on one side the still waters of Puget Sound and on the other patches of woodland and single family homes in well-tended gardens.

Madison parked next to her grandparents' Mercedes and

balanced her gym bag on one shoulder; her arm was wrapped around the grocery bag as she unlocked the door, toed the sandy trainers off and gently pushed the door shut with one foot.

She padded into the kitchen and unpacked the shopping. Without turning on the lights she crossed the living room and opened the French doors, letting in the fresh air. The answering machine flashed red. She ignored it, settled herself into a wicker chair on the deck, her feet on the wooden rail, and unwrapped the sandwich.

The garden sloped down to a narrow beach that ran along the waterside properties; tall firs on either side worked better than a fence. In the half-light Madison looked at the plants and the shrubs: soon they would wake up for a new life cycle – the Japanese maples, the magnolias – each one seeded and nurtured by her grandparents.

Madison knew nothing about gardening yet she would weed, water, prune and make sure that everything stayed alive because they weren't there to do it anymore. She worried good intentions wouldn't make up for ignorance. In her job they usually didn't.

Once the stars were bright enough, Madison stepped inside. Her Glock went under the bed in its holster and her back-up piece – a snub-nose revolver – was oiled and dry-fired. Madison peeled off her sweats and climbed into a long hot shower.

The message had been from Rachel: 'Tommy's birthday party is next month. I hope you can make it.' Nothing but love and kindness in her voice.

You have occasional nightmares, possibly an exact memory

of the event but more likely your own perception of the event and whatever troubles you about the nature of your own actions in it. And, most of all, I'm willing to bet you are careful never to be alone with your godson since you got him out of that forest.

The nature of your own actions. Madison wasn't exactly sure she understood the nature of her own actions and she was honest enough to admit to herself that there had been moments that night that she probably did not want to fully understand. It had been a blur of fear and rage and she didn't know exactly how much of one or the other.

Tommy would be seven soon. On that awful night she had sung 'Blackbird' to him and he had come back to them, to life, to his red bicycle and his little boy's games. Her godson would be seven and Madison tried hard to come up with an excuse not to go to the party and failed.

As every night since that day in December her last thoughts went to two men: one in jail, locked behind walls and metal doors guarded by armed correction officers, and yet more terrifyingly free than any human being she had ever met; and the other in the prison of his injuries, somewhere deep past the corridors and the silent rooms of a hospital a few miles away. His sacrifice had meant Tommy would have a seventh birthday party. She could not think of one without the other.

Madison closed her eyes and hoped sleep would come quickly.

To be continued . . .

A PROMISE TO A LOVED
ONE, CARVED IN BLOOD
AND BONE...

Seattle Homicide Detective Alice Madison is bound
to jailed murderer John Cameron and attorney
Nathan Quinn by a debt that cannot be repaid, by a
nightmare that changed their lives forever.

When the remains of Quinn's younger
brother are discovered in a shallow grave,
Madison vows to follow the trail of brutal deaths
that leads to the truth.

A sadistic killer stalks the investigation as Madison's
own demons threaten her future career with the
police and darkness closes in.

How far is she prepared to go to save a life?

the dark

September 2014